Doves Migration

Linda Daly

Dearest Anne Marie
Dreams do
come true
when you
Believe
Love
Linda

Light Sword Publishing

Timeless Tradition; Word by Word

First Edition

Editing by:
Nancy Lepri

Formatted by:
Laurie Christopherson

Cover designed by:
Sean Dickey

ISBN-10: 0-9800733-5-9
ISBN-13: 978-0-9800733-5-5
Published by Light Sword Publishing
www.lightswordpublishing.com

Printed in the United States of America

*Dearest Meriwether, everyone should be blessed
to have a friend that listens with their heart as you do.
My life has been truly enriched with your friendship and love.*

Linda Daly wishes to thank all of her friends, family members, and colleagues who have generously offered their support and expertise in helping to keep her dream alive, as she continues the Doves Collect series, book 3 – Doves Migration. Especially:

Marie Fernandez
Sharon Boury
Shawn M.Guideau, *MA, LPC, NCC*
Bonny Kirby
Nancy Lepri
Laurie Coombs

Doves Migration

Linda Daly

~ One ~

Farewell, Dixieland

April 12th, 1865

"Come on ladies. At this rate, we won't make it out of town by sunset!" Michael Honeycutt's pleas to his wife, Sarah, and stepdaughter, Elise Hamilton went unnoticed. Shrugging his shoulders in frustration, Michael shook his head and looked over at his future son-in-law, Joshua Carmidy. "I tried, son."

In response, Joshua dramatically raised his hands in despair. "By God, this is gonna take some getting used to," he said, while continuing to place trunks behind the rig they were going to New York in.

"Yes, the fairer sex is definitely non-regimented. Not at all like the military life you have become accustomed to, Major. But I can tell you one thing; they are definitely worth the wait." Michael grinned devilishly at the Union Major standing before him in his worn and tattered uniform, and handed him another satchel to store securely in the rig.

"Yeah, and they smell better too. That's for damn sure," Joshua replied, chuckling in agreement while pulling on a leather strap that held the carpetbag in place at the foot of the carriage.

Hearing the familiar sound of Joshua's laughter sent waves of emotion through Elise, knowing just how fortunate and blessed she was, and a soft smile crossed her lips. Just as she had done hundreds of times in the past few days, she quickly thanked God for sending the love of her life back for her. Not just because he had fought under Grant for the past three years and lived to tell about it, but more importantly, Joshua knew she was a former Southern Spy and despite this fact, he still loved her.

Following the ringing of the bells this past Monday, signaling the war had finally ended with Lee surrendering to Grant at Appomattox Court House, Elise had waited and prayed Joshua would return to her.

Never had she known such happiness as when he woke her, the following afternoon. With the war behind them, their vast differences resolved, the two of them intended to start a new life in New York where Joshua lived prior to the war.

Their happy reunion was short lived when a few hours later Elise's former officer friend and comrade threatened to take her life as Joshua stood watching.

Thomas Hastings, a well-known Confederate officer fighting under the Mosby Brigade, had vowed to revenge the death of his fallen men, whom he blamed Elise for, following an ambush that had happened back in '63 behind Doves Landing. Despite her pleas of innocence for the death of his men and explanations as to why she had stopped spying for the Confederacy, Thomas wouldn't believe her. In his anger of not being able to win her heart years ago, he believed she had turned traitor because of Joshua.

Elise quivered, remembering the look of hate in Thomas's eyes when Joshua happened upon them in the back gardens of Doves Landing.

Glancing at Thomas now, while standing beside her mother in front of their homestead, the two of them exchanged friendly smiles. Although everything on the surface appeared normal between them, Elise was certain she would never forget how crazed he had been that day. Convinced she surely would have been a casualty of war herself if it hadn't been for Joshua's keen perception and masterful art of persuasion--a quality that in the past she had found most discerning, especially when he had used it against her in her espionage days.

Time seemed to stand still as images of that day and the past four years flooded her mind. Magically before her eyes, Thomas was no longer the embittered, broken man who stood before her now, but that of the confident, Confederate Major she had visited in Manassas back in '61.

For a few moments she stood silently, blocking out all the pain and misery the war had caused and reminisced of the small community of Fairfax, Virginia, prior to the war. Brief glimpses of Miranda Brown (her oldest and dearest friend), Thomas, Constance Hildebrandt, and Nicholas Wilder danced before her eyes like drawings on a canvas. *My, but life was good back then. Why couldn't I have just enjoyed my life rather than nearly destroy it and also the lives of those I loved, trying to prove how clever and brave I was?*

Regretting some of her past actions, Elise frowned slightly and looked across the yard toward the barn. Her eyes fixed on Jesse, their former slave, as he unhitched the weathered wagon from Maggie. Seeing her horse and wagon stirred up old memories of when she had sneaked across town right under the enemy's nose to pass on vital information to the "cause". *I was brave though . . . No one can ever take that away from me.*

Her frown eased, recalling how exhilarating it had been relaying information to Thomas and spying on the enemy. Her greatest accomplishment had been when the Confederacy had captured a Union Major off guard and confiscated their horses and ammunition from the information she had managed to give to Thomas. Unfortunately that very night, only miles from the safety of her home, she had been stopped by a Union patrol while returning to Doves Landing. There in the dark of night, she had her first encounter with Major Joshua Carmidy. From the onset, it had been clear that this cunning and quick-witted Union Major was not the least bit taken in by her charms, as were the other officers. Smiling inwardly she thought, *Well, perhaps he was a little.*

Recalling their earlier encounters of bantering back and forth on the steps of her mother's boardinghouse brought a twinkle to her eye. She nearly chuckled aloud when she remembered how she had even thrown her shoe at him once out of frustration. However, as the memories continued, her smile faded, recalling when Joshua had discovered that she was a Southern Spy and she had nearly lost him forever.

Such disturbing thoughts made Elise's heart begin to race. Suddenly, without warning, the demons of her past haunted her in a collage of painful images. No matter how Elise tried to stop the mental pictures from forming, there before her flashed Joseph's slain body lying at her feet. Miranda had hovered over him sobbing irrationally that she was responsible when it was Elise who had actually shot him. Closing her eyes, Elise could not get the sight of blood from her mind, recalling the slain Confederate sniper who had shot her beloved Joshua.

Glancing at him now, she thought, *Oh Joshua, how close I was to losing you then . . .* As those painful memories continued rushing into her consciousness, Elise struggled not to let her emotions get the best of her and cry. Especially today, when she had so much to be thankful for, now that Joshua had come back to her, and they were preparing to start a new life together in New York.

For years she had dreamt of this day, and now that it was finally here, she was not going to spoil it by recalling events from her past that should be buried. Scolding herself for being so melancholy, Elise tried to direct her attention toward her mother and Mr. Wiley's conversation.

"I must say, I half expected that following the war you and Michael would be going north, but for Miss Elise to hook up with a Yankee...er..."

Verus Wiley, realizing he had called Joshua a Yank in public, coughed and cleared his throat before hastily continuing. "Not to say that I don't have the fondest regards for Major Carmidy, because I do. It's just that hearing of their engagement was rather surprising."

Unable to refrain from commenting at the slip of the tongue from the editor of the *Fairfax Gazette,* referring to Joshua as a Yankee, Elise chuckled. "Why Mr. Wiley, I find it hard to believe that someone with such a keen sense for the news didn't know my true intentions regarding one of my favorite Yanks." Emphasizing the word Yank, Elise's eyes sparkled over at the older man.

"Why Missy, it's good to see the war hasn't snatched away your spirit none," Versus replied quickly, returning her smile. "Putting all kidding aside Miss Elise, truth be known, you've always been a great mystery to me. As I recall, back when the war began, I would have sworn your loyalties were with the Confederates."

"They were! That never changed," interrupted Elise, while turning to look at Thomas. "Sometimes we just can't control our hearts, is all."

The tension between them was evident, and again Mr. Wiley cleared his throat, while nervously fidgeting in his pocket looking for his pipe.

"No, I suppose we can't," Thomas said shyly. Looking warmly at Elise before turning his attention to Mr. Wiley, he jovially added, "But hell, I know what ya mean though, Verus. A Yankee and a Southern Spy getting hitched . . . Don't that just rot your socks!"

As the two of them chuckled between themselves, Elise, never having been publicly called a spy before, glanced away to avoid any further commenting regarding her involvement in the war. In front of the rig, she noticed Michael standing alone puffing on his pipe, looking miserable, and she tugged at her mother's sleeve. "Look Mama," Elise whispered, "Michael, looks like a lost puppy."

"I know," Sarah snickered. "Isn't it sweet? Michael's become such a part of the Southern way of life, struggling right alongside us through the destruction and losses of war instead of returning to the safety of New York, as he could have. He's going to miss our friends, just as we are."

"Yes . . . I suppose he will," Elise said, absent-mindedly, seeing him come toward them. As he drew nearer, her mind wandered back in time once more.

Shortly after the Union soldiers had encamped in their small community in 1861, Michael Honeycutt, a war correspondent had become a frequent guest of Doves Landing. After the first battle, Elise realized that his interest had become much more than to capture a story; he had in fact, captured the heart of her mother, Sarah Hamilton.

At first Elise had disliked him intensely, especially when she had discovered he and her mother intended to wed. However, gradually over time, Elise came to realize that this quiet, studious man was more than a friend and confidant to her, but he had become a friend to those in their small community as well.

Michael chose not to sit out the war in New York, where he could have lived in luxury, unscathed by the daily heartaches of war, which was primarily fought in the South. Instead, he had remained at Doves Landing by choice, determined to protect his beloved Sarah from those made so desperate by the ravages of war that they preyed on others, especially the many Southern women and children who were left alone with no men folk to protect them. Michael revealed to no one, not even Sarah, that he came from a family of great wealth. Knowing if his wealth were known to others, people so desperate for food and money might look to him for gold, or worse, vent their hatred and frustration for the Yankees by lashing out at Sarah and Elise. To avoid placing his newfound family in any further jeopardy than they already were in simply by being in the South, Michael remained silent.

Michael truly has been a Godsend, Elise thought, knowing that if it had not been for Michael's swift action by securing passage for the Browns', Miranda and Lucas's lives would have been in jeopardy if they had remained in Virginia. Especially since Lucas had taken such an active role for Virginia to secede from the Union.

On the night following the first battle of Manassas, he helped brave the searing flames of a horrible fire that ended up taking the Mason's house and young daughter's life. Even today, as busy and excited as he was to be returning home, his generosity continued by offering Thomas Hastings a job at Doves Landing.

Smiling warmly at the man she was proud to call father, she moved aside so he could stand beside Sarah. *My, what would we have done without him?* Elise wondered. Looking among her friends, one by one recalling how Michael had truly made a difference in all of their lives, she thought, *Thank heavens, we will never have to find out.*

Then suddenly realizing she may never see any of these people again, Elise began to etch the images of their faces into her memory, to assure she would never forget them. When her eyes rested on the round, full face of Mammy Tess, their former slave, a single tear rolled down her cheek.

Since childhood, Mammy Tess, and her son, Jesse had played vital roles in Elise's family. Almost as if she had stepped back in time, bittersweet images of her past unfolded in Elise's mind . . .

The day was no different from countless others in the kitchen of Doves Landing as the slave lovingly prepared the meals for the hungry travelers passing through. Kneading bread in a floured, stained apron Mammy Tess would hum softly while allowing Elise and her dear friend Miranda ample time to snatch a warm biscuit straight out of the oven. Playfully, Mammy Tess then would snap a linen towel in the direction of the girls, shooing them from her kitchen. Squeals of delight echoed throughout the boardinghouse as the girls juggled the hot biscuits in their hands while running up the back stairs. Hearing their laughter, Mammy Tess, with a broad smile across her lips would resume preparing the traveler's meals, humming softly again.

Recalling such happy times and the thought of living her life without Mammy Tess, whom she thought of as a second mother, became more than she could bear and Elise struggled against the urge to cry. *My, but we were happy . . . no fear of starving, or being raided, or killings . . .*

As if knowing what Elise was thinking, Mammy Tess stretched out her arms and called to her, "Sugar, come give yer Mammy Tess some lovins."

"Oh Mammy Tess . . ." Elise whimpered as she eagerly ran to her, taking comfort in the arms of the robust Negro woman. Rocking her gently from side to side, Mammy Tess squeezed her tightly while patting her lovingly on the back.

"Now don't be makin' a fuss, Missy. You need to be strong fo' Miz Sarah. This is goin's to be real hard on her."

Pulling away slightly, Elise dutifully nodded up at her. "I promise."

"That's my girl." The older woman lovingly cupped her hands around Elise's face and wiped away her tears with her rough, callused thumb. "I love you, child. Now you go on over to that man of yer's, and make me proud. Be a good wife to him and mind yer manners with his folks, or I'll come up there and take a switch to ya."

Chuckling slightly, Elise kissed Tess softly on the cheek. "I love you too, Mammy Tess. There's so much I want to say . . ."

Mammy Tess shook her head and pressed her lips together firmly. "Shh, child, no needs to say nothin' now. I already knows that no matters where you be, yer my little girl . . ."

Trying to hold back her own tears, Tess stopped in mid-sentence and Elise watched as Mammy Tess took the corner of her apron and wiped her tear-swollen eyes. "Now jest look what ya gone an done . . . got me blubberin' like some old fool." She scolded, as only Tess could, pretending to be sterner than she actually was.

"Oh Mammy Tess, I'm going to miss you so much," Elise whispered, through the lump in her throat that was the size of a peach pit.

Smiling knowingly at Elise, Tess nodded her head, than wagged her finger as she gently scolded her again. "Now go on and get yourself over where you belong. Before that good lookin' major changes his mind."

Without saying a word, Elise tenderly kissed her one last time and turned searching for the reason she was leaving her childhood memories, her beloved homeland, and the friends that she loved. Finally, her eyes settled on Joshua and her heart skipped a beat, just as it did every time she looked at him.

Having finished the task of loading Sarah and Elise's belongings into the rig, Joshua was leaning up against the carriage watching his fiancées every move. As soon as their eyes met, Elise's heart began beating faster, admiring his rugged, manly appearance. *My, oh my, but you are a devilishly, good-looking man, Major Carmidy!* Recalling how they had almost consummated their love the day of their reunion, she blushed. *It took some time, but he's definitely captivated by my charms now!* She thought, as a smile crossed her lips.

Lost in her own thoughts, Elise hadn't realized Joshua had joined her. Standing to the side of her, he leaned inward and placed his arm around her waist, whispering huskily, "Any regrets?"

Elise closed her eyes, taking in a deep breath while enjoying the feel of him so near to her. She replied earnestly, "None." Placing her hand over his, she rubbed it gently and leaned up against him. Turning to nuzzle closer she moaned in a soft seductive voice, "Well, come to think of it, maybe just one."

"Hmm, and what would that be . . ." Joshua said, nudging her shoulder with his. "As if I didn't know, you shameless hussy. Behave yourself! What will people think?"

"Oh pish-posh! Who gives a hoot?" Elise scoffed.

Chuckling, he squeezed her tighter. "Why, Elise Hamilton. I do believe that a serious discussion with your mother and father regarding the virtues of a proper, upstanding, Southern Belle is in order."

Certain that no one could overhear them, she whispered, "Is that right? Well, as I recall, you certainly didn't object to me practically throwing myself at you the other day, Major Carmidy." Elise's smile was radiant as she gazed up at him. Grateful that although the war had kept them apart for so long, once reunited, they were able to resume their bantering with each other as if nothing had ever separated them.

Nuzzling close to her, he rubbed his clean-shaven face up against her delicate ivory skin.

"You, know I was just thinking about that, and I've decided I reacted in haste the other day. Surely you would agree I wasn't thinking clearly considering the fact that I was exhausted from riding all night straight through from Appomattox Court House, and therefore, I deserve a second chance. And since today being clear-headed, clean-shaven, well rested, and having a keen desire that won't wait much longer, surely you might grant me a few moments to indulge myself with your charms."

Taking a breath and winking at Elise devilishly, Joshua continued. "Could it be that in your haste of packing, you've forgotten something we could fetch together?" he whispered suggestively.

Laughing gently at his proposal, she lifted her gloved index finger, shaking it lovingly.

"Absolutely not! You had your chance Major Carmidy. And since it was your choice-- not mine--to wait until we were wed . . . which, I might add, I've not yet decided if I should forgive you for, or not. You, my dear, will simply have to wait until you make an honest woman of me."

In a husky voice he growled, "Just as long as it's not too long."

"It won't be much longer," Elise said dreamily, feeling Joshua's strong arms wrap tighter around her waist. "Darling, look at Mama and Michael. Do you think she will be happy in New York? All she has ever known is Doves Landing and the life she built here in Fairfax with her dear friends."

"Your mother is a strong woman who loves her husband very much. She will be fine, wherever, Michael is."

"Yes, I know how she feels . . ." She cooed up at him, her voice trailed off, as she watched Sarah conversing with Irma and Charles Mason. *My, how they have aged since Tricia's death!*

Her smile faded as the immense guilt stirred inside her again, remembering Tricia Mason's death. *If only I hadn't stolen the piece of paper off Mr. Brown's desk that disclosed how each man had voted regarding secession, and had not passed it on to Thomas Hastings. Perhaps then that innocent, young girl might still be alive.* Such thoughts sent immediate shivers up her spine.

Joshua leaned closer and asked, "Are you all right, darling?"

"Yes, just got a chill, is all," Elise said, trying to sound convincing, not wanting to alarm him. Nonchalantly she began rubbing his hand, still wrapped tightly around her, still troubled by her thoughts, knowing for as long as she lived, she would never forgive herself for the role she played in

Tricia's death, or for shooting Joseph when he tried to run. The lifeless eyes starring up at her was a sight that still haunted her till this day.

Looking down at Joshua's hand she closed her eyes, desperately trying to block out all the pain she had caused. Immense guilt filled her at being able to feel safe from harm with the arms of the man she loved wrapped around her, knowing all that she had done. Her guilt-ridden mind couldn't seem to forget--much less forgive--her past actions and suddenly tears from her inner anguish streamed down her cheeks.

Knowingly, Joshua whispered reassuringly in her ear. "Elise, don't do this to yourself. Put it behind us darling, if not for you and me, but for them. We were at war, but now we must try to rebuild a life. One that will be of peace."

Speaking not a word, Elise listened to his soothing words, needing to make some sense of all the tragedies of war that not only she had committed, but that others had also.

"There is not a soul in this grieving nation, who has not done something of which they are not particularly proud of, north and south alike. War has brought out the best, and the worst, in us all. I look at Hastings over there and I honestly sympathize with that poor bastard. That shell of the man standing there could just as easily be me."

Just then Thomas glanced at them and nodded politely. Returning his nod, Joshua quickly continued. "Don't you think it troubles me that I can go home and step back into my life in the North with only my personal demons and nightmares to remind me of all that has occurred? What does he and others just like him do? With no family, no home to come back to? Where does a man like him, with so much rage inside him, even begin to build a new life?"

"Oh Joshua," she whispered lovingly. "Is it any wonder why I love you so?" Feeling a tug around her waist, she softly whispered, "As far as Thomas goes, don't worry about him. Michael has offered him a position as overseer of Doves Landing, as well as helping at Glenbrook. I told you that Glenbrook has been converted to an orphanage for girls, didn't I?"

"Yes. I recall you saying that when you explained how Mr. Brown and Miranda found their way to Washington and New York too. Wasn't it? Lucas Brown in New York? By God, now that's something I cannot imagine."

"Well it's true. Miranda and her father are in Washington right now, actually. From what I understand, Miranda travels from Washington to New York quite regularly. Seems Mr. Brown is quite active with old colleagues of his. I believe they call them the War Democrats. So we will join them for a visit . . . that is, if it's alright with you darlin'."

"That works out perfectly, since I have business to attend to in Washington myself. That is, if we ever get on the road today!"

Elise turned to face Joshua, hearing the frustration in his voice. "Don't fret dear, I'll go and see if I can move Mama along. Now wait here, I'll be just a minute . . ." Before he had a chance to stop her, Elise was off, her hoop skirts swaying back and forth. "Mama." Her voice trailed in the wind. "Please do try and hurry, it's getting quite late."

Hearing Elise, Noah and Gweneth Crenshaw looked over at Joshua and smiled. Then turning back to Elise, Noah said, "God has indeed blessed you, Miss Elise."

"Yes, sir. He certainly has," she replied, politely.

Realizing Joshua was standing alone by the rig, Michael took advantage of the opportunity to edge his way closer to the carriage while Gwyneth was giving Sarah one last hug.

"God speed, to you Michael. I will miss you all terribly," Noah said, following closely behind Michael. Upon reaching Joshua he added, "You're one mighty lucky man, Major Carmidy. You take real good care of her, now. Elise is a rare and precious pearl who needs to be loved and held dear to your heart to retain her luster."

"I'll remember that, sir."

"Good. You do that son, and you won't regret it." Turning back to Michael, he said, "Now take good care of our dear Sarah and say hello to Lucas for me when you see him. It's so hard to believe that all our friends are leaving."

Ignoring his last comment and to avoid any further delays, Michael said, "I will, Noah. With the war behind us, perhaps we will all see one another again, one day soon."

The two men shook hands vigorously and Noah slapped Michael on the back. "Even if we don't, it was a pleasure and a blessing to have you amongst us these past few years. I shall keep you all in my prayers."

"Thank you, friend." Turning back toward his wife and daughter, Michael called to them anxiously, "Ladies, are we about ready to go?"

Sarah and Elise, arm in arm, stopped to look at Doves Landing one last time. Overcome with emotion, they embraced. "Well, my darling daughter, are you ready to begin a new life with the man you love?"

"I could ask you the same, Mama. Are you?" Smiling at each other and with a nod of their heads, mother and daughter chimed in unison, through their tears. "Ready!" As they walked together, still arm in arm, Joshua and Michael stepped closer to their loved ones.

Playfully, Joshua extended his arm and then dramatically bowed to Elise, as if addressing royalty. "Come my precious pearl. Your chariot awaits you."

"Pearl? I rather like that," Elise retorted, smiling as she stepped into the carriage.

"I thought you might," Joshua said, winking at Noah, who gave a knowing nod as Joshua assisted her into the back seat of Lucas's old carriage that they were taking to him for his stay in New York.

Sarah, who had been watching the two young lovers, smiled as Michael came up behind her and placed his hand in the small of her back. "Darling, we'll be back soon. I promise."

"I know, dearest. I just never thought I'd see the day when . . ." Pausing, she stopped in mid-sentence seeing the worried look in her husband's eyes. Immediately Sarah changed her tone of voice to one of enthusiasm and cheerfully said, ". . . when I would actually be excited to be leaving my lovely home and starting a new life with my wonderful husband."

"You won't be sorry. I'll see to it," Michael whispered.

"I know." Realizing Elise was watching her intently, Sarah placed her gloved hands before her and in a playful shrug asked, "What seems to be the delay here, anyway? I thought we were in a hurry."

Michael glanced at Joshua and shook his head in disbelief. "What did I tell you, they are definitely worth the wait." Joshua winked and climbed up on the buckboard with Michael.

Since Joshua was still an officer in the Union Army, it was agreed that for the safety of all concerned, it would be wisest for him to ride up top in plain view, until they reached Washington. So on this bright sunny spring day, nearly four years from the first time Michael Honeycutt had come to Fairfax, Virginia on assignment, he was now headed back home with a new family.

With a broad grin, he looked at his future son-in-law, and said, "You know son, I'm not one to borrow trouble, but if I were you I'd be a getting while the getting's good."

Confused by Michael's comment, Joshua said, "Why is that?"

"Well considering the fact that two Yanks are about to take two of the finest treasures that the South has to offer, I'd say we had better be getting a move on. Wouldn't you?"

Chuckling knowingly, Joshua agreed. "Yeah, I see what ya mean." Needing no further encouragement, Joshua snapped the reins, leaving the lives they had known in Fairfax behind them. As the carriage slowly pulled away, Elise leaned slightly out of the window, holding on to her hat with one hand and waving merrily with the other to their friends.

"Sic semper tyrannis! The South is avenged!"

~ Two ~

The South is Avenged

On April 14, 1865--Good Friday morning, as they rode into Washington, an awestruck Elise gazed out the window of the coach.

"My goodness, Mama, look at all these people. Have you ever in all your life seen so many folk all in one place milling about, like that? Just look at the women in their lovely gowns and hats," she said enviously. Then excitedly, Elise pointed to the other side of the coach.

"Look at her . . . Why her parasol matches her gown." Turning toward Sarah, she asked, "Have you ever seen a lovelier ensemble in all your life?" Then looking at her worn traveling suit, Elise pouted. "I feel like some old strumpet, or worse, some farmer's wife in these old rags! Can we please go shopping before we go in search of Miranda and her friend Felicity? Heaven knows, I would shrivel up in embarrassment meeting them like this."

"Now Elise, there's nothing wrong with the way you look, and might I remind you that some of our dearest friends are farmers. Why as I recall..."

Interrupting her mother, Elise said, "Oh Mama, no lectures today. Surely, you agree that our clothing is outdated and terribly worn. What kind of impression will either of us make looking like this?"

Hearing his daughter, Michael called down to her reassuringly, "Fear not Elise, as soon as we secure acceptable rooms, we shall remedy your shopping dilemma at once." Looking at Joshua, he added, "The town looks mighty busy. I hope they saved our reservations."

As they pulled up in front of the Willard Hotel, at 14th Street and Pennsylvania, a gentleman in a top hat and coat, with a white silk scarf above the lapels of his overcoat, came to greet them. "Will you being staying with us, sir?"

"Yes, good man. I have a reservation, under Honeycutt--Michael J. Honeycutt. Three rooms, sir. Kindly see to it that our trunks are taken to our rooms."

"Of course, Mr. Honeycutt. Good to see you again."

Michael looked closer at the man before him as he stepped down from the backboard and stretched his back. "Why Cromley, you old son of a gun. How are you? How kind of you to remember me after all this time."

"Darling . . ." Michael pulled on Sarah's hand as she exited the carriage under the assistance of Joshua. ". . .This is Cromley. Cromley, I'd like to introduce you to my wife, Sarah Honeycutt, and my beautiful daughter Elise Hamilton." Stretching out his arm, Michael added. "And this fine officer is my future son-in-law, Major Joshua Carmidy. While we are here in Washington, please see to it that you give them all special attention now, won't you?"

"I'd be honored to, sir." Bowing politely to the women first, he then extended his white gloved-hand to Joshua. "Good to make your acquaintance."

Turning, Cromley blew his whistle three short bursts. Within seconds, three men came scurrying out the main door of the lobby, all dressed in red overcoats and black hats. Elise and Sarah glanced at one another, not saying a word, just taking it all in, in amazed silence, having never seen such formality as this.

"Will you be requiring your carriage, sir? Or shall I see that it goes to the stables?"

Michael, putting his index finger in the air signaling he required a moment, turned to Joshua. "How long do you think it will take for you to clear things up at the war department?"

"Why, there's no telling . . . I'm sure I'm not the only one trying to get my discharge papers and back pay. I don't know. Three, maybe four hours, I'd guess."

"Of course. Tell you what. How about if we all meet back in front of Ford's Theatre . . . You know where it is, right?"

"Yes, of course," Joshua replied.

"Good. Then let's say around eight o'clock, shall we? That should give us plenty of time to do what we all have to do and I'll send word to the Browns' and the Myles' to meet us for a late supper. How does that sound?" Michael asked, turning to Sarah.

"Fine. But darling, where are the shops? And what and where is Ford's Theatre?" she asked.

Michael, realizing the bellman was still awaiting orders, addressed him first. "Cromley, it doesn't appear we will be needing the carriage any further at this time."

"Very well, sir," the bellman retorted, bowing politely.

Michael took Sarah by the elbow, smiling down at her. "I will take you there straight away, after checking in. I certainly can't have my wife getting lost in Washington, now can I?"

After checking into their rooms, Joshua went in one direction while Elise, Sarah, and Michael went in another. Just as promised, Michael pointed out the Ford Theatre and other interesting sites in Washington as they searched for shops that would be suitable for their purchasing needs. After a short visit at his bank where Michael withdrew money, the three of them were off again.

For the first time in their lives, Sarah and Elise went shopping in a large city. Within hours, they were completely transformed into well-dressed women, attired in the latest fashions direct from Paris, France. With only a few coins left in Sarah's new silk-beaded purse, she smiled at Elise, and whispered, "My, I don't recall ever spending this much money in a month, let alone in one day."

Stepping onto busy 10th Street, both women wrapped their parasol cords around their wrist as instructed by the shopkeeper and clutched their new silk purses in their lace-gloved hands. Feeling every bit as stylish as any other woman on the cobblestone streets of Washington, Elise and Sarah strutted proudly over to Michael, who had waited for them outside the boutique.

Seeing them approach, he immediately stood erect and then in grand fashion, took off his top hat and gallantly waved it in front of him dramatically as he bowed. "Two visions of loveliness have graced my presence."

Sarah tapped her toe and tried to look crossly at him. "Be still Michael, or you will have the entire town staring at us."

Chuckling, he placed his hat firmly back in place. "I thought that was the idea, Mrs. Honeycutt." Winking at her, he turned and offered an elbow to each of them. "Shall we go and find Joshua? I'm sure he must be finished by now."

As the three of them strolled down the street, Elise couldn't help but admire her reflection in the various shop and boardinghouse windows. Leaning forward slightly to get her mother's attention, she whispered, "Mama, have you ever seen so many boardinghouses?"

"That's easy to explain," Michael said, obviously pleased to be their tour guide. "You see, the majority of Congressmen and State Representatives rent rooms rather than taking up permanent residence in Washington."

"Michael, is that also why there are so many shops and eateries?"

"Indeed."

As a group of gentlemen passed them, tilting their hats and displaying admiring smiles, Elise declared, "I think I rather like the North after all."

Sarah responded by shaking her head at Elise being so predictable, while Michael declared, "Ah yes, well judging by what I've just seen, a certain Major Carmidy is definitely going to have to keep an eye on his fiancée."

"Oh pooh," Elise scoffed, teasingly.

Just as Michael had thought, Joshua was already waiting on the corner of E Street and 10th Street. Seeing them, he began to walk toward them, his broad smile clearly exhibited his approval of his fiancée's choice in apparel. As soon as he was close enough to be heard, he complimented her. "My pearl, you glow. Never have I seen you look lovelier."

Pleased by his comment, Elise glided her gloved hand to the waist of her tailored black skirt with large pleats in the back that ran from the back of her knees to the hem of the long skirt.

Knowing that her attire accented her tiny frame, Elise casually adjusted her parasol on the sleeve of her coat. The matching coat cinched in at her waist and spread gently across her buttocks then gathered tightly again around the front of her waist ending in a scalloped, velvet taupe lapel collar. With the matching high-collared sheer taupe blouse, Elise felt radiant as she curtsied at Joshua, being certain to show off her matching narrow taupe felt hat.

Proudly placing her hand in the crook of his arm, Joshua nodded at Sarah. "Ma'am, if I didn't know better, I would think I was in the company of royalty."

"Oh, Major Carmidy, you do go on so," Sarah blushed, looking at Elise.

As the two couples continued walking toward the Ford Theatre, Elise looked at Joshua with a concerned frown. "Joshua darling, why are you still in uniform? I thought you were here to end your military career?"

"Indeed I did, but did you think the army would hand me over a new suit?"

Michael, overhearing the two of them, chuckled softly and said, "New suit . . . I like that."

Noticing Elise pouting slightly at being teased, Joshua patted her hand gently. "Darling, we will have time in the morning to shop for a new suit. Perhaps you could look for another dress, as well." At this suggestion, her scowl turned to a broad smile.

"Well, if that's an apology, I accept. I was wondering, does New York offer such fine shops, as we've seen here?"

"Far more, I dare say. Washington is hardly famous for its shops, my darling. Some believe Washington needs a complete revamping. I tend to agree. The Capitol of such a grand nation as ours should hardly resemble a quaint Southern town."

This is a far cry from Fairfax, or Centerville, Elise thought to herself, taking offense at his comment, but deciding to ignore it for the time being. "Yes, of course . . . in New York, there are more shops, you say?"

"You are relentless, aren't you, dear? Yes, hundreds more. However, darling, please do remember we are going to be just starting out. Such luxuries will have to wait until I'm established in the law firm again."

A slight frown crossed her brow and Elise pouted again.

Michael chuckled at his daughter's reaction. "Now don't fret, Elise." Smiling lovingly at Sarah and drawing her nearer to him, he said, "I promise you and your beautiful mother an entire wardrobe, once we reach New York. So you will have several opportunities to go shopping again."

"Oh, thank you, Michael," Elise cooed in delight.

Just then, the bells from a clock struck eight o'clock. Elise and Sarah stopped and watched in amazement as men began lighting the lamps lining the streets of Washington, leaving a warm, soft glow hovering over the streets.

Engrossed in watching the sights and sounds of the city, Elise didn't notice a coach pull up on E Street alongside Ford Theatre.

"By God, it's good to see you all again." Hearing a familiar voice, she turned to see Lucas Brown exiting his carriage.

Elise's heart began to beat rapidly. *Oh, my, but doesn't Mr. Brown look gallant in his tailored suit with long tails and top hat.*

Out stepped Miranda, followed by another couple whom Elise assumed was the Reverend Myles and his wife, Felicity. As the four of them approached, Elise brought her hands to her face.

"Oh, look how beautiful Miranda is," Elise cried happily.

Then, without waiting to be properly escorted, the two old friends ran toward each other, throwing their arms around one another and hugging tightly.

"Miranda, I've missed you so. You look absolutely beautiful!"

"I've missed you, too. And just look at you! How in the world did you manage to get such a beautiful suit as this, all the way in Fairfax?"

"Mother and I went shopping today . . . *here* in Washington. Do you like it?" Elise exclaimed as she twirled around in the playful manner of a child.

"Very much. Words just don't describe how wonderful you look to me."

"And to me, also." Lucas boomed. "Come over here and give me a hug, Miss Elise."

Without hesitation, Elise went to Lucas, hugging him. "Oh Mr. Brown, it's so good to see you again."

Elise, never having been accused of being shy, turned to Felicity. "Why, Felicity Phelps, I mean Felicity Myles, I hardly recognize you. You are truly lovelier than I remember."

After they hugged each other politely, Elise turned to the bearded man beside Felicity and said, "And you must be the good Reverend Myles that I've heard so much about."

Benjamin smiled broadly at the outspoken young woman standing before him and extended his hand to her. Kissing her offered hand politely, he said, "How delightfully enchanting and refreshing you are, Miss Hamilton. I am indeed the lucky man who has won your friend's heart. But please, do call me Benjamin, since we are sure to be good friends."

"Thank you, only if you call me Elise." She smiled politely, trying not to show her fascination with Reverend Myles's English accent and his polished mannerisms. Turning to Joshua and extending her arm, Elise proudly said, "Felicity and Benjamin, allow me to introduce you to Major Joshua Carmidy."

Joshua shook Benjamin's hand heartily before turning his attention to Felicity. "Mrs. Myles . . . I don't suppose you remember me?"

"Of course I do, Mr. Carmidy. How kind of you to remember me."

"Yes, it's been some time. I haven't seen you since before you went abroad." Turning his attention to Elise and the others, Joshua quickly explained. "Mrs. Myles' uncle was a client of ours prior to the war." Redirecting his attention back to Felicity, he continued. "I trust your uncle, Mr. Robbins, is well?"

Felicity's smile faded, as she said, "We lost Uncle Edwin a few years back in a tragic accident."

Everyone listened with great interest to Joshua and Felicity's conversation, Elise taking particular interest in how lovely Mrs. Myles was, feeling suddenly jealous of this woman who knew her fiancé.

Felicity looked at her husband, Benjamin, and explained. "The Major is Mr. Carmidy's son. Prior to my trip to England, Uncle Edwin had me meet with his solicitor here in New York."

"Right. Well, this is a small world isn't it?" Turning his attention to Joshua, he said, "As it goes, Felicity and I still use your father's services."

"I see. Well, then you have seen more of my father these past few years than I have."

"Indeed. He's been most helpful. With my work calling me away for long periods, it has been wonderful to rely on your father's expertise. Do you plan on returning to his firm, Major?"

"Yes. And . . ." Joshua turned his attention back to Felicity. "May I express my deepest sorrow to you, Mrs. Myles, for the loss of your uncle. Edwin Robbins was a fine man."

"Thank you, Major," Felicity replied.

Feeling suddenly awkward, Felicity and Elise began to speak at the same time. Both women laughed nervously and looked at their mutual friend while Miranda smiled, taking Felicity's hand.

"See, I told you Elise would remember you." It was clear that Felicity and Miranda were extremely close and suddenly, for the second time in the few short minutes since they had met up again, Elise felt jealously toward Felicity.

Sarah, recognizing the look in her daughter's eyes, turned her attention to Lucas. "Why Lucas, you look . . . *wonderful.* It does my heart good to see you looking so fit."

"And you, dear Sarah, are as lovely as ever. And Honeycutt, by God, it's good to see you again. How are you?"

"Quite well, thank you. As you requested, we've brought up your carriage and the Masons received your wire. That was mighty fine of you, Lucas."

"It's the least I could do. Glenbrook . . . well, Glenbrook needs life inside those walls."

"Life is exactly what she has too, with all those young girls running around."

Lucas Brown's smile faded as he asked about the former slaves from his plantation. "How are Chester and Betsy?"

"Chester is still doing rather poorly, the old guy. Doc says it's his rheumatism . . . but Bessie . . . well, what can I say? She's as cantankerous as ever."

Joshua and Benjamin began conversing politely. "Good to finally meet you, Major Carmidy. Your father has spoken of you often. I'm so pleased to see that the perils of war have escaped you."

"Call me Joshua, please. Yes, I'm fortunate, alright. So tell me, how is my father . . ."

Just then, a screech of joy rang out and their attention went to the three women standing a few yards ahead of them. "What in the blazes?" asked Lucas.

"Well, Mr. Brown, from the sound of your daughter's enthusiasm, I'd say that Elise has just informed her of our engagement."

"Engagement! Well, don't that beat all." Lucas grasped Joshua's hand and shook it once more then slapped him on the back. "I thought it mighty peculiar that you were escorting Michael and Sarah here . . . Well, all I can say is congratulations. You've got yourself a mighty fine and spirited woman there. You take good care of her or you will have to answer to me."

Michael coughed, as if objecting to Lucas's last comment and Lucas changed his last remark. "Forgive me Michael, I stand corrected. First you will have to answer to Michael, and then to me."

Michael patted Joshua on the back. "Son, if that hasn't scared you off completely, nothing ever will."

"Nope. Been through a lot worse than that recently," Joshua said, smiling.

Somberly Lucas looked at him and said, "Yes. You and so many others . . . but enough of such talk, this is an evening of celebration and rejoicing."

"Indeed it is, Mr. Brown." Joshua stretched out his hands and nodded his head, gesturing up the street as he continued speaking. "We seem to be blocking the entrance to the theatre. Why don't we adjourn this reuniting of old and new friends to a local establishment down the street, shall we?"

As they walked farther down 10th street, a tall slender gentleman came out of a carriage just ahead of them, wearing an amazingly tall top hat. He was escorting a short, refined woman toward the entrance of Ford's Theatre.

Joshua immediately stood at attention and saluted the gentleman.

"At ease, Major," the lanky, bearded man responded.

Elise, puzzled at Joshua's peculiar behavior and stopped chattering to Miranda, who was standing by her side in total shock.

"Oh, my," Elise gasped, finally recognizing the man. "Why, if it ain't Old Abe himself. In the flesh!" Her voice traveled further than she had intended.

Hearing her comment, Abraham Lincoln stopped and smiled, while tipping his hat in respect, he said, "Why yes, my dear young woman, it is. How charming it is to hear the sweet sounds of a Southern Belle's voice ringing through our fair city again. Begging your pardon for intruding on your privacy, but what, might I ask, has brought you here today?"

Elise curtseyed and shyly replied to the Commander-in-Chief. "Excuse my words, sir. I didn't mean them to sound unkind."

Amused, Lincoln smiled and said, "Oh, you are enchanting, my dear. Mother here, she's from the South, too." Lincoln waved his hand toward his wife, Mary Todd Lincoln, who smiled dutifully at Elise.

"Yes, I do recall hearing that, sir. In answer to your question, I'm here with my fiancé," Elise said, tugging proudly on Joshua's arm and flashing a warm look in his direction. "And my Mama and stepfather. What with the great General Lee surrendering and the war all but over, we're traveling to New York."

"New York, you say?"

"Yes, sir."

Lincoln eyed Joshua more closely, apparently recognizing him. "Major, didn't I see you in Richmond earlier this month?"

"Yes, sir," Joshua replied respectfully, still standing at attention.

Lincoln shook his head in distress. "It saddens me to see such a fine city like Richmond destroyed." He tugged at his whiskered chin.

Mrs. Lincoln gently tapped her husband's arm as she held onto it tightly. Acknowledging her polite reminder that they were on a time schedule, the President nodded politely to the group gathered before him. "If you'll excuse us. Mother gets rather upset if we miss curtain call."

Waiting for no reply, the Lincolns began walking toward the theatre to see *Our American Cousin*.

After they disappeared into the theatre, Elise turned and looked at the rest of her family and friends and exclaimed, "Why, I don't know why people make him out to be such a mean sort. He seems rather likeable."

Miranda shook her head and started to laugh, then said "Oh my goodness, not only did you insult the President of the United States of America, but you then proceed to have a conversation with him. And if that wasn't enough, you act as if it's common place! You are unbelievable . . . Only you could say such a thing about the man you once proclaimed to be the enemy."

"Yes, well, I thought Joshua was the enemy once too and surely I found out differently. Perhaps I can see my way to accepting Mr. Lincoln as well."

"Well that's an improvement from 'Old Abe.' Elise, what am I going to do with you?" Joshua groaned, shook his head and tenderly squeezed her hand as she placed it in the crook of his arm. Everyone laughed at her shocked indignation as they made their way to the boardinghouse eatery Michael had picked out.

After the eight of them had been seated and their orders taken, Elise, being the boldest of the group, looked at Benjamin and Felicity. "Since we're old friends, Felicity, I trust you won't mind me asking how you and your husband came to meet? Was it here in America or while you were in England?"

Felicity looked at Benjamin as if hoping he would explain.

"Well, as luck would have it, I had the great honor of meeting Felicity in England," he dutifully replied.

"England? And then you two came here? How interesting." Elise prattled on, nearly bursting with enthusiasm.

Benjamin lovingly patted his wife's hand and spoke for her. "Right. Well, it's a rather long tale, but the long and the short of it is, Felicity and I, after meeting originally in England, were reunited and wed in New York. At your mother and father's home in fact, Mr. Honeycutt."

Nearly choking on his biscuit in surprise, Michael asked, "My parent's home, you say? My, but that is a coincidence. How did that come about?"

Felicity spoke up this time. "My dear aunt, Gwendolyn Phelps and your parents were dear friends many years ago. When Aunt Gwen and I arrived here in America, we stayed with them."

Intrigued, Elise couldn't help but ask more questions. "Forgive me Felicity, I hope you don't find me intrusive, but did I hear you say *were* good friends?"

"My aunt died shortly after Benjamin and I were wed."

"Oh, I'm so sorry . . ."

"Please, don't be sad. My aunt was an incredible woman and brought Benjamin and me together. So you see, as we share our lives, Aunt Gwen will always be alive in our hearts."

Touched by her words, they looked at each of their own loved ones. Before anyone had a chance to speak, three waiters brought their dinners.

After the meals were set before them, Sarah looked at Michael and said, "Well, this is rather wonderful, not having to be the one to prepare the evening meal for hungry travelers."

Sarah's words sounded upbeat, but from the look in her eyes, Elise knew her mother had suddenly become homesick for Doves Landing.

Clearing his throat, Lucas said, "Reverend Myles, please do us the honors and lead us in prayer."

Once grace had been said, the eight of them chitchatted while enjoying their evening meal.

"So, Benjamin, how is it that you and Felicity came to be here, in Washington?" Joshua asked.

"Well, following the riots of '63 and the Negro orphans that were nearly killed at the Asylum, and with so many Irish immigrants arriving daily in the city, there was a desperate need for spiritual leadership, as you can well imagine. The majority of the clergy were working in the field and at hospitals for the wounded. As luck would have it, at a recent dinner party at your parent's home, Mr. Honeycutt, Lucas here suggested I come with him to Washington and present my concerns to Congress."

"Really?" Michael's curiosity piqued. "Ah, so father and mother were instrumental in you two meeting, I take it?"

Lucas cleared his throat. "Well, not exactly, Michael. As it was said earlier, Felicity's parents were dear friends of the family. However, Alfred did introduce me to James Sterling, who is a partner of his and just happens to be from England as well. Quite a small world as it turns out, since Felicity, Benjamin and James's wife, Lavinia, all knew one another in England, too."

"Really? You don't say?" Michael looked at Benjamin and Felicity. "Well, it would appear then that you all know my son, Thaddeus. Tell me, how is he? It's been so long since I've seen him . . . Thank heavens the war is finally over."

"Amen to that!" everyone cheered spontaneously and raised their water glasses in unison.

Looking over the rim of her glass, Elise glanced suspiciously between Felicity and Miranda. She was certain the two women had secrets they didn't wish to share in public. Always loving a good mystery, Elise regarding herself as a rather good sleuth and her eyes danced as unanswered questions filled her mind. *If Benjamin and Felicity knew one another in England, then why were they reunited in New York?* Remembering the wary expression that had briefly appeared on Felicity's face when the Sterlings were mentioned, Elise wondered what Miranda and Felicity were hiding.

"Elise dear, have you and the good Major set a date yet?" Miranda asked.

Elise lowered her glass and with a gleam in her eye, looked at her friend, deciding Miranda was trying to distract her by bringing up the wedding again. She may not have seen her for years, but she knew how Miranda's mind worked. *Just what is Miranda trying to hide from me?* Elise thought, growing more certain with each passing moment that Miranda was trying to divert her attention away from Felicity.

When Elise didn't answer right away, Joshua spoke up. "Please, everyone, my army days are over. There is no further need to address me as 'major'. Joshua will suit me just fine from here on out. As for our wedding date, just as soon as we can. Right, sweetheart?" he said, smiling proudly at his betrothed.

As Joshua spoke, Elise smiled at Miranda as their eyes met. Just as Miranda had done as a child, she immediately looked away then glanced back at Felicity for a split second. *I knew it! You are hiding something, Miranda.* Raising her eyebrow, Elise smiled at Felicity, pointedly. *So what deep, dark secret are you and the Reverend hiding, Mrs. Myles?*

Before Elise could respond to Joshua, Michael enthusiastically interrupted. "Sarah, darling, with you not knowing a soul in New York, why not let Mother help plan Elise and Joshua's wedding? That is, if there wouldn't be any objections from your parents, Joshua."

"I can't speak for them of course, but I'm sure they wouldn't mind."

"Of course. It is customary for the bride's family to make the arrangements, isn't it, dear?" Michael looked at Sarah for confirmation.

"Yes, that's right," Sarah said, smiling brightly. Too brightly, Elise thought, noting her mother deliberately avoided answering his first question.

"Well, then if you would like, I'm sure Mother would love to help you. What a wonderful way for you two to become acquainted."

Sarah smiled weakly at her husband and Elise suspected her mother was indeed, delicately trying to conceal her misgivings about Michael's suggestion.

"Well, darling, that would be splendid. However, don't you think it is a bit presumptuous of us to assume that your mother would even want to plan such an affair? It is rather an inconvenience, don't you think? After all, she doesn't even know us."

"Nonsense, if there's one thing Mother does enjoy, it is planning a grand party. Besides, it will give all of you an opportunity to meet everyone right away."

"How splendid," Sarah replied, prompting Michael to hug his wife's shoulder. "Darling, don't look so apprehensive. It will be fine."

"A grand affair? That could take months to plan. I had always thought of a more refined, smaller event." Joshua interjected cautiously, looking to Elise for agreement. "Isn't that how you saw it too, Elise?"

By the look on his face, Elise knew he was alarmed by the prospect of waiting several more months to make her his wife.

"Well, I don't wish to appear ungrateful, Michael, but I agree with Joshua. We have waited so long and really don't need anything elaborate. A simple ceremony with friends and family is all we want."

"Nonsense, Elise. I won't hear of such a thing." he insisted, vehemently. "You two deserve the best and by God, you two shall have it. Right, Sarah? Only the best for our girl."

Michael's reaction shocked Elise, but before she could respond, her mother softly said, "Well . . ." Sarah hesitated, looking across the table at her daughter and then at Joshua sympathetically, before continuing. "Of course, Michael, dear. But Elise and Joshua do raise a point we should take into consideration. If it were you, would you want to wait any longer than necessary? Did we wait?"

Sheepishly, Michael conceded her point. "When you put it that way, I guess I can't refuse. But, with just a short time to plan, would it be possible to still have a celebration that would allow me the opportunity to show off my lovely new family to old friends?"

Apologetically, Miranda interrupted. "Please, forgive my intrusion into such a delicate, private matter. Perhaps you would allow me to offer a suggestion? Having the privilege of getting to know Mrs. Honeycutt over these past few years, I'm certain if anyone could accommodate both of your needs, she would be the one. Why not simply explain to her that a celebration would be wonderful, if it could be done within a few weeks?"

"Splendid idea, Miranda," Michael eagerly said, turning to Joshua and Elise. "Don't you agree?" he said, almost pleading. "A few weeks doesn't seem unreasonable, considering both you and Elise have already stated you wanted to go shopping, and Joshua does need to get reacquainted in the law firm before you take a wedding trip. This way, Elise can shop for a complete trousseau--my treat--and Joshua, you can settle back into work."

Elise looked at Joshua, waiting for him to respond. Seeing the look on her face and the eager look on Michael's, he responded firmly. "Fine, a few weeks, only."

"Of course. I will tell Mother myself of our agreement." Raising his cup, Michael proposed a toast. "To the bride and groom."

Sarah joined her husband, saying, "Cheers!"

The small dinner party became festive again as Benjamin added his sentiments. "And may God shine down upon you both."

With that, they all raised their cups and chimed, "Here, here!"

As they sipped their wine, several men rushed into the establishment shouting, "President Lincoln's been shot, at Ford's Theatre. He's not expected to live!"

Gasps filled the small room and between the sounds of women crying, anguished questions echoed from neighboring tables.

"Oh, God, no!"

"Why would anyone do such a thing?"

Shocked and horrified, Elise looked at Joshua, close to tears herself. "But that can't be, we just saw him . . ."

"I know, my darling." Unable to hide his stunned grief and sense of loss, he took her into his arms and held her close.

As the room's anguish heightened, Benjamin placed his linen napkin on the table, pushed back his chair and stood up.

"Ladies and Gentlemen, if I may have your attention, please." A hush fell over the room as everyone looked at the Reverend.

"In this time of terrible sorrow, please join me in a prayer for this great man, his good wife, and a nation that needs our prayers now, more than ever before."

Without hesitation, everyone lowered their head in dazed disbelief.

Clearing his throat, Benjamin bowed his head and began to pray.

"Dear Lord, one of your flock, Abraham Lincoln . . . a great man who led the noble fight for the freedom of our Negro brothers and sisters and reunited a nation once divided, has fallen victim to a brutal act . . ."

~ Three ~

Thieves in the Night

Stunned and shocked by the news of President Lincoln having been shot, it was impossible for those gathered in the Washington eatery, just blocks away from the Ford Theatre, to finish their meals.

Michael looked at Lucas and seeing a frown on his face, said, "Lucas old friend. No offense, but I must say your reaction surprises me."

Raising his hand, Lucas replied thoughtfully. "None taken, friend. Although I have not always agreed with Lincoln's politics, being here in Washington these past few years has provided me the opportunity to observe him first hand. And I have come to admire the man's desire to rebuild the South, instead of punishing it." Shaking his head sadly, Lucas slowly stood. "If you'll excuse me, I'm sure my old friend Andrew Johnson will be in need of a friendly face about now."

"Yes. Of course," Michael said, standing up along with Lucas as he made his way over to his daughter.

"Miranda dear, under the circumstances, I'm not sure I will be able to return with you as planned to New York. If Mr. Lincoln does in fact pass, then Johnson, as Vice President, will be sworn into office. And if I know anything about the Republican Senate, then all hell will break loose with a Southern Democrat at the helm."

Kissing his daughter lightly on the cheek, he turned to Michael and Benjamin. "I know this is a lot to ask, but would you please see to it that Miranda is safely returned to New York?"

Benjamin answered first. "As you know, Lucas, my business is complete here, so we can leave at any time. Miranda is more than welcome to join us."

Joshua, who had been listening to the other patron's hushed conversations in the eatery, suddenly stood up and quietly interrupted. "Excuse the intrusion. If what I just heard is true, then I suggest we leave immediately while we still can."

Michael frowned. "What's wrong, Joshua?"

"It's being said that a Southern actor by the name of John Wilkes Booth is responsible for the attempted assassination, and since we are in the company of Southerners . . ."

"Enough said, I get your point." Michael looked at Elise and Sarah. "Ladies, shall we?"

After taking care of the bill, Michael joined the group where they gathered around the Myles' coach. Fear shone in everyone's eyes as Michael asked, "Son, what do think we need to do?"

Joshua replied calmly. "Leave Washington at once. With the shock so new, I'm sure no one has thought to block the roads leading out of the city yet." Turning his attention directly to Michael, he stated urgently, "There's no time to pick up our belongings. Is your tab settled?"

"Don't worry about that. I can settle up with them tomorrow," Lucas offered.

Looking at Joshua, concern showed in his eyes. "Well then, what are we waiting for, Major? Get these women the hell out of here while you still can. I have all the faith in the world in your abilities."

Joshua gripped Lucas's hand firmly. "Coming from you sir, that means a lot. I promise I won't let you down."

"God speed, Joshua," Lucas said, patting the man he once detested, firmly on the back. "I'll be holding you to that promise."

Turning to Miranda, Lucas gave his daughter a kiss while the other men helped their loved ones into the coach. Tenderly Lucas looked at her, trying to reassure her by saying, "Darling, please understand. New York is where I can assure your safety. I'll miss you terribly, but know how much I love you."

Close to tears, Miranda hugged her father. "Papa I love you too. Please be careful."

After securing Miranda in the coach, Joshua gave directions to the band of weary travelers in a low steady voice. His demeanor left no doubt as to why he was such a good officer, and Elise looked adoringly at him.

"From here out, Elise and Mrs. Honeycutt, unless it's absolutely impossible to avoid, I do not want you to speak with anyone if we should be stopped. Your accents are far too noticeable. Mrs. Myles, of all the women, you speak most like a Northerner. Although, Miss Brown, I've noticed your accent is almost undetectable. Therefore, if we are detained, you two should be the ones to do the majority of the speaking. Now, Reverend Myles, this is a lot to ask, but I need you to keep our backs covered. Just until we make it safely out of Washington and parts of Maryland. I'll need you to take a seat as lookout in the back of the rig."

"Right. Consider it done."

"Good." Joshua nodded affirmatively, before continuing. "Michael, you and I will cover the front and answer any questions that should come our way. Both hailing from New York, it makes sense that we're anxious to return after the war, and are therefore traveling at night. Also Mrs. Myles, please don't take offense, but if asked why we travel at night, it's your health we are concerned about. You are in the family way. Understood?"

Felicity blushed, but shook her head obligingly.

"Look, I'm sure it will take a few minutes to organize a search party for the perpetrators of this heinous act. By then we will have plenty of miles between Washington and us. Any questions?" Joshua asked, urgently looking at everyone. Hearing none, he said, "Well then, let's be on our way, and above all else, appear calm."

Benjamin took his seat as Michael climbed up to the backboard, and Joshua, noticing Elise's frightened look, stopped long enough to poke his head inside the carriage. "Don't worry, my darling. Close the curtains and we'll be safely out of Washington in no time at all."

Trying to smile reassuringly at him, Elise nodded. "Don't worry about me. I'm fine knowing you're here."

Winking at her lovingly, Joshua climbed aboard the buggy and the seven of them left Washington like thieves in the night.

As Joshua held the reins firmly between his thumb and forefingers, Michael looked at him. "This must be exceedingly difficult for you, son, considering you fought under Grant's command. Not exactly the actions that a fine officer like yourself would expect to be taking only hours after becoming a civilian, I would imagine."

"Tonight, I don't look at our leaving Washington as an act of cowardly retreat, sir. Rather, this is a tactical diversion, necessary to protect our loved ones."

Nodding his head, Michael said, "I agree. So much for a pleasant evening. Will this madness ever stop?"

Sitting in the coach, Elise grasped her mother's hand and whispered, "Don't fret Mama, what Joshua said makes sense. I'm sure everything is going to be just fine."

"Darling, I'm not worried about that. I feel very confident in Joshua's ability to lead us to safety. I was just thinking that if that actor fellow did kill the president, what might the ramifications against the South be? You said it yourself earlier, Elise. President Lincoln seemed to be a nice man. What purpose is served by killing him? Hasn't there been enough pain and misery in this nation already? Did we need his blood shed, too?"

As the coach eased its way through the streets of Washington at a slow and an easy pace designed to avoid suspicion, the streets became lined with people. It was evident the mood of the Capitol had changed drastically from earlier in the day. The cheers celebrating victory had been replaced by an eerie stillness as everyone reacted to the rapidly spreading news with disbelief and shock.

Men and women alike milled about in the streets, waiting to hear the latest word of the President's condition. Some wept openly, while others were already beginning to seethe with anger. The distinctive sound of men's raised voices demanding revenge could be heard.

As every moment passed, the four women sat in complete silence listening to the crowd's anger and rage increase as the shock began to wear off, just as Joshua had predicted.

How peculiar, Felicity thought, *that Major Carmidy had thought her accent was nearly undetectable and that she should pretend she was expecting.* Felicity closed her eyes, feeling suddenly emotional. *If only I were.*

In the two years since her marriage to her beloved Ben, the only thing that lacked in their life was a child of their own. Blocking out that pain, Felicity focused on her accent, recalling how frightened she had been upon returning to America and experiencing the hatred of others upon hearing her Southern accent. She wondered now if it had been a conscious decision on her part masking her drawl. Recalling that very first night back in America, how she and poor Aunt Gwen had been nearly accosted by four hooligans as soldiers in the federal army did nothing to come to their aid. *My, that seems a lifetime ago, but at the same time, only yesterday.*

Forgetting the fear she felt that night, Felicity focused on the years since and her life with Benjamin. Except for not being blessed with children, the life Benjamin and she shared was nearly perfect. Not a day passed that she didn't thank God for bringing her and Ben together despite all odds, to experience how love between a man and a woman was meant to be. She decided her changed accent was surely due to living with her Ben and hearing him speak so often. Whatever had caused her to lose her Southern drawl, Felicity was now fervently glad that she had.

As the horse picked up speed, the women breathed a sigh of relief, realizing they must be out of the city.

"Whew. Being North all this time, I've forgotten how frightening this war business is," Miranda said.

"Frightening? War business? From the sounds of it, you *have* been North far too long. Why this isn't frightening at all," Elise exclaimed. "A bit unnerving, perhaps. But surely not frightening. After what we've been through the past four years, the last two being the worst, I can assure you Miranda, this was nothing. Isn't that so, Mama?"

Sarah nodded at Elise, saying softly, "Dear, why don't you fill in Miranda and Felicity to the hardships we've had to endure while I rest for a spell. Suddenly I find I've got a nasty headache and would prefer to rest my eyes."

"Mama, are you sure you're all right?"

"Nothing that a few winks won't cure. Now you three get reacquainted while I rest."

After everyone wished Sarah a good sleep, Elise described at length and in detail their experiences during the past four years. Miranda shared her memories from the first year of the war, when she had still been in the South. Felicity sat in utter shock, unable to fathom living through such hardships for so long a time.

Elise held nothing back, telling Felicity of her involvement as a spy, including meeting Joshua and their turbulent relationship until they had fallen in love. How she had nearly lost him and how unbearable it had been, not knowing if he was alive or dead for three years. Then she expanded upon how those three years had been a living nightmare. Not just due to constant worry for Joshua's safety, but never knowing from one day to the next where their next meal would come from. She spoke of how they had been raided countless times, all their food and valuables being taken from them, and of the attack she sustained at the hands of her one time friend, Thomas Hastings.

Leaning closer to her mother, to be certain Sarah was in fact asleep, Elise cautiously raised her skirts and pantaloons. Seeing the jagged scar on her thigh, Felicity and Miranda gasped.

Not really asleep, only pretending to be, Sarah wanted desperately to see her daughter's scar and ask Elise why she hadn't shared her horrific ordeal with them, but she refrained. Sarah realized her daughter was indeed a woman, just as Michael had said to her many times. Certainly, Elise had earned the right to keep secrets from her mother if she felt she must. So instead, Sarah continued to lean on the window of the coach listening to the chatter of these young women and pretend to sleep.

"Oh Elise, how could you have kept such a wound from your mother and Mammy Tess? Surely you were in excruciating pain," Miranda whispered.

"I was indeed and believe me it wasn't easy. However, how was I supposed to explain that by my own foolish actions I was nearly raped, or worse, could have been killed trying to help someone who I believed to be a friend? Besides, if Thomas' men accused me of ambushing them, the less Mama and Michael knew the better. Don't you see? By telling them, I would be putting their lives in danger, too. No, I had gotten myself into that pickle and I had to get myself out."

Felicity smiled warmly at Elise, saying, "Well, it would appear you have been through a lot. How did you ever handle it all?"

"Hope and a whole lot of praying," Elise stated, sincerely.

"Hope," Miranda whispered nostalgically. "Oh Elise, I remember the day when you convinced me that hope was what was needed if we were to carry on. How wonderful that you never wavered and kept believing, despite everything you endured."

"Oh, I didn't say that." Elise chuckled softly. "There were plenty of times I nearly gave up. But it was Joshua's love and Michael's unselfish devotion that kept me strong. Without Michael, I honestly don't know if Mama and I would have made it. I still can't believe how he stayed with us, when he could have lived in comfort. But he made a promise and he followed through and I shall never forget what he sacrificed for both Mama and me. Why, I couldn't love him more if he were my real father," Elise exclaimed.

As Sarah pretended to sleep, a tear rolled down her cheek as she heard her daughter speak of Michael with such endearment. At the same time, Joshua looked at Michael, as the two of them listened to the women chattering inside.

"Just in case I haven't told you, Michael, thank you! If anything should have happened to that woman, hell, I don't know what might have become of me."

"We both did what we had to do. Hell, I had it easy compared to what you went through. I had Sarah by my side everyday," he replied humbly. "I'm just glad it's almost over."

"The sooner we're in New York, the sooner we'll both breathe easier."

From inside the coach, Felicity said softly, "Mr. Honeycutt seems like a wonderful man. Truly, you have been blessed. Not only did you find a father, but you also found the love of a wonderful man, who obviously loves you completely. Yes, Elise. I would definitely say you have indeed been one of the fortunate souls who will take with them something of value out of all this madness."

"And don't you think I don't know it, too. As soon as we reach New York I plan to spend the rest of my life making both Joshua and Michael proud of me."

Miranda sheepishly said, "Well, all I can say is, Michael definitely takes after his father and not his mother." Shaking her head knowingly at

Felicity, she added, "Now, don't look at me so disapprovingly, Felicity. You know what I say is the absolute truth."

Felicity softly chuckled and whispered, "Shh, Miranda. What if Michael can hear you?"

Anxious to hear what Michael's parents were really like, Elise smiled encouragingly, knowing if she asked point blank that would be wrong, but if Miranda volunteered the information . . . *Well, what could be the harm in listening?*

"Oh Felicity, you know perfectly well Vivian grates on your last nerve, always comparing you to her precious Lavinia." Realizing she had said too much, Miranda quickly added, "I'm so sorry, Felicity. Will you ever forgive me?"

"No harm done. I'm sure it's just a matter of time, and Elise will be told the whole sordid past regarding Lavinia, Benjamin, and me. After Elise bared her heart to me, it's only fair that I reciprocate. Besides, I would rather Elise hear my side first."

Unable to contain her curiosity any longer, Elise squealed softly, "I knew there was something peculiar going on, regarding the Sterlings. Isn't that their names? I sensed it back at that restaurant."

"Elise, you are truly amazing. I won't even ask how we gave it away," Miranda whispered.

Slowly, Felicity began explaining to Elise how she came to meet her husband, Benjamin, after her parents' tragic deaths. She explained the arrangements her uncle, Edwin Robbins, had provided for her--to live with the Reverend Myles and his newly-wed wife, Lavinia.

Confused, Elise asked, "Excuse me, Felicity. Are you saying that when you first went to England, Benjamin was married to this other woman, Lavinia?"

"Yes. It's very confusing, and since we have a long ride ahead of us, I'll try to explain everything to you."

Elise sat silently as Felicity explained the details of her past. From the look in Felicity's eyes, it was clear to see this was something that brought her deep pain.

From her first meeting with Benjamin, when Felicity had mistaken him as the headmaster of the school she was to teach at, she saw in him a tenderness she had never seen in any other man. And as good friends as she and Benjamin had become, the opposite was true of Felicity and Lavinia.

A tender smile crossed Felicity's lips as she spoke of meeting other family members; her Aunt Gwen, the sister of Felicity's late grandfather, and her cousins Rupert Robbins and Anne Spencer. It was clear that

Felicity genuinely missed them and loved them dearly. As she explained the rift that had kept the Phelps and the Robbins apart for so many years, the tone of her voice betrayed great sadness.

"You see, my grandfather and grandmother had such a deep love for one another that they risked everything to be together, forsaking their past, their inheritances, and their families, just so they could be together. Unfortunately, their love caused my dear Aunt Gwen a tremendous amount of pain."

Elise and Miranda remained silent allowing Felicity to continue. She explained her beloved aunt's pain was precisely why she and Benjamin were together now. Seeing their look of confusion, Felicity began to describe the night of the ball, when she was introduced to society.

"That was to be a magical night, bringing two families together. Instead, it ended up being a night that separated another and nearly destroyed an innocent man's reputation--her Benjamin's. The man with whom she had fallen hopelessly in love with, despite knowing he was never to be hers."

As Felicity relived the Squire's attack, she nearly faltered, her voice cracked with pain and humiliation. Yet she continued.

When Felicity revealed it was Lavinia's father--the Squire--who had accosted her, Lavinia had risen to his defense, accusing her own husband, Benjamin, of being the attacker instead. Within weeks of that dreadful night, Lavinia disappeared, presumably to Australia with her married lover, James Sterling. Benjamin had been sent away by the Church of England to avoid further scandal, even though he had, by then, been proven innocent.

Felicity had no hope that her love for Benjamin and his love for her could ever be accepted in British society. Benjamin's reputation had been tainted and she, as an heiress of two prominent families, must forget the love she had found in her Ben.

Pausing, Felicity looked earnestly at Elise, saying, "When you explained the depth of your pain, not knowing where Joshua was or if he was alive or dead, I understood exactly what you felt. I knew from my own experience, the depths of such pain. Unless you experience it first hand, no one, no matter how sympathetic they are, can ever truly understand. You see, that is what I felt when I was separated from Benjamin. Fortunately, my Aunt Gwen had known such pain and brought us back together. She risked her own life, so I could live in true happiness."

"And have you?" Elise asked softly, genuinely moved by what Felicity had been through.

"Elise, there are no words to describe the utter peace and joy I have experienced since I became Mrs. Benjamin Myles. I know this may sound strange to some. Nevertheless, when two people have struggled as you and Joshua, Michael and your dear mother, my dear grandparents, and my Ben and I have, I truly believe God blesses them with an extraordinary gift. And that gift is bliss in loving one another completely and freely. And I know that with all you and Joshua have been through, you too, will have such a marriage."

"Oh Felicity, that's so kind of you to say. Mama said something very similar to me, many years ago, when I couldn't decide between my loyalty to my countrymen and the man I loved . . ."

Her voice trailed off, recalling the day Joshua had told her he didn't trust her. That day, fearful she would lose him forever, Elise had chosen love. A frown crossed her brow and she said, "Felicity, there's just one thing I don't understand. How is it that Lavinia is in New York and married to James Sterling?"

As Felicity explained, Benjamin sat silently on the back of the coach, smiling. *My dear Felicity . . .* he mused, *What a treasure you are. With all her wealth and position rightfully due her, the only thing that matters to her still, is our love.* Looking up at the darkened sky filled with twinkling stars, Benjamin bowed his head and earnestly said a prayer of thanks to God. Ending his prayer he asked, *Dear Lord, please grant dear Felicity the child she so desperately wants.*

As Felicity and Elise finished sharing their tales, Miranda looked at her friends and said, "Both of you are so fortunate, to find someone to share your lives with, while I'm convinced more than ever that I'll end up an old maid."

"Oh pish-posh Miranda," Elise exclaimed. "Why, you are lovelier today than I've ever seen you. Surely by now, someone has taken a fancy to you."

Before Miranda had a chance to answer, Felicity interrupted. "Oh, believe me, someone has. A most desirable gentleman, too . . ."

"Oh, and you haven't said a word. Why you naughty girl. Tell me who this lucky man is," Elise said, bubbling with excitement.

Miranda rolled her eyes as her cheeks turned bright red, and she protested in embarrassment. "There is nothing to tell. I've told you dozens of times, Felicity," Miranda scolded, turning her head to the woman beside her. "I'm not the least bit romantically interested in Tad."

"Tad?" Elise blurted, her curiosity getting the best of her. "You can't mean Michael's son, can you? Oh that would be perfect. Then we truly would be sisters."

"As lovely as that would be, Elise . . . There is no future for Tad and me."

Confused, Elise asked, "Why? You made a comment earlier that Michael's mother is . . . perhaps difficult. Is she preventing such a union?"

"No, not at all. As difficult as Vivian can be at times, I honestly believe she has grown fond of me in her own way. In answer to your question, no, Mrs. Honeycutt is not preventing a romance between her grandson and me."

"Is there something wrong with Tad?"

"No. He's extremely good looking, very educated, always charming and exhibiting the finest character."

"Well, Tad sounds perfect, for goodness sake Miranda. What is wrong then? Surely, it can't be because of him being a Northerner. Is that it?" Elise's back stiffened, taking offense to the implication, suddenly feeling very protective of men from the North. "Does this have anything to do with your Papa? Surely, he wouldn't deny you . . ."

"Stop! Father has no objections to Tad. Why, he has even hinted that as difficult as it would be for him to accept any man, least of all a Northerner, he would never stand in the way of my happiness."

Elise looked at Felicity and Miranda, completely puzzled. "Then what in tarnation is wrong? You say Tad is wonderful and neither of your families is opposed to your union. Why, then? I don't understand."

"Well, as polished and as debonair as Tad appears to be in public, there's something about him . . . Let's just say Tad definitely takes after his grandmother rather than his grandfather, Alfred, or even Michael."

Before Miranda had an opportunity to expand on that, Sarah--still awake and unable to bear the thought of Michael overhearing anything negative about his son--started to stir. Raising her head up straight and opening her eyes slowly, Sarah smiled at the three women, saying, "My, I must have dozed off. Surely, we're well out of danger by now. Perhaps we should inquire if we could stop and rest for the night? Michael and Joshua must be exhausted by now, driving from Fairfax and now this." Without waiting for a response, Sarah tapped on the roof of the coach.

Within minutes, they came to a halt. After determining it was unwise for them to seek lodging, possibly arousing suspicions needlessly, Joshua found a location nestled deep in the woods where they could pass the night unnoticed.

Benjamin and Felicity, clinging close to one another a few yards from the coach, whispered their goodnights while Sarah and Michael found shelter under a tree close by. Lying in her husband's arms, Sarah assumed from his quiet demeanor that he had overheard the conversation earlier. Rather than saying anything, she cuddled closer to him, whispering, "Darling, I'm so sorry, but after lying in these damp weeds and leaves I'm afraid I'm going to ruin the lovely dress you bought me."

"Don't give it another thought, dear. As soon as we get to New York, I will take care of everything." Sarah knew he meant more than just replacing her dress.

With Miranda across from her, fast asleep in the carriage, Elise could hear Joshua pacing alongside and she crept off the seat where she had been trying to sleep. Peering out the window, she saw Joshua leaning against a tree. As she watched him, her heart soared and she thought of that first night so long ago, when he was leaning against the French doors of her mother's parlor.

Sneaking out of the coach as quietly as she could, she saw him grinning at her from the shadows. As she approached, he shook his head. "What are you doing skulking about, Miss Hamilton? Seems I've caught you again. You're not going to try and wiggle your way out of this by claiming you're sleepwalking are you?" he whispered, teasingly.

"Oh no, I know precisely what I'm doing. I've learned my lesson long ago. You were always more clever than I, anyway."

Pulling her close to him, their eyes met. "Oh Elise, I still can't believe we're together." Wrapping her in his arms he whispered, "Why aren't you resting? I thought you were fast asleep hours ago."

"I couldn't sleep. Darling, you must be exhausted, too. Why don't you rest for a spell and I'll keep watch."

"You little spitfire, always afraid you're going to miss something." Joshua chuckled softly.

Pouting, she said, "No, I'm not. Honestly . . ."

Before she had a chance to finish, Joshua whispered, "I know."

His head bent toward her and from the look in his eyes, Elise knew how raw his passion for her was. As their mouths hungrily found one another in the dark of the night, Elise wrapped her arm around the nape of his neck, moaning slightly. Joshua tenderly pulled back from kissing her further, whispering, "As captivating as your charms are my dearest, you are a distraction. Why not return to the coach while I stand guard?"

Defiantly, Elise begged, "No. Oh please, let me stay here with you, Joshua. I promise I'll be good."

Lovingly, he smiled at her. "I've never been able to refuse you, have I?"

Sheepishly, she grinned. "Well, that's not exactly true. Why, as I recall, two times in particular, you certainly did turn down my advances. Shall I refresh your memory, Major Carmidy?"

"No, that won't be necessary, you little minx. Now, if you insist on staying out here, come sit beside me. That is, only if you promise to behave yourself, you shameless hussy," Joshua whispered teasingly at her.

"I promise to *try*," Elise replied, enjoying their playful bantering. They took a seat against the trunk of the tree. For the better of an hour, Elise nestled in his arms, while Joshua gingerly brushed her hair along her forehead. Feeling her breathing steadying, he knew at last that his beloved had fallen asleep.

Joshua stiffened slightly as a male figure approached, and Michael Honeycutt, hearing the chilling sound of the hammer being cocked on Joshua's pistol in the still of the night, whispered,

"Hold on there, son. It's only me. By the looks of it, perhaps, I should be drawing my rifle on you," Michael said jokingly, nodding toward Elise, still nestled in Joshua's arms. Joshua released his hand from his gun and placed it back near his side.

"Sir, I can assure you nothing happened. You know how determined Elise is . . ."

Raising his hand, Michael smiled. "Oh, I know only too well, Joshua. Get some rest now and I'll stand guard for a spell. We've got a lot of miles to cover tomorrow."

Nodding knowingly at Michael, Joshua wrapped his arms tighter around the slight figure so close to him and allowed himself to drift off to sleep while holding Elise protectively

~ Four ~

Haunting Reminders

As the weary travelers finally arrived at the Honeycutt's mansion, it was clear that Michael was not himself. His mood was far more sullen than Sarah had ever seen in the three years they had been married. The closer he approached his family home, the edgier he became. And it wasn't just Sarah and Elise who noticed his abrupt attitude change. Judging by the way the others looked away--embarrassed as Michael snapped at Sarah, when she harmlessly commented on how different the three story brick homes were from those in Fairfax.

"Well, they might not be as quaint as Doves Landing, but there's something to be said for orderly tradition."

Sarah was so hurt by her husband's comment she only smiled her reply. Seeing the shocked look on Elise's face, Sarah shook her head as if pleading with her daughter not to say anything.

By the time the tired group had stepped through the Honeycutt's front door, Michael immediately started barking orders to the butler.

"Jerome, where are my parents and son?" Michael snarled, not allowing the butler an opportunity to properly welcome him home, or greet the other guests. Then without consulting anyone, Michael decided the women should rest while he visited his family, ordering the butler to freshen their gowns and bring them a tray. After determining that Elise was going to meet Joshua's parents that evening, Michael insisted they all meet for dinner the following night.

As if there was nothing further to discuss, Michael then made it clear he was anxious to be alone with his family and every one hastily bid their farewells.

"Right this way, Mrs. Honeycutt."

Stunned, Sarah nodded politely at the servant, while glancing at Elise and Miranda, who had not said a word since their arrival. "Come along girls, let's not keep Michael any longer from his family."

Once Michael was well out of overhearing them, Elise whispered to her mother, "Have you ever seen a house like this in all your life?"

Sarah frowned and motioned to the butler ahead of them. Clearly, she wanted Elise to wait until they were alone, before commenting on the

Honeycutt's home. As the three of them silently followed Jerome, Miranda pointed out things to the wide-eyed Elise, all the way up the long staircase.

After Jerome had politely excused himself showing Elise and Sarah their rooms, he looked at Miranda, asking, "Miss Brown, shall I expect your father as well?"

"No, Jerome. Father has remained in Washington," Miranda said sadly.

"Well then, if you'll excuse me, I'll get a tray for all of you. Is there anything special you would like?" Jerome, out of respect, directed his attention to the senior woman.

Sarah smiling politely, said, "Some coffee with cream and sugar would be most welcoming." Glancing at Elise and Miranda, she asked, "What about you, girls?"

"Jerome, has cook prepared her famous strudel?" Miranda smiled affectionately.

"Of course. Apple or cherry?" he said affectionately with a trace of a glimmer in his eyes.

With a devilish grin she looked at Sarah and Elise, and said, "Why both of course," snickering fondly back at the butler. "You know me. I just love Hilda's strudel."

"I remember, Miss Brown." Then risking appearing improper by being too familiar, he added hastily, "Welcome back miss, we've missed you."

"And I've missed you. Have you heard word from your sister recently?"

The butler looked nervously over at Sarah and Elise. "No Miss."

Seeing the butler's concern, Miranda reassuringly said, "Don't fret, Jerome. Mrs. Honeycutt and Elise are old friends of mine, and your secret is safe with them."

Nodding politely, he heartily welcomed them both, which Sarah and Elise responded to warmly.

"Well, then if you'll excuse me, I'll see to it that a welcoming tray is sent up immediately."

"Oh thank you kindly, Jerome. And I promise to have our guests changed into something of mine and their gowns ready for Beatrice."

"Thank you, Miss." With that, the butler bowed politely, dismissing himself.

"Miranda dear, it would appear that you've adjusted well to your surroundings since we saw you last. It's clear that Jerome is very fond of you," Sarah exclaimed.

"Oh he's a nice man. Most of the staff here at the Honeycutt's are in fact. Once they discover you can be trusted, they will warm up to you too.

Mrs. Honeycutt expects perfection and a certain aloofness from her hired staff. This, as I've found out, is exactly how most of those in the North treat their hired help. Not at all the relationship we had with Bessie and Chester at Glenbrook or you with Mammy Tess."

"I see. Well, I will definitely keep that in mind, my dear." Sarah made a mental note, realizing that not only were the homes different from what she had been used to and where she was going to be now living, but so were the attitudes.

Looking around the heavy decorated room, which she had taken an instant dislike to, Sarah asked, "Not that I'm criticizing mind you, but Miranda dear, I was wondering, are all the homes in the North so . . ."

"*So* in excess?" Miranda chuckled, adding. "Why heavens no. Mrs. Honeycutt tends to favor a little grandeur, is all."

Sarah sighed, taking in the bits and pieces she had gathered about her mother-in-law, saying apprehensively, "Ah I see . . ."

Her daughter was not so delicate and reacted by bursting out laughing, saying, "A little? Why in all my born days, I've never seen anything like this house before. Nothing like flaunting your wealth."

"Elise, how unkind of you." Sarah scolded. "Why I've taught you better manners than that. We are a guest in Michael's parent's home and I forbid you to say or do anything that will dishonor him."

"Yes, Mama. But from Michael's outburst earlier and the way he acted when we arrived, I'd say anything we did would be upsetting to him."

"Please, Elise. I know you mean well, but you are not helping the situation. Obviously, Michael is already upset about something, so out of regard to him and as difficult as it might be, we must be certain to do nothing that will further add to his burdens. Promise me, Elise, that you will do nothing to upset him further."

"I promise Mama."

Smiling at her daughter wearily, Sarah said, "Good. Well, if we are to be changed, before the servant comes back, I would suggest we do so now."

Immediately Miranda went to her wardrobe and selected silk robes for Sarah and Elise to change into. Moaning, Elise marveled at all the lovely suits and gowns Miranda had.

"Mama come look," she exclaimed, "Why I've never seen such beautiful things in all my life."

"Tomorrow we will go shopping, so don't fret. While you admire Miranda's gowns, I'll take my leave. Just do me a favor dear, as you convince Miranda to loan you a gown, please choose wisely. Nothing too fancy, mind you. Soft and alluring, but sensible too. Miranda dear, do you have something like that in your magnificent collection?"

"Why certainly, Mrs. Honeycutt," she responded eagerly. Turning to Elise, she enthusiastically began showing off her gowns. "Look at this one Elise . . ."

"Oh Miranda, I adore it. How chic and elegant. Joshua won't be able to keep his eyes off me . . ."

Shaking her head while smiling, watching her daughter's excitement, Sarah commented, "Darlin', I said sensible. As lovely as that gown is, perhaps it is a bit revealing. Do keep in mind, you are meeting his mother as well."

Frowning, Elise reluctantly handed back the dress, mumbling, "Oh pooh! Surely Mrs. Carmidy doesn't expect her son to marry a frump."

Seeing the disappointment in Elise's eyes, Miranda began looking for another gown more suitable. "Don't fret Elise, there are others."

Just then, a soft knock at the door alerted them that the maid had come, and Miranda called out, "Come on in Beatrice." Sarah smiled at the fiery red-haired woman who had let herself in, carrying a tray.

"Hello, Beatrice is it? I'm Sarah Honeycutt, Michael's wife, and if it wouldn't be too much trouble, could I have my tray sent to Micha . . . er . . . Mr. Honeycutt's room?" She suddenly recalled Miranda's warning how her mother-in-law expected her house to be run.

"Yes Mum. Shall I do that now?" From her accent, Sarah knew this young woman was an Irish immigrant and she smiled to try and sooth her discomfort.

"Mercy no. Take your time." Then looking at Miranda and Elise who were still busy selecting a dress, Sarah said, "Well, I'll be on my way. Elise dear, did you say what time Joshua was coming for you?"

"I'm not sure, he did say a few hours."

"Well that gives you little time to do anything but freshen up. When were you intending to rest?" she asked motherly.

"Oh Mama, please don't fuss. I want to be with Joshua."

Smiling, Sarah came over to her daughter and softly caressed her cheek. "Well soon enough, you'll be with him everyday, my darling." Not waiting for a reply, Sarah went to the door, pausing to watch the two women together. How lovely it was for her to see something familiar.

When Miranda called Beatrice to the cupboard, Sarah watched the young Irish woman's eyes light up. "Hello Beatrice, how good it is to see you again," Miranda said. "Come help my dearest friend in the world pick out a dress to wear to meet her future in-laws--the Carmidy's."

"The Carmidy's you say, miss? Oh, me John loves working for them. Fine people they are, miss."

Hearing the servant's comment, Sarah slowly stepped out of the room. A sense of peace filled her. No longer did she have to worry that her daughter would be walking into a situation much like the one she found herself in. As she closed the door, she paused and leaned against it before she went down the corridor to hers and Michael's room.

"Oh, Miss Miranda, I fancy your pale blue one, with the matching parasol. With your friend's hair, she will be so striking."

"Hello Beatrice, I'm Elise. My hair? Oh dear, I must look a fright. How will I ever become presentable with it all tangled so?"

"I'll help, miss," Beatrice offered quickly.

Ah, how wonderful, Sarah thought, *at Elise being excited about her new life.* The soft muffled sounds of her footsteps echoed in the hallway as she stepped into Michael's room. *How wonderful to have nothing more pressing on your mind but what gown to wear.* Forcing herself not to think about her fears, Sarah hastily changed from her soiled and creased gown. Looking at the grass stains, she dreamily recalled the look on Michael's face when he had seen her and Elise come out of the shop in Washington. *How happy and excited he had been that day.* Not yielding to her troubled mind, Sarah immediately went to the dry sink and quickly washed before slipping into the pale green silk robe Miranda had loaned her. While tying the wrap tightly around her, a gentle knock at the door alerted her that the servant had returned.

Taking a seat at the bureau to brush her hair, Sarah softly said, "Come in, Beatrice." Casually stroking her tresses, not looking at the servant, she added. "My gown is folded in the chair. I fear, though, no amount of cleaning will restore it."

"Then burn it, my dear." From the reflection in the mirror, Sarah saw Michael smiling at her, and she quickly ran to him. "Oh darling, I thought you were the maid."

As he put his arms tightly around her, Sarah knew her husband was troubled by the way he clung to her. She desperately wanted to ask how his visit had gone and why he had been so distant the past several days, but instead of badgering him with questions, she just held him tightly, needing to feel him near to her too, obviously as much as he needed her.

Feeling her pull away, Michael asked, "Darling where is your tray? Haven't you eaten anything?"

"There's hardly been time. After Jerome showed us to our rooms and Miranda lent me her robe . . . Besides, that lovely maid, Beatrice, is busy helping Elise get ready since Joshua is coming for her early. And as you see, I've managed quite nicely on my own. Why not come lie beside me. You look exhausted."

Stretching his neck then looking at his wife, childlike he mused, "Only if you remove your robe."

Laughing softly, she blushed. "Why Michael Honeycutt. Shame on you!" As the couple began to kiss, a soft knock at the door alerted them that Sarah's tray had arrived. Huskily Michael whispered, "Enter."

Beatrice, seeing Michael and Sarah embracing, walked in carrying a tray and sheepishly said, "Mrs. Honeycutt, here is the coffee and strudel you requested. I've taken the liberty of adding another setting for you, Mr. Honeycutt."

"Fine, Beatrice, set it over there," Michael said pointing to a table by the window. "Mrs. Honeycutt's dress is folded on the chair. See that it's burned."

"Oh darling, does it have to? I rather hoped to keep it. Beside the fact that you bought it for me, I have nothing else . . ."

"You heard Mrs. Honeycutt. That will be all, Beatrice."

As soon as the young woman exited the room, Michael bent down and fiercely began kissing Sarah. Within moments, Michael had gratified his needs, without the tenderness the two of them usually shared. Feeling bereft and empty--more of a sexual object than someone he loved and cherished--tears stung Sarah's eyes.

As Michael pulled his body from her, he looked at Sarah, hoarsely whispering, "Oh God, I'm sorry. I don't know what to say. I just needed you so desperately, I wasn't thinking. Only reacting."

Seeing her tears, Michael tried to pull her to him. Feeling Sarah pull away from his touch, he apologetically said, "Please don't cry, darling. Did I hurt you?" Tenderly Michael wiped her tears, still pleading for her to forgive him.

"You didn't hurt me, Michael. I just don't understand what has happened . . . Why are you behaving so strangely?" she pleaded, looking at him.

Rolling onto his back, Michael shook his head and sighed, "I overheard Miranda."

Sarah gasped, "Oh no . . . Surely darling, you realize Miranda would never say anything deliberately to hurt you. Anyway, it's only her opinion."

"Please stop. When a woman, speaks from the heart and says it as delicately as she did--that my son is not a man she chooses to share a life with--this was not something said in haste. Especially, if that woman is Miranda Brown."

"Yes, but darling, surely you can't blame . . ."

Interrupting her, Michael said solemnly, "My darling Sarah, of course I'm to blame. Not only did I fail my son, but I broke a promise."

"A promise? I don't understand."

"On Emily's death bed, I promised her I would take care of our son and make certain he never turned out like my mother. My late wife and mother never got along--as a matter of fact, Emily despised her. The feeling was mutual, I'm sure." Michael looked at Sarah, his eyes showing his deep pain and anger. "So no matter what you say, Sarah, after hearing Miranda say my son was more like my mother than my father and me, I had to face the fact. I've failed them both, Emily and Tad."

"But Michael, you can't be responsible for taking Emily's death so hard and throwing yourself into your work. We all deal with inner grief and pain differently . . ."

"No." Michael shook his head, his voice barely above a whisper. "For the past several days, I've asked myself over and over again if my reason for leaving Tad for so long was due to grief or an act of cowardliness." Sarah said not a word, but silently allowed her husband to express his pain fully to her. "You see, Sarah, my mother is a difficult and manipulative woman. I say this not out of malice, nor disrespect, but as a man who is not blinded by her faults. I honestly don't know how my father has lasted this long. The closer we came to New York, the old resentments and bitterness that I've felt most of my life returned, along with the hatred and contempt I feel for myself in not being a better father to my only son. Do you have any idea how it feels to come to the realization that you are nothing but a spineless coward?"

Leaning toward him, with tears streaming down her cheeks, Sarah gently cupped Michael's head between her hands. As their eyes locked and she reassuringly whispered, "Michael Honeycutt, you are no coward! I will not now or ever allow you to say anything like that again. Over the past few years, I have come to love and respect you as the most tenderhearted, caring, loving and fearless man I have ever known. If you overheard Miranda, then you must have heard Elise's comments too. What she said is true. As hard as it was living through that hellish war, the only thing that I hold near to my heart from that time is you, Michael. The wonderful man that you are. Now I don't know anything of your mother or your son, but I do know you. And if Tad does have problems, nothing can't be rectified. Just look at Elise. We--you and--I helped Elise, and I swear to you

Michael, if you will let me, I'll be there for you now. All that matters is that you are home now. And I give you my word, for as long as Tad needs you, I will never keep you from your son again. Can you ever forgive me for being so selfish?"

Tenderly he pulled Sarah in his arms, as he passionately kissed her. "Oh Sarah, I love you so much. Promise me you won't leave me, too."

"Never. You're stuck with me darling."

This time the two of them shared a tender and gentle lovemaking, followed by the two of them discussing his short visit with his son and parents. Openly, for the first time since they had wed, Michael spoke of his life as a child and the hardships that his late wife Emily had endured living with his parents. Explaining further that before they had an opportunity to move into the house he had built for them, Emily had died giving birth to their son, Tad.

"Is that the home Lucas uses while he's in New York?" Sarah asked.

"Yes. In fact, I have never been inside it after it was completed. Lucas has expressed an interest in the home, and if it's agreeable with you I'd like to sell it to him."

"Darling, you don't need to discuss such matters with me. I told you before, I have no claims on your holdings, or your wealth. Whatever you decide is fine with me."

As the two remained holding one another in Michael's room of his parent's home, it was decided that as soon as Elise's wedding was behind them, they would find suitable accommodations. Relieved that Michael had no desire to remain in his family home, Sarah snuggled closer to her husband. As her eyes grew heavy, she savored the closeness, instinctively knowing the road ahead of her would not be easy. Michael's guilt was deep seated, and would need more soothing than a moment of tenderness. *I won't let you down my darling.*

~ Five ~

A New Dawn

As giddy as a schoolgirl, Elise in her wedding dress, looked at her reflection while nervously chatting with Sarah. "Oh Mama, can you believe what a difference a fortnight makes? Why these past two weeks have just flown by. Between meeting Mr. and Mrs. Carmidy . . ." She paused to turn and look at her mother with concerned eyes. "Mama, you really do like them don't you? I mean you weren't just being polite, were you."

"No darling, Mary and William are wonderful . . ."

Not waiting for her mother to finish her response, Elise jerked her head back in front of the mirror while fidgeting with a pesky curl that had a mind of its own. "I agree. I like them very much too. And you know Mama, Mother Carmidy agreed with . . ."

Laughing giddily Elise interrupted herself. "That's what she wants me to call her. Oh mercy, I've already told you that, haven't I?"

Nodding her head, Sarah said, "Yes dear, as a matter of fact several times this mornin'. What was it that Mary agreed about?"

"Agreed? Oh yes, I remember now . . . Mother Carmidy agreed with my concerns about choosing a red wedding dress, even though it's the fashionable thing to do these days. As soon as I told her I had seen enough blood spilled to last me a lifetime she suggested a cream color dress, just like you did. Especially since Joshua has been calling me his precious pearl."

Turning to face her mother with a tear in her eye, Elise softly said, "Oh Mama, I still can't believe that in less than an hour, I'm going to be Mrs. Joshua Carmidy."

"Yes, and while you're still Elise Hamilton, I'd like to say something to my beautiful and wonderful daughter. Sweetheart, there has never been a more proud mother than I am now, looking at you today. Throughout all the toil and hardship that you and Joshua faced, the one thing that remained constant, once you finally realized how much you both loved and needed one another, was that you remained true to yourselves. Both of you, as I've said several times in the past, are both headstrong, fiercely independent people with a great capacity to love. No mother could have chosen a finer man for her daughter to marry, than Joshua. As you begin the next phase of your life together, darlin', please remember that your husband is a proud man who loves you more than I think you even know today. And if at times in your life you and he don't see eye to eye, please remember . . ."

Elise smiled at her mother, and quickly said. "You attract more bees with honey than with vinegar. Right?"

"Right," Sarah said, chuckling. "Well, I'll go and take my seat and get Miranda so we can begin. Just please remember darling, I love you and no matter that you're now going to be a married woman, you're still my Elise."

Hugging her mother tightly and kissing her on the cheek, Elise whispered, "I love you Mama. Nothing will ever change that."

Before Sarah had a chance to respond, Michael poked his head into the small room in the back of the church and lovingly smiled over at his wife and daughter. "Just as I expected, the two of you hugging while we wait patiently for the bride's grand entrance."

Elise beamed, looking at her stepfather and started firing questions. "Oh Michael, have you seen Joshua? Is he nervous? Did he wear his uniform or choose a suit?"

Stepping into the room, shutting the door behind him, he chuckled. "Well, let's see now if I've got them straight. Yes, I saw him. No, he's not nervous, surprisingly enough. And in answer to the last one, I'm not telling. I promised Joshua to keep you guessing."

"Oh you two men. Always sticking together," Elise pouted.

"Only when he's doing the right thing where my daughter is concerned. Now let me have a look at you, Miss Hamilton, before you become an old married woman." Their eyes locked and Michael softly said, "Elise, I couldn't be more proud of you, if I were your own father."

Tears stinging her eyes, Elise hugged him tightly and whispered in his ear, "Oh Michael, don't you know by now that I think of you as my father? I love you very much."

Kissing her gently on the forehead, he said, "I love you too." Then pulling away from her he said, "Well there's a certain fine young man who loves you also, and before he sends in a search party after us, I'd say we better get this show on the road. I'm certain your mother has given you wonderful advice darling, so I won't add to that other than to say that you and Joshua deserve happiness. Make every day special and never forget how much you love one another."

"I promise."

Taking Sarah's arm, he jokingly added, "Good. Oh, and have I mentioned a few grandchildren would be a welcoming addition to our family?"

Blushing, Elise smiled nervously at Michael then at her mother who began playfully scolding her husband. "Shame on you! Now poor Elise is blushing." Chuckling while escorting Sarah out of the room, Michael said, "Why certainly, haven't you ever heard of the expression 'a blushing bride'?"

Passing them, Miranda came into the room, asking, "Are you ready?" Her excitement was clearly noticeable in her voice.

Nodding nervously, Elise took in a deep breath and said, "Oh yes. Let's begin."

Within moments, following her Maid of Honor, Elise slowly walked down the aisle, her eyes focused straight ahead on Joshua who stood smiling broadly wearing his uniform. Seeing him, her heart skipped a beat. Joshua had insisted he would never wear the uniform again, even though Elise had begged him to, just this once. *Oh Joshua you wore it for me.* As their eyes locked, the love they felt for one another was obvious to everyone in attendance in the small church.

As she reached the altar, Benjamin Myles, who agreed to perform the ceremony, smiled at Elise and Joshua asking them to take each other's hand.

"Today, it is my sincere honor and privilege to stand before this man and this woman, who have overcome great obstacles to become husband and wife. Through their steadfast love and determination they renew my faith, as I'm sure they do yours, that anything is possible with the help of our Lord."

Michael immediately grasped Sarah's hand and squeezed it gently, while she silently wept tears of joy. Feeling his son's eyes on him, he turned and smiled warmly at Tad as Benjamin continued to perform the ceremony.

From the corner of his eye, Michael also saw the strained smile on his mother's face, and directed his attention back to the altar, knowing the pasted smile on his mother's lips was for appearance sake only. As grateful as he was that Vivian had managed to put together such a lovely wedding in such a short period of time, he knew such gestures didn't come from her heart, but rather as a way to impress others.

From the first moment Vivian had met Sarah and Elise, she had gone out of her way to appear welcoming, all the while snidely insinuating Michael had chosen unwisely, just as she had with his first wife, Emily. However Sarah--older and wiser than Emily had been--took it in stride and never complained. Looking at Elise and Joshua, he silently prayed the two of them would be blessed as he and Sarah were, and not have to endure the hardship of meddling in-laws. Then thinking of the surprise that the Carmidy's and Sarah and he had planned for the newlyweds, he smiled. *Well only if the meddling is for their own good,* he thought. Amused with himself, his attention went back to the wedding vows.

"Do you Joshua Carmidy, take Elise Hamilton to be your lawfully wedded wife?" Benjamin asked solemnly.

"I do," proclaimed Joshua in a firm tone, his eyes never trailing from Elise's.

"Do you promise to love her, to cherish her, and forsake all others before her?"

Hearing those words, Lucas Brown, arriving late the previous night from Washington, shifted in his chair and winced, recalling when he had promised to do the same when he and Catherine had wed. Blocking out the haunting images of his late wife and slave mistress Elmira, he rubbed his knee unconsciously, just as he had countless times in the past few years whenever he was reminded of his sordid past. *Stop this at once!* He scolded himself, determined not to let the phantoms of his past cloud this particular occasion.

Shifting again in his chair, he looked at Elise. *My, but you were a handful, little one.* Time seemed to stand still for Lucas as he allowed himself to recall those particular memories of his life in his beloved plantation, Glenbrook, where Elise and his daughter were concerned. A smile crossed Lucas's lips as he recalled images of his daughter Miranda and Elise as children, growing up together as neighbors. His Miranda, shy and awkward, where Elise was just the opposite, full of life and spirit and determined to have things her own way. *Well little one, I sure hope you know what you're getting yourself into with this man,* he thought, recalling the night he had first met Joshua.

From the onset of meeting him at a dinner party that Joshua had horned his way into, Lucas had taken an instant dislike to him. Viewing the major as an arrogant Northerner, not just because of his politics--Joshua, a Union Major, and Lucas a staunch Southern Democratic Statesman, who had openly pushed for the great state of Virginia to withdraw from the Union-- were like oil and vinegar. But the fact was he was certain Joshua was after more than delivering threatening messages.

Glancing at Joshua now, Lucas smiled. *Well I guess I was right after all, you did have hidden agendas. And by the looks of it, you won more than the war, you sly dog.* Always wanting to be proven right, Lucas smiled contentedly recalling how as a child, Elise had looked upon him as a father figure after her own father, Caleb Hamilton, had been killed in a tragic hunting accident. Seeing her now, standing before the man she had chosen to share a life with, Lucas couldn't help but wonder if Caleb would approve. Then glancing at Sarah, their eyes met and knowingly the two old friends, who had been through so much together, smiled warmly at one another and nodded. *Yes, Caleb would definitely be pleased*, he thought, his eyes trailing back to the altar.

As Elise made her commitment to Joshua, a tear rolled down her cheek as she lovingly gazed back into his eyes. With trembling hands, Elise extended her hand and accepted Joshua's ring as a pledge of his love and devotion. Never had she felt such love for him as she had right then. Her heart pounded so rapidly, she was certain everyone in attendance could hear it. As she slid the ring on Joshua's finger, her voice cracked. "With this ring, I thee wed."

As Benjamin announced they were now man and wife, without waiting for permission, Joshua whisked Elise into his arms and huskily whispered, "I told you one day I would win your heart. I love you, Mrs. Carmidy."

"That you did Major Carmidy. That yo . . ." Before she could finish her sentence, Joshua leaned down and began kissing her passionately.

"Well it would appear our groom needs no prompting from me to kiss his bride," Benjamin exclaimed, as he and the others in attendance smiled and chuckled amongst themselves.

~

Within the hour, the bride and groom, snuggling close together inside the coach, pulled up in front of the Honeycutt's, with Charles, Joshua's youngest brother and best man, and Miranda. Glancing away from Elise for a moment Joshua said, in apprehension. "By God, I thought we agreed to a *small* reception."

"Oh for Vivian, this is small," Miranda exclaimed, smiling.

"Hell brother, what did you expect? A war hero returning home, with a Belle from the South. I'm surprised the whole town didn't come out."

Shaking his head, Joshua said sternly, "Charles, I'm no hero. How many times do I have to tell you? And we're no longer Northerners or Southerners. Today, I'm nothing more than one hell of a lucky man who married a wonderful and beautiful woman. We've worked too hard for this day, so please no more talk of war. Today is Elise's day."

Snuggling closer to Joshua, Elise whispered, "Our day, darling."

Just then, Benjamin and Felicity pulled up, and Charles and Miranda joined them outside the carriage while Elise dreamily cooed, "I suppose we should go in. Mrs. Honeycutt has gone to so much trouble and all."

"Yes. However, as I recall a few weeks ago in your bedroom, I said once we were wed, I would truly make you mine. Well, we are wed . . ." He paused as he pulled Elise closer to him, suggestively saying, "Do we really need to attend this party, darling? I still recall a few tactical maneuvers that should get us half way to Niagara Falls before they even miss us."

Enjoying the feel of his mouth tenderly kissing her neck, she moaned slightly, and said, "Why Joshua Carmidy, I do believe I've married a devil."

"You have no idea, Mrs. Carmidy." Skillfully, Joshua shut the door to the coach with his foot, while passionately kissing her.

From outside Benjamin jokingly called to them, "There will be no retreating this night, Mr. and Mrs. Carmidy. You two deserve a celebration."

Playfully growling, Joshua waved his hand toward the window, motioning them to leave as he said to Elise, "We better go in before I change my mind. But later, you and I have a great deal of unfinished business to tend to."

Smiling back at him Elise whispered, "See, I knew if we tried long enough, we could find something to agree on, Major." Then pulling away from him, she brazenly said, "Major Carmidy, aren't you going to be a proper gentleman and escort your wife into our wedding celebration?"

Chuckling, he stepped out of the coach while offering her his hand. "At your service, my captivating little minx." Taking his hand, she gingerly slid out of the coach and looked up at him grinning from ear to ear. "I always knew someday you'd come around to my way of thinkin'."

Bending down, he whispered, suggestively, "Keep it up darling and I might be forced to turn you over my knee like I threatened to a long time ago."

"Promises, promises. I'd like to see you try." Moving out of his reach before he had a chance to affectionately pat her hind end, Elise chuckled.

Miranda smiled affectionately at their childlike bantering, no longer embarrassed by their display of affection for one another, as the six of them walked up the stairs to the Honeycutt's mansion. "I always said you two were like two roosters peckin' at one another."

Elise, spotting Lavinia Sterling standing next to Mrs. Honeycutt greeting their guests, said softly, "Speaking about a couple of roosters peckin', what is *she* doin' here?"

"I swear I had no idea Lavinia and Mr. Sterling were going to be here tonight," Miranda said apologetically to Felicity.

Before Felicity had a chance to speak, Elise snidely said, "Well don't fret none, Felicity. Mrs. Sterling may think she's being so clever but truly, she's no match to me. Just follow my lead." Glancing up at Joshua, Elise smiled. "You know me darling, I never could back down from a good fight."

Nodding, he escorted Elise to their hostess while Elise cooed affectionately, "Why grandmother Honeycutt and Mrs. Sterling, how lovely you both look this evening. Joshua and I can't tell you how much this means to us, opening your home like this so we could celebrate our special night."

Reaching Vivian, Elise immediately kissed her on each cheek, then turned to Lavinia and did the same. "Why, I see you thought of everything, too. You both greeting everyone is truly special. I'm sure Mama and Mother Carmidy appreciate it so much."

"Precisely what I told our dear Sarah only moments ago. I believe my words to her were, 'Why my dear, one with good breeding never denies the opportunity of another with only the purest of intentions to be recognized for her generous offer to assist in the arrangements.' So of course when our Mrs. Sterling offered, I simply couldn't deny her, now could I?"

Elise's back stiffened but her smile never wavered. "Why certainly not." Turning her attentions to Lavinia, Elise gushed. "Mrs. Sterling, I am truly honored that you would be so generous on our account. In all my excitement, I didn't see you at the church, wasn't it just the most loveliest of ceremonies?" Elise motioned for the others to pass by, while Joshua held his wife more snuggly around her waist, amused by her clever distraction.

Seeing the other four had safely avoided any embarrassing moments by Vivian or Lavinia, Elise said condescendingly, "My, but Reverend Myles surely does know how to give a heartfelt service, doesn't he? Speaking woman to woman . . ." Elise leaned forward, whispering, "I like to think behind every good man, is a better woman. My friend Felicity is truly a lucky woman to be married to such a charming man, wouldn't you agree, Mrs. Sterling?"

Lavinia's smile faded, as Vivian's smile spread. Then cordially Elise excused herself, making an excuse she needed to find her mother and in-laws.

"Well of all the nerve. I'm telling you Viv, that new little granddaughter of yours must know that Benjamin and I were once married. Otherwise, why would she say such a thing? Unless she's completely void of proper rearing, which is no wonder considering who her mother is."

"I may have no use for that daughter-in-law of mine, but my granddaughter on the other hand shows great promise."

"Why Viv, I'm shocked at such a comment. Surely you can't think anyone from that backward part of the country could possibly be anything more than a simpleton."

"Are you sure of that Lavinia? Look for yourself. Felicity and Benjamin are already in the ballroom thanks to Elise's little diversion. From where I stand, I'd say not only does she match your beauty but she's equally as cunning."

"Well, time will tell, won't it Viv?" Lavinia's eyes glared at Elise watching intently as the bride made her way to her friends and parents.

Casually looking over the rim of her fluted champagne glass Felicity softly said, "As much as I appreciate what you've done, Elise, I fear you have made a fierce enemy."

"Oh pish-posh. Even the greatest adversaries enjoy a little competition every now and then." Turning her attention to Joshua, she added, "Isn't that right darling?"

"Yes darling. And we certainly were that, weren't we."

For the remaining afternoon, Elise and Joshua mingled amongst their guests, telling everyone how they had met and fallen in love, all the while aware that Lavinia was watching their every move. While Joshua was visiting with his parents, Elise strolled over to where the senior Mr. Honeycutt stood, looking out at his guests. As she approached Michael's father, she smiled sweetly, saying, "Thank you again, for such a lovely reception, and for opening your home to me. I do hope I haven't been any nuisance to you. When Joshua and I return from our honeymoon, I do hope you will honor us by coming to dinner at the Carmidy's."

"Ah, so then you and Joshua have decided to move in with his parents?" Alfred asked.

"Why yes, Mr. . . . er . . . Grandfather Honeycutt. With Mama and Michael intending to find a home of their own soon, and since Joshua's just getting started back at the firm, it will take sometime before he will be established again. So for the time being, we, I mean Joshua and I thought, this would be wisest."

"Yes. Well it does seem well thought out. Your husband is a fine man. I'm certain in no time you and he will have a home of your own."

"Thank you, sir. There was one more thing I wanted to ask, that is if you wouldn't mind another inconvenience? Would you find me terribly rude, sir, if I asked to be excused from dinner tonight? It's not that we both don't appreciate everything you've done, because we do. It's just that we have such a long ride ahead of us and all . . ."

Alfred smiled at her. "My dear, am I to assume you've not asked my wife or even your husband about this proposal of yours yet?"

Blushing at his candor and at being so astute, Elise said hesitantly, "Not exactly, sir. Perhaps I spoke too hastily. Please forgive me if I've said something to offend you. It truly was not my intention. It's just that Joshua and I have been through so much and since we hardly know anyone . . ."

"Dear Elise, in the past week, it has become abundantly clear just why my son fell so hopelessly in love with you and your dear mother. I too find I can't refuse you anything, so don't worry your pretty little head about another thing. If you will give me a few minutes, I'll announce to everyone that your leaving early is my idea, being the most sensible thing to do. Will that please you, granddaughter?"

Without thinking, she hugged him tightly. "Oh thank you so much. You really are such a dear man, just like Michael."

By then Joshua had joined them and jokingly said, "As much as I admire you, sir, I'll not stand by idle while you steal this lovely creature from me without a fight. It took too long to capture her heart."

Chuckling, Alfred said, "Well Joshua, if I were some thirty years younger, I might have given you a little competition where this charming woman is concerned. I was just telling your lovely bride here that I think it unwise to prolong your trip any further. You two have a long ride ahead of you, so why don't I toast the bride and groom and send you off to that honeymoon Elise was telling me about."

Joshua looked suspiciously at Elise then grasped Alfred's hand. "I don't know what just went on here Mr. Honeycutt, but hell, I could hug you myself. Thank you!"

"My pleasure, Joshua. But since you're part of the family, please call me Alfred."

Joshua, still shaking his hand, said, "Alfred it is. Thank you very much."

With that, Alfred cleared his throat, and with Joshua and Elise beaming by his side, got everyone's attention. After toasting the couple, he announced that after careful consideration, he felt it wise if the newlyweds started on their journey without delay.

Michael and Sarah who had been conversing with the Carmidys looked shocked and immediately went to their children's side, asking to see them both before they left. Then Joshua and Elise, after thanking their guests for sharing such an important day with them, said a special goodbye to other friends and family who had gathered close to them.

As Elise hugged Lucas, her eyes smarted as she whispered in his ear, "Thank you Mr. Brown for everything. Not just for leaving Washington to make it to my wedding, but for being a surrogate father to me as a child. Perhaps that's why I chose someone like Joshua to share a life with."

Startled by such a comment, he looked puzzled at her. "Frankly Elise, I never thought the day would come that you could surprise me, knowing you as I do. Yet again, you've managed to bowl me over with such a comment. Not that I disapprove of your choice mind you, but clearly given the vast difference between your Joshua and me, I hardly see any similarities."

"Oh I wouldn't say that. Aren't you both equally stubborn, and true to your convictions?" she replied coyly.

Lucas's robust laughter filled the room. "Well come to think on it, I guess we do have some similarities after all," Lucas said, smiling fondly at her and then over at Joshua.

"Not to mention the fact that we both admire a certain young lady's spunk!" Joshua chimed in.

"Yes indeed. It would appear we do agree on some things after all."

Again Elise kissed Lucas softly on the cheek, before being led into Alfred's study where Joshua's and her parents were already waiting for them. As they approached the doorway, as if forgetting something, Elise stopped and whispered to Joshua, "Hold on one second, darling."

Turning, she ran back to Alfred and tenderly kissed him on the cheek. "Thank you so much. I'll never forget this, Grandfather."

Since Vivian was watching her husband closely with disapproving eyes, Alfred cleared his throat. "Now run along dear. We'll talk more when you return."

"Yes, Grandfather." Smiling fondly at him, Elise scurried back to Joshua, who had been watching her and was now shaking his head adoringly at her.

"Now why is it I find it hard to believe that Mr. Honeycutt's sudden concern for our traveling arrangements was not all his own idea?"

"Why Joshua Carmidy, whatever are you implying? I can see already you are going to plum wear me out with that suspicious mind of yours."

Michael, overhearing her, said, "Well my dear, I tend to agree with your husband. Father is a staunch believer in following tradition, and the bride and groom leaving before dinner is anything but traditional. I don't know what you said to him, but perhaps your new daughter in-law might be useful at your law firm, William."

"Funny you should say that, I was thinking the same thing," William Carmidy said, smiling fondly at Elise.

Closing the office door to his father's study, Michael listened as Joshua responded, "By God, are you trying to ruin my career before I even get it back on track? There's a reason why women aren't lawyers; I'd never win a case up against her."

After they all had a good laugh at Joshua's comment, Michael nodded at William Carmidy who looked seriously at Elise and Joshua.

"Well, before you two leave, Michael, Sarah, and your mother and I have a little surprise for you both. Now I know you both said that you wanted to go to Niagara Falls for your honeymoon, but we all agreed after everything that you two have been through, you deserved something more. Precisely why we've arranged passage for you to travel to England. Your luggage has been packed, your boarding passes bought, even traveling expenses have been obtained thanks to the generous gift of Alfred Honeycutt, who opened a special account in your name just for this special occasion."

Dumbfounded by such news, Elise and Joshua both gasped as William reached inside his coat pocket and pulled out an envelope with documents tucked neatly inside. Taking the tickets, Joshua looked at Elise in hesitation. As much as she wanted Joshua to say yes, seeing the look in his eyes, Elise knew this was out of the question, so she smiled and nodded reassuringly at him.

Before Joshua had a chance to refuse, Michael and William told them how his career was well on track now that the Myles' along with Alfred Honeycutt had requested that upon returning from his honeymoon, Joshua should be in charge of overseeing their holdings and business matters from here out. In complete shock, Joshua didn't know what to say.

Rapidly Michael added, "We've tried to think of everything, to assure both of you begin your new lives together as man and wife should. Even your living accommodations once you return have been arranged. You see, Lucas has decided it was time he found his own home here in New York, so my home off Bloomindale Boulevard will be vacant. So when you return, perhaps you will do me the honor of accepting this home as a gift from your mother and me, since we both have found another in which to begin our new life here in New York."

The couple stood in complete shock, unable to speak. Not only had they just been offered a trip to England; they had discovered Joshua's law practice was well on the road to recovery with influential clients, along with the fact they now had their own home.

"Speaking for both Elise and myself, I . . . er . . . We're speechless. And as well meaning as your thoughtful gifts were intended, I'm afraid we, simply can't . . ."

"Son." William Carmidy interrupted. "Before you try to refuse, please consider what I'm about to say. All of us here in this room, along with those whom we have mentioned, look at you two as a symbol of hope for this grieving nation. When we look at you and your bride, our daughter," William paused to look over at Elise before continuing, "we see how extremely, strong-willed, fine people, despite their differences, managed to find some happiness in all this madness. Don't you see, just seeing you two together renews our hope that we can rebuild and somehow come to terms with our differences and put the past four years behind us. So please, son, allow us to offer these gifts as a token of our appreciation and well wishes for a new life for you and your bride. A life that both of you have earned and deserve."

Solemnly, Joshua looked between his parents, Michael and Sarah, and finally Elise before answering. "Well father, I just have one question. When do we leave?"

Hearing his response Elise squealed in delight and wrapped her arms around his neck tightly. "Oh thank you, Joshua."

Rushing to her mother excitedly she said, "I can't believe this is happening! How did you ever manage to keep something like this from us? When did you pack our clothes? When did Mr. Brown decide not to rent Michael's home any longer? Oh Mama, thank you so much."

Sarah looked at Mary smiling. "Oh you'd be surprised what can be accomplished when two mothers put their heads together."

Turning to Mary Carmidy, Elise's lips started quivering. Running to Joshua's mother, who was on the verge of tears herself, Elise hugged her tightly. "Oh thank you so much, Mother Carmidy."

"No it's I who thank you my dear, for making my son so happy. Just go and enjoy yourselves."

For several minutes, the six of them chattered about, as Elise and Joshua repeatedly thanked them and went over the particulars of their generous gifts.

~

As arranged by their friends and family, Joshua and Elise left their wedding reception to begin married life at their new home on Bloomindale

Boulevard. As the carriage pulled up in front of the three-story, brick federal dwelling, Montgomery, the Honeycutt's chauffeur stepped down and politely addressed Joshua. "Sir, I've been instructed by Mr. Honeycutt to return tomorrow in the event you and your Missus will be requiring anything."

"Yes, Montgomery. Not too early, make it past noon, good man." Turning his attention to Elise, Joshua offered his hand. "Ready to start our new life?"

Accepting his help, Elise smiled at him and nodded. "More than you could ever know."

After opening the door, Joshua turned to Elise and scooped her into his arms and carried her over the threshold. Giggling, she wrapped her arms tightly around his neck, her pulse quickening and she whispered, "What if someone is watching?"

"Let 'em! You're mine now." Closing the door behind him with his foot, still carrying Elise, Joshua made his way up the stairs leading to the second floor, heading in the direction to the only room where the door had been left ajar.

"Where are you taking me, darling?" She asked, acting as if she didn't know.

"To settle some unfinished business," he said huskily, while bending down to kiss her eager lips passionately.

Stepping into the room, while still locked in their embrace, Joshua tenderly released Elise. As her feet touched the floor, her arms still holding his neck, Joshua wrapped his arms around her waist and pulled her petite frame snuggly against him. Feeling their bodies so close to one another, the urgency in their desires intensified, and Joshua slid his tongue into her mouth, which Elise eagerly accepted, moaning and pulling him even closer. As their breathing increased, Joshua pulled slightly away from her to gaze into her eyes. Tenderly his hand slid to the small of her back. "Perhaps we should see where we are?"

Chuckling nervously, Elise nodded, and the two of them looked about the small but quaint bedroom where a poster bed nestled up along a wall, with two matching mahogany night stands on each side. Six feet to the left of the bed, under a window, was a table and two tapestry-padded chairs. On the table stood a silver ice bucket with an unopened bottle of champagne wrapped in linen, and there were two glasses set next to a vase of fresh-cut lilacs. Directly across from the bed was a fireplace, and to the right of the room was a small sitting area with a settee, small round end table and Queen Anne chair.

"Oh Joshua, it's perfect!" she exclaimed. "Absolutely perfect."

"You're perfect."

Taking her hand in his, they walked over to the table holding the champagne, and Joshua pulled out the bottle and smiled, while Elise sat on the edge of the bed, hoping their first time together would not be disappointing for him, since she was inexperienced in lovemaking.

Admiring how skillfully Joshua opened the bottle and poured the contents into the two glasses, she said, "They thought of everything didn't they?"

Accepting the champagne from him, Elise took a small sip, and wrinkled her nose as the bubbles tickled it. "I wonder if any of our clothes were left unpacked in the wardrobe over there?"

Not responding with words, Joshua's eyes sparkled as he drew closer to her and gently took the glass from her hand and placed in on the nightstand. Turning back, he whispered tenderly, "I don't think we'll be needing a change of clothes this evening, darling."

From his look, Elise knew precisely what was on his mind and her heart raced. *What if I don't please him,* she thought nervously.

Kneeling in front of her, Joshua cupped his hands around her face. "Do you?" he asked, huskily, showering her with tender short kisses trailing down her cheek and neck. Feeling his touch, her concerns started to vanish and she moaned his name as her breathing increased.

"Will you let me help you slip out of your wedding dress, darling?"

"If you would like," Elise said shyly, hoping her voice didn't sound as nervous as she felt.

Tracing her face with his fingertips, Joshua started to unlace her shoes. Removing them, his fingers suggestively began inching up her calf as he caressed her leg while he tenderly removed her stockings. Hearing her breathing increase, he seductively asked, "Did Mammy Tess undress you like this, darling?"

"Not quite, like this . . ." she whispered, her voice trailing off, feeling his hands caress her frame until it reached the first pearl button of her lace gown. Feeling his breath on her cheek, as he bent forward releasing the loop around the button, her heartbeat soared. Never had she imagined a man's touch could be so inviting and gentle as his.

Gazing into her eyes, Joshua jokingly said, "If I didn't know better, I'd swear this gown was picked out deliberately to keep me from you."

"Shall I help?" Elise asked, her voice barely above a whisper.

"No. Please, darling let me. Unless it makes you uncomfortable."

Hearing no complaints from Elise, Joshua slowly unfastened each of the buttons that trailed from her neck to her midriff. His tenderness aroused her, and as he delicately opened her blouse fully exposing her ivory-white neck and chest, it rose up and down with every intake of her quickened breath. Saying not a word, he gingerly slid his fingers across her bare skin and gasped at the feel of her.

"Your skin feels like silk," he huskily whispered.

She closed her eyes, allowing herself to fully enjoy his touch, which sent immediate waves of desires through her. Elise moaned softly, "Oh Joshua . . ."

Gliding her blouse fully from her arms, he discarded it near his feet then delicately traced the length of her arms across her shoulder until he reached her corset. Feeling his fingers slide inside the rigid garment between her bosoms, she gasped as his fingers found the drawstrings, nestled between her pert breasts. Masterfully, he untied them and gently loosened the tight hold of the garment around Elise's torso.

After unfastening the cord from every hole, the corset was also discarded.

Never could Elise imagine such tenderness existed between a man and a woman, which only caused her to desire Joshua more. As his fingers caressed the tops of her breasts, Elise's breathing increased and she moaned in delight. Then tenderly, his hands lifted her arms over her head, as he stood directly in front of her and removed her camisole.

Taking her hands in his, Joshua helped Elise to her feet. His eyes traced her nakedness, while his breathing increased. As their eyes met, she saw the depth of his love, and her hands trailed up his arms to his shoulders while losing any inhibitions by his sensual touch. Slowly and deliberately, Joshua unfastened the buttons of her skirt one-by-one until the cream-colored garment, free from restraints, fell around her feet.

Anticipation increased while he gingerly slid his fingers inside the waist of her pantaloons and slowly eased himself downward following the garment over her thighs until it was free from her body. Still grasping onto his shoulders for balance, Elise stepped free of them one leg at a time, while Joshua traced her frame with his fingers, sending pulsating longing through her.

Shifting her head while arching her back, slightly exposing her complete nakedness to Joshua freely, she drank in the pleasure of his caress on her naked thighs and midriff, moaning, never experiencing such pleasure. As his hands trailed up her body, he paused and tenderly kissed her abdomen, which sent immediate aching to her loins. "*Joshua . . .*"

Responding by lifting her into his arms, he tenderly lay her on the bed, while gazing wontedly at her creamy white skin. No longer was Elise concerned of pleasing him. Her urgency and desires increased as she watched him quickly remove his clothing. The sounds of their rapid breathing filled the room, until Elise gasped at seeing his masculine physique and enlarged manhood.

With one knee planted firmly on the edge of the bed, he leaned over and tenderly kissed her scared knee and thigh while huskily saying, "My poor darling. No one will ever hurt you again."

Knowing his bride was a virgin, and that their first encounter together may be painful, he softly whispered, "Not even me. I'll try, my darling, to be as gentle as I can."

Touched by his concern for her at such a moment of intense yearning, she reached for him. "Oh Joshua, please come love me." As his body slid next to hers, feeling his firm nakedness on her skin sent new longings through her.

Huskily he whispered, "I do love you, Mrs. Carmidy." While cupping his hands around her face, he tenderly began kissing her. As their fervor increased, so did the intensity of his kiss, while his hand inched down her neck to her pert rounded breasts, causing her to moan softly again. Especially aroused by how Elise responded so readily to his touch, Joshua then began gently kissing her bare skin where his hands had just been and she stirred beside him, her breathing increased, moaning his name softly. "Oh Joshua, Joshua."

Feeling his tongue glide across her ribs and down to her navel sparked a fervor inside her that she had never experienced before. Softly moaning under her breath, her head moving from side to side, taking in the full pleasure that Joshua was bringing to her, she gasped, feeling his fingers slide inside the moist crevice of her body.

Never had she experienced such pulsating pleasures, and instinctively, Elise grasped his shoulders as he began sucking her nipples. Breathlessly, she pleaded with him, "Oh please Joshua, please . . . Come to me. . . ."

Certain she was completely aroused and would be able to accept his full erection, Joshua kissed her stomach as he removed his fingers from inside her, while gently raising his body over hers. Tenderly he edged his enlarged manhood between her legs and slowly, while kissing Elise tenderly, Joshua entered her.

Feeling their bodies being joined, they both gasped as Elise wrapped her arms around his neck. Slowly Joshua inched himself further inside until she gradually accepted all of him, while softly groaning. Feverishly she pushed her body up to his until she lost control and let her desires release as she called out his name.

Feeling her tighten up around him, Joshua, no longer able to hold back his desires, matched Elise's urgency and exploded in a fiery raw passion of ecstasy, as they climaxed together. Their bodies erupted in the culmination of the pent-up longings for over four years and they clung one to the other, breathlessly, kissing each other frantically.

Elise, overwhelmed by her love for Joshua, began to tremble as she softly wept in his arms. Aware of her tears, Joshua began to pull from her, but Elise grasped his neck tighter.

Unsure what to say at a moment as this, she whispered, "No Joshua, please don't leave me. You're not hurting me, honest. Just let me feel us like this a little longer. I love you so much, it hurts . . ."

Tenderly he wiped her tears, and kissed her eyelids. "I love you so much Elise, it scares me. More than you could ever imagine, even more than I had ever dreamt possible."

Feeling his desire mounting again, Joshua lowered his head and eagerly Elise parted her lips as his mouth came crushing down on hers. As their passions became more urgent, the two of them again fulfilled their needs in the rapture of their love.

~ Six ~

Deceptions

The morning following Joshua and Elise's wedding, Miranda, who had been offering her services at the Minority Orphanage during the past several years, returned to her daily activities. As soon as she entered the courtyard--just as she had in the past--a sense of solace and peace enfolded her.

The thought of Joseph's tragic death never far from her mind and the role she played ending his life tormented her, yet here her guilt eased. By helping with the children, it gave her a sense that if she could just help one of them, then a part of Joseph lived on in their future.

"Good morning Miranda. What a pleasant surprise. I didn't expect to see you today with your father still in town. The children are attending early services so we have time for a cup of coffee, if you'd like."

"I've had mine, but a nice chat would be welcome."

"You look troubled. Is everything all right?" Felicity asked.

"I suppose I'm being silly, it's just that I was thinking about Elise and Joshua's wedding, which led me to wonder about my own future . . . or lack of one where men are concerned," Miranda said hesitantly.

Patting the bench beside her for Miranda to join her, Felicity said soothingly, "Surely you can't mean that, considering that Joshua's younger brother, Charles, and Tad couldn't keep their eyes off you last evening."

"I hardly think they are a testimony to my charms considering I was the only available female in attendance."

"Oh come now, Miranda, you and I both know that was not the reason for their interest. What's really bothering you?"

"I wish I knew. Seeing you and Benjamin, and Elise with Joshua made me wonder why I refuse the attention of men."

"All men, or are you reconsidering Tad's attentions by any chance?"

Shyly she smiled. "Am I that transparent, Felicity?"

"Not exactly. But considering that you've only met Charles, and that Tad has repeatedly exhibited affection toward you over the years, it was a pretty good guess."

"Do you think . . . er . . . I mean, if I should begin taking his advancements more seriously, what if he feels it was out of desperation or worse that I'm a strumpet?"

""Desperation or a strumpet?" Felicity said, trying to mask her desire to chuckle. "Heavens no! Why on earth would you even think such a thing?"

"You said it yourself. For years I've ignored his advances. Yet now, after witnessing Elise's wedding, I suddenly become interested. If that doesn't appear desperate or the actions of a tart, then what does?"

Seeing her friend was serious, Felicity put her arm around her shoulder and hugged her fondly. "Dearest Miranda, if you ask me, you worry too much. If I know Tad, no thoughts will ever cross his mind. He'll be so pleased that you finally are giving him a chance."

"And what about Michael and Sarah?"

"Oh, you are being silly. I can't think of anyone they would prefer a budding romance with their son, than you."

Continuing to rest on Felicity's shoulder, Miranda sighed, "Perhaps, but what if Tad and I didn't work out. Can you imagine how awkward our relationship would be then? I just couldn't bear having a strain between our families, especially with me living with them so much of the time. I owe Michael so much. If it weren't for him helping my father, I shudder to think what would have come of him or me for that matter."

"Sit up and look at me," Felicity said softly. "My dear Aunt Gwen once told me to follow my heart. Under the circumstance, I think you would be wise to do the same. You trying to second-guess everything obviously has caused you more unhappiness than if you and Tad were to make a go of it or not. Love isn't planned, or can't be forced upon two people. So why not try just letting your heart lead you for the time being and have faith in God that you will know what is right for you? However, before you can do either, perhaps you should ask yourself one question. Are you afraid to love someone?"

Defensively Miranda answered, "I'm not afraid to love. I just don't love Tad. When I am with him, I feel he's not truly being honest with me. It's as if he is portraying the person he thinks I want him to be. Does that make sense? Always saying the right thing, exhibiting the finest mannerism of a perfect gentleman, yet I just feel there is something I should be leery of."

"Surely you don't think he's sinister?"

"Of course not." Miranda paused pensively gathering her thoughts before continuing. "It's just that I think he's learned to be a master of concealing his true feelings to please his grandmother. At times it's as if he is suppressing something he is ashamed of from his father as well as the Honeycutt's."

"Dearest, Tad surely can't be faulted for suppressing his thoughts, considering you too have done the same. However, if you honestly feel he is acting strange to cover up something he is ashamed of, then perhaps you should discuss your feelings with Sarah or Michael."

"And tell them what? I have nothing concrete on which to base my suspicions other than his peculiar behavior."

"Well, perhaps if you tell me what it is that you find so peculiar, that will help?" Felicity asked sincerely.

Eager to confide in someone she trusted, Miranda asked, "Have you noticed when we are all together, how he frequently is looking at the clock and at the slightest provocation he'll excuse himself to leave early? Where does he go? If you ask him, Tad cleverly avoids the question never giving a direct response. Careful not to be caught in a lie, I suspect. In addition, I find it particularly odd that he didn't welcome the opportunity to move in with his father and Sarah considering Michael has been away for so long. Only after Alfred's insistence did Tad agree. Now of course I understand he has a lot of resentment toward his father, but how can he hope to establish a relationship with Michael, if he remains with his grandparents? In truth, I think he doesn't want to move in with them simply because Michael would know how late he returns every night."

"I hadn't realized Tad refused to move in with his father. How sad for Michael and Sarah. They both must feel just awful . . . Speaking of which, have they found a house yet? With all the excitement of the wedding yesterday, I forgot to ask either of them."

"Oh I do wish you had, otherwise it's as if I'm gossiping. However, I'm sure they wouldn't mind you knowing they purchased a vacant home near Elise and Joshua's with the intent to move in by week's end. In answer to your other comment--although I have never discussed it with either of them personally--I should think it must be devastating for both Sarah and Michael knowing Tad's reluctance to join them. It truly saddens me, especially knowing what decent and loving people they are."

Nodding, Felicity hastily added. "Never fear, I'll not breathe a word of what we've discussed. I do have a question though. With your father now looking for a place of his own, where are you intending to stay? Surely, this must be awkward deciding where you should go. On one hand, you have a lifelong relationship with Sarah, yet on the other, the Honeycutt's have been most generous allowing you to be a houseguest for so long. You must be torn."

"Actually it wasn't that hard a decision. You know what a special relationship I have with Alfred. Well, the dear asked me if I would be so kind to remain with him and Vivian. Of course, I agreed. Especially when Vivian seemed so eager for me to stay as well. Not that I believed for an instant that she really wanted me there. I suspect she had ulterior motives. With me around she'll be free to come and go as she pleases without feeling guilty that Alfred is alone. Besides, Michael, Tad and Sarah need time to get to know one another, without any outsiders interfering."

"I would hardly consider you an outsider, Miranda. However I agree, time alone with one another should improve their awkwardness if nothing else. As for Vivian, she does spend a lot of time with Lavinia, which could be hampered if Alfred were alone I suppose."

"In truth, Lavinia Sterling was the only drawback of remaining at the Honeycutt's."

"Yes well, I can appreciate your sentiments regarding Lavinia. You know it's odd, for a time there following Aunt Gwendolyn's death, I honestly felt Vivian and I could be close. That was until she and Lavinia became such dear friends, of course. For the life of me, I simply cannot understand what those two women have in common, other than their husbands are in business together."

Felicity paused for a moment to ponder such a thought then shook her head, and continued. "Oh never mind about that woman, the least said about Lavinia Sterling, the better I like it."

"Yes indeed. However, it was rather enjoyable witnessing Elise beat Lavinia at her own game, while she kept her occupied so that we could avoid her nasty digs."

"As shameful as this sounds, it was glorious. Yet now, thinking on it some, perhaps it would have been wiser if we allowed Lavinia her victory. From past experience I have learned that when Lavinia is denied, she will be hell-bent on getting revenge. Precisely why in part, Benjamin and I were thinking of begging off tonight. We still have so much to do after being in Washington for so long, and we were rather looking forward to a peaceful night alone together."

"Oh no," Miranda whined, disappointed. "Please reconsider. Don't leave me to tend to her myself, it will be so awkward if you're not there."

"Well, I'll talk to Benjamin . . ." she said, hesitating as the sound of laughter filled the courtyard. "Oh dear, the younger children must have been released from church early, and I've not even had a chance to prepare any lessons for today. Where has the time run off to?" She stood up gathering her few belongings.

"It's all my fault. Why don't amuse I them for awhile so you can work on their lessons?" Miranda asked, helpfully.

"That sounds perfect. Thank you, dear friend." Not waiting for a response, Felicity called out as she made her way to open the door of the small schoolhouse. Turning with a smile, she said, "We can talk later if you like."

Nodding, Miranda rounded up the smaller children to play Maypole in the courtyard. From the corner of her eye, Miranda became distracted by a man delivering ice who was staring at them. Trying to appear cordial, she smiled at the gruff, handsome dark-haired man. Even from this distance, she was attracted to his green eyes.

"Good day, sir. May I help you?" Miranda asked shyly.

The man seemingly surprised that she would speak to him, said, "No, miss. I'm sorry for disturbin' ya."

Realizing he was about to leave and finding herself attracted to the stranger, Miranda boldly said, "Why, you're not disturbing me at all." A faint smile crossed the stranger's lips and hoping to draw him into a conversation, she asked, "Are you Irish, sir?"

At once his smile faded and immediately Miranda regretted what she had asked and quickly added. "Forgive me for asking, but your accent is like that of some of the children here."

"Well you're a fine one to talk about accents lass, considering yer's is different than the rest."

"I've offended you. Oh please do accept my apology." Walking toward the stranger, Miranda extended her hand. "My name is Miranda, Miranda Brown. So nice to meet your acquaintance, sir."

"Missy, I'm not one of yer high falutin' society friends that you need to be shaking hands with. So there be no need to be callin' me sir, neither. I'm nothing but an ice deliverer and don't think you'll have much cause for exchanging names with the likes of me."

Miranda stood horrified that not only had he not accepted her gesture of kindness, but she detected contempt for her in his eyes. Embarrassed, she felt her cheeks flush and lowered her hand to her side. Sheepishly, she said, "There is no cause for you to be rude. I was only trying to be polite."

Suddenly her embarrassment turned to outrage and Miranda, not giving the man a chance to speak, huffed, "You seemed like a nice man at first, but obvious I was mistaken. Good day to you, sir!"

Turning abruptly, she returned to the children as they sang *"Ashes, Ashes we all fall down."* Seeing them fall and roll on the ground merrily laughing, Miranda clapped her hands. "Oh that was wonderful! Shall we do it again?" she called out to the eager children around her.

Cheers of delight erupted from the children, and at once they merrily held hands while skipping in a circle singing loudly, *"Ring around the roses, a pocket full of posies . . ."*

The man, still standing alongside the fence hailed to her. "Pst, Miss Brown is it?"

Hearing him, Miranda, still angered, turned slightly not looking at him, but keeping her eye on the children, and said, "Yes?"

"Gilbert O'Flaherty, is me name. I lost me senses fer a wee minute. It's been a while since anyone, especially one so lovely as yerself has shown me kindness in this 'great land of opportunity' and I forgot me manners."

Aware of the sarcasm in his voice referring to America, Miranda noted he had complimented her, and she glanced over at him. Immediately her heart began to race, seeing tenderness she had not expected as he gazed at her.

Never had Miranda met anyone who confused her more. At one moment he could appear kind and gentle, yet at a drop of a hat he seemed capable of displaying anger and resentment. Even his comment of her appearance seemed contrary and completely inappropriate for two people who had just met, and rather than continue with this obviously rude and unrefined man further, Miranda sharply responded, "Yes you did Mr. O'Flaherty! Forget your manners, that is."

Expecting him to leave, Miranda was startled to see him remain where he stood with a devilish grin on his lips as if deliberately trying to annoy her further. Their eyes locked on one another's and she firmly placed her hands on her hips.

"Well aren't you going to offer an apology for embarrassing me by not accepting my hand and then inappropriately commenting on my appearance?"

Chuckling, he said. "Well lass, not only am I not sorry fer what I said, but less you're daft, I did apologize."

Miranda's eyes widened and her mouth dropped. "Daft? Well clearly, you are no gentleman!"

"Aye. Never said I was, lass. As I told you before I'm a laborer who works hard for his money rather than parade around town with more money than brains."

It was clear to Miranda that he resented the upper class, and against her better judgment, rather than end the conversation, she stepped closer to him. "Mr. O'Flaherty, I'm sure you work very hard for a living, which is admirable. What I don't find gallant is that you insist on behaving rudely. Not that it matters, but all I was trying to do was be kind, and in return you have managed to insult me repeatedly. What possible reason does this serve other than prove you're mean-spirited?"

"Mean-spirited you say? Well coming from a fair maiden who has her fists clenched at her hip while her pupils are watching, I'd say you are a fine one to talk, Miss Brown. Now is that how a fine upstanding lady of America behaves?"

There was no mistaking the amusement in his eyes and Miranda's back stiffened while glaring at him, realizing he had managed to goad her into losing her temper. Taking in a deep breath to try and regain her composure, she turned her attention to Felicity who stood ringing a bell for the children to line up.

Without saying another word or looking back, Miranda, flushed by such an encounter, rounded up the children and walked across the courtyard of the orphanage, feeling his eyes still upon her.

"Who was that?" asked Felicity, watching the man slowly move toward the other buildings at a slow pace, whistling.

"A very rude man, named Gilbert O'Flaherty. Who apparently loves to annoy women almost as much as he hates America, judging by his sarcastic comment of the land of opportunity." Miranda tooted, then paused glancing back in his direction, speaking her thoughts. "Hmm, I wonder if he's any relationship to Margaret–Ann O'Flaherty, the housekeeper at Michael's old home, the one that Elise and Joshua moved into?"

"I'm sure there must be countless O'Flaherty's, with so many Irish immigrants these days. Did you notice a resemblance?" Felicity asked, while assembled the children in a single line.

"What I noticed is that he's obnoxious, with hate in his green eyes."

"So Miranda, Mr. O'Flaherty mustn't have been too unappealing if you noticed he had green eyes . . ." Felicity purposely let her voice trail off while raising her brow. "How green were they? Like the meadows of the moors?" she asked, teasing her friend.

"Oh pish-posh! Now don't go trying to make something out of an innocent comment in passing." Miranda scolded, shaking her head as she followed her friend into the schoolhouse.

~

Hearing the laughter of his wife, Benjamin smiled and entered his newly-arranged office to start on the Sunday service. Just as he sat down in front of the blank sheets of paper, there was a knock at the door and he said, "Yes. Come in, Megan."

Before him stood an older girl that would have been forced to leave the orphanage if she hadn't agreed to stay on as a maid to help with the housework in exchange for room and board and a few dollars a month.

"Begging your pardon, Reverend, Mr. James Sterling is here to see you."

"Right. Well show him in." As an afterthought, he quickly added. "Oh Megan, I missed you at service this morning. Was there a problem?"

"No, sir. I was helping the cook after the morning meal, before I started with my chores."

"Hmm, that is most disturbing," he mumbled more to himself then to the young woman. "It would appear more help is needed around here."

Making a mental note to address that problem with the bishop, he absentmindedly said, "Please, show Mr. Sterling in."

As James Sterling approached, Benjamin stood up and shook his hand. "James, how good of you to come by this morning. To what do I owe this honor?"

"Reverend Myles, good to see you too." Shaking Benjamin's hand, hoping he didn't look as desperate as he felt. "I dropped off some extra meat and other canned goods that I thought you could use."

"Are you serious? We can always use extra provisions. How good of you to think of us. With the budget so meager, it's becoming a challenge to feed the children we already have, not to mention the extra ones that arrive daily." Realizing he was rambling and seeing the distressed look on James's face, he hastily said, "Forgive my rudeness, I've forgotten my manners. Come in please, and sit down if you have a moment."

"Yes, if you have some time."

As James took a seat in the chair Benjamin was pointing to, he politely asked, "How are you and Felicity settling in after returning from Washington? I trust your trip went well?"

"Let's just say the trip was disappointing. Congress seems to be sympathetic, yet not willing to offer any more funding. No one seems to have an answer, yet everyday more and more children are at our doorsteps. Even though this was once a Negro orphanage, we have so many Irish immigrants that we should just change the name. I cannot imagine what I would do without Felicity. She is wonderful with the children. They take to her beautifully, and of course, now with Miranda back helping out, I hope that will help relieve some of Felicity's burdens."

"You are indeed a fortunate man to have such a loving and devoted wife. How many children do you care for now?"

Benjamin rubbed his beard for a moment, in thought. "Well, when we left at the latter of last month, there were just under two-hundred and seventy, but that number is now nearly up to three-hundred, in less than a month."

"Three-hundred, where do you house them all?"

"In this building, we house the boys. Their dorms are on the second floor, and the hall on this level is filled with tables to feed all of the children, which we do in shifts with the numbers increasing daily. Then in the other smaller building, next to our living quarters over there . . ." Benjamin walked to the dingy windows and pointed to the red bricked building. "All the girls are in that building right next to the church."

"Well Reverend, it does appear you have your hands full. Who takes care of the cooking and cleaning for all of these children?"

"We have a small staff, unfortunately. So, the children are responsible for making up their own beds of course, and we've just hired Megan, that nice young girl who showed you in, which brings us up to twelve, including Felicity and myself. Unfortunately, Megan is very young and needs direction, so she's not much help as of yet. After the age of sixteen, children are not allowed to stay on here any longer as a pupil. So instead, Megan has elected to stay on in exchange for room and board. She's our housekeeper."

"Ah so sixteen is the cutting-off, age is it? Then what do they do?"

"Well, that is a problem. Them being orphans, of course they have no families, so we are supposed to help them get established elsewhere."

"Right. And just how are you to do that?"

"Thank goodness, I've only got to worry about two young men for now. Since the rest of the children are younger, but eventually of course, I'll have to make arrangements with local merchants to see if they can take them on as apprentices."

"Hmm . . ." James asked while rubbing his chin in thought. "You say you have two lads now, that you must find positions for?"

"Yes. Jessup, and Christopher. Both will turn sixteen within a month."

"Why not send them by the warehouse? Maybe I could get them started in my shipping plant?"

"That's mighty fine of you, James. I'll do that first thing tomorrow, right after services. I can even have you meet the young lads today if you like." Benjamin's enthusiasm clearly showed in his tone.

"Right. Well then that's settled. Now who feeds all of them? If you don't mind me asking of course?"

"No of course not. Molly is our cook, and Felicity comes in before the noon meal to help while Miranda keeps the younger children occupied in the courtyard. It works out, but the strain on Felicity is so great, she works from sunup to sundown tending to the children."

"Well then why not hire more help?"

"That's another dilemma. There are simply no funds. The bishop sympathizes with our needs, but the whole diocese is in need of financial aide, so he's stretched things as far as he can as well. As it is, Megan's meager monthly wage of three dollars comes directly out of our salary, but we need her and there was no other way. As it is, I've already dipped into Felicity's inheritance for the children, and I will not see it dwindle to nothing . . ."

"I had no idea things were that desperate."

"How ungracious of me to ramble on about our problems. Especially after you have so generously offered to help with Jessup and Christopher. Not to mention you were kind enough to deliver some much-needed food. I'm in your debt, James. Thank you! If there is ever anything I can do to assist you, I hope you won't hesitate to ask."

James looked at Benjamin, sheepishly. "As it turns out, the donation of food was no more then a ruse to come and speak to you today. Hell, I don't know if it's for guidance, or because you are the only man in the world who can appreciate how difficult it is at times being married to Lavinia. I know I have no right to ask for your help, after all that has transpired between us . . ." James fumbled over his words, apparently embarrassed by bringing up the past and quickly added. "But I'm desperate."

"I see. Don't get me wrong, James, your kindness is most appreciated for whatever the reason. However, you need not have felt it was necessary to bring food as a bribe or for that matter, offering apprenticeship for our two orphans, if you were in need of spiritual guidance. That's assuming that's what you've come to see me about this morning?"

"Yes and no. You see I was told this morning by my wife that last evening I did something shameful, unthinkable really, and I was hoping you could offer me some advice."

"I'm not sure I follow you, James. Maybe it would be better to start at the beginning."

"Right." James looked at Benjamin with troubled eyes. "It's regarding Lavinia."

"I guessed as much. But as you know our past relationship was strained to say the least. Lavinia and I were like strangers living under the same roof, I'm afraid. So regretfully, I won't be much good to you on advice where she is concerned. However, why not tell me what it is that has troubled you enough to come to me of all people, this morning. Perhaps I can be of some help after all. Certainly I will try, if at all possible."

Without looking at the man before him, James began. "Marriage to Lavinia, has been shall we say . . . difficult. As you know, the woman has many moods, easily to be upset."

"Yes. That I do recall. I always felt this was from her upbringing though."

Ignoring Benjamin's opinion, James quickly added. "Since the death of the Squire, and him leaving the lion share of his fortune to Annabelle, she has been volatile. Consumed with anger and hate."

"I wasn't aware of how he divvied up his holdings. Nor was it any of my concern. So are you saying Lavinia resents the division of his holdings, rather than her father's passing?"

"I would like to have said his death, however to be frank, Lavinia resents being left with the townhouse in London while Annabelle has everything else."

"I see . . . go on," Benjamin said pensively.

"As I've said, her behavior has been radical, or possibly I'm seeing her for what she really is for the first time, with my eyes opened. She enjoys manipulating people. I hate to admit that, especially by manipulating me and taunting me sexually."

"James, Lavinia is a strikingly beautiful woman. There is no doubt about it. But of these matters I'm not one who would be able to comment, nor would I want to." Benjamin blushed, recalling how he had been seduced by her charms the time he had been physically involved with Lavinia, and quickly added, "Surely you can understand?"

Noting James hadn't responded and sensing James needed reassurance regarding his prior involvement with Lavinia, Benjamin asked, "Is this what's troubling you? Trust me, I know how sensitive it is with all of us living so close to one another, knowing the same people as we do. However, I can assure you, I love only Felicity."

"No, no I understand that. And as awkward as it is, your prior involvement with my wife is not the only thing that is troubling me where you and Felicity are concerned. And although I had no intention of bringing any of this up today, since we are on the subject may I speak freely?"

"Of course." Benjamin leaned forward, showing great concern as James continued.

"From the day we returned from our honeymoon and discovered that you and Felicity were here . . . Well, in truth, our relationship took a turn for the worse. Of course, receiving a copy of Randolph's will from his solicitor only made matters worse, compounded by the fact that Annabelle was traveling extensively through Europe with Rupert, which caused Lavinia to become bitter and angry. Reliving the past daily, she recalled those events that caused her to be excommunicated from the life she had once known. I'm sure you have seen how agitated she is every time she happens to run into you or Felicity. It's as if she must face her past all over again. As a result, I've been spending more and more time at the club to avoid her tantrums."

Leaning forward in his chair, James added. "In truth I've enjoyed the drink far too much in excess, which seems only to add to our difficulties as she constantly reminds me of your virtuous behavior. So much so that I have grown to hate the sight of you. And have taken pleasure in Lavinia's demeaning you and Felicity at every opportunity."

James's words obviously caused him distress, and as he glanced down at the floor, Benjamin, feeling the other man's pain, putting his own personal feelings aside, spoke as a man of the cloth.

"As I'm sure you have come to realize, alcohol is only an escape. It serves no purpose other than to mask your burdens and can only create more."

Judging by Benjamin's demeanor, James felt confident he had drawn him into his confidence and said, "Reverend, I know that only too well. Last night is proof of that."

"What happened last night?" Benjamin asked with genuine concern.

"I think the more appropriate question would be, what didn't happen last night?" James said, looking up at the puzzled Benjamin.

"I don't follow?"

"This morning I have been accused of attacking my wife last evening. Forcing myself on her." James' voice was barely audible watching Benjamin's eyes closely paying particular attention to his reaction by saying Lavinia had been attacked.

"Are you saying Lavinia has accused you of defiling her sexually? Forgive me James, for asking such a question. But is there any truth to her accusation?"

Compelled to exonerate himself of any wrongdoing to the man whom he knew capable of such an act himself, having been told on countless times by Lavinia how Benjamin had been a wild beast, James said, "No. I'm certain of it. I'll admit I was drinking. Quite heavily in fact, but I did *not* force myself on her. This may seem hard to believe, but the truth is Lavinia seduced me, as only she can do being a master temptress."

Suddenly realizing the irony of speaking such a topic with James, Benjamin stirred in his chair as James continued.

"Don't misunderstand, my manly needs were met all right, however there was never any force on my part. This I'm certain of."

"Just how can you be certain? You have just confessed that you were filled with the drink, and possibly under this influence . . ."

James was not going to give the high and mighty hypocrite that sat before him any opportunity of giving himself an excuse for the heinous crime he had committed against his wife, so he responded loudly. "No! I recall her drawing me to her, pulling me even to her . . ."

As James recalled the events of the prior evening, his anger and hatred increased for the man who had caused his marriage to sour.

Following the wedding of Elise and Joshua, James had gone straight to his study with Lavinia complaining how he had done nothing to prevent her from looking like a fool by Felicity's friend, Elise. James recalled how he had thrown up his arms in desperation, yelling back. "For God sake Lavinia, what in the hell were you doing greeting guests anyway? Surely you and Vivian had to have known this was not your place."

"Why would I expect you to understand? For the past two years all I've heard out of your mouth is I'm in the wrong. Always siding with Benjamin and that precious little tart of his! Have you forgotten what they did to me?" she snarled. "Why must I continue to bear the shame and humiliation of our pasts in England while the two of them are adored by all living a lie?"

"Look, that was a long time ago and still you harbor a grudge. Let it go!"

"Are you insane? How can I let it go when I know what a conniving little bitch Felicity really is and what a monster she is married to? Or, are you too drunk again to see what I mean? How many drinks did you have at the club before coming to the reception?" Lavinia had asked accusingly.

James had yelled back to her snide comments defensively. "Apparently not enough! Besides, what is the harm if I had a little too much to drink? As I recall, you enjoy a good belt every now and then yourself." Gulping back his drink in hand he had said, "Is it any wonder I find refuge at the club? You never want to talk about anything but the damned Myles'. Hell, we rarely are together anymore, not like before we were married . . . back in England things were so different."

"Always the same tripe, *I've changed, I'm not the sweet girl I once was* . . . Honestly, James, you really are becoming such a bore. Sounding more like that old crotchety Alfred Honeycutt everyday," Lavinia spouted, turning on her heels to enter the sitting room of their master suite.

Swiftly, he gripped her arm and she whirled around facing him again. "Don't you dare turn away from me! Let's settle this once and for all, here and now. Just what is it that I've done?" he had demanded, in a raised shout, "that has soured you against me? And since we are on the subject of Benjamin and Felicity, let them live as they choose. They sure the hell seem to be a lot happier than we are. From where I stand he's one hell of a lucky man. He's jumped from one heiress to the other, and wound up with a wife who is not only rich but is genuinely sweet and gentle. I told you before there's a lot to be said for a woman with those qualities. Hell, I'd gladly pay for you to have some of those attributes!"

Recalling their argument years earlier at Ashwillow, when she had accused him of lusting after Felicity, she glared at him. Struggling to free herself from his grasp, she gritted her teeth, her voice becoming cold and barren. "Take your hands off me at once or I'll scream! You smell of drink and you disgust me."

Feeling how tightly his hand was around her forearm, James had released it and apologetically said, "I'm sorry."

"You're sorry? Are all men the same? They hurt a woman and then they justify it by saying, I'm sorry?" Seeing the look of resentment in his eyes, she had added. "You don't want sweet and innocent James, you never have. Rebecca was sweet as sugar and that certainly didn't prevent stolen moments with me, *while she lay dying.* You wanted me! And now that you have me, would you rather I become deathly ill too, so you can carouse around some more?"

Seeing the hate in his eyes at her comments and realizing she had said too much, Lavinia had rushed to him, pleading, "Oh darling forgive me. I was angry. I didn't mean those dreadful things. Really I didn't."

"Lavinia, get away from me now! I mean it, or I won't be responsible for my actions." Walking over to the crystal decanter he filled his glass with an ample amount of brandy, which he immediately tucked away in one large gulp. After feeling the sensation from the aged liquor as it trickled down his throat with ease, he promptly poured himself another.

"James darling, please don't drink so much alone. Won't you pour me one too?" Lavinia had cooed.

Lifting the decanter, without even looking at her, James extended it saying with contempt, "Pour it yourself!"

Slowly she had taken the decanter from his hands and reached for him, but James had promptly pulled away, moving across the room where he slumped into an overstuffed chair. Not going after him at first, Lavinia had slowly poured herself a stiff drink as well, her mind racing to figure out what to do next. *Watch yourself Lavinia, with your inheritance robbed while Father was dying, by that gold-digger thief Annabelle, James is your only security now.* With a plan forming in her mind she belted back her drink, then poured herself another.

Turning to face James, knowing precisely what his weaknesses were, she had cooed, "Here darling, have a little more." Gliding over to him, feeling his scornful eyes on her, Lavinia decided to seduce him.

After refilling his glass, she slithered between his knees and rested herself on the floor facing him. With the grace of a cat, she had placed the open decanter next to his foot on the thick Persian rug, beside the heel of his shoe. Seductively she had said to him, "You are absolutely right, I haven't been myself darling."

Sultrily she traced his thigh, resting her glass on his knee and slowly and sensually, she had begun moving her glass over his knee all the while batting her eyes as if she were helpless. "You know the pain I suffered at the hands of Benjamin. And seeing him and Felicity act as if they were perfect makes me sick. Then if that wasn't bad enough, with poor Father's death on my conscience and then learning how traitorous my own sister was, well I suppose it's been more than I could bear. You can't imagine my pain and how helpless I've felt, considering that she tricked father into changing his will in his weakened state to secure all his holdings except for that worthless townhouse."

Forcing herself to shed a single tear she had whimpered, "I suppose it has soured me, and I've been taking it out on you. Oh please forgive me, James."

"Lavinia, we've discussed this before, several times in fact." Dismissing the act that Lavinia claimed Benjamin had committed against his wife, he addressed Annabelle's inheritance instead. "Even if Annabelle was able to achieve such a dubious deed, which is doubtful, knowing her and the Squire as I did, the townhouse is clearly not worthless. Of course it's not Ashwillow, but with my holdings, you are well cared for."

"I know darling. You know so much more of financial matters then I do . . ." Taking the last sip of her brandy, she swirled it across her mouth to ease some of the sting her words were causing her. Laying the glass on the floor she smiled up at him, allowing her hand to slide down over his knee and into his inner thigh, resting it there trying not too appear too obvious.

"Darling, I try, truly try to forget the past, honest I do. But when I saw how everyone was making such a fuss over Felicity and Benjamin at that backwoods, little tart's wedding, as if they were so pure and perfect, it just sickened me. Do you remember how I told you the day I had caught that little harlot, kissing Benjamin's thumb, soaked to the skin? Well when Elise had mentioned that behind every good man is a better woman, I nearly lost my mind. All I kept thinking was what would people think of the virtuous perfect Felicity if they knew the real truth? Why as hard as I try, I don't think I will ever be able to forget that awful stormy day at the vicarage. Why it's just like it happened yesterday . . . There she stood, her dress clinging to her bosom, full of silky mud showing through that thin cotton frock of hers all the while batting her eyes up at him, enticing him with her purity and goodness. I can assure you that was anything but pure! More like a lioness after its prey."

"Right. I do recall you telling me that story before, but never with such vivid detail." James, feeling the effects of the drink, relaxed in his chair, able to see Felicity in his mind with her pert nipples pressing against a cotton frock.

"Go on Lavinia, tell me more," he mumbled feeling aroused by thinking of Felicity as a seductress.

Lavinia knowing the time was definitely right to further seduce him, slid her hand up his leg and began to unfasten the ties of his trousers, while caressing his manhood to further arouse him.

"Darling, she may well be able to fool some of those naive people with her sweet and innocent act, but take it from someone who knows, she seduced Benjamin only to take something away from me. Whom she despised. You remember that dreadful outburst at the vicarage I told you about and how she kept trying to prove worthy of my acceptance of her? Why would have that been necessary if I hadn't found her out? She and I both knew what sort of harlot she actually was, with no real breeding. I tell you I don't trust her. Why I even blame her for Benjamin's actions now. She drove him insane, bewitching him all the while, fooling her aunt and uncle into leaving her such a large inheritance. And I helped her to succeed. It does make me wonder though, who she might try to get her claws into next. Precisely why I became so distraught this evening. At the reception when you greeted her and kissed her hand, with all her droll dear friends around her, well darling, I just lost all of my senses becoming insanely jealous. Which is understandable, loving you as I do . . ."

"Oh darling you can't be serious, she and I were only being polite," James mumbled, enjoying the sensual touch of Lavinia's hand caressing him.

"Darling you mustn't be fooled by that so-called innocent act of hers. I know her type. She appears to be a soft harmless kitten, when in reality she's nothing more than some alley cat."

Feeling his manhood exposed from his skillful wife, he looked down at her and feeling his drink, his words slurred. "An alley cat you say?"

"Yes darling, ruthless and scheming. I was just so worried that she was now after you that I was beside myself. She hates me you know, and I still remember our arguing over her in Father's garden."

"Don't be absurd . . ."

Kneeling in front of him, her body seductively leaning against his manhood to further arouse him, she extended her hands to him outwardly. "James, you do forgive me for my foolish jealousy, don't you darling?"

"Of course, I do . . ."

"Then show me darling," she suggestively cooed, gently tugging at his arms to draw him near her as she leaned back on the carpet. "Come prove to me that you want only me."

Lunging from the chair, James fumbled at her petticoats, freeing her from the cumbersome undergarments. As James entered the moistness of her body, the vision of Felicity that was so perfectly painted for him, remained fresh in his mind, until his hunger was satisfied. Upon fulfilling his desires, he lay lifeless across Lavinia, despising himself for allowing himself to be gratified by his wife, while lusting after another.

Lavinia struggled to free herself from under him and after successfully pushing him off her, she sat up, looking appalled at the sight of her husband.

"Well that was hardly worth the bother," she had said disgusted, while arranging her torn undergarments.

Stretching for the open decanter, she had leaned against the chair occupied by James only moments earlier. Pouring another brandy, she then looked at the man before her in contempt. Raising her glass as if cheering him, she had said, sipping slowly at her drink, "You're right about one thing, James. Things *are* different between us. I find you as loathsome as Benjamin once was."

Hearing his wife say such words, James lay on the floor as anger and rage filled his tormented mind. No longer would he try to help his wife forget the past. It was his turn to lash out. The love he had once felt for Lavinia had now vanished. He had been unable to avenge her honor before, but he would avenge the marriage that had been taken from him. And as he lay there hating the life he was forced to endure knowing Benjamin went unscathed living a peaceful existence, James fell asleep vowing to rectify that.

Finishing her drink she entered their suite and went into her powder room where she looked into her reflection, and felt defeated. *Nothing is going my way. Maybe it's time to change my strategy. He wants sweet; well that is exactly what he'll get! I can be just as sweet and wholesome as that tart Felicity, and that puritan Miranda, whom everyone adores. Then maybe I can manage to get some of that money he holds so tightly.*

Tearing her dress deliberately, Lavinia stared into the mirror. *Now James, live with the guilt of forcing yourself on your wife just as you think Benjamin did, you pathetic bastard.*

As she walked to her dressing bureau to get a clean nightdress Lavinia smiled, leaving her torn dress where James would surely see it when he came to. *How easy it is to be a poor helpless kitten. Now protect me, you shell of a man.*

So deep in recalling the prior evening events in his mind, James barely heard Benjamin saying, "James, are you alright, old man?"

"Yes, I was just reliving the whole incident in my mind again. As I told you, our intimacy was consensual, never forced. The only sin I committed was seeing another in my mind as I had her, but it was not by force," James said, omitting whom he had fantasized lusting over to be able to perform for her advancements.

Inhaling a deep breath, searching for the appropriate words to guide him, Benjamin asked, "James, was this other woman Rebecca?"

From the moment he had arrived, everything up to this point was a ploy to win his trust so that he could avenge his ill-fated marriage, until Benjamin had asked him about Rebecca. The guilt James felt regarding the way he had treated his first wife was genuine. Precisely why he had allowed himself to continue living such a hellish existence with Lavinia these past three years, telling himself daily he deserved such pain for the sins he had committed against Rebecca. So as he answered Benjamin, his reply was sincere.

"No. What I did to Rebecca, God rest her soul . . . the guilt of such unwarranted deeds against her and our marriage lay heavy on my soul, but it was not her in my mind."

"Have you asked for our Lord's forgiveness for the sins you committed against Rebecca and your previous marriage?"

"Countless times," James said earnestly. "Rebecca deserved better and I failed her. She knew when we married I was in love with another, but she never questioned who . . . or why."

"James, look at me. The heavy burden you carry with you daily cannot be masked with alcohol to alleviate the pain. The drink will destroy your very existence if you are not careful. God has forgiven you long ago, when you asked Him for forgiveness. So now you too must learn how to forgive yourself and carry on. We all have reminders of how imperfect we are, but the true test of a man is his inner strength. To learn by his past mistakes and move forward, is what God expects from us."

Hearing Benjamin say that, he wondered if that was how he could live with himself, after he had done what he had done to Lavinia. James barely heard Benjamin continue.

"You and Lavinia have been brought together as husband and wife. You must honor this marriage and work at making it a strong and sacred union in the eyes of God. Have you addressed with Lavinia what you recall from last evening's events, with the exception of seeing this other woman I mean? Not one of force, but that of consent?"

"Yes. This morning as she accused me."

"And?"

"She supplied the dress and the torn pantaloons."

"Well this does present a problem. If you are certain you did not force yourself on her, then you have only one thing to do and that is try to convince Lavinia of your love for her. No matter what it takes. Throughout our difficult past, one thing above all else that I was always certain of, was that you and Lavinia loved one another.

"You have just confessed to me, it was the love you felt for her that prevented you from being the husband you should have been to Rebecca. And from my own experience, from our short-lived relationship, I know it was you Lavinia desired, certainly never I."

"Are you so sure though, that what we desired from one another was love, or lust?"

Such a candid question left Benjamin feeling awkward having wondered the same thing himself.

"Only you, Lavinia, and God know the answer to that. And even if that were the case, Lavinia is now your wife and you must make what once was wrong, right. Not by force or liquor as a shield to hide from, but rather seek the truth in your heart, and live your life as God intended, in peace with your wife."

"That may prove to be difficult. I'm not sure I can do that alone."

"James, you are never alone." Benjamin smiled at him knowingly, adding. "God will be with you always. Lavinia is your wife, for better and for worse, for richer and for poorer, in sickness and in health, until death do you part. These words are not just said to make your marriage ceremony filled with sweetness. Those words were a serious oath that you agreed to take with God. You must obey this oath and do as He has intended, without hesitation or regret. With His guidance, you will reap the rewards. This I am certain."

"I will try."

"Good." Satisfied that he had been able to assist James, Benjamin said, "Nothing in life that you value comes easy. I have painfully learned this lesson myself. But trust me James, just put your trust in Him and I am confident you will be blessed."

A gentle knock at the door alerted both men to look in that direction. "And speaking of God's blessing, if I'm not mistaken, I believe my dear wife has come to tell me it's time for the noon meal. Which, I must lead our rather large family in prayer." Standing, Benjamin shook James's hand heartily.

"God be with you, friend." Then turning his attention to the door, he said, "Come in."

"Darling, sorry to disturb you . . . Oh, Mr. Sterling, how fortunate that you are still here. Cook told me of your generous donation to our needy cause. I can't tell you enough just how much we appreciate this."

James's face turned crimson, remembering how he had found such pleasure fantasizing about her in his drunken state and said, "I'm pleased that the tins will come of some use."

"Good use? Surely you jest! Why single-handedly you have managed to feed our dear growing family for at least a week. How can I ever thank you enough? Please come and join us for noon meal, and meet some of the children, that is, if time allots of course?"

"What a splendid idea, dearest. This will give you a chance to meet Jessup and Christopher as well." Turning to Felicity, Benjamin explained. "As it turns out James has agreed to take on both these lads as apprentices at his warehouse."

"Why that's wonderful. You really are our benefactor, heaven-sent, I'd say," Felicity exclaimed, smiling fondly over at James.

"Now that is definitely a false statement, if ever there was one." James, looked away embarrassed, thinking, *If she only knew. . . .*

"Now don't be too hasty there James. God does work in mysterious ways."

"Benjamin, that may be true, but I can assure this was a sheer stroke of luck. But in the future I'm sure to remedy that."

Felicity looked on in puzzlement, but knew not to meddle in her husband's work. "Well whatever the reason for your generous donation, I'm grateful. Please join us, before the soup gets cold."

~

After the meal was finished, James met the two young lads and started to head back home just as Felicity was leading the children out to the courtyard for a brief recess before their afternoon session. Motioning to Miranda, who instinctively knew what she meant and took the remaining children outdoors, Felicity called to James, "Mr. Sterling . . ."

"Please Mrs. Myles, can we dispense with the formalities in the future, of using our Christian names? I've known you for many years now and I would hope you feel comfortable enough to at least consider me a friend."

"Yes. Friends indeed." Feeling rather peculiar and shy, Felicity forged on. "James . . . Thank you again for all that you are doing to help us." Taking her hand again as he had at the wedding reception, he kissed it.

"It is entirely my pleasure, dear woman. Why, you're trembling like a kitten. Have I offended you?" As he watched her, he began enjoying the little cat-and-mouse game he had conjured up in his mind.

Suddenly feeling uncomfortable by his familiarity and the look in his eyes, Felicity withdrew her hand from his and quickly added, "You've not offended me at all. It's just that I have much to do this afternoon." Excusing herself, she politely added. "If you will please forgive me."

"Of course. Will I be seeing you this evening at the Honeycutt's, Felicity?"

Hearing him address her by her first name, her back stiffened, but feeling grateful for his help, she nodded. "Yes. I look forward to it."

As soon as she agreed, Felicity regretted her words, *Now I suppose we will have to attend this evening. Fiddlesticks!*

"As do I." His words were sincere, yet Felicity still felt uncomfortable around him. Chastising herself for holding on to old misgivings about him and deciding perhaps she had been wrong about his character, she walked back to the courtyard where Miranda was still attending the children.

The thought of not having to care for the children for an evening and being carefree enjoying adult conversation was appealing to her, even if it were to be only for one night. Realizing her thoughts, Felicity felt ashamed. *Stop this at once*, she scolded herself. *This is Benjamin's vocation and he loves his work. And as his wife you must too! Besides, these poor children need you. Who else would care for them?*

No matter how much she missed being alone with Benjamin as they were in Washington, without the demands of running the orphanage, she forced herself not to think of her own needs. She knowingly and willingly had chosen this life to be with her Ben. And even though it was burdensome at times, she knew she had been blessed by God to have the love of such a fine man that she loved with all her heart. She only wished that he could find fulfillment to serve God by preaching as he had in England, without the demands of three-hundred children requiring so much of their time and energy on a daily basis.

Entering the courtyard, she paused momentarily to look at the younger children playing carefree in the courtyard. Without realizing it, she found herself envying them. With so much on Benjamin's mind, worrying where the money was going to come from to care for all of them, she hadn't seen him truly relax since their return. Although he was always tender to her, she knew he was consumed in worry, and by the time the two of them went to bed at night they were too exhausted to share the closeness they once had. Missing that time with her husband, she said a prayer. *Dear Lord, please bring relief soon. Not just for the children, but for Benjamin and me as well. I miss his smile and our intimacy with one another.*

Seeing Felicity while watching the younger children run about, Miranda called to her. "My, what a surprise Mr. Sterling was."

Startled, Felicity said nonchalantly, "Yes he is. Isn't he?" Still feeling overburdened, yet not wanting her friend to see it, she smiled softly while walking closer to her. Noticing the look of apprehension in Miranda's eyes for his motives, ashamed for her own uneasiness for his sudden generosity, and not wanting to discuss it with her, Felicity quickly changed the subject.

"Never mind James. Tell me more of that handsome Mr. O'Flaherty. What is it about that particular gentleman that seems to annoy you so?"

Noting Felicity had called James by his Christian name, never hearing her refer to him that way in the past and realizing her friend obviously didn't want to discuss the Sterlings, she answered her question. Chuckling merrily Miranda said, "First off, he is no gentleman! Secondly, that is what troubles me the most. How could someone with so little manners, intrigue me so?"

"Ah, so you admit you are still thinking about him. I thought so."

"As much as I hate to admit it. Yes. There is something about those sad green eyes of his that I am drawn to. There is something seriously wrong with me. A very available and most suitable gentleman, refined, educated, from a well-respected family like Thaddeus Honeycutt showers me with attention and I push him away. Yet, a man with such lack of regard for social graces as Gilbert O'Flaherty has just displayed, fascinates me."

"Ah, he now fascinates you, does he? Pray tell, in which way?"

As Miranda prattled on, Felicity soaked in the sheer joy of conversing with someone her own age merrily without any demands on her or consumed with worry. Grateful to have Miranda with her, especially today when the strains of running the orphanage seemed greater than most, Felicity smiled lovingly at her friend. Feeling lighthearted again, she thought, *God does work in mysterious ways.*

Sketch as it appeared in "Harper's Weekly" on May 13, 1865

Seven

Explosive Encounters

Temperatures soared on this unseasonably hot and muggy May evening while a fire blazed in the Honeycutt's hearth. The room was stifling--heavy with the scent of burning wood--yet no one seemed to notice as they chatted amongst themselves. From bits and pieces of the conversation Miranda overheard, she knew Michael and her father were debating if it was actually Booth who had been killed as reported.

"For God's sakes Lucas, who the hell else would it be then, if not Booth? Didn't you read that among those who identified his corpse was a Dr. John Frederick May? The same doctor who had recently removed a tumor from his neck, and there was also his dentist who had pried open the corpse's mouth to identify the two fillings Booth had prior to the assassination. Besides, what purpose would it serve the government to portray such an elaborate hoax by falsifying who the corpse was?" From her father's anxious look, she knew it was more than the heat that was causing his face to redden.

"All I said was, if it really was Booth, then why the need to weight the poor son of a bitch and drop his remains in the Potomac?" Lucas demanded.

"Hog wash!" Michael tooted. "You know that was never confirmed. It's just some hideous, ridiculous rumor, just like countless others circulating. Come on Lucas, next, will you be joining in with Booth's followers that he wasn't involved, when we both know that's not true? Hell, we were in Washington, we heard eyewitness accounts ourselves."

Trying to block out the two men's heated debate, never wanting to think about that dreadful night again, Miranda gazed at the flames of the burning log that was enclosed behind two glass doors. Mesmerized by the reflection of the flickering blaze that danced across the panes of glass which contained the log, Miranda's attention was diverted by the sounds of an occasional horse and buggy driving past the Honeycutt home.

The sound of hooves clicking upon the stone pavement combined with the reverberation of splashing water from the recent downpour of rain against the surface of the road felt soothing to her. Especially since she hadn't been able to get Gilbert O'Flaherty off her mind, or what Felicity had said earlier about her being afraid to love someone. *Could it be that she was incapable of loving a man?* Miranda asked herself repeatedly.

Although she had flatly denied it earlier, she now wondered if it were possible. Feeling flushed, she gingerly patted her neck with a lace handkerchief, waiting anxiously for the arrival of Felicity and Benjamin. A sudden laughter from Lavinia and Vivian caused her to turn her attention in their direction. Pasting a superficial smile on her lips, she nodded politely to them while she surveyed the room filled with the usual guests that gathered nightly to share the day's events with one another.

As she observed the Sterlings and Honeycutts from afar, Miranda was amused that they thought her too shy to mingle, and seemed not the least bit offended by her aloofness. Realizing Sarah was watching her, she returned a warm smile, but feeling another set of eyes on her, Miranda turned her head to avoid eye contact with Tad.

Noticing he was being detained by Michael, Miranda took the opportunity to escape his attention and head for the gardens. The sudden laughter from Lavinia and Mrs. Honeycutt rang out again, which had a sinister quality to it, and Miranda glanced at them as they busily chattered away like two magpies. *Hmm . . . I wonder what dastardly deed those two are cooking up this time,* she thought.

Judging by the watchful eye Lavinia had on James, Miranda assumed he must be the next victim to one of their endless schemes. Trying to be as discreet as possible, carefully holding onto both handles of the French doors that led to the side gardens, Miranda opened the door slowly, holding her breath as the door hinges squeaked.

Glancing back into the room to see if anyone else heard the door, she nodded to James, who had paused for an instance to return her gesture, quickly resuming his discussion with Alfred. Judging by the look on his face, he seemed to be anxious. *My, this afternoon he was so pleasant . . . how peculiar,* she thought, while hastily stepping into the garden and down a path of cobblestones between the lush ferns and hostas, escaping before Tad would see her.

After walking for several minutes, certain Felicity and Benjamin should be there by then, she headed back to the house. Much to her surprise, along the side fence leading back to the street, was Tad and Gilbert conversing with one another.

What a small world, she thought, while concealing herself behind a large overgrown lilac bush, straining to make out what was being discussed by the two of them. From her vantage point, she watched in fascination at Gilbert who leaned over a hedge. Although she couldn't make out what he was saying, by the look on his face and by his demeanor, it was obvious he was upset, while Tad remained poised with a smirk on his face. *What could these two men possibly have in common?* She wished she could hear them.

Her heart quickened when she realized Gilbert was about to make his way back to his ice cart. Without stopping to think, Miranda stepped out from behind the bush, and said, "Good evening Mr. O'Flaherty. Still busy working, I see."

"Why Miranda, there you are," called Tad clearly surprised at seeing her. "I've been looking everywhere for you. How is it you know someone like O'Flaherty here?" he asked suspiciously.

Politely she answered Tad, but her eyes were on Gilbert, hoping he would acknowledge her greeting. "We met while I was helping out at the orphanage today."

This time, the angry man had a reply, and by the look of resentment on his face, Miranda braced herself for his wrath.

"Some of us *work* from sunup to sundown, not like those with money who were born with a silver spoon in their mouth, and *help* out."

Angered and hurt by such a spiteful comment, Miranda felt the blood rush to her cheeks, while Tad retaliated with a snide comment of his own.

"O'Flaherty, watch your tongue when addressing a lady. Didn't your mother ever teach you any manners? And you wonder why manual labor is for the likes of you ill-mannered thugs?" he exclaimed, a smirk on his face.

Finding Tad's words incredibly rude and insensitive, Miranda spoke up in Gilbert's defense. "How unkind of you to say such a thing, Tad. Why I'm sure Mr. O'Flaherty was merely pointing out that he works very hard."

"That I do. And I don't need the likes of you, or your kind, to do my bidding for me. I got a tongue of me own," Gilbert retorted indignantly. From his reaction, Miranda knew she had hurt his pride and wished she hadn't said anything, while Gilbert continued. "I'm not one of them wee children needin' yer charity, lass. Kindly let me tend to me own affairs. Or don't you have anything better to do with your time than buttin' yer nose in where it don't belong?"

Hurt pride or not, Miranda couldn't believe how he had just insulted her again and was ready to say something when Gilbert turned his attention to Tad, his tone almost threatening.

"As fer you, leave me poor dead mother out of this, hear?"

Seeing the shocked look on Miranda's face, while taking her by the elbow to escort her back into the dinner party, Tad said, "Grandmother will be ringing for dinner momentarily. Shall we go inside, my dear?"

"Dear?" Miranda whispered hoarsely.

Hearing her say "dear", Gilbert shook his head in disgust, obviously mistaking her question as a term of endearment and began to walk back to his wagon, much to Miranda's dismay. Completely outraged, not having a chance to respond either to Gilbert's rudeness or to Tad by addressing her so familiar in public, she turned her anger on Tad, jerking free of his touch.

"How dare you refer to me as your 'dear'? I've never given you any cause to think of me in that manner."

"You're absolutely right. Forgive my insolence. However, it served its purpose, now didn't it? That low life won't be bothering such a fine woman as yourself again."

"Mr. Honeycutt, I'll have you know I am more than capable of choosing whom I associate with in the future. I need no assistance from you." She snarled at him, her eyes reflecting the anger she felt.

"Miranda. . . ."

Interrupting him, she snapped, "Miss Brown, if you please!"

Smiling smugly, as if ignoring her comment he said, "I've angered you, which was not my intent. As a guest in our home, I have a certain obligation to assure your safety. Especially from a man that can't be trusted. The Irish are all alike--good-for-nothing drunks--that fight all day, gamble all night, and think the world owes them something. If it were up to me, along with half the nation, they would all be sent back from where they came."

"Is that right? Well, Mr. Honeycutt, I am indeed a guest in your *grandparents'* home that much is true; however, has it escaped you that I'm also considered as undesirable by some of your smug friends? As a matter of fact, as I recall, when I arrived here during the war, you yourself made no attempt to hide your contempt for me, simply because of my origin. So, should I assume then that you would prefer me to be sent home as well?"

"The truth finally surfaces at last! You're still angry with me because I made comment of your family being slave owners, years ago. Surely after all this time Miranda, you can't be holding a grudge over my curiosity?"

"Angry? No. I even understand you being curious. As you recall, I told you then, I too was curious coming to a Northerner's home. However, your prejudices against those different from one of your upper-class snobs, I find particularly offensive. And so that we have no further misunder-standings, in the future, if you have an urge to make decisions for me, since it's viewed by your class that Southerners are dimwitted, unable to make decisions wisely, and since I'm clearly a Southerner, kindly confine your attentions to someone who wants them, and is worthy of all your so-called superior knowledge. Now if you will excuse me, I'll see if Mr. and Mrs. Myles have arrived yet."

Turning on her heels, not giving Tad a chance to respond, Miranda rushed back to the house only to be angered further by Tad's laughter.

Walking into the drawing room, she saw Felicity and Benjamin being joined by James. Much to her amazement, Lavinia went to greet them as well, gushing over Felicity and even welcoming Benjamin. From the suspicious look on Felicity's face, Miranda knew she wasn't the only one who wondered why the sudden change of heart from Mrs. Sterling. When James greeted them both by asking, "I was wondering if you were going to make it. Trouble at the school this afternoon?"

"Nothing we couldn't handle. I do hope we didn't detain anyone," Benjamin said. Accepting James's hand, the two men shook a hearty greeting. Then turning his attention to Felicity, James took her hand, kissing it politely. "Hello, Felicity. How good to see you again. My, you look tired this evening."

Hearing him address her by her first name, Felicity politely responded accordingly.

"Good to see you too, James. It was a long day, and now I look forward to the company of adults, rather than children this evening."

"Indeed! Well, we'll try to make the evening enjoyable then. Won't we, my dear?" Lavinia's smile faded, hearing the familiarity in the conversation between the Myles' and her husband. Glaring at Felicity, she thought, *So now it's James, is it? Why you little bitch.*

Having little else to do but try to grin and bear this humiliation, Lavinia said, "Why of course, darling. If you'll excuse me." Turning, she went to the fireplace while Miranda, Sarah and Michael greeted the Myles' as well.

Hearing them carry on about how lovely the wedding had been, Lavinia felt sickened. *Get a hold of yourself, Lavinia!* She scolded herself, *Or you'll come across as a scorned alley cat rather than a poor helpless kitten.* Glancing back at Felicity, who seemed to enjoy all the attention she was receiving, Lavinia shook her head. *Well, I'll give the bitch this much. She is a master at appearing sweet.*

Trying to regain her composure, painting on a smile for the Myles' benefit, Lavinia turned and faced the fireplace. Upon doing so, out peeked Alfred leaning away from where he was sitting, nestled in the high back Queen Anne chair.

"Why Mr. Honeycutt, I had no idea you were over here," Lavinia cooed, trying not to sound surprised.

"Every now and then, I enjoy a good crackling fire. The flames are mesmerizing. Don't you agree? The mystery of the fire so vibrant and alive, until it nearly consumes the log then dwindles away loosing its luster and power with nothing left but a non-menacing spark every now and then. Look there . . ." Alfred paused, gesturing at a small withering spark. "The flame trying to regain its strength but never quite achieves its youthful splendor. Ever notice that, my dear?" Alfred asked, while gazing at what was left of the fire with a smug look on his face.

Why you old coot . . . Instantly she knew he could see through her and felt suddenly sick to her stomach. *Dear God, was she so transparent that she couldn't even fool an old man any more?*

Deciding she would not be intimidated by him, she played along with his little game. "Yes, but the fire does devour the log eventually."

Alfred shrewdly turned to look at her again, his eyebrows arched. "Only if it goes undetected, or the log wishes to be consumed. I like to think that someone can always douse the flame with a little water if need be."

Standing, he took a glass of water from a side table next to the chair then poured it dramatically over the flame with a snide grin. Turning to her, he said, "See, the fire is out. The wood is no longer threatened by the flame."

In absolute shock, Lavinia's eyes drifted from the gray smoke to her host.

Politely, Alfred asked, "Are you ill, Mrs. Sterling? All of a sudden you look pale. Shall I ring for a bit of *brandy*? I understand a little of its nectar works wonders for what ails you." Alfred smiled wickedly at her as more smoke from the fire filled the air.

Dear God, James told him everything! How could he . . . Finding her voice, Lavinia said, "No, that won't be necessary."

Not waiting for a response, Lavinia turned on her heels. *Why, that no good bastard is going to ruin everything!*

Tad, who had the misfortune of being detained by his grandmother, looked grateful for the distraction, as Lavinia approached. "Oh my, Lavinia, you're so flushed. Has that husband of mine kept you by that fire of his too long? He has such a fascination with them, even in this God-forsaken heat . . ." Vivian prattled.

"It is rather warm this evening. We never had this type of heat back in England." Lavinia mumbled, still in shock. "I'm just a little parched-- nothing that a cool glass of water won't cure," Lavinia cordially answered, trying to regain her composure as Vivian Honeycutt watched her grandson Tad join Miranda.

Gesturing in their direction she muttered, "Why must that girl constantly push my dear grandson away like that? The thought has occurred to me that it may serve someone's interest to persuade Miranda into having a change of heart."

"Funny you should bring that matter up. I was just thinking how the two of them are suited for one another." Disliking Tad Honeycutt from the beginning, viewing him as a weak man, sure to make someone miserable, Lavinia looked at Miranda and smiled coyly.

"Vivian, your grandson is exactly what that woman deserves. Perhaps if someone like myself were to help a budding romance along, then perhaps someone like yourself would be willing to return the favor."

"Splendid idea. Now what is it that you need from me, my dear?" As the two of them put their heads together to advance their own desires, Tad spoke softly behind Miranda.

"Do you intend to stay annoyed with me all evening?" Tad whispered, coming up behind the unsuspecting Miranda, who immediately turned and peered up at him. Realizing that everyone's attention, including that of her father's was now on them, she politely excused herself and Tad to the side, far enough away as to not be overheard.

With a pasted smile to her lips, she whispered, "Tad, I find it extremely ill-mannered, even contemptible, that you find it necessary to further agitate me by bringing up the incident in the gardens. Clearly, you must know that such behavior will only make matters worse." Since she had his undivided attention and her anger wasn't satisfied, she added. "Solely for the purpose of not being misunderstood, let me make myself perfectly clear. I am not angry, nor annoyed with you. I just believe firmly that our differences are far too vast to ever expect anything more between us, than that of an acquaintance. Therefore, for the sake of risking an unpleasant evening, I would prefer you drop the entire incident."

"Only if you promise me one thing."

Trying very hard not to appear angry, although she was livid, Miranda took a deep breath and asked, "What is that?"

"Let me make it up to you by taking you to the theatre next week?"

"The theatre? Why on earth would I go to the theatre with you?" she answered sharply, her resentment unmasked. Realizing her tone was extremely rude, she quickly added. "Tad, I'm very sorry. What an unkind thing for me to have said. No matter how annoyed I am with you, I had no right to be so rude."

"Ah ha! By your own admission you are annoyed with me, after all?" he said smiling at her.

As hard as it was for Miranda to admit it, Tad did know how to be charming and she couldn't help but smile.

"Perhaps just a little."

"Well then, please, let me make it up to you. Come with me to the theatre and dine out for an evening, rather than sit here night after night listening to the same old rubbish."

An evening out did sound delightful, Miranda thought, gazing up at him, suddenly aware that he looked exceptionally handsome tonight.

"I'll think on it and let you know after dinner," she whispered.

Nodding, Tad's smile faded as he gazed lovingly at her and cupped her elbow in the palm of his hand. "Miranda, truly I am sorry."

The sincerity in his voice startled her, as she looked into his eyes that reminded her of the sea. As their eyes met, her heart stirred and no longer could she be angry with him. *Was it possible she had misjudged him?*

Just then, Jerome announced dinner was being served. Still gingerly holding onto her elbow, Tad whispered, "Shall we?"

Accepting his arm, Miranda and Tad followed Vivian and Alfred into the dining room, rather than being accompanied in by her father which normally took place when he was in town. A smile passed between Michael and Lucas as they accompanied Sarah into the dining room, while Lavinia glared at James, knowing any hope to continue the farce that he had attacked her was futile.

Suddenly everything became clear to Lavinia. *If James had told Alfred, which she was certain that he had, then could it be possible he had confided in Benjamin too?*

Recalling the sudden familiarity among the three of them sent chills through her, as her mind raced. *Why you miserable bastard, gathering sympathy were you?* Then another thought crossed her mind and she felt nauseous. *Or, were you simply trying to be closer to that tart?*

Seeing a smile being exchanged between Felicity and James, she knew instantly it was the latter. Remembering how he had been so keen on hearing every detail of Benjamin and Felicity's mudslide episode, especially where Felicity was concerned, her stomach coiled. *Dear God, he wasn't aroused by my advancements, but rather he lusted for her.* Enraged by such a revelation, she immediately looked at Felicity with contempt and hate then back to her husband.

"Why Lavinia dearest, you look pale. Are you sure everything is all right?" James asked sympathetically, but his eyes reflected amusement by her suffering.

"Perhaps some fresh air would help." Directing her attention to her hostess, she said, "Vivian, please begin without us. We shan't be but a moment."

It was Alfred who replied for his wife. "Take your time, dear. The Myles' were just commenting on how generous your dear husband was to them today and since we both know how James detests notoriety, this will save him further embarrassment."

Raising his eyebrow, emphasizing the word embarrassment, Lavinia knew his comment was directed toward her. *How dare he*, she thought while turning on her heels. Lavinia stormed out of the dining room, past the sitting room, rushing to the garden where she stood fuming watching James approach. From the smug look on his face, she knew her suspicions were right. Unable to control her rage as soon as he entered the gardens, she snarled, "How could you?"

"How could I what, my dearest?" James asked innocently, only provoking the rage inside her.

"You know perfectly well what I mean. You knew how vulnerable I was, begging you to prove your love for me last night, when all the while you were lusting over that filthy tart!"

Judging by the look in his eyes, Lavinia knew she was right and demanded an explanation. "How could you?" she yelled.

Drawing closer to her, James took her elbow and callously said, "You're distraught Lavinia, besides delusional. First you accuse me unjustly of accosting you, and now you claim you begged for my affections. Didn't I satisfy your insatiable desires, so you maliciously attack me for punishment? Or is it, in your demented state that you simply don't know anymore? Maybe I should take you home and call a physician that Alfred has recommended. Perhaps a few weeks of rest in the countryside might do you a world of good."

Jerking away from him, Lavinia snarled, "No. I know precisely what you and that old coot are scheming and I won't stand for it. You are the delusional one if you think I'll be fooled into being sent away to the country so you can be free to lust after that strumpet Felicity. Next you'll be insisting I go to some sanitarium . . ."

Chuckling sinisterly at her, he said, "Is that so? Why would you think I'd send you away to asylum, my dear? Could it possibly be that you aren't able to control your temper in public? Have you become so unstable that you find it necessary to hurl false accusations at your husband trying to discredit his good name, calling a matriarch of society foul names? The list is endless my dear, and I've only mentioned today's outlandish behavior. Shall I bring up your sordid past episodes as well? Why, any doctor would agree you need confinement."

Before she had a chance to respond, Alfred came through the garden door asking, "Is everything alright, James? Should I send Montgomery for the doctor?"

Lavinia gasped, knowing the two of them were deadly serious. They did intend to be rid of her by locking her away in some nut house. Panic filled her as she pleadingly began shaking her head, and tears ran down her cheeks.

"Please James, don't do this," Lavinia begged. Their eyes locked onto one another and she held her breath. Seeing no warmth for her in his eyes, Lavinia feared the worst. "I beseech you, don't lock me away. I'll be good." She whimpered.

Turning his head back to Alfred, James finally said, "No. Not this time, my friend."

Hearing his reply Lavinia, sighed and wept softly in her hands.

"Very well, as you wish," responded Alfred in a cool tone. "Do see to it though, that you both return promptly. You know how Vivian detests waiting."

"Yes. of course," replied James looking back at Lavinia. "Get control of yourself at once or I might have a change of heart, my dear."

Obediently, Lavinia wiped the tears from her eyes, having no other recourse. Never had she felt such hatred or fear for another as she did now. Realizing that she had been out-maneuvered by the two of them and had played right into their hands, Lavinia asked, "Now what?"

"Now, you *will* conduct yourself in the manner that any man should expect from his wife, and that is to be soft and gentle just as Benjamin Myles' wife. From where I stand, I've got the short end of the stick when he rid himself of you and took Felicity as a bride. Furthermore, I'll be damned if you think I'm going to continue letting the likes of that sniveling swine, ex-husband of yours outshine me any longer. Am I clear on that, Lavinia? You do as I say, or else my dear, you will suffer the consequences."

She quivered, hearing his ultimatum. James had made himself perfectly clear. Either she did exactly as he wished, or she would be locked away. Nodding her response, stunned beyond belief, Lavinia stepped back into the Honeycutt's home, being led by James who had placed his hand in the small of her back. Coarsely he whispered to her, "Smile dearest, you wouldn't want to make a scene now, would you?"

Pasting a smile to her lips, Lavinia took her seat across from Felicity. Judging by the look of concern on her face, Lavinia knew her smile wasn't fooling anyone. Avoiding eye contact with her nemesis, she unfolded her linen napkin, saying, "My, but dinner smells wonderful as usual, Vivian."

As the salad was being served, Lavinia remained silent, keeping to herself. *James might be able to control my tongue, for the time being, but he will never be able to control my thoughts.* Smiling at Felicity then back at her husband she thought, *you bloody bastard, you will rue the day you prefer that little bitch to me.* Then recalling James's words describing Benjamin, a genuine smile crossed her lips. *Well, James was right about one thing. Benjamin was nothing but a swine who apparently enjoyed rolling around in the mud, with his sow slut.*

Spooning dressing over her salad, she continued to smile until Benjamin, said, "Um, roast pork, one of my favorites."

Immediately Lavinia began coughing to mask her laughter until knowingly, James frowned at her.

"My, but I am parched this evening," she mumbled and reached for her goblet of water.

After dinner, as was the case every night, the men went to Alfred's library while the women chatted in Vivian's private sitting room. As the women relaxed, sounds of the men deep in conversation over the conspiracy of the death of Lincoln could be heard trailing into the sitting room as one disagreed with another. Tonight was no exception.

From the night Lincoln had been shot and killed, no matter who attended the Honeycutt evening dinner parties, sides were drawn as the events of the conspiracy and the military rights on such offenses were reported in the newspapers. Tonight's debate was no exception--even if a woman was found guilty in a military court of law, should she be hung.

Proclaiming Mrs. Surratt's innocence as usual, Michael argued that she was as much a victim as poor Lincoln was and therefore should have never been found guilty in the first place. He argued there was no proof she was actually involved in the plotting with John Wilkes Booth and the other men. As others would interject, Michael held steadfast to his opinion that this was a gross injustice. Simply because she ran the boarding house where Booth resided and had become friendly with her boarders and son's friends, was no justification for such acts to be committed to a good Catholic woman as they had been, always ending his argument by stating emphatically that her only crime was trying to protect her son, John.

Albert and James however, sided together that *any woman*, no matter how naive Mrs. Surratt claimed to be now, should be treated as the men whom she associated with. Using Michael's argument against him, especially since her son was involved, it was certain proof that she must be involved too. Claiming Mary Surratt knew exactly every detail of the assassination plot and was proven a co-conspirator by storing French field glasses at her property in Maryland, along with other escape articles needed for Booth and Herold, Louis Weichmann, her escort, testified he had overheard her telling John Lloyd that very morning "to have those shooting irons ready". According to Weichmann's testimony, Booth and his accomplice David Herold did flee to the boardinghouse in Surrattsville, Maryland, first, to retrieve the hidden items after the murder of Lincoln. Clearly, this was proof she was guilty and should get what she deserved.

Benjamin on the other hand, felt as many Americans did--that a civilian should not be brought up on charges by a military court--of law. Apparently, Lucas agreed with his assessment of the situation by adding, "The woman is entitled to be tried in a court of law as prescribed in the constitution, by a dozen of her peers." Stating, this being the case, then a pardon was in order until a civil court could hear the evidence.

Bored with the same old arguments night after night, Tad, not caring if Mary Surratt were to be hung on July seventh or not, patiently waited until Michael was deeply involved expressing his opinion and would silently make his escape. This night however, Tad had to wait, while Benjamin, with the aide of Lucas, debated their viewpoints with Alfred and James.

While Sarah and Lavinia exchanged their views on woman's suffrage, Miranda asked Felicity, in a hushed whisper, "Have you noticed how peculiar Mrs. Sterling is behaving this evening?"

Nodding, she said, "Take it from me. She's a predator, waiting for her prey to become distracted. So watch yourself."

Immediately Miranda smiled at her friend's ability to come directly to the point without arousing suspicion.

Seeing Miranda's smile, Lavinia turned her attention toward her and cooed sweetly, "Oh do share with us what's so amusing, Miranda dear. It wouldn't have anything to do with that incredibly handsome Tad, now would it? I must admit, when I saw you speaking with him earlier, I thought to myself, 'my but they do make a striking couple'."

Feeling exceptionally uncomfortable, Miranda's eyes drifted toward Felicity as if looking for assistance and acknowledging her earlier observation.

"Wouldn't you agree, Mrs. Honeycutt?" Lavinia asked.

Both Vivian and Sarah began to speak at once. Embarrassed and realizing her mother-in-law was annoyed, Sarah politely said, "Oh I'm sorry, Mother Honeycutt."

Vivian looked at Sarah, coolly saying, "Perhaps this could be prevented if Lavinia felt comfortable calling you by your first name."

Aware that this was another attempt of Vivian's to make her feel uneasy, Sarah turned and looked at Lavinia, her face crimson. "I'm so sorry Lavinia, for the confusion. Since I've heard you address my mother-in-law as Vivian, I assumed you were referring to me. But to avoid any further confusion in the future, please, will you address me by first name?"

Glaring at Sarah, Vivian coughed, clearly not amused by Sarah pointing out the obvious that it was she who had spoken out of turn. Felicity and Miranda only glanced at one another sensing the tension between Sarah and Vivian.

Not ready to drop the opportunity of speaking about Miranda and Tad, needing Vivian's help more than ever, Lavinia said, "Certainly Sarah. You've known our dear Miranda since she was a child I understand?"

"Yes, of course." Sarah said, knowing where this conversation was leading and feeling extremely uncomfortable.

"Well, then perhaps you would give her some motherly advice and tell her what a wonderful catch Tad is."

Sarah knew that if she didn't agree with Lavinia, Michael would hear from his mother how his new wife had said that she didn't think Tad was good enough for Miranda. While on the other hand, if she agreed with Lavinia then poor Miranda would feel uncomfortable.

Tactfully Sarah responded by saying, "It has always been my practice never to try and persuade my daughter Elise or Miranda into doing anything while in the presence of others. Surely you must agree that deliberately trying to embarrass them serves no purpose other than to alienate your loved ones from you." Sarah's last comment was directed to Vivian, but she turned to Miranda and smiled lovingly. "I trust Miranda being such a wise young woman will follow her heart."

The smell of cigar smoke filled the room and Vivian looked at Lavinia knowingly and nodded toward the doorway just as Tad came in to join them.

"Ah, I knew I'd find you lovely ladies in here. Such a lovely evening isn't it?" Tad walked over and kissed his grandmother's cheek. Then turning to Miranda, he asked, "Since we still have unfinished business, perhaps a bit of fresh air would suit you?"

Not ready to answer him yet, but not wishing to be questioned what unfinished business Tad and she had, Miranda said, "A walk sounds quite nice, thank you." Avoiding everyone's eyes, especially Felicity's, she accepted Tad's hand. Once Miranda stood, Tad placed her hand in the crook of his arm as he escorted her to the gardens.

"Thank you, Miranda. From the look on your face when I came in, it looked like you needed rescuing."

For the second time that evening, Miranda was stunned by Tad's sudden change in attitude. "I don't know what to say Tad. In fact, I was just going to scold you for putting me in such a compromising situation, which left me no alternative but to take a walk with you. After what you've just said, though, I would sound terribly rude, wouldn't I?"

"Oh no, I wouldn't dream of answering that question. Especially since it took you three years to get over something I said in haste when we first met."

Glancing at him in the moonlight, Miranda softly chuckled, suddenly finding herself enjoying his company, despite her reservations. Watching a hummingbird glide to another branch of the lilac bush as she and Tad walked closer to it, she said, "Well, I suppose that was a baited question."

Not answering her, Tad changed the subject and asked, "This time of the evening is so pleasant. Don't you agree?" He pointed to a bunny that hopped into the shadows of the dense bushes.

"It is indeed," Miranda replied softly. "Until Father and I came north, I've never seen a lilac bush. Of all your grandmother's flowers I enjoy them the most."

"Did you enjoy gardening at your home?" From his question, she knew he wasn't trying to pump her for information of their way of life on the plantation, but rather what she enjoyed doing while she was there.

"Well before the war, I did. Unfortunately, after the war began, when mother and I were forced to work the fields out of necessity to survive, gardening seemed to lose its luster." Thinking of Catherine Brown, her mother, Miranda was able to picture her in filthy and torn clothing, which brought a tear to Miranda's eye.

"And now?" Tad asked.

"And now I think we should head back inside. Don't you?"

Lovingly Tad gazed at her, his blue eyes dancing in the moonlight. "Miranda, why not let me accompany you to the theatre, let's say this Friday, and we can begin again?"

Accustomed to his sandy hair and good looks over the years, never had he looked as appealing as he did tonight, and her heartbeat quickened.

Embarrassed suddenly by his closeness, she softly asked, "Friday you say? Of this week?"

Recalling how difficult it was for her father at the last minute to secure tickets to a particular show that they had wanted to attend last fall, Miranda asked, "Will that give you enough time to reserve seats?"

"Oh trust me, my dear, I mean Miranda. If you would honor me by accepting, I will find a way."

"Well Tad, with such kind words. How can I possibly refuse? Yes. I would love to attend the theatre with you."

Smiling fondly at him, Miranda suddenly was aware that she still had her hand nestled in his arm and began to remove it as they reached the door to reenter the Honeycutt's home. Feeling her hand withdraw, Tad took her hand and tenderly brushed it with his thumb before releasing it while gazing at her lovingly as only a man does to a woman he adores.

"Thank you, Miranda. You have no idea how much you have pleased me by accepting."

Not certain how she should respond, Miranda stepped forward, waiting for Tad to open the French door. Seeing him stand to the side, she frowned at him. "Aren't you coming inside?"

Shaking his head, Tad said, "No. I have another engagement."

"Oh. I didn't realize . . . I hope I didn't detain you," Miranda said, puzzled as to why he had not appeared anxious to leave while they were walking.

"Not at all. I look forward to this Friday, and I'm sure I'll see you tomorrow."

Noting that Tad didn't mention where he was going and knowing he owed her no explanation, Miranda only smiled politely while turning--her cheeks flushed and heart pounding like a schoolgirl--then she went inside. As she entered Vivian's private sitting room she was aware that all eyes were on her, including Michael who had joined them.

"Ah Miranda, I thought Tad was with you?"

"He was, Mr. Honeycutt. However, he had another engagement," she said, hesitantly, seeing the concerned look on his face.

"Another engagement? This time of night?"

"I'm sure he won't be out too late, darling," Sarah said reassuringly, noticing the look of concern in her husband's eyes as she smiled lovingly at him.

Not the least bit interested in listening to Sarah and Michael, Lavinia said, "Miranda dear, we were just discussing having dinner at our home this Friday night. I do hope you and Tad will be able to attend."

"Friday, you say?" Miranda said hesitatingly, not believing her bad luck and softly added. "I'm afraid I'll have to excuse myself."

"Oh no. It just wouldn't be any fun without you and Tad there."

Meekly Miranda, said, "I'm sorry, I've just agreed to dine out with Tad, and attend the theatre this Friday evening."

Flashing a smile toward Vivian, Lavinia said, "Oh how lovely! Well, let's you and I go shopping for a dress then tomorrow, shall we?" Turning to look at James, who had now joined them, Lavinia said, "James dear, you wouldn't mind me buying a new dress would you? I seem to have ruined my favorite last evening."

Acting as the dutiful husband, James answered. "Why of course not, dear. Anything you like will be fine with me."

Taking advantage of a lull in the conversation, Benjamin looked at his host and hostess, and said, "As lovely as this has been, I'm afraid my dear wife and I must be calling it an evening. Six a.m. comes rather early."

Lavinia winced inside at hearing Benjamin call Felicity his dear wife, but concealed it by looking at Felicity with a tender smile. "Oh dear, what a dreadful hour. Surely Benjamin, you know a woman needs her beauty rest."

As sympathetic as Lavinia's words sounded, Felicity knew this was Lavinia's way of snidely saying she looked dreadful. Suddenly feeling very homely and awkward, Felicity glanced at Benjamin. "Well, the children need a lot of care. Hopefully someday soon, we both will have enough help so the two of us can catch up on some badly needed rest."

Judging by James's eyes as he traced Felicity's face adoringly, Lavinia knew that her husband thought of his tart as anything but homely and haggard. Silently she cringed as her jealousy mounted, yet she knew she could do nothing about it but grin and bear the humiliation for the time being. Realizing there wouldn't be an opportunity to discuss her problems with Vivian now that the gentlemen had joined them, Lavinia vowed to make the time tomorrow morning.

~

Across town, Tad joined in a game of five-card stud. Sitting next to his friend Daniel Hobbs, at a round table in the back of the dingy, poorly-lit room of Jake's pub, he dealt the last card to himself. Determined to win some of the money he lost last night to that damned Irishman, Gilbert, Tad casually slipped himself the ace that was buried on the bottom of the deck.

Casually picking up his hand, he showed no emotion at the ace-high straight he dealt himself. Only the glimmer in Tad's eyes betrayed his excitement, knowing he was certain to win this hand. Glancing at Gilbert over the top of his cards, Tad's desire to shame his enemy intensified. Not for the money he had consistently lost to the Irishman. But more importantly, after seeing Miranda's interest in Gilbert earlier in the garden, Tad was hell bent on proving he was far more worthy of her attention than this man he deemed as a worthless son-of-a-bitch. Clearing his throat, he turned to Daniel.

"Hobbs, it's up to you."

"Not so fast, Honeycutt." Gilbert grabbed Tad's arm from across the table. "Let's be showing us all the ace of spades that was buried low hole. I'd be wagering it has found its way miraculously into yer hand!"

Glaring back at him, Tad said, "Are you accusing me of cheating?"

"I'm doing more than calling you a cheater, ya lousy bastard! I'm here to prove it." Gilbert shouted, reaching across the table before Tad had a chance to react, and grabbed him by the coat lapel, while knocking his cards across the table.

Daniel, noticing the ace at the same time as Gilbert, reacted by knocking into the table, resulting in the cards, money, and ale crashing to the floor at Tad's feet.

"Why you dirty low down scum! Can't win the honest way can ya? Gotta deal off the bottom of the deck?" Gilbert shouted.

"You damned liar!" Tad shouted back, knowing it was now his word against Gilbert's, since all the cards were scattered on the pub's floor in a pile. "You're drunk and don't know what the hell you're talking about!"

"That may be so, yer lordship. But why is it then that you got yourself the ace of spades that was buried on the bottom of the deck? I saw it with me own damned eyes when you were shuffling!"

Tad, outraged, reached on the dirty floor to retrieve the money and cards that had fallen, spotting the ace of spades on top, he placed his boot over the card and then threw the money at his accuser. "You don't know what you're talking about! Here, take your damn money! Who needs it! You're only pissed off that the lady prefers me to the likes of you."

"What the hell you talking about? What lady?" Gilbert shouted back.

"You know perfectly well what lady, you slimy bastard. Can I help it that Miss Brown would rather associate with someone of means, rather than a good-for-nothing like you? And since you can't have her, you're trying to destroy my good name. Before you start accusing someone unjustly of cheating, you better be damned sure you're right in the future you slimy-Mick."

Realizing everyone in the entire bar was staring at the both of them, Tad pulled the table back to an upright position and kicked the tin tankards at his feet. Dramatically he then straightened his suit coat and took his seat again. After confidently leaning back in his chair, with a snide look on his face, Tad added for the benefit of those who were listening, "Hear me real good O'Flaherty. People get themselves killed for trashing the good name of honest folk here in America."

"Bullshit! There ain't an honest bone in yer body. And I caught ya dead to rights!" As he flung himself across the table, his first blow clipped the corner of Tad's eye. Knocked off balance, Tad fell back in his chair onto the floor of the pub. Recovering quickly, Tad jumped to his feet and flung himself onto his attacker. Gilbert, anticipating Tad's reaction, made his way around the table to deliver another blow to Tad, but found the taller man pinning him down across the table with a forceful strike to the head instead.

The remaining men that had been sitting around the table, jumped from their seats as the two men continued striking each other with their fists. Within moments the fight ended abruptly when the owner of the pub, breaking a whiskey bottle on the side of the bar, yelled, "Get out, Irish! We don't need the likes of you and that bad temper of yours tearing up my place. Get out and don't come back."

"Me! I ain't the one who's just been caught cheating. You'd let that bastard remain, but yer throwing me out? What the hell is going on here?" Gilbert demanded.

"That's right, Irish. I said get on out of here and don't you be coming back! Or the next time I'll send for the constable and throw your ass in jail, and have you deported back to Ireland, where you belong!"

With victory in his eyes, Tad again picked up his chair and after brushing his blonde blood-soaked hair across his head, yelled at his attacker, "You heard the man. Get on out of here ya damned lying bastard!"

From the look on Gilbert's face, it was obvious he was outraged. Glaring at the rest of the men around the table who had been playing cards, he yelled, "Tell 'em! Tell 'em what ya saw, damn it!"

None of the men would come to his aid and glanced away from his accusing eyes. "What in the hell is the matter with you dumb bastards? His lordship steals your money right from under your noses and you protect him." Disgusted, he waved his arm at them. "Ah the hell with ya."

Turning his attention back toward Tad, Gilbert glared at him with contempt, grabbing his money, and spouted, "Watch your back 'yer lordship', cause I'll be getting yer ass! You can count on that, and the rest of you lying bastards too!" Then he stormed out of the pub indignantly.

Daniel, glancing at Tad, announced to the rest of the onlookers, "That dirty stinking liar has tried to dishonor my good friend's reputation here. A round for the house, on me!"

Dramatically patting Tad on the shoulder he added, "I tell ya all, Honeycutt is a man of honor! It was that low belly O'Flaherty. I saw the whole thing. Isn't that right?" he yelled, looking at George Hornsby and Harry Pike to back him up. Readily, the other poker buddies agreed, but they knew differently, seeing Tad deal from the bottom of the deck as well.

~ Eight ~

Distinctive Differences

Onlookers who might see the exchange of well wishes between James Sterling and the Myles' outside the mansion of their mutual friends, the Honeycutt's, would think they were old friends, rather than estranged adversaries with a sordid past. No longer able to witness the shameless way her husband was trying to wiggle his way into the Myles' good graces merely to be closer to Felicity, the scorned woman turned her head in disgust. *You will pay for this, you miserable bastard. If it is the last thing I ever do!*

Trying desperately to figure out a solution to her current predicament, Lavinia called upon the dead spirit of her father, Randolph Bailey-Smythe. *Father, this is all your fault! If you hadn't left all your holdings to that pathetic daughter of yours, I would have some leverage against that worthless husband of mine rather than be forced to kowtow to his every whim. Help me father please,* she pleaded. *Haven't I suffered enough with the humiliation of losing everything I value? Do you want to see me locked away in an asylum too? If James and that old coot Alfred have their way, that is precisely what will become of me, while your precious Annabelle and her traitorous fiancé Rupert live in luxury off your holdings and protecting his vast fortune no doubt!*

On the verge of tears from frustration and the sheer irony of how life had changed since her father's death, Lavinia gave in to the images of the past that flashed before her now. A single tear ran down her cheek as she recalled her beloved Ashwillow, the family home her father had bequeathed to her only sister, Annabelle, and the life she had once known in England. Her memories were halted when the image of Annabelle living in the lap of luxury with Rupert at her side, crept into her tormented mind.

In desperation, she again pleaded to her deceased father. *How could you do this to me, father? Annabelle has everything, while I am forced to live here in this godforsaken country with these inept simpletons who think they are of quality breeding.*

Living in the colonies these past three years, it had become painfully clear to Lavinia that the prestigious life she had once led as the daughter of the Squire Randolph Bailey-Smythe meant little to those in New York society. All they seemed to care about was who had money and power.

James, who had invested wisely in the meat-canning venture, was now looked upon as quite influential in New York.

Glancing at her husband, she glared at him with hate in her eyes. *Enjoy yourself now, you miserable bastard, pretending to be decent to win that little tart's affection, because when I'm through, you will wish to God you were never born. How dare the likes of you think yourself superior over a Bailey-Smythe!* Watching James kiss Felicity's hand, a plan for revenge against her husband began to form in her mind.

Although she had been socially excommunicated from the elite of society in England, Lavinia knew that her sister and Rupert would come to her rescue if they believed she had learned the errors of her ways. Also aware that Rupert would do anything to protect his cousin, Felicity, recalling the night of the ball when he had gone against his own kind to protect her, decided to play on both their weaknesses.

What a splendid idea! She congratulated herself. *Surely they couldn't refuse a letter of apology, begging for their forgiveness. Especially when I tell them my fears about James trying to sabotage Felicity and Benjamin's marriage out of revenge and old jealousies.* As if she no longer had anything to fear, knowing that by using James' threat against her, and Rupert's weakness for Felicity to win access back into their good graces, she glanced at Felicity and Benjamin. *As inviting as it might be to see you suffer Benjamin, losing another wife to James, I'm afraid I will have to prevent my wayward husband from winning Felicity's heart for the time being.*

A sinister smile crossed her lips, as her eyes remained focused on Benjamin. *But mark my words you stupid fool, the day will come when I no longer will have a use for James, and then he and that harlot wife of yours will rip your heart out, right under your own nose! And that is precisely what you deserve, you boring sniveling swine.*

Preoccupied by the thought of Benjamin suffering, Lavinia hadn't realized James was returning, and as the coach door opened, she gasped.

"Oh it's you. Finished making a fool of yourself, gushing over the Myles'?"

"Felicity wanted me to be sure and let you know she hopes you're feeling better by the morning. Wasn't that thoughtful of her?" James snidely commented.

Glaring back at him, she responded curtly, "Most thoughtful indeed! And Benjamin, the unsuspecting naive swine, as you so eloquently called him earlier--did he wish me well too?"

Hearing no response, Lavinia looked out the window in silence. As hard as she tried to remain focused on her plan of winning back Rupert and Annabelle's trust, Lavinia's mind wandered. The similarities of James' behavior to her's years before when he was wed to Rebecca, and the way he was now with Felicity was uncanny. Glancing at the man she once believed she loved, she wondered if Rebecca had felt the same humiliation when James had actively flaunted his desires for her back in England years ago.

You pathetic bastard, always wanting what you cannot have. For an instant, Lavinia felt sorry for Rebecca Sterling, and a cold chill ran up her spine as the haunting voice of Rebecca Sterling mocked her. *Serves you right, Lavinia!* Doubting her own sanity, she scolded herself, *Stop this at once or you will end up in a sanitarium.*

As the carriage pulled up to the couple's home, Lavinia waited for James to assist her. However, when he stepped out of the coach and called to the hired driver to assist his wife instead, sheepishly Lavinia stepped out of the coach on her own.

"That won't be necessary. I can make it on my own."

Upon entering her home, Lavinia hastily dismissed the butler and followed her husband up the stairs to their private suite. Anger had replaced her earlier fear and humiliation and she glared at him staring out the window, his back to her. Slamming the door as she entered their room, she asked vehemently, "Just so I understand the new rules that you and Alfred have apparently set for me, what precisely am I to expect in return for my obedience?"

Hearing no response, she continued. "Shall I now be required to fill your glass with the drink like some peasant servant and then watch you pass out? Or, perhaps you would prefer me to soak myself in mud, reduced to painting a picture in your mind so you can perform as a man? Although, I would be hard pressed to consider that pathetic attempt last evening as an act of a virile man!"

Turning on his heels to face her, James spouted, "There is not enough mud in all of New York to disguise who I'm actually bedding. Has it occurred to you Lavinia, that my sudden lack of enthusiasm in having you is that I'm not the least bit aroused by you any longer?"

Hearing his derogatory comment, Lavinia immediately lunged forward with her hand in the air to strike him, which James grasped firmly before she made contact.

"Considering the fact that I've not had a drink all evening--all day for that matter--and my reflexes are no longer hampered, it hardly seems *worth the bother* now, does it Lavinia?"

Gasping, realizing those were nearly the exact words she had used after pushing James from her last night, she asked suspiciously, "What is that supposed to mean?" There was no need for James to make eye contact--she felt his eyes bore a hole that penetrated her soul.

"When you try to seduce your next victim, you delusional little bitch, perhaps it would be wise to make sure he's actually passed out before insulting him." Although James wasn't certain what she had actually said, only remembering bits and pieces of last evening's events, he acted as if he had total recall.

"I don't know what you're speaking of!" She spat indignantly. "And you call me delusional? I think not! Your brain must be pickled from all the brandy you've consumed over the years. Now let me go! You're hurting me," she squealed, trying to free herself from his grip.

Realizing what force he was using to refrain her, he released her arm and said, "Oh you haven't begun to experience pain. Be forewarned, you will! The exact hurt you have inflicted on me and others over the years. And don't think for a minute that I've forgotten what you said about Rebecca last evening. As God as my witness, you will rue the day you ever said something so vile."

Rather than apologize for her earlier remarks, undaunted by his comment, Lavinia stated coolly, "You know James, I always knew you had a dark side to your character, but never had I dreamt you were capable of being so naive. Do you honestly believe for one moment that your precious little tart will ever leave Benjamin for the likes of you? Take it from someone who knows first hand, Benjamin may be weak, but what he lacks in character, he well makes up for in other areas. I can assure you that little alley cat you desire, is well taken care of by her well endowed husband!"

Seeing the hurt in James's eyes, Lavinia quickly added. "Come to think on it, no wonder Felicity always has that annoying smile pasted on her lips."

James raised his hand this time to strike her. Without backing away from him, Lavinia stood defiantly and calmly said, "Go ahead, James, hit me! And I'll be forced to let your precious Felicity know what kind of bastard you really are. Even if you try to lock me up, eventually I'll get word to her and don't you think for one instant I wouldn't."

Seeing him back down, Lavinia realized she had regained the upper hand for the time being, with James having no way of receiving coaching from Alfred. Taking advantage of his weakness, and his obvious jealousy over Benjamin, she said, "Rather than threaten one another further and cause each other such unnecessary pain, why don't we make a deal?"

"A deal?" he asked. "And what would you have to offer, Lavinia? Need I remind you we are no longer in England and more specific, you are no longer the heir to the Squire's fortune? What possibly could you have to offer me here in New York, being only the wife of a successful business man who has already proven that his wife is unstable at best?"

As hurtful as his words were to hear, Lavinia knew her husband's strengths and weaknesses. James needed to feel vindicated for her hurting him as she had last evening, but more importantly, he needed to prove he was superior to Benjamin, of whom he was insanely jealous. Suddenly his desire for Felicity became clear to her. By having what Benjamin desired most, it satisfied James's need to prove his superiority. Not only to the man he despised, but also to Lavinia.

She understood such an obsession, having once had the same desire in proving herself superior over Rebecca, and exactly why she no longer had any interest in James now. With Rebecca dead, James was no longer a token that proved her superiority. The only thing Lavinia currently desired from her husband was his money.

Forgoing her previous plan to be the poor helpless victim, another scheme began to form in her mind--one that would enable her the freedom to come and go as she pleased until she had worked on Rupert and Annabelle. That plan was to win James back by arousing his jealousy and insecurities through his manly desires.

Hastily recalling those from the party and canceling Alfred, Tad and Michael, not wanting Vivian as an enemy, she set her sight on the only available man in their set.

"Well for starters, Alfred is not the only man in New York who is prominent. Have you forgotten that Lucas Brown is a friend of the new president? Which makes him not only a powerful man to have on your side in Washington, but rather influential here in New York as well, I would imagine. And since it's obvious you want to prove your manhood by having the only thing Benjamin has, and that's his wife, what better way for you to get closer to your little tart than to have her husband away? Now what would it be worth to you if I persuaded Lucas that Benjamin should go to Washington? I mean wouldn't the most powerful man in all the nation help his old friend?"

"By God Lavinia, you are mad! Not only are you insinuating that you would assist me to have an affair with your ex-husband's wife, but you're offering to help by openly admitting that you would compromise your principles for a price. Have you no shame?"

By his reaction, Lavinia knew he didn't suspect her motivation and she continued cautiously trying not to appear too obvious.

"Shame? Oh please James, let's stop all this foolishness. You know neither of us has an ounce of shame or virtues when something comes between us and what we desire. Hasn't that always been what attracted us to one another in the first place? Unfortunately, it would appear you no longer desire me, so what would you have me do? Passively watch you have all the fun, while I'm miserable? I think not!"

"Not that I agree with you, but for the sake of argument, from all accounts Lucas Brown doesn't even like you. So pray tell, why would he listen to you?"

"Lucas is a man, is he not? And by all accounts a lonely one at that." Giving him her most alluring smile, Lavinia raised her eyebrow and began to unfasten her bodice buttons by taking great pains to be provocative while wetting her lips to paint a picture of Lucas in James mind.

"Although you may no longer find me sexually appetizing, I'm sure someone as lonely as Lucas would find my charms inviting. Even exhilarating, I'd hazard to venture. So I ask you James, do you honestly think I couldn't find a way to get his attention?" she said smugly.

"Jesus, Lavinia, are you suggesting you would allow that old man favors, in exchange for a romp in the sack?" Sensing his jealousy peak, she looked at him helplessly.

"I didn't say I would allow him the pleasure of my company, James. Although come to think on it, having a man desire me again and shower me with attention might be enjoyable. And considering he probably hasn't been with a real woman for years, I'm sure Lucas Brown would be very attentive to my every need. There must be something behind that saying, 'There's no fool like an old fool'."

Waiting for the right moment, she allowed her dress to fall to the floor. Pausing long enough for his eyes to trace her petite frame, she seductively began loosening the cords that held her corset, paying special attention to caress the cleavage of her breasts as they became loosened from their restraint. Inching her hand inside her corset, exposing more of her pert breast to him, she seductively whispered, "Except for perhaps a man who would fantasize over someone as boring as Felicity to me."

Realizing that his manhood was enlarging, she continued to disrobe, sultrily gliding her hands over her midriff, and she gazed into his eyes wontedly. Seeing his desire for her increase she added. "You do recall how good we were together, don't you James?"

Shaking his head, he whispered huskily, "This changes nothing between us, Lavinia. On occasion, I may still find you erotically appealing. However, living with you has proven to be pure hell. I cannot bear the way it's been between us and I refuse to live my life like this any longer."

"I agree wholeheartedly with you, darling. It's been hell for me too! Watching you lust after that woman when all I ever wanted was you. Why I gave up my reputation, my standing in society, even my inheritance to be with you . . . Not just to have your name . . ." She paused to discard her camisole to her feet, revealing her bare breasts to him completely before continuing. ". . . But all of you, James, including your love and devotion." Slipping out of her pantaloons with only her stockings on, she looked over at him, pleadingly. "Without your love James, I react badly and do such foolish things. Oh please, James, why can't you love me like you once did?"

Unable to resist her charms any longer, he reached for her and huskily pulled her naked body next to him. "Heaven help me, but I do love you, only you . . ." His words garbled between his ravenous kisses to her mouth while groping at her breasts.

As his mouth trailed down her neck to her nipples, feeling his urgency heighten, she moaned, "Darling, take me to our bed so I can truly please you."

As James swooped her into his arms, Lavinia smiled victoriously, knowing she still had more power over him than Alfred did. Lying on their bed, Lavinia began caressing her inner thighs to entice him further and watched as he quickly undressed. Once his trousers were removed, James immediately, thrust his manhood deep inside her. While James satisfied his desires, Lavinia moaned periodically as if she were enjoying their oneness. Certain that he wanted Felicity now, since he never denied it, she callously planned her next move to destroy him, before he had a chance to destroy her.

~

At the Honeycutt mansion, as the minutes passed into hours, Sarah kept silent vigil in the couple's bedchamber. Intuitively she knew that Michael was still pacing the library floor waiting for Tad, just as he had every night that week. Like her husband, she too paced the floor, praying Michael would be able to come to terms with what had happened in the past so that all of their futures could be brighter.

Knowing the torment Michael was putting himself through, blaming himself for his son's radical behavior, Sarah desperately wanted to help ease his burden but knew this was something he had to work through on his own. Fighting his inner demon was not his only concern and she wondered how long Michael would be able to refrain from speaking his mind, watching his only child stagger in well past 4:00 a.m., reeking of alcohol, night after night.

To keep herself busy, Sarah decided to catch up on correspondence with her friends back home, hoping to find some comfort in them since there was none to offer her or the man she loved.

Within moments of opening her first letter from the Mason's, her heart sank. Fairfax was besieged with such unthinkable changes in such a short time since the war had ended. The small ravaged town was now filled with Carpetbaggers from the north, strangers not accustomed to the southern way of life and furthermore, not interested in any of the traditions. These men were there for one purpose and that was to make sure that the traitors, whom they clearly despised, adhered to the new laws of the Union. Holding positions as judges and federal marshals, accountable for several towns in their jurisdiction, they were responsible to make changes immediately.

All across the south, these men came into towns carrying carpetbags and stayed only long enough to determine new law and order, then moving on, leaving a path of uncertainty behind. Many newly appointed lawmen were hand-picked by these strangers to the communities. Their choice of who should hold positions of importance was based primarily on if they had ever pledged their allegiance to the rebel cause. Many were mere overseers or sharecroppers, now able to tell their past employers what to do.

Even more shocking was that some of these newly-appointed lawmen were Negro men, educated from the north. Panic and hate flooded the hearts of the southern townsmen, no longer free to govern themselves since it was feared they may rise up again and rebel against the new laws.

Lee's troops were engaged in a new battle. However, this one was fought on no battlefield, using no weapons that could be seen. This attack was aimed at the very core of these prideful men and what they had fought so hard for to begin with. Men and women alike, who had suffered immensely from the war, were now in an invisible bondage, forced to adhere to the new laws as hate filled their hearts.

Irma wrote of a new General Store that had opened up on Main Street filled with much needed household goods, staples and farming tools, along with new fabrics from up north. However, the prices of the goods were high. Many of the white families having no income, their fields barren, and no seeds to plant or no money or any valuables left to barter with, went without--leaving them with hate in their hearts as they watched others able to buy the things they so desperately needed. Many of whom were former slaves, who seemed to have more than the white families did. They were the ones being hired at the new establishments in Fairfax and in Centerville alike. Everyday, news came of white families leaving their properties to travel west, leaving everything behind to start fresh with only what they could carry.

Oh dear, how awful, she thought, rubbing her eyes that were strained from the dim light of the room. Finding her place again, she read on and was shocked to find that Jessie now worked at the new General Store in town. Apparently, his salary was twice what Michael had been sending him and he had been seen around town with Clarisa, Gweneth and Noah's former slave. Clarisa and Jessie were now living at the old Green's homestead since the day following Lincoln's assassination. The new Mayor gave Jessie ownership of the property now that the federal government owned this unclaimed property. Stunned, Sarah shook her head unable to comprehend such changes in such a short span of time.

Why didn't Jessie just ask us for more money? We would have gladly given it to him! What is poor Mammy doing with out him? Quickly she read that Jessie and Clarisa were expecting a child some time in the fall. *Jessie and Clarisa, going to be parents? Oh poor Mammy must be heartsick, worried about her boy and his newfound freedom along with trying to take care of Doves Landing too.*

Painfully aware that the boy she helped raise was never one to hold his tongue being so willful, Sarah feared trouble would certainly find him, if he wasn't already looking for it on his own. Closing her eyes, feeling hopeless, she said a prayer for her beloved former slaves and friends back home. *Maybe I should return . . .* she thought, then as if answering her own question she said to herself. *No! My husband needs me. I cannot leave him now. Please dear God help those I love back in Fairfax.*

Staring into the flickering light of the lamp, holding back the tears stinging at her eyes, Sarah knew that if Michael saw she had been crying, he would only worry more than he already was. *For Michael's sake I must be strong . . .* she pledged.

Redirecting her attention back to her letter, she discovered the remainder of the news was primarily about the girls at the school, and how every day or so another showed up at their doorstep--some from as far south as North Carolina--claiming they had nowhere else to go. There were now twenty-eight young girls at the school. Reading about the girls, Sarah whispered to herself, "Whew, Glenbrook sure isn't quiet anymore."

The rest of the letter explained daily life at the school. And how fortunate they were that Lucas continued to send what money he could, making good on his promise to do so through the harvest when the fields should produce enough food for all of them to sustain the winter. *Oh I hope you are right, dear friend,* she thought while folding the letter neatly to show Michael later.

Straining to hear and recognizing the familiar sounds of the rocking chair from the sitting room in the lower level of the home, Sarah leaned back in her chair, suddenly feeling very tired. Not giving into her heavy eyes, she thought, *I wonder what time it is . . .*

Looking about the second-story bedchamber, she couldn't help but notice how ominous the room looked. Shadows danced across the walls from the flames that flickered off the kerosene lamp. Feeling slightly uneasy and not willing to give into the temptation of having a good cry, she opened the next letter she held in her hand. Seeing the smudged edges of the folded paper in front of her brought a smile to her drawn face. *This could only come from Verus Wiley.* Peeling away the wax seal, she eagerly began reading his letter.

> *Dear Michael and Sarah,*
>
> *I hope this letter finds you in good health. I'm certain that you are aware of how this small town of ours is under Reconstruction and all the ramifications that goes along with such acts.*
>
> *Not one for small talk, I will come directly to why I felt compelled to write today. . . .*

Smiling, she realized her old friend wrote as he would an article for his newspaper, reporting the news. Without saying so directly, she could tell that his concern over "Reconstruction" was foremost on his mind. She had heard Michael speak with his father of this often in the past few weeks and understood that the taxation already had begun for the education of all children, including Negroes, through a public school that was now mandatory.

Sarah didn't need to be told just how this tax would affect people from her hometown, knowing only too well how grave a situation this actually was. Such radical changes so quickly after the war could only add dissension among the already tense situation. Remembering how only a few years ago, such actions as teaching slaves to read and write was considered a crime, Sarah was certain Fairfax was no place to be right now.

How on earth could that be of any use? No wonder there is tension in the south. She thought while placing the letter in her lap. *Doesn't Congress realize what the south needs now is for their lives to be restored with necessities like food and clothing for their families; certainly not the burden to educate their former slaves? We were better off before the war!*

Feeling disheartened, Sarah picked up the letter again and scanned to where she had left off . . .

> *Michael, have you heard of a group, called the "White Camellia"? This group founded in Tennessee, proclaims to recapture the comradeship and excitement of the war, be that as it may. Are you aware that Thomas has been asked to be the head of this secret social club for his district? His title is the 'Grand Poppa'!*

Hmm, White Camellia . . . Sarah paused, thinking about this new society. *How lovely this group sounds. I'm sure Thomas will do splendidly being such a natural leader!* Eagerly she read on.

> *"Did you also know that Thomas has hired an old army buddy and his wife to help out around Doves Landing? Such a shame that Mammy has gone to live with Jessie. The old boardinghouse doesn't seem the same any longer.*

What? Sarah's heart pounding in her chest, she quickly reread his last line then shook her head. *Mammy gone from Doves Landing? How can that be?* Needing more of an explanation to why Mammy Tess would move from the only home she had ever known, Sarah quickly read more of the letter.

> *Under the circumstances it is probably best for her, besides since Clarisa is not well, I'm sure Jessie could use some help.*
>
> *Fondest Regards,*
> *V. Wiley*

Sarah quickly turned the single sheet over to see if something was written on the backside then searched the floor to see if a sheet had fallen. Realizing there was no other, she reread his letter again. Puzzled, she wondered had her friend gone daft? What was he talking about, she asked herself, *The best under the circumstances. What circumstance?* Rereading the short letter yet again, Sarah was even more confused, seeing nothing out of the ordinary that could explain such actions from her beloved Mammy leaving her home like that. *And what was wrong with Clarisa? Hadn't Irma just said she and Jessie were expecting? Surely, Verus wouldn't refer to being in the family way as ill?*

The sound of horse hooves echoing from the silent street below distracted Sarah from the concerns of those back home in Fairfax. *Oh please God, let it be Tad,* she prayed. Pulling herself from the chair, she stood motionless, afraid to breathe as the carriage came to a halt. *It is him. Thank goodness!* She sighed, hastily tucking away the correspondence.

From the study, hearing the carriage come to a stop, Michael lunged to the door overwrought with anger, concern, and self-pity for not being a better father to his son. As Tad's footsteps approached, it was apparent to Michael, who was standing in the doorway, that his son was intoxicated, by his unsteady steps. Seeing his father through his drunkenness, Tad attempted to tidy up by struggling to put his shirt back into his trousers. Weaving back and forth, he brushed his hair off his bloody face and smiled.

"Father, how good of you to wait up for me. It *wasn't neces . . . sary* though!"

"Tad, you've been in a fight, and you're drunk! I'd say it was quite necessary! Here, let me help you, son," Michael said, concerned while walking toward the young man, offering him his hand. The emotional turmoil that he had felt waiting for his son these past several hours dissipated as concern for his son's safety became foremost on Michael's mind.

"I can take care of myself. I always have. . . . Since when do you care anyway?" spat Tad indignantly.

"Tad, I've always cared."

Trying to focus on his father, Tad asked, "Is this a slow month for current events? Or is it to show Sarah what a devoted husband and father you are?" Glancing about and seeing no one else in attendance, Tad defiantly pulled away from his father and rushed past him.

Stepping inside the foyer, Tad proceeded to the stairwell where he dramatically waved his arm above his head. "Go to bed, Father. Tomorrow you can be the doting father in front of your new wife and I'll be the grateful son. Now I'm far too tired."

"Tad, you can't mean those cruel words. I've always thought you understood that it was my job that kept me away from you. How dare you insinuate my concern for you is an act simply for impressing Sarah! Every night this week I have agonized over where you have been and what it is that keeps you out all night. Son, please do not walk away while I'm talking to you. Let me see that cut over your eye."

Shaking his head, Tad stumbled up another stair. "Always the reporter, never the father. Am I now to be research for a character in your novel? The great man who has a drunk for a son." Sarcastically he laughed aloud before continuing. "Father, you really must come up with better material than that if you intend to continue with the successful life you've built for yourself." Obviously amused at his comments, he continued to snicker.

"What did you say to me?" Michael snapped in retaliation.

Not turning to acknowledge his father, ignoring Michael completely, Tad staggered up the next stair raising his foot far above the step trying to judge its distance.

"Son, please. Why won't you talk to me? We used to have such grand talks. Don't you remember?"

Tad's back stiffened hearing Michael's plea and he responded coldly, "I wanted to talk to you when I was ten, and when I was twelve. Even the last couple of years would have been nice." His words trailed off as he stood weaving, holding onto the railing as the room began to whirl about him, never turning to face Michael. Taking in a deep breath, he got his bearings. "Now I don't care to talk to you any longer. I'm a man now, so go find yourself an interesting story to write about rather than your drunken son. Maybe there's another war going on . . . what? No war? Oh well Father, maybe next year."

Trying to find the words to help ease the pain his son felt and struggling with his own guilt, Michael pleaded with him. "I'm sorry I wasn't here when you needed me, son. But you must have known I always loved you."

Tad jerked around. "Love? What do you know of love? You think writing me your letters, telling me of your great adventures is *love*? You loved your work. Not me! Why didn't you quit your job when mother died? You did for Sarah. Why couldn't you do it for me or for my mother when she was so ill?" he shouted while gripping onto the railing as his free arm flung across his chest.

"Yes Father, I knew exactly how much you loved me. I grew up with no mother and a father who thought a week's camping trip once a year was what I needed." He glared down at Michael, the liquor giving him the courage to say the words that he had kept bottled up inside of him for so long.

"I needed you! I wanted you! Even when I begged for you to stay with me, you left me alone."

"Son, you never begged me to stay with you . . ."

"Every night I begged God to send you home to me. If you were home where you belonged, you would have heard my prayers." Never had Michael seen such hate in his son's eyes before as they burrowed a hole through his tortured soul.

"Dear God Tad . . . I'm so sorry. I had no idea. How can I ever make it up to you?"

Turning on his heels Tad walked up the remainder of the steps leading to the second-story landing, standing erect and tall, no longer affected by the drink as he was earlier. Glaring down at Michael he said, "Father, I desire nothing from you--except an increase in my monthly allotment. My funds are rather low this month, and of course, money has never been an issue with you. I trust this will remain the same. As for trying to tell me what is best for my welfare, well, you have been replaced. In the event I require advice, my friends who have been here for me over the years will do nicely."

"What are you proposing, Tad? That I should hand over some money and pretend nothing is wrong here? These friends of yours, were they there for you tonight when you were hurt in a fight?"

"How dare you speak ill of my friends when they have stood by me. More than you ever have."

"I'm here for you now. Tad, I can't just stand by and let you throw your life away."

"Father, tend to your own affairs and I shall do the same." Giving his father an icy stare, he shouted, "Good night."

Michael, unable to respond or move, just watched as his son walked to his room, wanting to run to him and try to explain. Instead, he remained planted to the spot where he stood as if there were anchors at his feet holding him in place. "Oh God what have I done?" His voice trailed behind him as he returned to his chair in the library. "Forgive me, son, please forgive me."

Hearing the angry words of her stepson, Sarah wept silently for both Tad and Michael. Unsure exactly what she should do, she left her bedchamber and crept into the darkened hallway. Glancing at the closed door of her stepson's room, she hesitated. *I should go to him, the poor dear needs a mother figure now . . .*

Knowing Tad's current frame of mind, she concluded he might consider this an invasion of his privacy so instead, Sarah slowly went down the stairs to find Michael. Silently she stood at the doorway to the library where she found him staring out the window into the darkened night. Seeing her reflection in the window Michael turned and sheepishly said, "Dearest, I thought you went to bed hours ago."

Realizing this could be the difference in their relationship, if she let him go through his pain and suffering alone without discussing together what had just taken place, Sarah decided to go to him. Offering her hand she said tenderly, "Come darling, let's go to bed. Nothing can be done this evening. Perhaps tomorrow we can help our boy together."

"Oh Sarah, he hates me."

"No. He loves you. He is just filled with resentment. Give him time . . ."

"Time? But what if my time has run out? What if I'm too late?"

"It's never too late, darling. You taught me that. Together we can help your son learn to forgive and forget the past. But first we must work on today, one step at a time." Standing now and taking his wife in his arms, he pulled her closer to him.

"Yes, but the step is mighty steep. I'm not sure how I can climb it."

"You'll find a way. I have faith in you. Now come darling . . . you need some rest."

Taking her by the waist, he turned to go up the stairs with his wife. "How much did you hear this evening?" Michael's voice sounded hoarse and shallow.

"Everything. I wasn't trying to pry or meddle, you must believe me."

"Oh I know . . . it's just . . ."

"Michael, please hear me out darling. Both you and your son are hurting very deeply, and have for quite sometime. The only way you can help Tad is to be open and honest with him and yourself. Before he can learn to forgive you for his pain, you must learn to forgive yourself. What has happened must remain in the past. Nothing you can do can ever change that. But you can change the future. You have a bright future with your son, if you both learn to let go of your pain. Tad must learn that parents make mistakes too. When he does, and he will, he will then learn to forgive and forget, and within time this will pass."

"I hope you're right." Michael turned to look at the closed door of his son's room. "But where do I begin . . ."

"Just be yourself, and don't stop trying to be his father. You are a good and decent man whom I love very much. Show him your love and who you are. The rest will surely follow."

"You make it sound so simple."

Responding with a reassuring smile, she knew neither of them was fooled in believing it was going to be easy, especially after hearing the venom that Tad had spoken to his father.

From inside Tad's room, hearing the door shut to Sarah and Michael's room, Miranda slowly walked away from Tad's closed bedroom door.

"They've gone to bed, Tad. Please let me help you," she whispered, her chest pounding through her dressing gown, seeing him remove his bloodstained shirt and discarding it on the floor near his feet.

"Leave me be!" he whispered hoarsely bending over to pull off his leather boots. "As kind as your offer is, I don't need or want your help."

Timidly Miranda made her way across the dimly-lit room, painfully aware that if she were discovered in his bedchamber dressed in only a dressing gown, and he half-naked, her reputation would be destroyed.

To add to her concerns, the gentle breeze that swept through his room from the open window near his bed caused her sheer gauze nightgown to hug her naked frame beneath the light material gown. Pausing at the foot of his bed, uncertain how she would make it past him without him noticing how skimpily she was dressed, seeing him bend over to remove his leather boots, Miranda swiftly tiptoed past him.

Reaching the dry-sink in the corner of his bedchamber next to his bed, Miranda's heart pounded as she nervously stood silently watching Tad's reflection through the mirror hanging above the sink. With trembling hands, she began to pour water into the basin trying hard to avoid his eyes upon her.

Discreetly she looked at his reflection in the mirror admiring his physique--his bare chest and broad shoulders--and caught herself just as the basin was on the verge of overflowing. Feeling the water on the tips of her fingers as they rested on the side of the basin, she nervously reached for a linen cloth hung on the rail of the sink. After submerging it into the cool water and sufficiently wringing it out and gathering inner strength, she turned to look at Tad.

"If you need my help or not, I'm not leaving here until you let me look at that gash over your eye. So what is it going to be? Are you going to have another shouting match with me now, and alert everyone in the house that I'm parading around in my nightgown like some floozy?" she asked, in a hushed tone.

Hearing Miranda refer to herself in such a manner produced an immediate smile across Tad's lips. "Floozy? Why I don't recall you ever saying such a colorful term before. Perhaps I should have disturbed your rest years ago to see the real you."

Ignoring his snide comment, Miranda walked over to where he sat on the edge of his bed, and hesitantly edged her way between his thighs to view his wounds. Whispering softly, she said, "Kindly bend your head and pull your hair from your face, Tad."

Intensely he gazed up at her while brushing his hands through his hair, tilting his head back as she had asked. Timidly, Miranda leaned closer to him, her eyes never wavering from his. Taking in a deep breath she softly whispered, "This might hurt a bit."

Hearing no response but feeling his breath quicken against her bare neck as their bodies became closer, Miranda examined the gash over his eye. "You look like you were kicked by a mule," she whispered, while placing the linen cloth over his open cut and patting the dry blood caked around it.

Wincing, Tad looked up at her while trying to balance himself on the bed, his hand instinctively reaching for her to steady himself. Glancing down at his hand on her waist she barely heard him say, "I was. By that no good O'Flaherty!"

Startled by his comment, she said, "What? Gilbert did this to you. But why?" Suddenly his nearness and his hand resting on her waist became secondary to the need of understanding what he meant by such a statement.

"Let's just say, a certain young lady provoked the mule in him to come out, or was it the donkey? Ass, mule they both look the same to me and have an equally bad temper from what I understand."

Hearing him joke so freely, especially over something so grave, Miranda paused and looked into his eyes. For a moment it was as if time stood still and she felt suddenly closer to Tad then she had ever felt before. Realizing for the first time that he used his quick wit to mask his pain, and aware that she was still holding his face in her hands, Miranda blushed and looked away.

"Not that I doubt you Tad, but surely you aren't suggesting that you and he fought on my account? I told you before, I only met him briefly this morning at the orphanage and then again this evening in the gardens. He means nothing at all to me."

Hearing her say that, he smiled at her and again the silence between them was deafening.

"I'm glad to hear that. But considering you addressed him by his first name just now, and by his reaction this evening, I would definitely tend to believe apparently you weren't the only one who resented me calling you, my dear."

Trying to appear calm, Miranda continued to wipe the blood from his face. With trembling hands, she brushed against his wound too closely, causing Tad to wince.

"Again those two simple words have caused an adverse reaction. Remind me never to call you, my dear, again. Far too painful, to my liking," he whispered.

Not amused by his attempts of trying to be charming, the thought that perhaps it was Tad who sought out Gilbert out of jealousy, crept into her mind. Glancing down at him she couldn't help but wonder if he was telling her the complete truth. Searching for a sign, she was awestruck at the warmth and sincerity in his eyes as he looked at her. Such truth she had never seen before, realizing that the man before her had learned to mask his anger and pain just as she had. Feeling for the first time that she truly understood Tad, Miranda smiled tenderly at him.

"You probably will end up with a scar, but I think you'll survive."

"Thank you, Miranda."

Touched by the warmth in his eyes, and feeling such closeness with him, she suddenly felt very awkward being so near to him while in her nightgown and he partially clothed. Silently she withdrew from him. Feeling his hand slip away from her waist, she placed the soiled linen in his palm and she turned to leave. Reaching the door, she paused.

The sudden desire to expose a portion of her heart to him was immense and shyly she whispered, "Tad, I know the pain of being alone and feeling unloved. Most of my childhood was like that. Although I had two parents living under the same roof with me, no one seemed to notice, or for that matter cared enough about me to see how much I needed their love."

Not wanting his pity, she quickly added. "If someday you want to talk about the pain we both endured as children, I am here for you. Before you say yes though, keep in mind that I think you are wrong regarding your father. I know you must have heard just as I did, your father and Sarah as they came up the stairs. If you want to admit it or not, your father is suffering, too. Don't misunderstand, I'm not siding with either of you. All I'm saying is that before you write him off, please know that I think Michael is a decent man who obviously has made a terrible mistake and now wants to make amends. Feel grateful that you have such an opportunity, because I never shall."

Not waiting for his reply, Miranda crept silently back into her own room leaving Tad alone with her words haunting him.

~ Nine ~

Awakening

In the sanctuary of her room, Miranda unlocked the torment and pain she had been harboring all her life. Hearing Tad's pain and wanting so desperately to help him, she realized she too had demons that had to be unleashed if she were ever to find peace and true happiness. As she lay still in her bed, the sorrowful memories of her past came rushing through her mind in waves.

The image of herself as a child alone and frightened in her room hearing the frequent shouting between her father and her mother caused her immense grief. Again, she jerked just as she had as a child when the slamming of a door echoed through the walls of Glenbrook, her family home. As she lay there recalling her past, she knew that her mother's tormented cries would follow shortly. Right on cue, the sounds of Catherine's sobs haunted her, and a tear rolled down Miranda's cheeks, fully understanding her mother's anguish, and still feeling as helpless today as she had all those years earlier. "Oh Mama . . ." she whispered, recalling the sorrowful life her mother lived.

Day after day, week after week, the lonely little girl, not knowing how to help her mother, who was so ill, tried desperately not to make a sound, fearful she might further upset her. As an older child no more than eleven, Miranda had come to understand that her mother's sickness was not physical, but was self-induced from drinking too much brandy.

Catherine Brown needed her "friend" to make it through the day and again at night to be able to sleep only to awake with a hangover. Recalling how sickened she had been at discovering her mother's shameful existence, the confused and angry child needing time alone to sort out her feelings had taken a walk in the woods of their property.

Much to her shock, Miranda happened upon a sight that still sent shock waves to her very core. Rather than block out the memory as she had over the years, Miranda allowed herself to relive what she had witnessed between her father and his slave that fall afternoon that haunted her still.

The memories of that fateful day were so vivid that Miranda pulled the cotton sheet up closer to her, despite the closeness of her bedchamber. Time stood still as she drifted back to 1851, long before the war, and witnessed herself walking the back grounds of the family plantation.

Absent-mindedly she had kicked the fallen leaves from her path ashamed of what her mother had become, but worse, hating herself for thinking such loathsome thoughts of her mother to begin with.

Startled at hearing a woman's laughter amongst the wind and the rustling leaves, Miranda had paused, looking up to see where the sound originated. Her heartbeat had quickened remembering how she had frozen at the spot when she saw Elmira kissing her father passionately as he leaned against a tree close to the slave's cottage.

Never had she witnessed any man grope at a woman so fiendishly before this, and certainly not her father. The shock was unbearable, but as the couple made their way to the slave's quarters, Miranda stupefied, followed and witnessed the two of them engage in fiery lovemaking.

Stunned and dazed, the young girl had managed to make it back to her room in the big house before being detected. The sights and sounds of what her father and Elmira had done in the slave's bed haunted her. With every step she took, the sounds of her father's groaning as his naked body kept rocking harder and harder against Elmira's brown skin taunted her.

Never having seen her father naked before, and to witness him performing such an act with his slave, who kept squealing and moaning, caused the young girl to withdraw from all other sights and sounds around her.

As Miranda climbed the steps to her room, only wanting to escape, she heard the familiar crying coming from her mother's closed room. Standing on the stairs, horrified, she suddenly understood why her mother had cried so much and her need to drink. Too ashamed to ask her mother if she had seen her father and his slave fornicate, as she had just witnessed, the young Miranda began hating her father. Not just for being intimate with his slave, but moreover, for betraying her mother in such a deplorable act that caused her to become a drunk.

Following that incident, Miranda's curiosity increased and she would frequently sneak back to the slave's cottage to watch her father shag his slave, despite how she hated him for what he was doing. Sickened by the sight, but unable to stop herself, the little girl would listen and watch, spying on the lovers for hours. Then one day, accidentally, she discovered Elmira's son was Lucas' too, making Joseph her half-brother.

On that particular day, much to her horror, she overheard her father threaten Elmira that if she did not obey him, he would sell Joseph, even though he was his son. The following day, just as her father had threatened, the slave-trader came to Glenbrook. After Elmira screamed and pleaded with Lucas, the frightened slave was allowed to remain.

Even now, years later, Miranda still could see the look of panic on Joseph's face as he had run for safety deep into the woods of the plantation. And the profound hatred she had felt for her father, for causing such pain. Unable to fathom that any man would sell off his own son, Miranda began to defy Lucas anyway she could.

Knowing that Lucas was opposed to Abolitionists, hearing him repeatedly rant with business associates from his study at how they needed to be stopped, Miranda secretly sought out those her father despised.

Over a period of years, she had formed a close friendship with Constance Hildebrandt, a friend from school, who Miranda discovered was an Abolitionist. By the time she was in her teens, Miranda had not only won the trust of fellow Northern Sympathizers, but was actively involved in the Underground Railroad.

Such undertakings gave the young woman immense joy knowing that of all the things her father hated in the world, those who helped runners was at the top of his list. Even following the misfortune of Joseph and her father's accident, Miranda continued with her pursuits intending to free her half-brother while she still had the chance. Especially after hearing her distraught brother's description of the events of the accident that had left his mother unbalanced and his father severely injured.

As she comforted her brother, she discovered Joseph was certain that Jeb Pickley was involved in some way, explaining the overseer's strange behavior leaving Elmira's cottage just before Joseph had discovered Elmira and Lucas. Drawing the same conclusion, Miranda then listened to Joseph explain that Lucas, before his accident, had promised his son he would be freed that very afternoon.

Realizing Joseph was probably never going to have his freedom, especially with his father so gravely ill, Miranda decided she would grant him this herself. On their way to the safe house she had used dozens of times before assisting other runners, they had been seen by a Confederate and took refuge in a shed.

While hiding Joseph and Jessie in the abandoned old barn, Miranda's heart stopped, hearing gun shots outside. When Elise had come inside looking for help, in the dim light the three of them had thought it was the Confederate soldier. Joseph, trying to be brave and defuse the situation had called out in sheer panic that he had a gun. Tragically, it was Joseph's last words, as Elise, frightened herself, shot and killed him where he stood.

The sight of his dull lifeless eyes staring up at her, still haunted her to this day. Miranda still found it ironic that on that afternoon as she wept over his slain body, she was not able to explain her loss. Instead she grieved in silence, knowing she had been able to free others, but not her own kin. Numb, hating herself, her father, but most of all the life she had led, which ultimately caused her own brother's death, a part of Miranda died along with Joseph.

Even following her mother and Elmira's death, when she sat alone in her room and heard her father agonize in his room, she remained lethargic. A part of her wanted to go to him and ease his pain, while another took solace in knowing he deserved the pain he was experiencing and so much more for betraying her mother's love, by loving another.

At last, Miranda allowed herself to grieve, releasing the bottled up pain she had held within her for years. As she wept, she mourned the loss of her mother, her half-brother, but more importantly her loss of innocence and the ability to trust men.

As she continued to cry, the thought crossed her mind that perhaps Felicity was right. *Maybe she wasn't allowing herself to love.* Fearing that love could hurt her just as it had her mother, and remembering the vile acts of love her father and Elmira had committed, she conceded that perhaps she had.

With no more tears to shed, and facing the fact she had rejected love to enter her life, it was natural that her thoughts went to Tad. *Have I been opposed to Tad simply from not being able to trust any man? Or, was it because of his secretive nature that reminded me of Father?* Deep in her heart, she knew the answer. From the moment she had met him, she had perceived Tad as a man who displayed a particular side of his character to society, while living the remainder of his life as he pleased, with no regard for those around him. Precisely like her father.

Her opinion changed though, hearing Tad this evening express the pain he had harbored against his own father. Suddenly Tad was no longer the enemy, but rather someone she could relate to. She understood what it was like to never disclose your deepest most intimate thoughts and pain one harbored, and her heart went out to him. That was precisely why she had gone to him following the incident with Michael--not thinking of the consequences--but reacting to her own pain.

With her past finally put to rest, her final thoughts before drifting off to sleep were, *Oh Tad, how sad and lonely it has been for you . . . And for me . . .*

~

In a boardinghouse across town, Lucas Brown had trouble sleeping. Just as he did most nights. No matter how tired he was, as soon as his head lay on the pillow, visions of the past haunted him, like phantoms in the night. Catherine, Elmira and his son Joseph, floated in and out of his dreams calling him from their graves until he awoke shaken by their memories.

The nightmares were always the same. Catherine off in a distance watching him with haunting, hate-filled eyes, just as she had the day she discovered him and his beloved Elmira in bed after an afternoon of passion. The phantom of Elmira in an eerie haze standing over an open grave where her son Joseph would be laid to rest was the most unsettling to him. Every night Elmira appeared to him wearing a torn dress, her hair matted just as it was on the day Pickley raped her.

When her long slender arms stretched out before her with blood dripping from her wrists into the empty grave, Elmira would then lift her bruised face and begin pleading with him. *"Lucas . . . Lucas, help me!"*

As the nightmare continued, Catherine then would appear to float closer to the blurred vision of Elmira with a menacing wicked smile, dragging something behind her. As she draws nearer, Lucas can make out that what his wife's ghost was dragging behind her is a man in chains.

Seeing the body was his son Joseph, Lucas becomes distraught and tries to come to them, but he never manages to reach them. Only the sounds of his son's pleas fill his tortured mind. *Father, free me.*

Lucas wakes shaking, drenched in perspiration, out of breath as if he had been running after the phantoms that haunt him.

Night after night, the nightmare plagues him. And every night after the specters have begged for his help, he cries out in the agony of his tortured mind. *I've killed them. It should have been me! Oh dear God why couldn't it have been me instead?*

Knowing if he remained in bed, the same would occur, Lucas pulled himself from his slumber and dressed for the day ahead. As the sun began to rise in the east, he walked to the sitting area of his rented room. After lighting the lantern, he pulled out a letter he had recently received from Charles Mason. As he read his correspondence describing how Glenbrook was getting on, Charles again asked if the stone cottage could be converted to a playhouse for the younger girls at the school.

Repeatedly, Lucas had avoided answering this question in the past, unable to think of allowing anyone inside its four walls as if it was sacred ground. With heavy heart, Lucas decided that possibly if laughter rang out from the cottage again, maybe his tormented mind could somehow find some peace at last.

Before he had a chance to change his mind, he quickly drafted a letter giving permission to Charles to do whatever he felt necessary with the stone cottage, as well as the remaining property of Glenbrook. Finishing the letter by including information regarding the political shambles of the capital, Lucas wished he had more encouraging words to offer.

Sitting pensively, Lucas thought of the turbulent times the nation was now facing. The Republican Party was split as to what should be done now that the war was over. Some still agreed as Lincoln did--that this was the time to rebuild, and by lending help to the crippled south allowing them to heal from their wounds, would only make for a stronger Union. While others debated adamantly that it was the Rebels who began this war by secession, and they should bleed even further, to crush their spirit so they can never rise up again to take action against its motherland. After all, wasn't it because of them that the blood of innocent men lay on the battlegrounds? Forgetting that the Confederates too shed blood for what they believed in, and lost everything in the process, Lucas explained how he would address this very issue at a political luncheon where he was to be guest speaker next month.

Having no rights himself to vote any longer, Lucas could only hope that his voice would be heard to avoid any further hardships being placed against his beloved south. His intentions were to point out that such Democratic groups as the Ku Klux Klan, or so dubbed "White Camellia", would only become stronger as hatred filled the hearts of the white male as they were forced into suppression.

Pausing, Lucas wondered to himself just how the hell he was going to manage such a feat. Knowing that as the hatred grew in the hearts of men toward the Negro, the Republican Party claimed they were obliged to protect them, but they were in far graver danger now than when they had been in bondage.

Such a thought caused him to deliberate just how he could come across as not issuing a threat, but that of a concerned Christian male pointing out human nature. A great leap, considering he had been a staunch believer in slavery all his life, until he had come to understand what torment being shackled in bondage was actually like. He had become a slave to his past, with no freedoms, no chance of ever regaining the freedom to escape from the life he had created.

And although Lucas knew his torment could never be compared to what true humiliation it was to be a slave--with no respect or dignity--as those had been forced to live, Lucas felt he could sympathize with the ones who had suffered for generations, since he now suffered in silent agony, having been stripped of all he had once felt he had been entitled to and valued most in the world.

After all, was he not a politician who could not vote? Just as he was a man who dared never to love again--never allowing himself to forget the pain that he had inflicted on two women he loved--a love that eventually caused their demise.

His condemnation for his actions was so immense, Lucas refused to allow himself the pleasure of returning to the land he loved, despite yearning for the Shenandoah Valley with every breath he took. As a means to repent for the sins he had once committed, Lucas continued to deprive himself of his beloved Glenbrook, exiling himself from the one thing he needed most to feel any peace again.

"Peace," Lucas whispered to himself. "Is that possible now for anyone?" Having no answer, he directed his attention back to his correspondence. Deciding not to include his concerns for the south, Lucas signed off instead, promising that this month's allotment would be increased for refurbishing the cottage and any other repairs needed at Glenbrook. Hearing the other residents stir, Lucas hastily freshened up as the sun rose.

~

Back at the Honeycutt's mansion, Miranda awakened to the sweet smell of lilacs. Opening her eyes, she glanced over to the nightstand beside her where a vase full of the freshly cut sprigs of the flowers sat, with a note in front of them.

Leaning over to read the note, she smiled. *Thank you, my angel of mercy, Tad.* Absent-mindedly Miranda brushed the note between her fingertips, while gazing at her favorite flowers.

Oh Tad you remembered . . . What an incredibly tender and romantic thing to do!

Realizing he must have come into her room while she slept, her smile faded. Bringing her quilt closer to her chest, her heart pounded as she looked about her room with uncertainty.

~ Ten ~

Built on Lies

Hours before the school was to begin, Miranda walked through the wrought-iron gate leading to the courtyard to find Felicity sitting at her favorite spot on a bench by the massive oak tree. Hearing the familiar squeaking of the gate, Felicity turned and smiled, gesturing Miranda to join her.

"I was hoping you would come early today. Come sit and tell me what made you decide to go with Tad to the theatre," she said enthusiastically.

"Oh dear, I had forgotten about that . . ." Miranda said, while joining her friend. "After last evening, I'm sure that will have to be postponed."

Confused, Felicity asked, "Postponed? But why, for goodness sakes? We only left you a few hours ago . . ."

"A lot has happened since I saw you last evening," explained Miranda, shaking her head. "Let me fill you in . . ."

For the next several minutes, Felicity shook her head hearing the events as they unfolded at the Honeycutt's in the wee hours of the morning, even including how she had relived her own painful childhood. Omitting the affair between her father and his former slave, Miranda spoke of the loneliness she had felt as a child and admitted she had been fearful of loving another. Explaining that witnessing her own parents' turbulent relationship had indeed scared her.

"Dear, you certainly all did have an evening, didn't you. I don't know what to say. I feel so sorry for Tad of course, but my heart goes out to Michael too. I can't imagine how he endured hearing his son's pain, which he caused, and then after reaching out to him, being pushed away like that must have been unbearable. Not that I blame Tad of course, obviously his resentment is deep . . . Ah, and poor Sarah, how dreadful for her to see her husband in such pain . . ."

It was clear from Felicity's tone that she felt immense sorrow for them all.

"I shall include them, and you, dear friend in my prayers. But tell me, this morning after discovering that Tad had cut you flowers and had been in your bedchamber, did you see him personally?"

"No, in fact, I avoided the dining room all together, coming directly here after I woke."

"What do you think about the flowers?" Felicity asked, cautiously.

Before answering, Miranda thought for a moment then a smile crossed her lips. "In truth that was the dearest thing any man has ever done for me. However, after it dawned on me that he had actually entered my room, well of course I became apprehensive. It is rather presumptuous of him to think that he could take such liberties by coming into my room, simply because of the kindness I showed him . . ."

Pausing for a moment and looking puzzled, she added. "Come to think of it, I could almost swear I locked the door after returning from attending his wounds." Shaking her head as dismissing it, Miranda smiled wearily. "Obviously not, since he was able to enter. My, I must have been extremely tired if I didn't even hear him." She added nervously.

Recalling her friend's concerns from yesterday regarding Tad's peculiar behavior, Felicity nodded politely, feeling equally apprehensive about Tad entering Miranda's private bedchamber.

Rather than address her concerns openly, in the event she was over reacting, Felicity asked, "So you say Tad sustained his cuts and bruises by our iceman, Mr. O'Flaherty? How odd? I would think those two men would have so little in common. Did you say how it was that Tad met up with him?"

"No. I didn't say. In fact, when Tad told me that it was Gilbert he had fought with, for a moment I wondered if Tad had deliberately gone looking for him. Feeling ashamed for doubting him again, I dismissed such thoughts. Do you think Felicity, that Tad provoked this altercation with Mr. O'Flaherty?" Miranda's voice expressed her concern.

"I couldn't say . . ." Felicity paused, hearing the sound of footsteps approaching. She nodded to Miranda, and whispered, "But perhaps he might."

Puzzled by her comment, she frowned seeing Gilbert O'Flaherty approaching. Without hesitation, Miranda swiftly crossed the play-yard calling his name.

"Oh Mr. O'Flaherty, could I please have a word with you?"

Seeing Miranda, Gilbert sighed, giving her a disgusted look and kept walking.

Angered by such rudeness, Miranda said firmly, "Mr. O'Flaherty, I know you can hear me."

"Saints be praised. Haven't I had enough grief by you and that suitor of yours? Do ya want me to be fired from me job too?"

"First off, Mr. Honeycutt is not my suitor, and . . ."

Shaking his head in disgust, he started to walk past her mumbling under his breath, "Like I should expect anything differently from your kind. I heard you call him dear with my own ears."

Outraged by his comment, Miranda raised her voice. "How dare you speak to me in that manner. If you can't even tell the difference between a question and a term of endearment, then it's obvious that it is you who is daft, as you so eloquently insinuated I was yesterday. All this leads me to believe that you attacked such a fine gentleman as Mr. Honeycutt for no good reason, just as he said." Flushed from losing her temper, not expecting a reply, she began to turn around.

"Honeycutt is no gentleman any more than I am. He may be well educated with means, but he has no honor. And if'n you think he is, then the two of ya are daft a far sight more than you think I am!" he spouted indignantly.

Trying to hold back the urge to argue further with this ghastly, mean-spirited man, she calmly replied, "Mr. O'Flaherty, I did not ask to speak with you to hurl insults at one another. I was merely trying to understand why it was necessary for you and Mr. Honeycutt to come to blows last evening."

"That is of no concern of yours. Why not ask that so-called gentleman friend of yours?"

Every instinct in her screamed to leave, but instead she said, "Obviously I have. Otherwise, how would I know it was you that attacked him? What I don't understand is why you would feel the need to attack someone simply out of some absurd jealousy."

Hearing that, Gilbert chuckled sarcastically, his green eyes conveying his sarcasm. "It's not I who am daft, but you and the rest of Honeycutt's loyal subjects believing such malarkey."

"Then you aren't denying the fact that you attacked Mr. Honeycutt, just the reasons why he gave me. Is that right Mr. O'Flaherty?" she asked solemnly, ignoring his hurtful comments once more.

"Damned right! And like I said last night to him and those worthless subjects of his, if I ever see him again I'll finish what I started. You can tell him I said so too!"

Miranda gasped at his threat, and looked at this man she now considered evil, rather than just angry. "Mr. O'Flaherty, I have a good mind to notify the constable about your threats against Mr. Honeycutt."

"Oh please do! I welcome the chance to divulge what an upright and decent citizen Honeycutt is." His grimace sent immediate shivers through her.

Not waiting for her reply, Gilbert walked back to the kitchen leaving Miranda stunned, shaken to her very core. As she walked back to Felicity, her mind whirled in confusion. *What did Tad do to him that was so awful he wanted revenge and didn't care who knew it?*

"Well, what did he say? Did he admit to attacking Tad last night?"

Nodding her head in disbelief, she said, "Yes. But apparently it had nothing to do with me."

"Really? Then why?" Felicity frowned at her friend who was pale as a sheet.

Shaking her head, Miranda whispered, "He didn't say . . . only that he wasn't through with Tad."

"Oh dear! You mean he threatened Tad? Perhaps you should notify the authorities?"

"No!" she added hastily. "Evidently Gilbert wants that."

Felicity gasped and watched as Gilbert made his way back to the street where his cart was parked. Once Gilbert had left, Miranda looked at Felicity. "Promise me you'll not breathe a word of this to anyone until I've had a chance to discuss this with Tad?"

"I promise. But do you think that is wise Miranda?"

"What other choice do I have . . . ?" Her voice trailed off, remembering the hate in Gilbert's eyes.

Later that afternoon, after Miranda had returned to the Honeycutt's and had changed for dinner, she went to the gardens to try to make some sense of everything that had happened. As she stood smelling the sweet scents of the lilacs, her confusion and anger increased and suddenly the flowers had lost their appeal, especially since they now reminded her of Tad.

She knew that what she had overheard between Tad and Michael was real, and when he thanked her, it came from his heart. Yet, she also knew from speaking with Gilbert that the fight he had been in had nothing to do with her as Tad had said. Suddenly, as she chastised herself into believing any man could be honest, tears stung her eyes and her heart began to harden again.

"I knew I'd find you here." Tad said walking up behind her.

Before turning, Miranda hastily wiped her eyes and tried to smile. "Hello, Tad. How are you this evening?"

"Fine, but I can tell you didn't appreciate my gift of gratitude."

"Oh no? The lilacs were lovely. Thank you. But that wasn't necessary."

Interrupting her, he asked, "Miranda, what's wrong? After last night I thought we had finally broken down our barriers. Yet today I feel you're as distant from me as ever. Have I done something to upset you?"

"No. Not at all." She lied, pasting a smile across her lips. "I have a lot on my mind is all."

"I see. After taking your advice, I had a long talk with my father this afternoon." From the look on his face, Miranda knew he expected her to respond.

Sincerely, she said, "Oh Tad, I'm so happy for you both." Hesitating to ask him more, not wanting to interfere in his private affairs, she waited, hoping he would volunteer more information.

"Of course nothing can be resolved in a day, but at least we're talking so hopefully in time . . ."

Looking up at him, she truly felt his sincerity, but after what Gilbert had said, she doubted her own abilities at reading him any longer. Smiling she said, "You're lucky to have that time, Tad."

Frowning slightly, he said, "Miranda, I know you said I've done nothing to offend you, yet I can't help but feel you're holding back from me. Are you upset that I came into your room last evening?"

"No . . . well perhaps a little. As much as I enjoyed the lilacs, I must say it was a bit unnerving to know you were watching me."

"Actually, I saw more of you while you were in my room than nestled under the coverlets, if that eases your mind any." His eyes danced merrily, which caused her cheeks to burn like fire and she turned her head.

"Oh please don't be embarrassed. Last night was perhaps one of the most memorable events of my life. I shall always cherish it."

Hesitantly, she returned his look. Their eyes locked, and she was swept away by such truth she witnessed. "Please Tad, can we change the subject?" she asked, whispering shyly.

"Yes of course. What shall we discuss then?"

Just then Gilbert--delivering ice--hearing them, stood off to the side of the fenced yard, able to hear their every word.

"Well actually, I was hoping you would tell me the real reason for your fight last evening. I ask only because I saw Mr. O'Flaherty this morning." Immediately she detected Tad's mood change from warmth to that of contempt.

"Oh really? And you would question me over the likes of him?" There was no denying it--his eyes darted daggers as spiteful as his tongue.

"No. In fact, he admitted he did attack you. Yet, I had the distinct impression, not for the reasons you gave. In fact, the whole incident left me shaken rather badly. Tad, he worried me by threatening that he wasn't through with you yet. What does he mean by that? Should you go to the authorities?"

Tad was clearly agitated, and said, "No. I can deal with his kind."

"Oh please, Tad, talk to me. I'm so confused and frightened over this whole affair. I want to believe what you said last evening, you have no idea how much . . . but with him acting like he did this morning . . ."

Seeing that she was trembling, he took her hand in his, softly saying, "Miranda, come sit with me and I'll try to explain everything." Nodding, she followed him to a bench nestled between evergreens. Taking a seat, he began. "What I'm about to tell you I'm not proud of . . ."

"Please Tad, I have no right to judge you or anyone for that matter. Just please be honest with me."

He gave her a small smile as he began. "For quite sometime now, as you probably have noticed, most evenings following dinner I go out. Where I go has been to a pub to gamble with friends."

Tad explained in detail the friends he gambled with and how he came to meet Gilbert O'Flaherty. Listening intently to him, she related to Tad's desire to rebel against his father by choosing a lifestyle he knew Michael despised, as Miranda had rebelled against Lucas by helping runners. As he spoke candidly of his second life, her trust for him increased. Tad was forthright in explaining the only harm he had caused was to himself and Michael's bankroll. That was, until O'Flaherty, who had been winning regularly, had insulted Tad's pride and intelligence. Tad explained that for weeks he had suspected that Gilbert had been cheating, yet could never prove it. He then reminded Miranda of the agitated state Gilbert had been in when she had observed them speaking with one another, telling her that he had in fact hinted of his suspicions to Gilbert yesterday after he had refused Tad an opportunity to win back some of his money.

Suddenly the story Tad was telling made sense. Especially as Tad spoke about Gilbert's pride being injured further when he tried to warn Miranda of his kind. This was something Miranda understood as well, recalling how her half-brother Joseph, the son of such a powerful and important man never could claim his inheritance or position in society, forced to remain a slave.

As Tad relived his version of what had happened at the pub, Miranda found herself believing every word this man--gifted in persuasion--spoke, even as he twisted the truth, placing the blame on Gilbert. To assure his tale was convincing, Tad included how Gilbert duped him as 'his lordship' and Tad's friends as his 'loyal subjects'. If Miranda hadn't been convinced of Tad's sincerity before, recalling Gilbert had made such a reference himself this morning, only added validity to his tale.

"Ah, now I see why you said the fight had something to do with me. The truth is Mr. O'Flaherty has no interest in me, as a matter of fact I honestly thinks he dislikes . . ."

Tad stopped her as she continued, by taking her hand in his. "No matter what that low-life has said, please take it from someone who knows what it feels like to desire someone from afar, and know he is unworthy of her heart. I've been in his shoes for three years."

Such an intimate referral to how he felt, caused Miranda to blush and look away. Tenderly, Tad placed his finger on the side of her chin and guided her face back to him.

"Miranda, I say this not to embarrass you, or in hopes to win your heart, but to explain that I understand O'Flaherty in part. As so many Irish, they come here to America in hopes of a new life. After generations of suppression, being forced to make a living as a sharecropper and hearing tales of America as the land of opportunity, with its streets lined with gold for the taking, they come here primarily to reclaim their manhood. What a disappointment it must be for them to discover that the opportunities are rare to immigrants. And even harder to accept that men of means, who they despise immediately out of jealousy, also have women they can only dream of. And Miranda, you are such a woman--beautiful, kind-hearted and gentle natured. Is it any wonder that man's pride was insulted when I dismissed him so abruptly yesterday? However, if he or any other man with such a lack of integrity tried to speak with you again, I would not hesitate in doing the same, feeling as I do for you."

Never had a man spoken to her with such tenderness and Miranda's heart leapt for joy as her pulse increased. As if she were in a dream, he leaned closer, and feeling his breath on her face, she eagerly accepted his advancement. Feeling no resistance, Tad parted her lips with his tongue as he slipped his hand around her waist to draw her, trembling, closer to him.

As the urgency of their kiss increased, Miranda gave in to her desires and guided her hand around the nape of his neck, never experiencing such pleasure from a man's touch before. Then suddenly hearing herself moan, she jerked away recalling Elmira's moan of pleasure as her father and she had indulged in such pleasures.

Shaken to her very core, Miranda stood, turning from Tad and whispered, "I'm sorry . . ."

Going to her, he whispered, "It's I who should apologize, for taking advantage of you."

Miranda, with tears streaming down her cheeks, shook her head. "You didn't take advantage of me Tad. I wanted this to happen just as much as you. It's just . . ."

Gently, Tad turned her to him with concern in his eyes. "Oh please don't cry, Miranda dear. Whatever has hurt you in the past must be deep, if a kiss makes you tremble. Will you tell me what it is? You know everything about me, and I know so little of you, except that I'm hopelessly in love with you and have been for quite sometime."

Hearing such words, her heart raced and more tears flowed. "Tad, please don't say such things . . . There's so much of my past you know nothing of. Things that I've done, I will have to live with until the day I die."

He held her close to him, and whispered, "And one day I hope you will trust me enough to share what it is that has caused you such pain. For now I won't press you to share the demons that torture you. Just please don't push me away, especially when we need one another so desperately."

Hearing him say he needed her, Miranda suddenly felt safe in his arms, and she knew what he said was true--they did need one another. Lifting her head, she nodded as his lips found hers again. This time she didn't pull away from the desires stirring inside her, but welcomed the comfort she felt in his arms.

Their moment of tenderness was interrupted by Michael, who embarrassed at finding his son and Miranda embracing in the family garden, coughed to warn them of his presence.

Nervously, Miranda turned from Michael, hearing him say, "Excuse me Tad and Miranda at such an inopportune time, but son, you have a visitor who is quite anxious to speak with you--a Mr. Daniel Hobbs."

"Yes father. Would you please ask him to wait? I'll be right there."

Nodding his response, Michael, with a smile on his face, turned back to the house while Tad tried to reassure Miranda who looked up at him anxiously. "Dearest, don't be embarrassed. I'll explain to Father that I was thanking you for tending to my wound."

"I'm not worried about that--well perhaps a little--but what troubles me most is Mr. Hobbs. Isn't he the man who was with you . . . I mean, Tad you have no idea the hate I saw in Mr. O'Flaherty's eyes. It worries me . . ."

"Listen to me, Miranda. For the first time in my life, I have something to live for. Father and I are trying to work out our differences and now we . . ." Tad paused, seeing her look of anxiousness speaking about the two of them, so he continued saying. "Nothing is going to come between us getting to know one another now that we are finally able to trust one another. You do trust me don't you Miranda?"

His question took her by surprise. "Yes Tad, I do," she said, realizing he had earned her trust by being so forthright.

"Good. So please trust me to handle this. Just promise me that you'll stay clear of O'Flaherty. Can you do that for me?"

"Yes."

As if the matter had been settled, Tad kissed her forehead and excused himself. As she watched him walk back toward the house to meet with his friend Daniel, she couldn't stop the feeling of pending doom. As she gazed into the garden, her mind flooded with the events of the past few days.

She absentmindedly smelled a sprig of lilacs from the bush, and a smile crossed her lips, recalling how Tad had picked some for her. *How could she possibly feel so close with this man after twenty-four hours, when for years she had been repelled by his advances?*

Even now, after he had told her everything about the fight he had with Gilbert, something inside her screamed there was more to the argument between her and Gilbert. *Dear God, how can I feel so safe in his arms but doubt him the moment he leaves? What is wrong with me?*

So engrossed in her thoughts, Miranda hadn't seen Gilbert step closer, watching her in wonderment. Disgusted that she was so easily swayed, he turned and walked back to the alley and pushed his cart to his next stop.

Sarah called out, walking into the gardens, "Miranda dear, would you care for some company?" She smiled fondly at her, feeling particularly maternal, especially since Michael told her what he had witnessed only moments earlier.

"Oh Mrs. Honeycutt, I didn't hear you coming. How are you today?" she said politely, knowing by the smile on her face she knew about Tad's and her embrace.

Sarah nodded, placing her arm around the girl she had known since she was a baby. "That was very kind of you to tend to Tad last evening. And since he and his father have begun to clear the air regarding their differences, it would appear you had something to do with that healing too."

Miranda smiled. "Nothing that you and Mr. Honeycutt haven't already done for Papa and me. Why I can't imagine what would have become of us if it hadn't been for the both of you."

"Sweetheart, we were only too glad to help." Seeing that Miranda felt uncomfortable, Sarah said, "Miranda, you do know that if there is anything you need or want I'm always here for you, don't you? I may not be your mother, nor would I ever dream of trying to replace her . . . but surely you must realize that I've loved you since you were born."

"I know Mrs. Honeycutt, and I love you too. I'm concerned about something but I need to work out on my own," Miranda said softly.

Nodding, Sarah said, "Yes. Especially since that something or someone is Michael's son. Now I'm not going to pretend I don't know about you two young folks kissing earlier, nor that both Michael and I wouldn't welcome having you in Tad's life. We both view you as a loving, wise young woman, whom we love very much. It's because we do love you, we want you to know that if a romance should develop between Tad and you, above all else darling, make sure that this is what *you* want. Don't let your heart be pressured or manipulated into caring for someone out of gratitude. In other words, Miranda, don't feel you need to do this for Tad, Michael, the Honeycutt's, your father, or me. Because it's your heart you are following and ultimately it's your heart that will either soar or suffer in the end."

Miranda, touched by Sarah's kind words, hugged her. "Oh Mrs. Honeycutt, thank you. I'm already so confused."

"Darling, take your time. When it comes to affairs of the heart, it's always confusing. All I can say is trust your heart, and above all be patient. Just look at Elise and Joshua, or myself for that matter. When I first met Michael, he was nothing more than a kind man who rented a room. Now he's my world. When a woman gives her heart to a man, truly gives it openly and freely, she lives to please only him. So dearest, be very sure he's worthy of such love."

"But how do you know if he is? I mean, how did you know, or Elise know Joshua was the right one?"

"My mother told me once that a man's pride will prevent him from sharing his inner thoughts sometimes, but a man's eyes are the mirror to his soul. And so far, she's never been wrong."

With those words of wisdom, the two of them joined the Honeycutt's and Sterling's for cocktails before dinner. As Miranda watched the three couples she couldn't help but notice that when James Sterling spoke to his wife, although his words were pleasant, his eyes showed no warmth. But for that matter, neither were Lavinia's toward her husband. Just before dinner, Tad joined them and smiled at her, but his eyes reflected agitation. Miranda smiled knowingly at Sarah who responded with a nod. Turning her attention to Tad, Miranda asked, "Is everything alright?"

"Couldn't be better," he replied, but instinctively she knew he was lying by the look in his eyes.

As they sat around the table, Sarah noticed the look between Vivian and Lavinia, and she braced herself expecting Lavinia to make mention of the cut over Tad's eye, or something equally none of her business.

"Miranda dear, don't think I've forgotten about our shopping date. What time will be good for you tomorrow? After all, the theatre does require a certain flair in our choice of fashion. Have you decided what play you plan to attend?"

Not giving the matter any thought since earlier this morning, Miranda looked at Tad shyly, hoping he would answer Lavinia.

"Well in fact, I was going to discuss this with Miranda in private, but I had thought perhaps we might take in those flashing pictures from the Cinematoscope or perhaps do some reading together." Tad said looking at Miranda for approval.

"Reading sounds lovely," Miranda said shyly while nodding to Beatrice for more soup.

"Ah well, as a writer myself you'll hear no complaints from me on your choice of entertainment. What novel did you have in mind, son?" Michael asked, looking across the table to Tad.

With a devilish grin, Tad replied, "I fancy Dickens myself. Perhaps, *Our Mutual Friends*. Gasps could be heard around the table, and receiving the shocked response he intended, Tad smiled victoriously while taking a sip of his soup.

Outraged by such a comment, Alfred arched his eyebrow and scornfully looked at his grandson. "I hardly think such a book would be considered appropriate. If memory serves me correct, Pearson wrote that Dickens' works are 'filthy and bestial, an honest man would admit one into his house for a water-closet doormat'. And I agree with him. I absolutely forbid it, Tad."

Tad's smile faded and he looked at his grandfather, saying in a respectful tone, "Actually Grandfather, I was thinking Hawthorne's *The House of Seven Gables,* or the tale of his life at Brook Farm, *The Blithedale Romance* might be more appropriate"

Glancing his son then at Tad, Alfred said, "A far better choice."

"Ah Hawthorne, yes I've rather enjoyed some of his novels," Lavinia said, adding her two cent's worth.

With a gleam in his eyes, James said, "Indeed, as I recall, you read *The Scarlet Letter* several times, dear. Wasn't that also Hawthorne's work?"

No one responded to James's comment, and immediately all looked at their soup seeing the angry glare Lavinia gave her husband.

With a pasted smile to her lips, Lavinia retaliated. "It surprises me you noticed dear, so preoccupied by *Dickens and America*--what was that passage I read regarding delusion of grandeur? Ah yes I remember, 'The lunatic is the man who lives in a small world, but thinks it is a large one'. Personally, I tend to agree with Alfred. Dickens is rather off color and not at all worth reading."

Again, there was complete silence around the dinner table as Alfred looked to James then back at Lavinia. "Begging your pardon Lavinia, dear. I believe Dickens was referring to those who are able to see their world for what it is and once they do, they become dissatisfied and sadly realize that what they had once thought was truth, was merely a fallacy. Wasn't that your interpretation James?"

Coughing to hide his chuckle, James nodded his head. "Yes, as a matter of fact, I did, Alfred. Opening your eyes to the truth is often painful." Then glaring at Lavinia, he added, "Perhaps, my dear, I could lend you my copy to reread the entire book so you might fully grasp Dickens's meaning."

"No that won't be necessary, *dear*," she said smiling at her husband, but it was clear for everyone to see that Lavinia's smile showed anything but warmth.

Obviously enjoying that the conversation had shifted to someone other than himself, Tad said, "Grandfather, I'm shocked that you know of Dickens' work so well, considering you clearly don't approve of me reading it to Miranda."

"I never said I hadn't read Dickens, Tad. What I said was, I do not approve of his writing and reading it with someone, especially if that person happens to be Miranda." Pausing to smile fondly at her then directing his attention back to Tad he added. "As I view it, a good business man should be knowledgeable on all subjects if he is to remain on top of his game. Literature being no exception, particularly since it's these writers that formulate a man's way of thinking."

Wiping his mouth with his linen napkin, Michael applauded his father's comment, saying, "Here, here Father. Precisely why I've decided to dabble in writing a novel, myself."

"How wonderful Michael!" Vivian cooed. "Does that small home that Sarah picked out . . ." Her eyes drifted quickly to Sarah with contempt, then she returned her attention back to Michael, and said sweetly, ". . . have a room that will afford you the quiet you will require with such an undertaking? After hearing all the decorating it will need, I am sure your father would offer you his study while he's away during the day. That way

Sarah could try to make a more presentable home while not disturbing you in the process."

Sarah's back stiffened hearing Vivian's comment, knowing this was Michael's mother's way of saying she didn't approve of their choice in homes, and she was trying to keep her son close to her and away from Sarah.

"That won't be necessary, Mother. Sarah and I have already discussed my need for privacy and she has graciously agreed to allow me to use her boudoir while the carpenters work on the first floor. Besides, since I intend to write a Northerner's point of view while living in the South, Sarah will be a great help in recalling situations."

Obviously not pleased with her son's response, Vivian's attentions were directed to her grandson. "Well surely with your father and Sarah so preoccupied with their new lives, whatever are you going to do while living there?"

Before Tad had a chance to respond, Alfred spoke firmly, "Vivian, we've already had this discussion. Tad is going to be with his father where he belongs. I was hoping to persuade him to come and join me at Honeycutt and Son's now that he's graduated and has had ample time off following school. How does that sound to you, Tad?"

"Well Grandfather, I was intending to discuss my future with you and Father of course later, but since we are all here . . . I was thinking of pursuing a career in law. As a matter of fact, with Joshua now in the family, I thought once he returned I'd discuss the possibilities of joining his father's firm."

Alfred looked at his grandson with disappointment in his eyes, and said, "I had no idea law intrigued you. But since it does, there's no need to wait for Joshua and Elise's return. If you would like, I can speak with William Carmidy on your behalf. After all, with his firm now handling a great deal of my holdings, I see him quite frequently."

"Oh Tad you can't be serious. The law of all professions, having to deal with all those undesirables and bad people," spouted Vivian.

Chuckling, Michael said, "Well it's a good thing Joshua isn't here. I'm sure he would have something to say about that remark, Mother."

"Indeed!" agreed Alfred, who added. "Where did I hear that if there were no bad people there would be no good lawyers?"

"Dickens, in *The Old Curiosity Shop*, as I recall," James said.

"My, but you are well versed this evening aren't you, darling? Where do you find the time to read so much?" Lavinia asked.

"Oh you would be surprised, my dear!" James gave Lavinia a snide grin, sending her mind whirling. *Does he know of my afternoon rendezvous?*

As was the norm every night following dinner, the women joined Vivian in her drawing room, while the men met in Alfred's study. However, this evening Sarah excused herself following the meal, explaining she needed to catch up on her correspondence. Miranda and Tad claimed they would begin reading and made their way to the adjacent room off the drawing room, in Vivian's private sitting room with the door open. As was the practice for couples who were courting, Tad took a seat across from Miranda who sat on Vivian's davenport.

Pulling out a worn copy of Hawthorne's *The House of Seven Gables*, Tad whispered to Miranda, "You have read this, haven't you Miranda?"

"Yes, of course," she replied, puzzled.

"Good, then if we should be asked about it, you can truthfully recall the story."

Not comfortable with deceiving others as a rule, she nodded.

To keep up the pretense, Tad began reading from the first chapter. After hearing chatter from the other room, he looked at Miranda and winked, laying the book on his knees. "If I know Grandmother and Lavinia, the two of them will be so busy conspiring they won't give us another thought."

A smile crossed her lips, recalling how she and Constance had done something similar when Lucas was in his study.

"You surprise me, Miranda."

"In what way?" she asked, being careful to keep her voice barely above a whisper.

"From that knowing grin, I would have to assume this was not your first time at concealing your true intentions."

Realizing she had let her guard down, her smile faded. "As I told you earlier in the garden Tad, there is much you don't know about me."

"Yes, I hope to remedy that soon."

Knowing this was Tad's way of asking her to share her past, Miranda quickly replied, "And in time perhaps you will, but this evening I was rather hoping you would tell me why Mr. Hobbs came to visit you. From the look on your face following his visit, I could tell you were quite agitated."

"Could you?" Tad smiled, yet his eyes disclosed anything but amusement as he made up some excuse for Daniel's visit. As Miranda listened to him, she suddenly became aware that when he lied to her, he often looked slightly over her head rather than into her eyes.

In the other room, Vivian filled Lavinia in on all that had transpired, including how Alfred had prevented her from going to her son or grandson when they obviously needed her the most.

"Oh how simply dreadful for you, Viv darling. So you have no idea what was said between Tad and Michael this afternoon?"

"No. That obnoxious wife of my son saw to it I was kept well away from them, talking endlessly with Alfred and me about that new house of theirs. I'm telling you Lavinia, I don't know what's worse, having that wretched woman as a daughter-in-law or dealing with Alfred's sudden interest in our family. Lately I can't move from room to room without him knowing everything I do. Honestly, I don't know what to make of it. Ever since Michael's return, he is constantly underfoot. Why, I don't think he's been to the club once this week."

Lavinia's eyes widened and she looked at her host suspiciously. "What did you say? Why, James told me he met with Alfred this very afternoon . . ."

"Oh I can assure you Alfred has been here the entire day," Vivian said, shaking her head in disgust. "Why, he's only been to the office twice this week as a matter of fact. And I can tell you having that man watch my every move, along with dealing with that ghastly wife of Michael's, well I'm at my wits end."

As Vivian kept twittering on, complaining about Sarah and Alfred, Lavinia's heart raced knowing that James had been lying to her. She recalled how James had excused his lateness this evening by saying he had been delayed at the club with Alfred. At the time, Lavinia had been grateful since Isaac's and her afternoon of lovemaking had gotten out of hand and he had left far later than they had intended. However, she couldn't help but wonder what James was really doing.

"Lavinia! Have you heard a word I've said?" Vivian asked annoyed. "Why if I intended to be ignored, I could have waited to discuss my troubles with Alfred. God knows that man has perfected the art of ignoring me."

"Oh Viv, I'm so sorry. It's just something you said got me to thinking. This afternoon, Isaac and my sitting went longer than usual. You remember how I told you how I've commissioned him to paint my portrait as a surprise to James?"

"Yes of course, but what does that have to do with what I said," she replied hotly, obviously still upset that Lavinia had not paid sufficient attention to her.

Annoyed by Vivian's tone, Lavinia chose to ignore it for the time being and continued, "Well, as I was saying, Isaac was detained and as luck would have it so was James. His excuse was that he was detained at the club with Alfred."

Raising her eyebrow, Vivian smirked. "Ah, so now you are wondering where that husband of yours really was, or more importantly, does he know about you and that lusty painter of yours?"

Lavinia gasped and looked at the older woman with her mouth still opened. "Vivian, why of all the ridiculous . . ."

Raising her hand, Vivian stopped Lavinia from continuing her lie. "Oh please Lavinia, do you honestly think for one moment I haven't known from the start what you and that artist friend of yours have been doing all these months? First off, no portrait takes that long to paint."

Lavinia was stunned and didn't know what to say. Knowingly, Vivian said ruefully, "Personally, I feel it serves James right for leaving such a beautiful vivacious woman alone as much as he does. But after what I've observed over dinner my dear, I would be very concerned if your husband hasn't become wise to your little amusement with your artist friend. And if I'm not mistaken, he has enlisted Alfred as an ally."

"Dear God, I think you're right," she whispered, more to herself than to Vivian. "So now what do I do?"

"Why nothing dear. If your artist suddenly didn't show up anymore, surely it would only confirm his suspicions. But I would definitely make certain that a portrait is completed or nearly complete, in the event you are questioned. I'm assuming this Isaac can paint, right dear?"

"Yes, of course he can." Lavinia's voice drifted off as her mind raced. *So if James suspects my infidelities than why hasn't he tried to stop me?*

So deep in her own thoughts, Lavinia barely heard Vivian say, "Take it from someone who knows. A man of James' position will not openly destroy his wife's reputation, especially when he has his own pride to consider among his colleagues. If you don't believe me, just look at our late president. Mary Todd spent well above her means, but to protect his good name and hers, Lincoln practically blackmailed Congress in paying them off, for the position of his office. Men have a code they must live by and James's pride would never allow anyone to find out the truth of his wife. That is, unless it serves him too for his own purpose. For instance, if he found someone more desirable in social standing, or unless his wife forced him to by flaunting her indiscretions openly. Which of course you wouldn't, so then my question would be, does James have his eye on someone else?"

Lavinia's heart raced as her eyes widened. *That little bitch, Felicity! Well, I'll just have to inform her cousin of this as well!* Trying to control her voice she said, "Why of course not, don't be absurd."

"How foolish of me to even ask such a thing." Vivian smiled brazenly, raising her eyebrow wondering whom James was interested in.

~ Eleven ~

Sins of the Past

Long after the residents had retired for the evening, Tad waited in the shadows of the Honeycutt property for his friend Daniel, as prearranged. Hearing the hooves of a horse approach, Tad stepped out from behind a tree, while Michael in his father's study, watched his son get into a buggy that had stopped briefly in front of the Honeycutt estate. Shaking his head discouragingly, Michael glanced at Alfred who had sat and waited with him in the darkened room to see what Tad was up to.

"Just as we suspected, Father."

Striking a match to light his pipe, Alfred drew in several small intakes of breath to assure the tobacco was fully lit in the bowl of his pipe. Blowing out the match, he raised his eyebrow while increasing the flame of the hurricane lamp beside him on the mahogany table.

"Son, as I said earlier, Tad is a full-grown man. The decision he makes is of his own choosing. He chose to lie, and that Michael, has nothing to do with you or me, for that matter," Alfred said sternly.

"That might be so, but the fact that I was not here to guide him certainly contributes to my son making bad decisions. And nothing you can say, Father, will ease my guilt."

Sighing heavily, Alfred motioned his son to take a seat beside him in the high-back Queen Anne chair next to his. Obligingly, Michael sat and glanced at his father who was obviously troubled. "Father, what is it?"

"Son, what I'm about to tell you, I had never intended for you to know. However now, under the circumstances, the truth must come out."

Frowning, Michael looked at his father, allowing Alfred the time he needed to gather his thoughts. "Before I begin, I need to tell you Michael, that the man you have become, I value as my greatest accomplishment. Now, hear me out . . ." Alfred said, seeing his son ready to respond. "I don't say this as a means to console you, but rather to point out why I feel I can trust you with what I'm about to reveal to you now. Understand?"

"I believe so... Please go on."

"As you know, your mother has always been a high-strung woman, requiring a great deal of attention. I knew this when we met and fell in love. In truth, that is what I fell in love with, her zest for life. When I took my bride back to England to meet my family and friends, never had I imagined it would nearly destroy our marriage and her in the process. Looking back now, I suppose they resented your mother not just because she was from America, but they had hoped I would marry another woman in our set. It didn't help that your mother was not as demure and cultured as those that my family associated with. After months of watching your poor mother struggle to fit in and win the love of my mother, which she never could, since your grandmother was so rigid in her thinking, Vivian and I left England after a terrible row. My father, heartbroken and fearful he would lose his son as did his friend William Phelps, funded any business adventure I wanted to start. Up until that time, in truth, I dabbled in business but never took it serious. I was young and was quite fond of enjoying life of the gentry."

Stopping to take a pull from his pipe, Alfred continued. "That all changed though upon returning to America. Feeling as if I had something to prove to my father, I became obsessed in my work while your mother was determined to improve her image. At the time, I thought your mother was merely trying to impress my mother and friends so she would be viewed as worthy. So involved in my own quest, I never realized how much she needed my approval as well. As it turned out, I was extremely fortunate and my investments paid off; all the while your mother built a lavish home for us, spending the money as quickly as it was made. Over time, we drifted further and further apart, me working long hours and then stopping at the club more frequently to unwind and avoid her complaints of me never being around. That all changed though when you were born and for a few years your mother and I were genuinely happy. She was busy tending to you while I kept building an empire, never satisfied with what I had, always wanting more. Before long, we both drifted apart from one another again. Then the worst day of my life happened when I discovered your mother was having an affair with the artist who painted that portrait." Alfred's voice trailed off, pointing to the painting that hung above the mantel.

Michael, so shocked at what he was hearing, looked up at the familiar painting that had hung in his father's study for as long as he could remember. In a low voice barely above a whisper, Alfred spoke again. "That afternoon I had just closed a deal that was sure to make me quite wealthy and I came home early to share my good fortune. Stopping by the nursery, I saw you were playing quietly with your nanny so I tiptoed to your mother's boudoir to surprise her. There I found her engaging in sexual activities with the man I had commissioned to paint her portrait. Stunned, I stood watching that bastard gratifying himself on your mother as she watched me looking on. I'll never forget the look in her eyes . . . cold and scornful. When I stormed in and flung him off her, your mother just lay there not even trying to conceal her nakedness. It was as if she had wanted me to find out what I had turned her into."

Stunned and angry, Michael lashed out. "For God sakes Father, I don't know what to say! You certainly didn't force mother into betraying you."

Alfred glanced back at his son coyly. "Didn't I? Michael, I had ignored her needs and desires to satisfy my own greed for power and wealth. Leaving her day and night for years alone, knowing full well, her insatiable zest for life, but not giving a damn."

"What did you do? I mean following that afternoon?" Michael asked hesitantly.

"Do? What I had done our entire marriage; made a business arrangement. After hanging up that damned portrait, more as means to torment her as a constant reminder of her infidelities, I made a deal with your mother. If she continued to raise you and appear as a happy couple for my business associates, in exchange, she could do as she pleased as long as she was discreet."

"Are you telling me father that since that day to this, you and mother . . . ."

"What I am saying Michael is, I forced that beautiful woman you see up in that picture so filled with life to change into the bitter, conniving woman she is today. Never to know pure happiness or contentment. I'll hand it to her though, Vivian kept her promise and from that day to this, if she had other affairs, I knew nothing of them, nor did I care. Sadly though from that day to this, we have never been intimate."

Michael's mouth dropped. "Father, that had to be more than thirty-five years ago."

"Forty-three actually. From that day to this, never have I allowed her or myself to be forgiven for what we have done to one another and to our only child. And for that I am truly sorry, Michael."

Puzzled Michael asked, "I don't follow . . ."

Interrupting his son, Alfred said, "You were raised by two people who cared more to fill their home with materialistic fineries to impress others and keep up appearances, rather than show one another love. The only thing of value that resulted from this shameful existence is you! And for years I've been a hypocrite, telling you that loving another was the greatest possession a man had, while living a private life and not giving a damn if your mother did or not."

"Are you telling me that you had affairs, Father?"

"Countless women who meant nothing to me. Their names I would prefer to keep private."

Michael nodded to his father not really wanting to know them by name.

Acknowledging his son's gesture, Alfred added. "After you went off to college and returned with a wife to live with us, for the first time in decades there was warmth and genuine love under this roof. Was it any wonder your mother resented your marriage? Not only had Vivian been taught not to be accepted by my mother, but also over the years I had taught her how to be manipulative to get what she required. What Vivian wanted most in the world was what you and Emily had, and that was something your mother could never have at any cost. After Emily's tragic death, your mother came to me pleading to at least let her raise her grandson since I had denied her a life she deserved. So I did. Again, my selfishness overruled my better judgment, convincing myself that it was best for all concerned. Over the years, I made it easier for you to leave Thaddeus with us. Then when Tad went off to college, you were spending more and more time in Fairfax and it became clear to me that you had again found love. With Tad away, I kept telling myself that you deserved some happiness. Frankly Michael, I lived for your happiness, even envied what it must be like to risk your own life for the love of a woman. When Miranda came to live with us, my heart soared at discovering what a fine and decent man you had become despite your parents. Then it suddenly occurred to me that all the while I had been appeasing your mother out of my own guilt and shame, I had prevented your son from knowing just how truly wonderful his father actually was. In addition, I prayed that God would allow you to return and not punish me any further. So you see Michael, if anyone is to blame for Tad's lack of character, it's me!" Alfred's voice cracked, as he looked at his son for forgiveness.

Shaking his head, Michael leaned over and patted his father's hand. "Don't be so hard on yourself, Father, I could have stood up to you and mother, but I chose not to. I took the easy way out, not able to face my grief losing Emily, and I hid behind my work. That is something I shall live with for the rest of my life. If it wasn't for Sarah, hell I might still be . . ."

"I don't believe that, son. From what I've heard and seen since your return home, I've observed a woman who has endured your mother's hateful tongue and schemes simply out of the love she has for my son. That love was based on two people finding one another and sharing their heart, not just one. My only advice to you now is, don't get so caught up in your own pain Michael, that you lose sight of what your wife's needs are, son, like I did. When you and Sarah move into your new home, allow Tad to witness how a man and a woman should treat one another, rather than what he has known living with us. If your son learns what you have achieved with your Sarah, I can tell you Michael, no matter how successful he may become in the life he builds for himself, what will matter the most when his life is nearly over is how he loved. Don't get me wrong, I'm very proud of your accomplishments, but I envy your ability to put what matters the most to you first in your life. If only I had been able to see that loving another came before my career, perhaps things could have been different for your mother and me."

Seeing the pain in his father's eyes, Michael wanted to ease his tormented mind but somehow he knew what his father needed the most was to finally release his pain by exposing the truth. Alfred, looking up at the portrait of his wife as she once had been, lovingly smiled.

"By God Michael, do you see how beautiful your mother was? Instead of punishing her, this portrait is now a constant reminder to me of how I had chosen my own ambition over her needs. How I wish to God I could change our pasts."

Then looking at Michael, his tone became more urgent. "For some unknown reason, Miranda has taken an interest in your son. And one thing I know for certain is that young woman has no tolerance for conniving or deceitfulness. If Tad is fortunate to ever truly win her heart, he will have to be honest with that woman or lose her. And if he loses her, it will haunt him forever. Take it from someone who knows. So rather than be consumed with the past in which you have no control of, help Tad to become the man I feel he truly wants to be. We both have more than enough money for him to live in comfort. What he needs more than wealth is to feel loved and to be able to love. You, Michael, can teach him that." Alfred's voice, so full of emotion, cracked.

Suddenly Michael saw his father as more than an untouchable successful businessman, but as a vulnerable man with a life full of regrets that tormented him, and who was now reaching out for the love of his son.

"Father, thank you . . ." Unable to find the words to express all that he was feeling, Michael knelt in front of his father and said, "I love you."

For the fist time in Michael's life, he saw his father cry as he whispered, "I love you too, son."

Tenderly patting Michael on the shoulder, Alfred said, "Go to your Sarah and let me wait up for my grandson tonight. We have a few things to talk over."

Nodding, Michael stood, wanting to ask him what he intended to discuss with Tad, but instead decided whatever it was that his father wanted to share with Tad, he knew it would be beneficial for them both.

~

As Alfred waited for his grandson, Tad was fighting for his life across town in the alley behind Jake's with Daniel Hobbs looking on. After Daniel picked up Tad, the two of them waited in the shadows of the alley being informed that Gilbert would be there after midnight. Just as they had thought, Gilbert, along with a fellow worker at the Ice Company, showed up soon after the church bell chimed twelve. As the two Irishmen came into the passageway, Tad walked out in plain view.

"O'Flaherty, I've got a proposition for you," he called to him.

"Oh yeah! And what would that be, your Lordship?" Gilbert remarked snidely.

"Give me back my money and stay the hell away from Miranda, and I won't make any trouble for you."

"The hell I will, you cheating bastard! As a matter of fact, that fair little lassie is far too good for the likes of you, so I think I'll be winning her from ya too."

Infuriated, Tad charged at Gilbert, but expecting his assailant, Gilbert easily stepped to the side, causing Tad to lunge into the wall of Jake's. Gilbert's friend laughed, goading Tad into a rage as he stumbled to regain his bearings. Grasping hold of a jagged piece of board, Tad swung the board at Gilbert and his friend.

"I'll wipe that smile off your damned face, you slimy bastard!" Tad yelled, taking Gilbert by surprise and clipping him in the ribs, which caused the wind to be knocked out of him. Hunched over, Tad punched him in the face, throwing the man onto a rusted iron tub used by the brewery to discard empty whiskey bottles.

"Get up, you son of a bitch," Tad said derisively, hovering over the stunned man, not noticing that Gilbert's friend had pulled an ice pick from inside his weathered coat and was inching his way closer to Tad to strike.

"Tad, watch your back!" Daniel yelled.

Jerking around just as the man lunged, Tad began struggling for control of the pick. Feeling his forearm slashed by the tip of it, Tad managed to knee his assailant in the groin while still struggling over control of the tool. Suddenly the man yelped as the pick pierced through his side. Seeing the stranger's eyes widen, Tad looked down in disbelief, as Gilbert, who had regained his bearings, struck him over the head with a bottle, causing him to fall to the ground.

Then Gilbert turned and looked at Daniel who had done nothing up to this point to defend his friend. "This wasn't part of the deal," he shouted. "Hell, me mate could have been killed!"

"Yeah well, who the hell told you to flap your jaws? What in the hell did you expect, when you threatened to go after his woman, you stupid son of a bitch?" Daniel shouted back at the outraged Gilbert while walking over to him. "All you had to do was promise him a chance to get his money back and we could have wiped him clean of next month's spending money too," Daniel snarled.

"Just how in the hell was I to know his Lordship would react like that?" Gilbert said, frustrated. "You want to keep robbing your friend, find some other patsy to do yer dirty work! I'm through with this shit."

"You're through when I tell you, you are. Do I need to remind you that your job hangs in the balance?"

"Look, I've done everything you asked, but this has gone too far. Winning at cards is one thing, but me and Dave here could have been killed tonight. You can shove that job right up yer arse!"

"Is that so? Well, what if I had to notify the authorities that you and Dave here got in some brawl and you stabbed and killed him?"

"Yeah well, Dave ain't dead now is he? Just a wee nick is all." Before Gilbert finished his sentence, Daniel grabbed the ice pick while he stood on the injured man's chest and glared at the stunned Gilbert.

"Oh I assure you that can be rectified," he snarled, lunging at his prey and shoving the ice pick into the injured man's body a second time under the ribcage while he struggled to be freed. A chilling moan rang out in the darkened alley, and Gilbert, realizing that Daniel had just killed his friend, lunged at him.

"Jesus, Mary and Joseph, you killed him ya cold-blooded bastard."

Yanking the ice pick from the mortally-wounded, bloodied man's body, Daniel pointed it at Gilbert replying cold and callously, "Just like I said, I came across you killing this poor bastard. Now who do you think the constable is going to believe--a law abiding citizen or some hot-headed Irishman who has built up a reputation for brawling? Why just last night you were thrown out of this fine establishment." Daniel paused, nodding toward the building behind him.

Glaring back at him, inching his way closer, waiting for the appropriate moment to jump Daniel, Gilbert goaded him, stalling for time. "Yeah, well I think I'll take my chances or kill you myself, you rotten bastard."

"Have you forgotten I've got the pick?" Daniel arrogantly waved the ice pick in front of him, snidely grinning. "You're a betting man. What do you think your odds are? Before you step any further though, you might want to keep in mind that I know where that feisty little tart sister of yours lives and works. And I can assure you, if you even so much as step another foot closer after I finish you off, I'll go after that whore-sister of yours next. When I'm finished with Margaret-Anne, no one will be able to identify her remains."

The two men, hearing Tad moan, looked at him and Daniel, taking advantage of the situation, cleverly called out as Tad started to regain consciousness and looked around. "I'm warning you, come any closer and I'll kill you. What Honeycutt did to your friend was in self defense."

"Why you lying bastard!" yelled Gilbert, while Tad managed to get to his feet.

Keeping up the pretense that Tad had killed his assailant, seeing that Tad was coming to, Daniel said, "Lower your voice, man! Do you want the whole town hearing you? Think how it will go for you, when I announce that I witnessed you trying to kill an upright citizen like Honeycutt here. You got a death wish, do you? Like I said, I saw the whole thing. My friend here was only defending himself when this thug pulled out an ice pick and tried to kill him. Honeycutt never intended to kill the poor bastard. It was an accident I tell you!"

Daniel's words were convincing as he looked at the outraged Irishmen. "Do you think going after Honeycutt now is going to help your friend?"

Dazed, Tad rubbed the back of his head and glanced at the man not five feet in front of him. As he looked at the lifeless body of his friend lying in a pool of blood, Daniel's words began to register. Not only had he just killed a man, but also his friend was trying to protect him.

Shaking his head in disbelief, Gilbert understood perfectly just how deceitful and cunning Daniel was. There was no chance the authorities would ever believe the truth against two of its leading citizens.

"Defend his Lordship's honor good and proper. The two of ya deserve one another," Gilbert sneered, before turning and running down the alley and out of sight while he still had the chance.

Looking at the dazed Tad, Daniel said urgently, "Get a hold of yourself man, before someone finds out you killed him."

"Killed him? You just said it was an accident!" Tad mumbled, trying to get to his feet.

"Who the hell's going to believe it was an accident, except some ignorant Irishmen? Let's face the facts, you and O'Flaherty made quite a scene last night, old boy. Just how long do you think the other guys will keep their mouth shut about you dealing off the bottom of the deck when murder is involved? Let's face it, you do not want the constables to investigate this man's murder. Even if you can convince a jury it was an accident, your reputation will be destroyed."

"What are you saying . . . dealing off the bottom of the deck? Why you know that's preposterous." Tad's head throbbed with pain as he tried to understand what his friend was saying.

"Bullshit, we all saw you. Why do you think I knocked over the table as I did? We've been friends for a long time and I was not about to let your reputation be destroyed over some foolish act. Now pull yourself together and help me get rid of his body, before you're found out."

It was clear to Tad that he had fooled no one last night, and realizing there was no point in trying to defend his actions, he started to walk over to Daniel, while rubbing the back of his neck. Feeling stickiness on his neck, he was shocked at seeing his own blood on his hands. "How the hell did I get cut?" Tad asked confused.

"Gilbert hit you from behind with a bottle after you stabbed his mate." Daniel mumbled, as he lifted the man's feet. "Grab his arms and help me to get him out of here."

Gazing down at the lifeless body, Tad recalled how he had struggled with the dead man over the ice pick. Shocked and reacting to Daniel's commands Tad bent over to take the dead man's arms in his, a cold shiver running up his spine upon seeing the lifeless stare in the man's eyes. "I don't even know his name . . ." he mumbled.

"David Sullivan. He worked with Gilbert at father's Ice Company," Daniel said frantically, looking about the alley trying to think how to get out of there without being caught, knowing time was of the essence. Urgently he whispered, "Listen up Tad, I need to go get the coach. We can't just carry a dead man out onto the street. Pull yourself together and I'll be right back."

Without waiting for a reply, Daniel turned and went after his rig while Tad, stupefied, continued to gaze at the man he believed he had just murdered.

The gravity of the situation finally hit home and suddenly realizing that he could in fact be hung, Tad began to tidy himself up by tucking his shirt into his trousers and pulling his hair off his face. While straightening his scarf, he became aware that his forearm ached. Looking at his arm he realized the sleeve of his coat had been slashed.

Raising the sleeve high enough, he saw his forearm was bleeding along with his head. Quickly he untied his scarf and wrapped it tightly around the gash to help minimize the bleeding.

By then, Daniel had returned with the coach and jumped down from the buckboard, saying, "Help get him inside. We'll drop him in the Hudson. No one will be the wiser."

Nodding his reply, Tad assisted his friend, grateful that Daniel was there to get him out of such a jam.

Within two hours, Tad was back in front of his grandparent's home after disposing David Sullivan's body in the Hudson River and thanking his friend profusely.

"Hell Honeycutt, if the roles were reversed I'm sure you would have done the same. For the next few weeks though I'd stay away from Jake's just in case O'Flaherty tries to make trouble for you. With pay due him, it works in our favor, so I'll keep an eye out for the bastard and persuade him to get the hell out of New York once and for all."

"Give him anything he wants, understand? Just see to it he never returns."

"Oh, I'll take care of O'Flaherty alright. You can count on that," Daniel said ruefully. "That drunken Irish mouth can't be trusted."

"Hobbs, you promised. No more bloodshed. Just get O'Flaherty out of New York. Hell, anywhere he wants to go, and let me put this behind us."

"Us?" Daniel asked indignantly. "Look Tad, I'm not the one who killed the poor son of a bitch, so don't be saying *us*. I'm here to assist a friend, nothing more."

"Yes of course . . . just promise me no more bloodshed."

"Fine. But first I have got to find him. You still haven't said how the hell you are going to come up with that kind of money? I can't cover that kind of expense without Father becoming suspicious."

Shaking his throbbing head, Tad said, "Just find the miserable bastard and I'll take care of the rest." Then grasping Daniel's hand in his, thanking him again for his help, Tad slowly edged his way off the buckboard, noticing the light from his grandfather's study. Hoping it wasn't his father, Tad made his way up the steps, ready to confess what he had done if necessary, to get the money he needed to make this hellish nightmare go away.

Alfred, standing at the entrance of his study, noticing the blood on his grandson's neck and hands, ran to him out of concern. "Christ all-mighty Tad, what in the hell has happened? Are you badly hurt? Should I send for the doctor?"

"No. I'll be fine," he said, pausing for a moment. Tad nodded toward the study. "Is Father inside?"

"No. I sent him up hours ago. I needed to discuss something with you." Alfred's voice trailed off, helping Tad inside the study. Seeing the gash just above the nape of Tad's neck where he had been hit with the whiskey bottle, Alfred asked again, "What the hell happened to you? You look like the devil."

Sarcastically, Tad replied, while taking a seat where Michael had been hours before. "No truer statement has ever been said. Grandfather, I am the devil! Or at least one of his followers, that's for damned sure."

"You're talking nonsense, Tad. Just tell me what happened to you tonight?" Alfred muttered sternly, while taking his seat next to his grandson. "I demand the truth Thaddeus, or so help me God . . ."

"Not even God almighty himself can change what I've done tonight," Tad said, despondently looking at his grandfather, sullen and full of self-contempt. "The finest education, or the finest breeding couldn't prevent me from turning out to be the despicable man I've become. Grandfather I've lied, cheated at cards and gotten caught, and now have committed murder." Seeing the blood drain from his grandfather's face, Tad hastily added. "And if that wasn't bad enough, I'm such a coward, I covered up my crimes by bringing a friend in as an accessory. Not to protect the family's honor, mind you, but out of fear of being found out, or worse being strung up at the end of a noose."

Realizing his grandson was not speaking out of delirium from his wound, Alfred sat horrified at his confession and as calmly as he could manage, said, "Start at the beginning Tad, and don't leave anything out."

After hearing everything, including how he thought Daniel had saved him from certain imprisonment and shame, Tad looked at his grandfather, waiting for the elder Honeycutt to decide what needed to be done next.

"As foolish as you have acted and as unfortunate as that poor man's death was, you did not commit murder. Your friend Hobbs was right, it was an accident. You were merely defending yourself. Thank God, Daniel had the foresight to remove the body. No need to bring unwanted and unnecessary gossip down on your good name."

"My good name indeed." Tad sarcastically chuckled, shaking his head. "How many times I've heard that Grandfather, and after what I've told you, all you can think of is my good name. Don't you see? I'm neither decent nor worthy of being a Honeycutt. I'm not like you and father. Hell, the way I look at it, I would have been better off if Daniel would have let Gilbert kill me."

"That will be enough, Tad." Alfred said sternly. "This evening I waited up for you, for the sole purpose to discuss with you things from my past that I have done, which I'm not proud of. Considering the lateness of the hour and everything that you have gone through tonight, that will have to wait until tomorrow. You are obviously distraught, with good reason, and before anyone else sees you, I want you to go upstairs and clean yourself up while I gather some medical supplies. All of your clothing, every last stitch needs to be disposed of. Understood?"

"Yes, Grandfather." Tad's voice was barely above a whisper as he stood up and looked at Alfred.

"Tad, what happened tonight was dreadful. Make no mistake about it. However, you must remember the death of that man was in self-defense. The way I see it, you have two choices here. You can choose to be swallowed up by self-hate and become bitter, or you can learn from this mistake. The choice is yours. Personally, I hope you choose the later. Either way, I will deal with Daniel from here out regarding this matter. With you moving in with your father, perhaps it would be wise to break all ties with your friends for the time being."

Nodding his response, Tad left his grandfather's study and promptly climbed the stairs as he had done so often in the past. This time however, the cold icy stare of David Sullivan's lifeless eyes accompanied him with his every step. Unable to block out the image from his mind, upon entering his bedchamber, Tad immediately disrobed and began cleaning the dried blood from his wounded arm. Rubbing the open gash repeatedly, he felt nothing. Even when he reopened the wound and fresh blood trickled down his wrist onto his fingers, Tad still felt nothing.

It was as if this were all a bad dream, not really happening. With blood dripping onto the wood floor, Tad in shock, stared at his reflection in the mirror about the dry sink, reliving the events in his mind repeatedly, still unable to accept that he had killed another. So engrossed in his tormented thoughts, Tad never heard Alfred enter his room.

"Christ Tad, what in the hell have you done?" Alfred whispered coarsely at his grandson while trying to stop the bleeding of Tad's wound. "Sit down and let me take care of that cut before you get it infected."

Dazed, Tad nodded and sat on the edge of his bed looking at his blood-soaked arm, unable to fully understand what his grandfather was doing or saying. Everything appeared to be happening to someone else rather than him. After Alfred had dressed his wound and helped clothe him in a night shirt, Tad obligingly lay his head on the pillow as he was instructed, all the while the haunting eyes of David Sullivan never left his tormented mind.

Time stood still for the younger Honeycutt as he stared at the ceiling, not even aware that Alfred had left his room. The only sound Tad heard was the gasp Sullivan made as the ice pick entered his body, and then the crashing sound of the bottle as he was struck from behind by Gilbert.

"Gilbert," Tad whispered, recalling how his nemesis had threatened to steal Miranda from him. Anger stirred inside him at that thought. Tad sat up in bed. Despite his throbbing head, he crept across the darkened room without making a sound. Without the need for light, he made his way around his bed, past the wardrobe to the corner of the room where he pressed a lever on the side of a dumbwaiter. Within seconds, he walked through a service passage that led him directly into Miranda's room through the dumbwaiter in her room.

As a child, Tad had used this passage to hide from his nanny, and now he found it quite beneficial to gain access into Miranda's room whenever he wished, which turned out to be often.

Once safely inside her room, he moved freely with stealth precision as he gazed down at the unsuspecting Miranda as she slept soundly. His eyes traced her petite frame with the aid of the moonlight that softly filtered into her room as she lay under the thin linen sheet.

Slowly he crept closer to her until he could feel her breath on his face. How he yearned to touch her creamy skin that glistened on this humid late-spring evening. However, noticing her stir slightly, Tad retreated to the corner of her room where he knew she would not be able to see him even if she happened to awaken.

From the very first night that Miranda had come to live with his grandparents, Tad was intrigued. Not only because she was a Southerner-- which was extremely fascinating in itself—but because Miranda appeared completely uninterested in him. Unlike others who gushed over him, which repulsed him. This pristine, Southern Belle, seeming not at all impressed with his good looks, charms or family position, appeared to be equal to his perceptiveness and shrewdness, which in itself Tad found irresistible.

After their first meeting, Tad was determined to win her heart, yet over the years, despite everything he had tried, nothing had worked, until the other day when Miranda actually returned his affection. By this time, Tad had found himself hopelessly in love with her and now that he had begun to win her heart, he was determined not to lose it to some Irishman that he viewed beneath her.

As Tad stood watching Miranda sleep, he recalled their passionate embrace in the garden that afternoon. Never had he desired any other woman, or wanted to protect another as when she trembled in his arms.

Recalling now her lips on his, he vowed that no one or nothing was going to prevent him from getting what he wanted, and that was Miranda.

The only one who stood between having the desire of his heart was Gilbert O'Flaherty. No matter what he had promised his grandfather, Tad was determined to find and hush his enemy forever. Even if he had to kill again.

~ Twelve ~

Revenge

Two weeks had passed since the night of David Sullivan's death. As promised, Alfred had opened his purse strings wide to avoid any connection with the Honeycutt name and the death of the Irish immigrant. Like Tad, Alfred never suspected he and his grandson were being victimized by blackmail. Or that Daniel Hobbs was actually responsible for the cold-blooded murder of Sullivan. The Honeycutt's predator thought of almost everything to assure never being found out. The only fly in the ointment was Gilbert O'Flaherty, who had not been seen since the night of the incident. Both Tad and Daniel, determined to silent Gilbert, searched in vain for the man they viewed as a threat to their future happiness.

For years, Daniel had been envious of Tad's generous monthly allotments and had resented that the same generosity had not been bestowed on him by his father, Jerome Hobbs. The senior Hobbs, a well-off business entrepreneur, with high morals and convictions, insisted that nothing had been handed to him, needing to earn it through hard work. Therefore, in turn, he demanded the same for his only son.

Opposed to his father's way of thinking, Daniel viewed manual work as tedious and demeaning. With no family allotments to rely on, the unscrupulous Hobbs found other means to ensure he had money to spend. Shamelessly, Daniel would get Tad drunk and cheat at cards to win the hands. Unfortunately, this plan was short lived when others in their set, wise to Daniel's ruthlessness would drop out of the hands when he dealt. When an opportunity presented itself through the desperation of an Irishman down on his luck and unable to make a living, the younger Hobbs thought of a new scheme.

Having been turned down to work at the Ice Company by the senior Hobbs, Daniel agreed to hire him unbeknownst to his father and under the stipulation that he would swindle the unsuspecting Tad at poker. Readily, Gilbert accepted Daniel's terms having little respect for Tad whom he had seen on occasion at Jake's, viewing him as nothing more than an egocentric, well-bred aristocrat who had more money than brains.

For months, the two of them had successfully swindled Tad out of his allowance. And as annoying as this was to Tad--only when he thought Miranda had become interested in a man he viewed as beneath her--did he decide to take matters in his own hands. It was one thing to lose at cards to the ill-mannered foul tempered Irishman, but it was quite another for the woman he had pined over for years to show an interest in the man he despised.

Convinced that if it hadn't been for Gilbert, none of this would have ever happened, Tad desperately searched for Gilbert to prevent him from ever telling Miranda what had happened. Both he and Daniel continued their hunt with both men hating O'Flaherty for different reasons, and both hell-bent to silent the Irishman. Perhaps they might have been successful too, if it hadn't been for the aide of Miranda Brown and Felicity Phelps.

Following a long humid day at the orphanage in early June, Miranda and Felicity decided to take a leisurely ride through Central Park, a popular meeting place for women to gather during the day. Although the park was built for all classes, the majority of those in attendance were those of wealth, dressed in the latest fashions with matching hats and parasols to protect their delicate skin. As the Honeycutt's open carriage passed those walking, Felicity and Miranda seated across from one another would occasionally nod their heads to those they recognized, all the while chatting amongst themselves freely in hushed tones.

"Why is it Miranda, you look so forlorn on such a lovely day? Are you and Tad having a spat?"

Softly shaking her head while pretending to be interested in the manicured gardens to avoid eye contact with Felicity, Miranda softly answered, "No. I almost wished we had and then perhaps it would explain Tad's distance."

Knowing that such a comment would only spark more questions from her friend, Miranda quickly added. "Of course, with Sarah and Michael's desire to leave early now that they are in their new home and having it redecorated, it's perfectly understandable. Yet, I can't help but feel Tad's grateful to be leaving so soon."

While adjusting her gloves, Felicity said reassuringly, "Surely you must be mistaken. Perhaps Tad has found living with his father and stepmother more demanding than he had anticipated and he just needs time to adjust to his new life."

"Or, perhaps he has discovered we really aren't suited for one another and doesn't know how to let me down gently." Miranda's voice trailed off, obviously too upset to continue.

"I cannot believe a man like Tad, who has openly been smitten with you for years, would alter those feelings for no apparent reason. It makes no sense. Are you certain there isn't something else troubling him?" Felicity asked, no longer able to conceal her concern.

Shaking her head in frustration, Miranda said, "I honestly don't know. I've asked him several times and he always says the same, 'What could possibly be wrong?' In truth, at first I thought he was hiding something from me, and now it's as if he avoids me so he won't have to answer my annoying questions, though I can hardly blame him. Heck-fire, I'm tired of hearing them myself! But I can't seem to stop myself from asking when I know something isn't right."

Not sure how to comfort Miranda, Felicity sighed and said, "Well, it is peculiar. However, before you give up on him entirely, why not have a talk about your concerns with Sarah. She seems like such a lovely woman."

Leaning closer to Felicity, Miranda strained to keep her tone just above a whisper. "Sarah is a very loving and kind woman, but I'm not about to ask for her help regarding this matter. What am I to say? Can you please see to it that Tad is more attentive to me? Absolutely not! This is one matter I cannot discus with Tad's stepmother, no matter how close I feel to her personally. It's already so humiliating to be with them nightly. You can't imagine how embarrassing it is to see the looks they give one another as they witness the change in Tad's demeanor toward me."

"Oh dear, I had no idea it had escalated that far. Surely there must be a way of finding out what's troubling Tad, without appearing to be worried about your relationship with him."

Sighing in frustration, and on the verge of tears Miranda softly asked, "Can we please not discuss Tad anymore today? Why don't you explain to me again, why it is that you think Mr. Sterling comes around almost everyday instead?"

Miranda knew that asking any question about the Sterlings' would preoccupy Felicity's mind, so she added, "It really is quite puzzling to me. Not that he comes to the orphanage so often, but rather when he is there, Mr. Sterling is jovial and friendly, unlike later in the day when he and Lavinia arrive at the Honeycutt's and his disposition is so solemn. It really is such a shame. If you saw how he and Lavinia sniped at each other every night, you would just keel over in embarrassment."

Hearing such a distressing comment from her friend, Felicity frowned. "Oh, I really hate hearing such things, Miranda. It is strange, considering our history in England and all, but over the past few months, my opinion of James has altered considerably. In fact, I have grown very fond of him. His generosity is immense; food, clothing, offering the orphan's apprenticeships at his shipping company, and now, James has contacted business associates with political connections to put pressure on Congress again to help orphanages like ours. Isn't that so kind of him?"

"It is indeed. I just find his actions peculiar is all."

"Peculiar? Why, for goodness sakes?"

"Not that he wants to donate his time and money, but that he does so much without Lavinia knowing anything. When I see Mr. Sterling at the Honeycutt's, he rarely speaks of seeing me during the day. As a matter of fact, I have gotten the distinct impression he prefers no one knows of his visits to the orphanage. If in passing, it is mentioned that we saw one another earlier in the day, James is very quick to change the subject."

"Well I'm sure it's simply to avoid any unpleasantness with Lavinia. You and I both know how trying she can be, if provoked."

"Precisely why I can't help but wonder why he would keep something like this from his wife." Seeing the look of confusion on Felicity's face, Miranda quickly continued. "Don't you see? By not telling her of his visits to the orphanage and his generous donations, with her way of thinking, she would probably assume he had ulterior motives or was deliberately trying to do something behind her back. So why go to all the trouble of keeping something so innocent from her, especially when she is bound to notice the familiarity of you three?"

"Ah, I see your point. Having been the recipient of her nasty disposition, I wouldn't wish that on another living soul."

"Precisely my point. Why deliberately provoke her? It just doesn't make any sense to me."

"Well, when you put it like that, it doesn't make sense to me either. Surely, James must have a good reason . . ." Felicity's voice trailed off, her voice barely above a whisper as she gazed out to those milling about Central Park. Judging by the look of concern on her friend's face, Miranda knew instinctively that Felicity was deeply troubled, and rather than push her, she waited patiently for Felicity to think it out.

"You know what troubles me too? When we were in England, Lavinia risked everything to be with James and now that she is his wife, it's almost as if she loathes him as much as she did Benjamin." Shaking her head, Felicity added. "How sad, to be so miserable all the time."

Hearing such a befitting description of Lavinia Sterling, Miranda nearly broke out laughing, yet seeing the concerned look in Felicity's eyes she said, "Dearest Felicity, only you would feel sorry for someone as nasty and evil as Lavinia Sterling."

Miranda's last comment went unanswered as Felicity gasped and pointed. "Oh dear! Is that man accosting that poor woman in broad daylight?"

Startled by such a comment, Miranda immediately turned her attention to where Felicity was pointing. From their vantage point, both of them witnessed a red-haired woman struggling to be freed by a well-dressed man in a top hat and coat. As their coach drew nearer, the blood drained from Miranda's face as her eyes drifted to a familiar man standing beside a parked coach only a few feet from where the man and woman were scuffling with one another. Even from this distance, she knew immediately it was Tad at the carriage. Confused as to why he would stand by watching, doing nothing as the other man grasped hold of the woman's arm, yelling at her, Miranda's heart began to race.

Sheepishly she looked at Felicity to see if she had witnessed Tad too. Judging by the surprised look on Felicity's face, Miranda knew she had. Her eyes trailed back toward the disturbing scene just as they were passing them on the trail. Horrified, she heard Daniel Hobbs yelling, while shaking his assailant. "Tell me where he is, damn it!"

Unable to keep their eyes off the scene, both women gasped when they realized the woman being accosted was Margaret-Anne O'Flaherty, as they were now able to see her face for the first time. Shrinking from sight and turning their parasols to avoid from being seen, Miranda whispered to Felicity, "What should we do?"

Without hesitating, Felicity hoarsely whispered to Montgomery, "Pull over at once!"

Following his orders, Montgomery pulled on the reins and the buggy came to a halt. Waving her hand, motioning Miranda to slide over, Felicity discreetly took the seat beside her. Then tilting her parasol to avoid being seen, she whispered, "Let's see what Tad and Mr. Hobbs want with Maggie first, shall we?"

Nodding her head in agreement, Miranda craned her neck to look discretely at Tad and the others.

Within seconds, both men leapt inside their coach and drove off in the opposite direction, toward the Boulevard. Noticing how distraught Maggie was, both women hastily left their buggy and called to her. "Miss O'Flaherty, are you all right?" asked Miranda as she ran to the woman who was crying.

Upon seeing Miranda and Felicity, Maggie quickly wiped her face. It was clear she was not happy to see them, and was either hiding something or extremely frightened at seeing them. Nervously, the servant managed to smile over at them and said, "Why Miss Brown and Mrs. Myles, what a surprise to see you today."

Ignoring the woman's attempts at concealing her encounter, Miranda boldly asked, "Why on earth was Mr. Hobbs yelling at you like that?"

The blood drained from her face hearing Miranda's question and immediately the frightened woman looked down as she tried to pass them on the narrow sidewalk. "Please Miss Brown, if you don't mind I have lots of work to do this afternoon."

"Maggie, why don't you allow us to escort you to the Carmidy's. That is where you're headed isn't it?" Felicity said softly in a comforting tone.

Nodding nervously, Maggie said, "Yes, Ma'am. But there's no need to be troubling you both like that. I can make it just fine on me own."

From the terror in Maggie's eyes, Miranda knew that the woman's fear stemmed from something deeper than the confrontation she had just witnessed. Following Felicity's lead, Miranda gingerly took Maggie by the elbow and softly whispered, "Nonsense, Maggie. We were heading over to see you anyway. So you see it's no trouble at all."

Reluctantly, Margaret-Anne entered the buggy while Miranda frowned disapprovingly at the Honeycutt's driver. "Take us to the Carmidy's at once, Montgomery," she ordered sternly, annoyed that Montgomery hadn't assisted them back into the carriage as he normally would have.

"Yes, miss," Montgomery replied boldly, seemingly not the least bit interested that he had annoyed her.

Never had the servant been so insolent before and Miranda's cheeks burned with anger. Rather than address his insubordinate behavior now, Miranda decided to deal with him later, and she stepped into the carriage. As she took her seat, her eyes stayed focused on Margaret-Anne, who sat stoic in the seat next to Felicity. *Dear God, why are you so frightened?* Miranda wondered, noticing the servant's hands were trembling in her lap while deliberately avoiding eye contact with either of them.

Needing time to think herself, Miranda also glanced at the scenery of Central Park, her mind whirled as she tried to make some sense of what she had just witnessed. *Why would Tad watch as his friend practically assaulted Maggie? And why would Montgomery react in such a disrespectful manner?* Having no answers to either of her questions, she shook her head. *Has everyone taken complete leave of their senses?* Slowly the shock began to wear off and she found her temper rising recalling Daniel's words. *"Tell me where he is, damn it!"* Her mind raced for answers. *Where who is?*

Intuitively she knew that Tad's strange behavior to her of late, and Daniel yelling at this woman was related, yet she couldn't put a connection between them. Mystified, Miranda glanced at Margaret-Anne again, and from the look of determination on the frightened woman's face, it was clear the servant did not intend to volunteer an explanation for what had just happened. More confused than ever, Miranda slowly glanced at Felicity. Seeing her friend shake her head disapprovingly, Miranda again resigned to wait, but vowed to herself that before she left the Carmidy's today her questions would be answered.

Once the carriage pulled up in front of the house, much to Miranda's surprise, Margaret-Anne leapt from the carriage and dashed toward the front door. Whispering to the stunned Miranda, Felicity said, "Why would she run off like that when clearly she is no longer in danger? Don't you find all of this extremely peculiar?"

"Indeed I do. And by hook or crook, I will get to the bottom of these queer goings on." Ignoring, Felicity's frown, Miranda went directly into the Carmidy's home to find the distraught servant removing her hat.

"Tend to your affairs Margaret-Anne and report directly back to the parlor."

Not waiting for a reply from the servant, knowing her way around the home she and her father had lived in from time to time over the past three years, Miranda went directly to the parlor. As Felicity walked through the open door, Miranda motioned her into the parlor where they took a seat and began whispering amongst themselves.

"I know you are upset, seeing Tad there and all. However, please keep in mind that Maggie has already been badgered and manhandled once today. Perhaps what she needs is another form of coaxing."

Perturbed that her friend felt it necessary to point out the obvious and hearing the servant's footsteps returning she said, "My, but it is stuffy in here with the curtains drawn and no air circulating." Seeing Margaret-Anne in the doorway, Miranda directed her attention to the servant. "Maggie, dear, why are all the windows boarded up? Surely, it must be unbearable for you to work inside all day with no fresh air."

"Oh I don't mind none, Miss Brown."

Smiling sweetly back at her Miranda said, "Well in the future see to it that some air circulates, dear. We wouldn't want Joshua and Elise to return to a musty dank home now would we?"

"No miss. With the cool air of the night, I find that opening the windows then helps to keep the home cooler, but if you prefer I can do both."

"No. As long as you give the home a good airing out that should be fine," Miranda said while removing her hat.

"Maggie dear, I know you weren't expecting any visitors this afternoon, but would it be too much of a bother to ask for some refreshments? Suddenly I find I'm parched," Felicity said while smiling at the servant.

Turning her attention to Miranda she asked, "Miss Brown, would you be wanting to wet yer whistle too?"

"Why yes. Thank you Maggie," Miranda replied. "A nice glass of lemonade would be most welcoming."

Without replying, the flushed and obviously upset woman turned and went down a darkened hall. No longer able to hear the woman's footsteps and feeling reassured that they could not be overheard, Felicity leaned over to Miranda. In a hushed whisper she said, "Not that I'm doubting her, but if she opens the windows at night, then why when Benjamin and I drove past here a few nights past, did the house look all boarded up?"

Shaking her head in agreement, Miranda whispered, "It was the same when father and I drove home from visiting Michael and Sarah's new home the night before last."

Hearing the servant's footsteps, the two sat back in their chairs and watched as Margaret-Anne entered the parlor and placed the tray on a table between them. With trembling hands and seemingly more flushed than before, she handed a glass of lemonade to Felicity.

"Perhaps you wouldn't mind opening the curtains for us now, Maggie. It really is most stifling in here."

As the servant walked across the room and over to the windows, Miranda quickly looked at Felicity who was trying to get her attention by pointing to her drink. Frowning, trying to ascertain what it was that troubled Felicity, Miranda discreetly shrugged her shoulders as if to tell her friend she didn't understand.

As the light filtered into the room when the heavy velvet curtains were being opened, Miranda's eyes immediately went to the tray. Glancing at the pitcher filled with sliced lemons in the drink and a single glass, and not seeing anything out of the ordinary, Miranda's eyes trailed back toward Felicity and discreetly shook her head, still not following. While Margaret-Anne was busy opening the other set of curtains, Felicity mouthed back to her, "No ice."

Acknowledging her friend with a nod, Miranda's mind began to race. *Why would no ice be significant?* Then as if a candle had been lit in a darkened room, Miranda began seeing the connection. Recalling Daniel's menacing words, "Where is he?" She knew instinctively the *He* was Gilbert. *But why would both Daniel and Tad want Gilbert?* Tad had repeatedly reassured her that all was resolved between Gilbert and him, yet after witnessing Mr. Hobbs threaten Maggie in broad daylight, she knew he had been lying to her. *If he has been lying to me now, what else has he been lying to me about?*

Such thoughts distressed her and to hide just how upset she was, Miranda rubbed her brow and closed her eyes, as if bothered by the sudden light. Scolding herself for being so sensitive, Miranda took a deep breath while pushing back her insecurities, determined to get to the truth once and for all.

As Margaret-Anne approached, Miranda regaining full control of her emotions obligingly said, "Oh that's much better. Thank you Maggie." Seeing a faint smile cross the servant's lips as she returned to pour more of the beverage, Miranda frowned slightly while accepting it. "Oh dear, don't you have any ice?" she whined, in an exaggerated sigh.

"No, miss."

"Why that surprises me, considering your brother Gilbert delivers ice and all. Surely, you would think he would see to it that his sister was never without." Miranda looked at Felicity, in hope that her friend would continue the conversation in this direction. "Don't you agree?"

"Why yes of course. I had nearly forgotten that Gilbert and Maggie are brother and sister."

Delighted that Felicity was following her lead, Miranda closely watched Margaret-Anne's every move. From her fidgeting and flushed cheeks, it was clear the servant was becoming more distraught, especially when speaking about her brother Gilbert. *Yes, indeed. This definitely had something to do with Gilbert. But what?* No longer buying Tad's explanation of cheating at cards, or Gilbert's interest in her, Miranda's mind began to race for a reasonable explanation. Thinking of none, she knew more questions were needed about Gilbert.

"You know, now that I think of it, I haven't seen him delivering ice at the orphanage lately. Have you Miranda?" Felicity asked as if reading Miranda's thoughts.

Delighted that she was going to be able to question Margaret-Anne further, Miranda continued the charade of cat and mouse and thought pensively for a moment before replying.

"Why no. Now that you mention it, I haven't." Directing her attention back to the servant, Miranda asked sweetly, "I trust your brother is well and that everything is all right, Maggie?"

"Yes, quite well. Thank you, miss for asking." Anxiously looking between them, and obviously looking for a way to end their visit, Maggie said, "Beggin' your pardon, miladies, I have chores that really should be attended too. So, I'll be makin' my leave."

"Nonsense," Felicity said. "As we said earlier, we have come here today to see how you are getting along." Pointing to the settee across from her and Miranda, Felicity gestured for her to join them politely. "Come sit and chat for a spell." Seeing hesitation at her request, she quickly added, "I insist."

Obediently Maggie did as she was told, but sat at the edge of her seat all the while nervously patting the front of her skirt. "That was very fine of you both, but Mr. Honeycutt and his Missus drops by every now and then to check up on me," she said timidly.

"How thoughtful of them," Miranda cooed. "And does your brother drop by as well?" she asked raising her eyebrow, determined to direct the conversation back to Gilbert.

"No, Miss," Maggie answered in a low hushed tone looking down at the carpet.

Feeling confident the servant was lying, recalling how her slaves had always done the same when trying to cover up something they had done, Miranda continued to bait her. "He doesn't? Why that truly surprises me. Surely, Mr. Honeycutt wouldn't have objections to you having a visitor from time to time. Shall I speak to him regarding this matter, Maggie?"

Hearing Mr. Honeycutt being brought into this, the servant quickly glanced at Miranda and shook her head. "Oh I wish you wouldn't miss. Mr. Honeycutt never said I couldn't have visitors."

"Then why, pray tell, wouldn't your own brother come to see you then?" Miranda asked, raising her eyebrow. Pausing to give the woman time to think, and seeing she was not going to answer her, Miranda leaned forward and in a concerned voice asked, "Are you certain everything is alright Maggie?"

In a soft tone, Felicity added, "You know Maggie, both Miss Brown and I mean you no harm. We ask you these questions out of concern for your welfare. Especially since we haven't seen Gilbert for at least a fortnight and now you are saying he doesn't even come to check on his own sister."

Still Margaret-Anne refused to answer, so Miranda tried another tactic. "Felicity, since Maggie doesn't seem to trust us, perhaps what we should do is take matters in our own hands. We both agree that something is amiss here, yet I can't for the life of me put my finger on it . . . Perhaps the wisest thing to do is contact the authorities."

Playing along with Miranda's facade, Felicity said solemnly, "Well perhaps you're right. After all, we did witness Mr. Hobbs practically assaulting our Maggie right there in Central Park. We can tell the authorities that we heard him yelling, 'Where is he?' That is what you heard isn't it Miranda?"

"Why yes, of course. But if we go to the authorities, won't that bring more people questioning poor Maggie about her brother's whereabouts?" Turning her attention to Margaret-Anne, she whispered, "Maggie, we both know Mr. Hobbs was looking for Gilbert. Do you really want more people looking for him too?"

Being asked such a question obviously upset Maggie judging by the color of her cheeks, which now matched her red hair. Avoiding eye contact, she mumbled, "Miss, please, I really should be gettin' back to my chores."

Leaning closer to the distraught servant, Miranda gingerly held her hand and patted it gingerly. "Alright Maggie, we won't pressure you, or go to the authorities just yet. But it's very hard not to be concerned, especially when we see how upset you are. How can we make you see that you can trust us?"

Shaking her head from side to side, and pulling away from Miranda, Maggie said, "There is nothing to talk about, miss."

Before Miranda had the opportunity to further persuade the obviously frightened woman to speak, a sound from the rear of the house alerted her that the back door had just closed. Rather than react to the sound, or acknowledge she had even heard it, Miranda looked at Margaret-Anne and smiled sweetly.

"As you wish, Maggie. But please remember what I said earlier. Mrs. Myles and I mean you no harm and if we can be of help, we will." Turning her attention to Felicity, Miranda added. "Well I really must get you back to the orphanage if I'm to be on time for dinner at the Honeycutt's."

"Oh my, where has the time gone?" Felicity said, looking at her watch pendent pinned to her collar. "Mrs. Honeycutt will never forgive me if I detain you."

Within moments, the two women made their hasty good-byes, aware that Margaret-Anne was watching them intently as they made their way to the carriage.

As soon as they reached the rig, Miranda sternly whispered to the driver who stood beside the carriage door. "I know you saw who left through the back door, Montgomery, so don't you dare try to deny it. If you value your position, you will follow him at once. Have I made myself clear?"

The educated Negro driver had always intimidated Miranda from the first moment she had met him years earlier, but never as he did now. His dark eyes were cold and piercing and sent shivers up her spine, yet she forced herself to show no fear, returning his icy glare.

"Montgomery, I'm warning you. Either you do precisely what I say or you will be looking for a new position by sundown. Now you tell me, what's it going to be?" she asked, while turning to wave at Margaret-Anne and praying silently that Montgomery would do as she asked.

Relief filled her as she heard the servant reply, "As you wish, miss. But Mr. Honeycutt is not going to like this."

Saying not a word, Felicity followed Miranda into the rig. Once they were on their way, she whispered, "Are you sure this is wise? Before long the sun will set and we won't be able to see a thing."

Shaking her head, Miranda said defiantly, "Nope. But how else are we to get to the truth?" Turning to look along the street edge, she squinted against the bright sun that was starting to set. Placing her hand above her brow, she looked frantically from side to side hoping to see a man hiding in the bushes.

"How did you know Montgomery had seen anything? And if he did, how did you know it was a man?" Felicity asked, while looking also.

Nervously Miranda chuckled. "Well, in all the years I've known Montgomery, never has he stood by the rig waiting. Normally he sits on the buckboard. I just guessed he would have noticed something peculiar and had stepped down to investigate. And I was right wasn't I? As for a man, I just figured it had to be Gilbert. As soon as I heard the door, it made sense to me why Margaret-Anne was acting so strangely. He was probably listening to our every word, and when we threatened notifying the authorities he took off."

"Yes, I tend to believe that was the case too. But why the urgency in following him tonight? If we should find him, have you thought what we're supposed to do then? We still haven't a clue as to why Tad and Mr. Hobbs are after him."

"I'm not sure . . ." Pausing to look at her surroundings, she directed her attention to Montgomery. "Why are we heading back to Central Park?"

"You said to follow that gentlemen, didn't you, miss?"

Squinting and looking straight ahead, Miranda couldn't see anything. "Where, Montgomery?" she whispered hoarsely to him. Without responding, Montgomery began pulling softly on the reins and drew the rig to the side of the road, just as they entered Central Park. Then stepping down off the buckboard, he opened the door to the rig, and whispered, "Miss, if I can see him, he can see you. Step out so I can latch up the cover."

Extending her hand so he could help her out of the carriage, Miranda looked into the driver's eyes and softly said, "Thank you, Montgomery. Will you kindly tell me where he is precisely? I promise I'll be discreet," she said reassuringly.

"To my left, between Boulevard over yonder and that evergreen." Nodding politely to her, he then extended a hand to Felicity who took it and stepped out of the carriage as well.

As Montgomery lifted and secured the canvas roof of the hansom carriage, both women waited by the side of the rig and began adjusting their gloves and parasols, discreetly looking in the direction Montgomery had said Gilbert was hiding. From where they stood sheltered by the rig, they could not see anything but shadows around the evergreen and a trail of rigs that had pulled up along Boulevard and the entrance to Central Park. Frustrated, they watched as more carriages passed, unable to see the man hiding among the bushes.

"Are you sure he's still there Montgomery?" Miranda whispered. Peering across the street into the park she gasped. "Wait, I think I see him . . . Yes right next to the tall blue spruce! What is he doing? Is he going to cross Boulevard and head the other way? Oh dear, we'll lose him if he does. See him Felicity? It is Gilbert, isn't it?"

"Miss, stay behind the rig or he'll see you," Montgomery scolded, offering his hand to Felicity to help her back inside the covered carriage.

As Felicity entered, her eyes scanned the area and seeing what the others had, she whispered, "I see him. Yes, I do believe it is Mr. O'Flaherty."

Gazing around the back of the cab, Miranda shooed her driver away as he tried to assist her into the cab as well. "Wait Montgomery!"

As the three watched--Gilbert--who was in full view, darted across the busy street and into oncoming traffic. Just as he did, shouting from another carriage rang out. "There he is!"

The three of them watched in horror as the man on foot began running with the carriage following closely behind. Miranda, so caught up in seeing Gilbert trying to outrun the carriage, held her gloved hands to her mouth. "Run Gilbert," she whispered, unable to move from where she stood, seeing the driver crack his whip to force the horses to run faster as they bore down on Gilbert trying to escape.

Her heart beat quickened in fear and she screamed into her gloves biting her own finger, seeing the horse and carriage run over Gilbert. Turning from the scene and leaning into the carriage, she shook her head as tears ran down her cheeks. "Dear God, no! They've killed him."

"Hush up miss, or they will see you!" Montgomery ordered in a hoarse whisper.

Turning toward to the street, she saw the carriage that had trampled Gilbert make a sharp turn, which would pass directly by them. Holding her breath, Miranda knelt down behind the back wheel of the buggy next to Montgomery. From her vantage point she recognized the driver and his passenger at once and gasped. The driver, Daniel Hobbs, so busy maneuvering the rig onto the road that led into the park, did not notice her, nor did his passenger, Tad. Both men, preoccupied at leaving the scene of their crime and assessing if they had been successful in running the man over, called out to one another as the hansom cab sped past them.

"Is he moving? Did we get him?" yelled Daniel.

"We got him alright," replied Tad as he pulled himself back into the covered front of the cab and lowered his hat shielding his face from any onlookers that might see him. "Now get the hell out of here, before we are spotted!"

Shaken to her core, witnessing such a deliberate and brutal attack, Miranda looked at her driver and asked, "What should we do?"

Standing he whispered, "Nothing! We wait here for a few minutes to make sure Master Honeycutt doesn't return then we head back to the orphanage and forget what we just saw."

"No!" spat Miranda, jerking away from her driver who was trying to get her back inside the carriage just as Felicity stepped out.

"I agree, Miranda. Come follow me . . ." Before the Negro driver could stop the two women, they dashed across the street and cut across the park to the other road where they found Gilbert moaning softly on the side of the street. As other carriages passed--apparently not seeing the injured man--the two women on the verge of hysteria began to run to him but stopped suddenly seeing the shadow of another man step out from behind another blue spruce.

"Miranda and Felicity, I wouldn't do that if I were you!"

Startled to hear their names being called, the two frightened women grasped hold of the other's hand.

"Who's there?" called Miranda, adjusting her eyes to the dusk. As the man drew nearer, they both sighed in relief seeing James Sterling approaching them.

"Oh James, it's you. Thank heavens! There has been a dreadful accident and we need your assistance," Felicity urgently called to him. "Our iceman, Gilbert O'Flaherty, has just been run down. Please help us," she sobbed.

By this time Montgomery had joined the two women, stood off to the side and nodded to Mr. Sterling. Judging by the look of concern on the hired help's face, Miranda felt it necessary to try to explain. "Mr. Sterling, I insisted Montgomery bring us here . . . And as you can see it's a good thing we did. Time is of the essence if we are to help Mr. O'Flaherty. Won't you please come see what we can do for him?" she begged, turning to go to Gilbert who was still lying curled up along the side of the road.

"Miranda I beseech you, turn around. You and Felicity go back to your carriage at once and forget everything that has happened here tonight."

Stomping her foot, Miranda said defiantly, "No! Are you mad? That man was injured on purpose. For all I know he could be dying and I will not turn my back on him. Now either you assist me or I'll do it myself. But by God, I will not just stand by and watch him die and do nothing!"

"Please James," Felicity chimed in with her friend, looking at him sympathetically. "Won't you please help him? Surely, you saw how he was run down."

Taking a drag of his rolled cigarette and then dropping the butt to the ground and putting it out with his boot, James looked at Felicity then at Montgomery and said, "Help me get him over to my cab." He pointed to a carriage parked on Boulevard not far from where Gilbert lay.

"No, sir. I will not do that and risk being brought into this mess."

"Oh but you could be persuaded to, if the price were right. Couldn't you Montgomery?" James proclaimed in a suggestive tone while glaring at the man, as only a man can, who knows another could be bought. Not waiting for his response James anxiously directed his attention back to Felicity. "You and Miranda wait in the coach while we tend to your friend, Felicity." Seeing the two of them hesitate, he said, "Please. I promise, I'll take care of everything."

"Fine, but take him back to the orphanage so we can tend to his wounds. That is if he's still alive," she meekly said.

"That's too risky! What if he doesn't pull through?" protested James.

Glancing at Miranda then back at James, Felicity said, "Well, if Mr. O'Flaherty doesn't pull through, I will be forced to tell the authorities everything we saw. Including the fact that you saw Mr. Hobbs and Tad run that poor man down in cold blood just as we did, and did nothing to stop them. On the other hand, if I can help him, all will be forgotten, now wouldn't it?" From her look, James knew she meant what she said.

"Fine! I'll follow closely behind you, but there was little I could do against a horse and carriage."

"Of course. How unkind of me to suggest otherwise," she added apologetically while turning to Miranda. "Come dearest, let Mr. Sterling tend to Gilbert."

Slowly the two of them turned to leave as James and Montgomery walked toward Gilbert who occasionally moaned. Hearing the man yelp in pain as they carried him to the Sterling's rig, soothingly Felicity said, "Don't fret Miranda dear, I'm sure Gilbert will be just fine."

Reaching their rig, Miranda looked at her friend. "How could Tad do such a thing? Why he's nothing but a cold-blooded murderer!"

"Now Miranda, you know Tad was not driving!"

"That much is true. But he didn't do anything to stop that fiendish friend of his either. Why, it was as if he too wanted to run Gilbert down as well? But why?"

Not having an answer for her friend, Felicity helped the distraught Miranda safely inside the coach and promptly closed the blinds to prevent anyone passing by from noticing her before she took a seat next to her friend. As the two women waited for Montgomery to return, they both trembled in the darkened carriage, reliving the incident in their minds. Unable to accept what they had witnessed, nor understand how two men of good standing could be capable of such a dastardly deed, the two sat dumbfounded searching for a reasonable explanation. But knowing there was none, Miranda closed her eyes and softly wept. Ashamed that she had once allowed Tad to hold her in his arms and eagerly kiss him, she began to sob.

"Oh Felicity, how could he do such a thing? I hate him . . . I tell you I hate him!"

"Shh, you're just upset," she said, tenderly trying to comfort her friend, but Felicity too found it hard not to despise a man capable of such treachery.

~ Thirteen ~

Revealed Truths

In the middle of the night Felicity tiptoed into her husband's office which had been converted to a temporary shelter for Gilbert, to check on Miranda. As Felicity had thought, Miranda was once again asleep in a chair beside her patient. Inhaling deeply, she shook her head disapprovingly.

From the first night they had brought the unconscious Gilbert to the orphanage, Miranda took it upon herself to tend to his every need, as if she were responsible for his well being. Despite her and James trying to explain she had done nothing to cause this, Miranda stubbornly remained by Gilbert's side.

In the past when Benjamin had been called out of town on business, Miranda stayed with Felicity, so when a note was sent to the Honeycutt's that she was staying for a few days with Felicity, no one was alarmed or suspicious. It was as if the whole incident of Gilbert being run over never happened.

Disheartened by such thoughts, Felicity drew closer to Miranda and noticed the rolled up bandage in her lap. Realizing Miranda must have wrapped Gilbert's ribs again, Felicity gently bent over and tapped her friend on the shoulder.

Immediately Miranda jerked awake. Seeing Felicity, she smiled wearily. "You gave me such a fright."

"Miranda dear, you need some real rest. Please come to bed. I'm sure Gilbert won't wake up and if he does we'll hear him."

Stubbornly Miranda shook her head. "I can't Felicity. Don't you see, if he does come to, and finds himself in a strange place, he could cause himself serious danger."

"Oh Miranda, you heard the doctor, Gilbert sustained a serious blow to the head besides breaking several ribs, and he might never come around. Surely you staying by his side day and night is not doing him or you any good."

"Don't say such a thing! I know he'll pull through this. He just has to."

"Sweetheart, all we can do is pray for him, but I'm genuinely worried about you, too. Surely you not eating or sleeping can't be of any help to Gilbert now," Felicity whispered.

"Oh Felicity, I know you mean well, but please let me stay here. Helping Gilbert soothes me as I've told you. I couldn't save Joseph, but maybe I can save him."

Kissing her friend on the forehead, Felicity nodded. "Very well, Miranda, just please be aware that what happened to Gilbert is no more your fault than what happened to poor Joseph."

Tiptoeing out of the room, Felicity watched as Miranda stood up and changed the cloth on Gilbert's forehead. Sighing, she closed the door behind her, saying a silent prayer. *Dear Lord, please heal Gilbert, not just for his sake but for Miranda's too.*

Inside Benjamin's study, Miranda tenderly wiped Gilbert's brow with a cool compress. Placing it over his forehead, she brushed her fingers through his hair, and whispered, "Oh please wake up Gilbert and let me see those beautiful green eyes of yours."

Not feeling the least bit apprehensive being so familiar with his body, having cared for his every need for the past three days, her fingers traced his face and she spoke again to him softly. "Please wake up and tell me why Tad would do such a thing to you."

Absent-mindedly, she caressed his forearm with her fingertips, admiring his muscular arms and chest. Reaching for his hand, she held it in hers tenderly. "You have such strong hands Gilbert." Stroking it tenderly, she placed his hand back by his side and returned to the chair she had become so familiar with. Feeling stiff and tired, Miranda stretched her neck and rubbed it. Gaining no relief, she leaned her head back into the chair, reliving the scene of the accident again in her mind, hating Tad more as every day passed.

She sighed heavily, closed her eyes, and felt a tear ran down her cheek. "Dear God, please let him live," she prayed. Then glancing back at Gilbert and seeing his green eyes staring at her, Miranda jumped from her seat. "Oh Gilbert, you're awake."

Instantly, she leaned over him. "Don't be alarmed. You're safe at the orphanage, no one can hurt you. Are you in pain?" she whispered.

Trying to lift himself from the couch, he winced, and seeing the bandage around his ribcage he looked at Miranda. "Aye . . . How long have I been here?"

"Three days. Please don't try to move, Gilbert, you have several broken ribs and a broken leg. You'll only hurt yourself more."

"Why are you here?"

Softly Miranda explained how she and Felicity had witnessed him being run down and how they had brought him there for his safety. Seeing no reaction to her explanation, she asked, "Are you thirsty? Can I get you something?"

"Aye."

Miranda immediately went to the table and poured him a drink of water. Returning to his side, she tenderly slipped one hand beneath his head while bringing the glass to his mouth. Their eyes locked onto one another and instinctively Miranda assured him again. "I mean you no harm Gilbert, honestly. I only want to help you."

Sipping at the water, Gilbert leaned his head back onto the pillow and whispered, "I don't need help, especially from you."

Miranda had expected such a reaction, but hearing it didn't make it easier, and her eyes smarted. "I don't know why Tad and his friend did such a despicable thing to you, Gilbert, but I swear to you, I had nothing to do with it."

Closing his eyes to her, he asked, "Who's Joseph?"

Miranda gasped, realizing that he must have been awake when Felicity had been in the room. Realizing she owed him no explanation to her personal life, but feeling obligated to tell him, she sheepishly said, "Joseph was our slave and my half brother. He died because I tried to help him to freedom."

Gilbert glanced at her and smiled faintly. "That's reassuring, lass, since I find myself depending on you too."

Comprehending that he was trying to add levity to the situation, she returned his smile. Suddenly aware that if he had been awake to hear her and Felicity's conversation, he must have been awake when she had run her fingers through his hair and caressed his face. She sheepishly looked at him. "You should have let me know you were awake."

"What was I supposed to think? I wake up, me head's throbbing, it hurts to breathe, and there you are sitting by my side, sleeping in a chair. Hell, I thought I was some prisoner."

"You're no prisoner Gilbert. We're only trying to care for your wounds and keep you safe but I'm afraid you are a wanted man for the murder of a David Sullivan."

Obviously upset at hearing that, Gilbert glared at Miranda. "I didn't kill me bud, your lordship's mate did! That's why they tried to kill me, to keep me mouth shut."

Confused by his statement and seeing he was obviously in pain trying to speak, Miranda tried to console him. "Gilbert, you mustn't overdo it, there will be time later to explain . . ."

"No. I did not kill me mate. Hobbs did. You believe me, don't you?"

Miranda had no reason to believe him other than the urgency she saw in his eyes as he spoke, and she nodded. "I believe you Gilbert. Just please rest now, and tomorrow, you can . . ."

"I've rested for three days, lass."

Clearly, he needed to explain everything, so Miranda sat and listened to the events that led to David Sullivan's demise as he spoke in a strained voice, from the pain in his ribs. Miranda was shocked how forthright Gilbert had been, including his arrangement with Daniel Hobbs to cheat money from the non-suspecting Tad. Stunned, Miranda sighed and looked at him, asking why he would have done such a thing to begin with, not in accusing voice, but rather as a means to fully understand the situation. As she listened, she came to realize that Gilbert had taken the job for the sole purpose to making a fresh start for him and his sister in New York.

"Gilbert, are you telling me that Mr. Hobbs killed this man, for the sole purpose to silence you? And for you to continue to extort money from Tad?"

"Silence aye, but I told him to find another patsy to rob his lordship, I was through with the lot of them. Then after his lordship came to, Hobb's acted as if Tad had killed him."

As hard as Miranda tried not to appear accusing, she found herself disgusted by such deceit and asked, "And you said nothing?"

"Don't be judging me, missy. Just leave me be. You got what you wanted, so run along and tell your beloved he was duped by his mate and then maybe the two of them will leave me and my sister alone."

Stunned beyond belief, Miranda shook her head in denial. "First off, Tad is not my beloved and secondly . . ."

Before she could finish Gilbert--obviously in pain by the look in his eyes--stubbornly said, "You all are alike, the whole lot of you are nothin' but liars."

"How dare you say such a mean-spirited thing to me. I know you are hurt and angry, but that gives you no cause to insinuate I'm a liar. Don't you understand Felicity and I have placed ourselves in grave danger by harboring a fugitive, and caring for you? Which we gladly did to save you from the injustices that we witnessed."

Miranda, exhausted and overwhelmed by the accounts of the death of an innocent man, and shocked by the actions of both Tad and Gilbert, looked at him with contempt.

"Furthermore, don't you dare pass judgment on my character when you allowed another man think he was capable of murder. Not that I care what you think of me, Mr. O'Flaherty, but just so you understand fully, I've never lied to you. As a matter of fact, I shared with you this evening something so personal and painful that I never discussed it with anyone, not even Tad. And God knows, I regret ever exposing my heart to such a wretched ungrateful man."

"Is this your idea of caring for me? Yelling at me and calling me wretched. I preferred you rubbing your hands through my hair, lass."

Miranda gasped in utter shock that he would even bring up such a delicate moment. Trying to regain her composure she said, "I'm sorry I lost my temper. That was inexcusable of me, considering how ill you are. But Mr. O'Flaherty, a gentleman would never bring up such an embarrassing moment, especially since I thought you were unconscious."

"Lass, I told ya before, me ain't no gentleman like his lordship, who says sweet nothin's to ya in the garden so he can steal a kiss."

Hearing his comment, and recalling the night Tad had kissed her in the garden, the blood drained from Miranda's face. "Oh my God, you were spying on me. How could you?"

Gilbert closed his eyes as if dismissing her and said, "Leave me be. I'm tired and need me rest."

Angered beyond reason, Miranda stood and peered down at her patient. "How convenient, when I pleaded for you to rest you demanded to be heard so I listened. Well now I demand an explanation for such unsavory behavior." Seeing he did not intend to answer her, Miranda stood over him, fist planted firmly on her hip. "Fine, Mr. O'Flaherty, have it your way, but I'm not going anywhere and neither are you, so eventually you are going to have to answer me."

After several minutes, Miranda, outraged, sat next to him and watched his chest rise up and down as he struggled to breathe, coughing from time to time. Seeing his cheeks turn red, Miranda knew his fever was returning. Putting her own anger aside, she went to the dry sink and dipped another cloth into the cool water. Then returning to his side, she removed the cloth that was on his forehead, and replaced it with another. Gilbert opened his eyes and grasped her wrist. "I told you before I don't want your help."

Glancing at his hand then back into his eyes she softly said, "Want it or not, you're going to have to accept it. You're burning up with fever, so stop being so pig-headed and let me care for you."

His grip lessened around her wrist and he mumbled a thank you, while Miranda softly placed his hand back to his side. Taking the other cloth to the dry sink, she dipped it into the basin, all the while looking at the man who could anger her faster than any other she had ever met. Retrieving the quilt she had used to cover herself, she tenderly laid it across him, noticing he was shivering.

Slipping her hand under his neck, he opened his eyes again and she whispered softly, "Gilbert, please let me place this cloth at the base of your neck to help break the fever, then I'll fix you some broth."

As she stepped away from his side, she noticed Felicity at the doorway and Miranda smiled at her, seeing she had fixed a tray for him already.

"How's our patient this morning?"

"Awake and cantankerous," Miranda whispered, going to Felicity. "Did we wake you?"

"No. I was already awake. Why don't I give this to our pig-headed patient while you get some badly needed rest, Miranda?" Felicity deliberately paused so Miranda understood she had overheard their conversation before continuing. Softly she smiled at her friend reassuringly. "Less you've forgotten, Tad will be here in a few hours to check in on us. And if you don't want him to find you looking tired and arouse his suspicion as to why, I suggest you rest and freshen up. Don't worry, I'll take good care of our Mr. O'Flaherty."

Nodding, Miranda left the room and went to Felicity and Benjamin's bedroom where she lay on the pillow, hearing Felicity speak softly to Gilbert.

"I don't think we've been formally introduced. I'm Mrs. Felicity Myles, my husband is Reverend Benjamin Myles, and we run this orphanage. Now, please take some of this broth and try to remain calm, Mr. O'Flaherty."

"Thank you, Mrs. Myles."

"Shh, Mr. O'Flaherty," Felicity interrupted. "It's not me you should be thanking, it's Miranda who has been by your side day and night since your unfortunate accident. Please do keep that in mind the next time you are compelled to lash out at her for the injustices that have been brought down against you."

Hearing not another word, Miranda closed her eyes and wept softly in a state of confusion. She was relieved that Gilbert was alive, yet filled with anger and resentment at both his and Tad's actions that had resulted in a man's death, and embarrassed he obviously had seen Tad kissing her in the garden--something she wished never had taken place, knowing the type of man Tad actually was. Overcome with anger and self-pity, she prayed, "Oh God, please help me to put all my feelings aside and only help Gilbert now. Not for me, or even him, but in memory of Joseph."

Ashwillow, England
June 1865

Sitting amongst the guests in attendance for the wedding of Rupert Robbins and Annabelle Bailey-Smythe were Joshua and Elise Carmidy. Newlyweds themselves and guests of Anne and Edward Spencer, they were seated in the front pew where family normally sat. Anne Spencer, a cousin of Felicity, smiled at Elise.

"Pity our dear Felicity couldn't make the journey. I know she would have loved being here today, loving both Rupert and Annabelle so."

Not certain how she should respond, Elise nodded politely while tucking her hand in Joshua's hand. Not recalling Felicity ever mentioning family members other than her beloved late aunt, or the close relationship she had with Lavinia's sister, Annabelle, Elise was more mystified than ever before. From the day the two of them had docked in Plymouth, England, Elise and Joshua were made to feel welcomed by the Spencer's as well as Felicity's cousin Rupert and Annabelle, who greeted their ship.

On the trip from Plymouth to the serene countryside of Devonshire, Felicity's friends and family listened intently to how she and Benjamin were getting on, yet oddly enough no one inquired about Lavinia or James. Only in private did Rupert ask about his future sister-in-law. Being polite, Elise had replied respectfully, "Mrs. Sterling is a beautiful woman who has become extremely close with my stepfather's parents, the Honeycutt's."

Right after she had made the comment, she instinctively knew Rupert understood her not willing to say more on the subject by replying with equal restraint, "Right. The Honeycutt's, you know were dear friends of my late father and Felicity's dear Aunt Gwendolyn. As it was, many years ago, I traveled to New York with Father and stayed at their home, as well. How are they?"

Judging from the look on his face, and how Rupert had chosen not to question her further regarding Lavinia, Elise responded politely, "The Honeycutt's are quite well, thank you. When we return to America, I will be sure to extend your well wishes to them."

It was apparent to both Joshua and Elise their hosts were keeping their distances although they exhibited exemplary kindness and generosity to them. Joshua observed it must be the differences between their cultures, while Elise believed it stemmed from Lavinia.

Never did Elise let on that she knew the sordid past of the Myles', nor that Lavinia had once been wed to Benjamin. Instead Elise accepted their warm hospitality and respected their privacy. Although today, attending

Annabelle's wedding, she found it particularly odd that not only was Lavinia absent, but that no one spoke of her absence. It was as if Lavinia didn't exist.

Following the wedding, a beautiful garden party was scheduled at Ashwillow. One of the guests in attendance was a Frenchmen, whom Elise discovered had once been an artist prior to a tragic accident which had left him partially paralyzed on his right side. As Elise discreetly observed the man, she was reminded of Thomas by the same haunting troubled look in his eyes. Much to her surprise, Francois joined her and Joshua.

"Ah, so Anne tells me you are friends with our Felicity, Madame Carmidy?" Francois asked.

Smiling politely, Elise nodded. "Yes. As children, her family would visit my dearest friends, the Browns. Recently we were all reacquainted in New York."

"Oui, I trust Reverend Myles and Felicity are well?"

"Quite well, Mr. Racine."

"And are you also familiar with Mr. and Mrs. Sterling?" he asked, his eyes twinkling.

Apprehensively, Elise said, "Yes, I know of them."

"Ah, from the curtness in your response am I to assume you are not as fond of them as you are the Myles'?" By the look on his face, Elise realized this man enjoyed taunting people.

Amused that he understood she would be flustered by his boldness, Elise raised her eyebrow and responded coyly, "Why Mr. Racine, I had no idea I was in the company of such a diversified gentleman who possessed the abilities of deciphering a complete stranger's speech patterns."

Hearing his wife's comment, Joshua chuckled under his breath while sipping his champagne, camouflaging it with a cough. Glancing at him with a devilish grin and a twinkle in her eyes, Elise asked, "Darling, are you alright?"

"Quite. I was just enjoying our hosts' hospitality and this fine nectar of the grapes. After years of tasting gunpowder, what a delightful change to experience a rounded full-bodied drink on my palate without the hint of bitterness. Perhaps you should sample some of your champagne, dear," Joshua answered, while placing his arm around her waist and squeezing it slightly as if to let her know he did not approve of her quick tongue.

The couple's interaction with one another did not go unnoticed by Francois who smiled at Joshua. "Monsieur Carmidy, it would appear you are quite a connoisseur. Not only in fine wines, but in your choice of women, choosing one equally resourceful to her beauty."

"Indeed I am, Mr. Racine. But please call me Joshua."

"Only if you will honor me by addressing me as Francois." He bowed politely then turning his attention back to Elise, he asked, "And I do hope you too shall honor me the same, Madame Carmidy."

Nodding her response, Elise took a sip of her champagne, glanced at the newlyweds, and commented, "My, Mrs. Robbins glows of happiness. Wouldn't you agree Francois?" Much to her surprise, the twinkle in Francois' eyes dimmed as he glanced at her.

"Oui, Annabelle always has though, in my eyes, Madame." Then as if he were aware of Elise's watchful eye, he added hastily, "She may not be the striking beauty of her sister, but there's much to be said for a woman of such tenderness."

"Oh please call me Elise, otherwise it hardly seems fair since I've already addressed you by your Christian name. As for Mrs. Robbins, although I've only known her for a short while, I would agree that she is indeed a tender and loving woman. No wonder she and Felicity were such good friends. In many ways they are very similar, wouldn't you agree?" she asked smiling, watching his reaction intently, mindful that Joshua was still holding her snugly.

"Again we agree, Elise. Yet am I mistaken or did you once again avoid commenting on Mrs. Sterling?" Francois said coyly, openly toying with her, which infuriated Elise.

Luckily though, they were joined by Elspeth Haversham who jokingly said, "Oh Francois, you naughty man, are you badgering Elise over Lavinia and James?"

"Badgering?" he asked, seemingly enjoying playing the part of the victim, while continuing playfully. "Why Elspeth, you know me better than that. Although I have been known to be perhaps persuasive from time to time, never would I be so vulgar as to badger information from a worthy opponent."

Elise, hearing him refer to her as a worthy opponent, smiled over the rim of her glass while sipping more of her champagne.

"Now be truthful dearest Elspeth, you are equally curious to know how James and Lavinia are getting on in New York, but are far too timid in asking. While I, on the other hand . . ."

Unexpectedly, Anne approaching from behind Francois, finished his sentence for him. "I should think 'scandalous' would be appropriate Francois. That topic of conversation is hardly appropriate, Francois, and you of all people should know that. Have you no compassion for Annabelle, after everything she has done for you? Now I absolutely forbid you from badgering Mr. and Mrs. Carmidy further regarding that woman. Understood?"

From Anne's tone--although her voice remained just above a whisper-- it was clear that she had a great influence on Francois and Elspeth.

Apologetically, Elspeth said, "Of course you're right, dear Anne. How foolish of me to even encourage Francois."

The tension was so thick that Elise nervously glanced at Joshua who winked back at her before saying, "Are Mr. and Mrs. Robbins intending to go on a honeymoon trip as my bride and I have done?"

"Hmm, I'm not sure . . ." Anne glanced toward the newlyweds as they approached. "Let's ask them, shall we Joshua?"

Hearing Anne's comment, Rupert said, "Ask us what, pray tell?"

"Joshua and I were wondering if you and Annabelle were intending to take a trip to celebrate your nuptials as he and Elise have."

"It's such a shame you hadn't thought of traveling back to America with Joshua and Elise. I'm sure your bride--never seeing the colonies-- might have found it rather enjoyable, old boy," Francois replied snidely.

Seeing the uncomfortable glance between Annabelle and Rupert, Joshua hastily added, "As enjoyable as your company would be on the return voyage, I fear you would be terribly disappointed. I love New York, but since the war I must admit, my fair city hasn't weathered the storm too well."

"Precisely why Annabelle and I chose not to visit the colonies," Rupert said smiling appreciatively back at Joshua.

"Oh dear, I had no idea New York was so dreadful," Anne said with concern in her voice. "I do hope our cousin isn't in any danger, Rupert."

"New York isn't dangerous, Anne," Elise gushed enthusiastically. "It's lovely! You can't imagine all the shops and brick buildings all together. Why, the streets are filled with people milling about, in all their fancy wares looking just as carefree as birds chirping. There are vendors on every street corner and did I mention the shops? Millinery, tailors, why they even have this one store that has just about everything anyone could possibly want. Honestly, I've never seen anything like it in all my life."

"It sounds as if you enjoyed yourself shopping in New York, Elise. Is that where you purchased your lovely gown?" Annabelle asked sweetly.

Blushing Elise said, "Why yes, as a matter of fact, as part of my wedding trousseau, compliments of my dear stepfather, Michael Honeycutt. Actually, it was Felicity and our mutual friend Miranda who helped me choose this very gown."

"How lovely . . ." Annabelle said dreamily. "I recall when Felicity and I picked out our gowns for her introduction party. What a time we had together. I know I've asked before, but how are they truly? Does Felicity help out at the orphanage?"

Enthusiastically Elise answered, "Help out? Why I honestly don't know what Benjamin would do without her. She wakes up at the crack of dawn to help feed all the children then schools them during the day, and if that wasn't enough, she tends to the wee ones before they go down for the night. I admire her devotion to the children and her husband's work." Seeing the concerned look on Rupert's face, Elise quickly added, "Perhaps in my haste of admiration, I've overstated Felicity's activities . . ."

"Fear not Elise, you have said nothing we haven't all suspected. Perhaps following our celebration you and Joshua would consider remaining so that we might have an opportunity to discuss a proposition my bride . . ." Rupert said, smiling at Annabelle lovingly. ". . . and I have for you both."

Although his question was directed toward Elise and Joshua, Rupert's eyes never swayed from Annabelle who blushed at her husband's display of affection toward her in public. After Joshua agreed, the newlyweds excused themselves to mingle with their other guests while Anne seized the opportunity and took Elise by the hand.

"My dear, I don't believe you've had the opportunity of viewing Ashwillow gardens, have you? Why don't you and I take a stroll? That is if you wouldn't mind, Joshua?"

From her mannerism, it was clear the invitation was only for Elise, so Elspeth excused herself leaving Francois and Joshua conversing while she and Elise made their way past the small groups of guests. Once outdoors and past the stoned patio, Anne looked at Elise and smiled nervously.

Never one to be shy, Elise whispered, "It's always been my way of thinking just to say what's on your mind. And so, I hope you won't be offended if I tell you that Felicity has shared with me, her and Reverend Myles' history."

Relief spread across Anne's face. "Oh I do love how you Americans can come right to the point," she exclaimed.

"Yes well, others may not share in your opinion, I dare say. Yet at times like this, it does cut through the muck now, doesn't it?" Elise smiled triumphantly.

"Indeed it does." Anne agreed, chuckling slightly as the two of them walked farther along the path. Allowing the other woman time to gather her thoughts, Elise said not a word, enjoying the lovely English gardens.

"It's uncanny I suppose some might say, but the day Aunt Gwendolyn announced she and Felicity were traveling to America--call it woman's intuition--I felt uneasy about their trip. So much so that I asked Felicity if we would ever see her again. Now it appears my fears have become a reality. With Felicity married and starting a new life with Benjamin, I suppose it's best . . ."

"Pardon me for asking Anne, but why is that precisely? I mean, I know that Reverend Myles' work at the orphanage is important to him and all, yet it has crossed my mind that perhaps he and Felicity feel they would not be welcomed back to England. Don't misunderstand, nothing was said, nor even implied, but it was my impression or perhaps woman's intuition that led me to believe this. Which, if you don't mind me saying, is darn-right silly considering the fact that when they met up in New York, both of them were free to marry whomever they chose. Especially since in the eyes of God, Benjamin's short-lived relationship to Mrs. Sterling was annulled, therefore never existed. Isn't that how you see it, Anne?"

"My but you are frank, Elise," Anne said solemnly.

Concerned that she had offended her hostess, Elise immediately apologized. "Yes, it's a gift and a curse sometimes. Please forgive me for butting my nose in where it obviously doesn't belong."

Smiling warmly at Elise, Anne said, "Nonsense. You obviously care about Felicity and your question is one I've asked myself over again. Unfortunately, there is no simple answer. You see, after the scandal that Lavinia and her late father began, accusing Benjamin of lusting over Felicity at the ball . . ."

"Felicity told me everything of that incident, but surely after everyone discovered who actually committed the attack on her, they must have realized Benjamin was innocent?"

"Forgive me for interrupting you, Elise. With them marrying as they did, surely you can see how it could be viewed that although Benjamin had not committed the attack, perhaps there was some truth to Lavinia's claims of them lusting over one another. In fact, after it was discovered that Felicity and Benjamin were married, you cannot imagine the gossip that ensued. Mind you, never in my presence, but it was clear our set had their doubts on both Reverend Myles and my cousin's integrity. And as happy as I am for Felicity that she has found love, I still can't believe that Aunt Gwendolyn, being such a staunch believer in tradition, brought them together, knowing full-well the ramifications of such a union."

"Well not knowing your aunt of course, all I can say is what Felicity told me of her, and that was, Gwendolyn Phelps had risked her own life so

that Felicity could find true happiness. To my way of thinking, someone
that lived her life upholding certain moralities and traditions and broke
them to bring Felicity and Benjamin together thought long and hard before
making such a decision. Surely others in your set could be more tolerant, if
nothing more than out of respect for such a wise and caring woman, as
your aunt obviously was."

"As lovely as that sounds Elise, I'm afraid you don't understand the
complexities . . ."

"If I know anything at all, complex situations of the heart, I have a
clear understanding of. You see . . ." As Elise spoke of how she and Joshua
had met and the obstacles they had to overcome, not just from the war, but
the bitterness and hatred that challenged their love, Anne listened silently.

"All I can say is what Felicity said to me. Now let me think, I believe
she said something to the effect that *'there are no words to describe the
utter peace and joy I have experienced since I became Mrs. Benjamin
Myles. I know this may sound strange to some, but when two people have
struggled to be together, I believe God blesses them with an extraordinary
gift, and that is bliss in loving one another completely and freely'*. And I
tend to believe her, Anne. Why, I risked everything, just to love Joshua. My
family, my beliefs, my life, and I can tell you I'd do it all over again.
Thankfully, Joshua and I have a happy ending, but it pains me to think
Felicity is being punished for loving that one man in the world who makes
her heartbeat quicken just by him walking into a room. Now I may not
understand all there is to know about proper English traditions, but no one
can deny that those two were made to be together. Why it's as plain as the
nose on your face when you see them with each other. Why would you
deny yourselves the pleasure of their company when you all clearly miss
Felicity so much?" Shaking her head dramatically, Elise said, "And my
Mama says I'm stubborn . . ."

A smile crossed Anne's lips. "How I wish it were merely being
stubborn, or that there were a group of people I could plead Felicity's case
to. However, that simply isn't the case here. Our codes of ethics are not
written down anywhere, and even if it were possible to change the thought
process of some very rigid thinking people, it would take more than one
person. Not to mention the fact that if Benjamin and Felicity's marriage
could be accepted--which is highly unlikely--but for the sake of argument
if it were, there would still be the matter of Lavinia. And I can tell you that
is one woman none of us misses nor wishes to ever set eyes on again."
Realizing she had said too much, Anne began to apologize for her outburst.

Elise hastily commented instead, "On the matter of Lavinia Sterling, having only met her a few times I can assure you, I agree wholeheartedly. However, that is where our agreement ends. You see I just witnessed what an influence you have on others in your set. Need I remind you of the incident earlier when you scolded Elspeth and that Francois fellow? It was very clear that they respected you and your opinion. Otherwise, why would they have kowtowed down to you so rapidly without a dispute? Perhaps it's out of respect for you that they do not say anything regarding Felicity and Benjamin, fearful that it is you who doesn't approve. From my own personal experience, I've been afraid to discuss them simply because I didn't want to offend you or your cousin Rupert. Either way, one thing's for sure, life is too precious to be wasting it on some silly imaginary rules, which if I'm not mistaken isn't there a saying that says rules are meant to be broken?" Elise said, smiling devilishly.

Anne reached out an arm to Elise, and smiled. "Mrs. Carmidy, I am so glad that you and that handsome husband of yours came to visit us."

Elise tenderly hugged the woman in return and walked arm and arm back toward the house.

Playfully Anne asked, "Well, since everything is out in the open, pray tell, how is Felicity coping with having that evil woman living so near? It still amazes me that the four of them ended up in New York together, of all places. Be honest and don't you dare leave out a single detail."

Giggling, feeling at complete ease with her new friend, Elise shared how after her wedding to Joshua, she had foiled Lavinia's opportunity at embarrassing Felicity and Benjamin as they entered the ballroom. Spotting Rupert nearby, she nodded reassuringly at him. He whispered something into his wife's ear, which caused Annabelle to react favorably by kissing him on the cheek and beaming from ear to ear. As busy as Elise was describing the events of her encounter with Lavinia, she noticed the interaction between her two hosts. Being inquisitive, she wondered what precisely it had meant but rather than question Anne, she followed her host as they walked closer to Mrs. Haversham and Elspeth.

Smiling lovingly at Joshua who was now joined by Anne's husband Edward, Elise heard Anne say, "Mrs. Haversham, would you mind terribly if we borrowed Elspeth for a few moments?"

Graciously accepting Anne's offer, Elise heard Elspeth whisper softly, "Can you ever forgive me dear Anne, for my insensitivity earlier?"

"Oh Elspeth, don't be silly darling . . ." Anne replied while walking back toward the stone patio, extending her hand to a table far removed from other guests mingling freely about. "Francois has a way of drawing those into his web. Since the accident he's gotten worse, I'm afraid."

Curious about Anne's comment, Elise walked ahead of her hostess and waited until all three of them had taken their seats. "Would it be considered terribly rude of me to inquire further as to this accident? I've heard several people mention it, yet I know little else other than it left him partially paralyzed."

Obviously taken back by the American's boldness, Elspeth looked at Anne, her eyes as wide as saucers, waiting for an appropriate reaction. Instead Anne reached across the table and gently patted her friend's hands, saying reassuringly, "It's alright, Elspeth. We've become dear friends and are beyond polite conversation. As a matter of fact, Elise has told me the most amusing tale regarding Lavinia, which I'm sure would be alright if I shared with you, dear friend."

Nodding at Anne reassuringly, Elise watched in amusement while the masterful aristocrat drew Elspeth back into the fold, reassuring the painfully dull woman that all was well between them. As the three of them sat around the table, Elise soon discovered that not all was what it appeared to be on the surface of the elite of society in England. The only difference between those in England and in America that Elise could tell was that they acted as if they were above reproach.

Within moments, Anne and Elspeth disclosed that the accident that had taken Edwin and his personal secretary, Elaine's life, was also the reason for Francois's condition. Shortly after the accident, Annabelle had traveled to Rupert's chateau in France where the injured Francois was convalescing under the care of Anne and Edward. As it turned out, Annabelle needed time away from Ashwillow, following the death of her own father, the Squire Randolph Bailey-Smythe who had been shunned following the incident of the ball and had never recovered.

Once Anne and Edward Spencer returned to their own home--Pixie Halt, back in England--they received word that Gwendolyn Phelps, the matriarch of their clan, had also passed away following the wedding of her niece in America. Elise's head was whirling.

"Am I to understand then that the Squire--Annabelle and Lavinia's father--passed away almost at the same time as Felicity's Uncle Edwin and both of your aunts?"

"Yes, Elise. They say bad news comes in three's and by-George it certainly did back in sixty-two . . ." Anne said sadly.

Hastily Elspeth added, "Four I suppose, if you include Francois's sister, Elaine Freeport to the equation."

Confused even further Elise asked, "Elaine Freeport was Edwin's personal secretary? Am I to assume then that Francois saw his sister perish too?"

"We all did," Anne whispered, obviously still shaken by the incident, so Elspeth filled in the events for Elise. On the carriage trip to Rupert's chateau, the first rig with its passengers including Rupert, Francois, Edwin, and Elaine, broke an axle and rolled over several times, killing Edwin instantly while Elaine, suffering severe injuries, died shortly after.

"So Rupert was in the carriage too, yet suffered no injuries?" Elise asked.

"Yes and don't you think that man hasn't suffered every day since. Following the accident, I tried to reassure him it wasn't his fault, yet he insisted that if he had been sitting across from his father rather than beside him, perhaps Elaine or his father would not have perished. And frankly, I believe he even blamed himself for Aunt Gwendolyn's death, too. You see, he and his father had known Gwendolyn's intentions for the trip to America, despite never telling Felicity or Edward and myself." Anne added hastily.

"Well that explains the accident. Yet I'm still confused as to why Francois seems so bitter over Annabelle's and Rupert's wedding. It was obvious to me earlier that he is pining over Annabelle."

Again, Elspeth's eyes widened as she looked at Anne before commenting herself. "My, but you are extremely perceptive, Elise. You must have been quite a cunning spy," Anne said admiringly.

Bubbling over with curiosity, Elspeth asked, "Spy? You Elise? Why I would have never guessed . . . You must tell me everything . . . Does Joshua know?"

"Yes. I was a spy for the Confederates at the beginning of the war. And yes, Joshua knows. Actually he found me out . . . but before I fill you in on all the details, you must finish telling me of Francois, Annabelle, and Rupert."

Eagerly, Elspeth began speaking while Elise listened intently, fascinated by how Annabelle had nursed Francois back to health while Rupert sat and watched from afar the woman that he loved have her heart broken. Francois, the son of a wealthy businessman, had been disinherited by his family when he pursued his art, rather than a nobler profession. Anne quickly explained that artists were not considered gentlemen in England. Even after Francois's accident, no longer capable of pursuing his craft, Francois's father still would have nothing to do with his only son.

With no family left, and his ability to paint gone, Francois was a broken man.

"From what I hear, Annabelle was wonderful through his depression and even following when he took up the drink," Elspeth said, adding to Anne's explanation.

Agreeing with her friend, Anne said, "As only Annabelle could. Never have I seen a gentler spirit."

"From what I've observed in the short time we've been here, I must say her tenderness shows in everything she does. But when did she and Rupert know . . . I mean, when did they decide to wed?"

Eagerly Anne filled in the gaps, explaining in a low tone so not to be overheard. "Rupert had been assigned the responsibility of overseer of Annabelle's inheritance from the Squire, and if rumors were true, Lavinia had received virtually nothing."

It was Elise's eyes that widened this time, and Elspeth said in earnest, "It's true. Go on Anne, you have such a way of explaining things."

"Well, let's see . . ." Anne paused to gather her thoughts before continuing. "Over time, Annabelle had learned to confide in Rupert, more than for financial matters, viewing him as a dear friend and confidant, never suspecting that he loved her desperately. As Francois's drinking worsened, he insisted on living on his own and moved to his sister's villa. From what I heard from Edward, Annabelle--consumed in worry after not seeing Francois for days--demanded that Rupert take her to Francois. That's where she found the scoundrel with several undesirable women, all in quite a state, following a night of . . ." Leaning across the table in a dramatic fashion, Anne continued. "Well let's just say, Annabelle was quite unnerved by what she witnessed. Now mind you, I've only heard bits and pieces of this part of the story, but I can tell you when she returned to Ashwillow shortly thereafter with Rupert by her side, Annabelle was devastated. Especially since Francois had apparently spoken words of love to the vulnerable and naïve woman, according to Edward. And of course, the poor dear believed every word he had said to her. I'm not saying Francois wasn't sincere, but Annabelle--after having to endure the shame and ridicule her father and sister had brought down on her family name and dishonor-- simply could not take another disappointment."

"No one could," Elspeth added in her defense. "For weeks, we all worried about the poor dear, but slowly over time Rupert seemed to bring her out of her shell. In truth, Annabelle seemed to bring life into Rupert as well. Don't you agree Anne?"

"Oh absolutely! Rupert is a changed man. You see Elise, prior to that time, Rupert was . . . well . . ." Anne hesitated, as if searching for the right words to say.

"Dull as dishwater!" Elspeth proclaimed. "Don't you recall how he spoke back then, rolling his r's in a most annoying and unflattering manner."

"Really Elspeth, you needn't be so unkind." Turning her attention to Elise, Anne continued. "In truth, Rupert's whole persona has changed drastically in the past few years, even his speech, as Elspeth so boisterously has mentioned. Although I've never discussed it openly with either Rupert or Annabelle, I recall distinctively how following the tragic incident of Felicity's ball that Rupert showed remarkable calmness. He took complete charge of rectifying the injustice brought against Reverend Myles, when the rest of us were all in shock. And never once did his speech seem different than that of anyone else, so I've assumed over the years that Rupert used this façade to keep people at a distance."

Nodding her head, Elise asked, "What a lovely story. Yet Francois doesn't appear to be under the influence now?"

"Oh he still does enjoy his wine, but what Frenchmen doesn't?" Anne snickered. "Shortly after Annabelle had left France and returned to England, Francois seemed to come to his senses and a few months later he returned to England. Obviously, hoping to win Annabelle's heart and perhaps even her hand. For a while there I truly believed he might succeed, him being such a suave and smooth talker . . ."

"I never thought he stood a chance," interrupted Elspeth. "After all, hadn't Annabelle been forced to endure a father who enjoyed his drink? Why would she choose a life with a man certain to only cause her more pain when there was Rupert showing her how life could be? No. I honestly believe Annabelle never gave Francois another thought. Why if I had to choose between two men, I can tell you . . ."

"Yes dear we all know . . ." Anne said motioning toward Annabelle and Rupert who were edging their way closer them. Quickly she changed the subject and asked Elise, "Not that we want to see you and Joshua leave us Elise, but when did you say your ship sets sails?"

"Why I believe Joshua said something about traveling to London in a few days to see the sights, then we would return here the first week of July for a few days before returning to New York."

Annabelle, hearing Elise's response, glanced up at her husband lovingly and softly said, "What a coincidence darling." Then directing her attention back to Elise, she asked, "Before it gets too late, perhaps you and

Joshua might have a few moments to discuss that very subject. Your traveling arrangements, that is."

Intrigued by her comment, Elise glanced at Anne. "Well if you'll excuse us, Anne and Elspeth, while I'll go find that wayward husband of mine," Elise said jokingly, standing up. "If I know him, he's probably bending Edward's ear off about the war."

After joining Joshua and being led to a private study away from the other guests, the four of them made themselves comfortable while sipping more champagne. Within a few minutes, it was decided that Rupert and Annabelle would be joining Joshua and Elise to London to show them the sights and returning with them to New York. Judging by the look on Rupert's face when he mentioned how he missed his cousin, Elise surmised that he was equally worried about her. As much as she welcomed the Robbins' company, Elise couldn't help but wonder what Lavinia was going to say when they returned with Rupert and her sister Annabelle.

~ Fourteen ~

Exposed

New York, July 1865

"Oh you can't be serious?" exclaimed Miranda, hearing the news that Elise and Joshua were returning early along with Rupert and Lavinia's sister, Annabelle.

"Just what am I going to do with another Lavinia snooping about the Honeycutt's? Gilbert is sure to be discovered now!" Overwrought from the stress of concealing Gilbert from Tad the past several days, compounded by keeping up the pretense of still being interested in the man she now loathed caused Miranda to weep hysterically.

"I just can't keep up this pretense any longer. Why can't Gilbert just tell Albert what really happened. Surely he would help us."

"Oh sweetheart, you're mistaken about Annabelle, she is nothing like her sister. And you know perfectly well that blood is thicker than water. No matter how sympathetic Alfred might be to the injustices Gilbert has sustained by Tad and his unscrupulous friend, he would never betray his own grandson."

Reaching for her friend, Felicity hugged Miranda while looking across the room at James for answers.

"Are you certain, James? As much as I welcome seeing my cousin Rupert and Annabelle again, having them under the same roof where Miranda is hiding Gilbert is rather unsettling to say the least."

"We all agreed that hiding Gilbert until the party was the best for all concerned, especially now that he is wanted for the murder of that poor friend of his."

Between her sobs, Miranda said defiantly, "And we all know who actually killed that poor man and yet we do nothing to see that his murderer is incarcerated. Instead, we keep an innocent man locked up after he was nearly killed while those guilty remain free!"

"We have no proof Daniel actually killed that man, except the word of an Irishman who has admittedly swindled a man of means out of money while playing cards."

Angered by James last comment, Miranda wiped her tears and glared at him. "You know as well as I do that Gilbert is innocent! So why are you suggesting otherwise?"

Seeing how angered Miranda had become, Felicity softly said, "Miranda dear, I think what James was trying to say is that if we were to bring in the authorities, no one would believe his story. Especially against two prominent members of society."

"Precisely," James agreed. "Haven't I from the first day we found Gilbert done everything in my power to keep him safe?"

Nodding, Miranda answered, "Yes. And I do appreciate it. Honest I do, it's just I'm frightened that he will be discovered before we have a chance to free him."

Felicity, still comforting Miranda, softly said, "Why borrow trouble needlessly? God has kept him safe while half of New York is scouring the city looking for him. I see no reason to think our plan won't work. All we need to do is keep our heads, and pray that God will help us."

Sighing heavily, wanting to believe it was that simple, Miranda agreed. "When are the four newlyweds expected?"

"The latter part of next week, and then the party is only four days after that. So less than two weeks from now, you and Gilbert will be safely on your way to San Francisco," James said reassuringly.

Seeing her friend relax, Felicity asked, "Dear, does Gilbert know your intentions of going with him yet?"

"No. I've decided not to tell him until we are safely aboard the train."

"I see," Felicity said frowning. "Are you certain this is wise? What if he makes a fuss about it and draws attention to you both? You know how volatile he can get."

Tired of justifying Gilbert's actions to Felicity and James, she shook her head, knowing that neither of them liked him. "He was frightened and hurt back when he was here, but now that he has grown to trust me, that's all changed."

"I hope for your sake that's true. As you know, Miranda, I can't for the life of me understand what you see in this man..." James raised his hand, seeing her temper flare again. "But then again, look whom I chose to marry, so I'm a fine one to talk."

Seeing a smile cross her friend's lips, Felicity said, "Well dear, as much as I enjoy your company, it is getting late. Perhaps we should finish this conversation tomorrow. You're still coming by in the morning so that we can look for a dress for the party, aren't you?"

"Why yes. As a matter of fact, I thought I might look for some suits for Gilbert as well. That is, if you wouldn't mind."

Seeing how impatient James was getting, Felicity smiled and said, "Of course not. Benjamin could use a few new suits as well, so we can look for the both of them."

After walking Miranda to the door, Felicity turned back to her husband's office to have a chat with James before he had to take his leave, knowing he was expected at the Honeycutt's by seven. Fearful James might take offense to what she wanted to discuss with him, she took a deep breath and said a silent prayer. *Dear Lord, please help me to find the words to express my concern of him spending so much time with me, especially since he has done so much to help both Benjamin and me.* Finishing her prayer, she walked through the office door and, mindful that they were now alone, kept the door open.

"How kind of you to stay for a few extra minutes, James. I would never have asked if it wasn't due to something I needed to go over with you."

A look of concern crossed his brow as he asked, "What is it Felicity? Aren't the two new women I've hired for you working out?"

"Oh no, they are wonderful. Why I can't believe how much free time I have now. It's heaven sent. Thank you again."

Sensing she was having a difficult time bringing up what it was that troubled her, and knowing how she was a stickler for protocol, he surmised she wanted to discuss the time the two of them spent together. Rather than put her through the embarrassment, James said, "Felicity, before you begin, I was wondering if I might address something with you?"

"Of course," she responded.

"As fond as I have become of both you and Benjamin, I fear that spending so much time here at the orphanage is unwise. Especially with Gilbert's future hanging in the balance. As you know, Lavinia is already suspicious of our friendship, and rather than do something that might further provoke her, I was thinking that perhaps from now until the party I should avoid being seen here."

Relief spread across Felicity's face. "Oh James, you have no idea how relieved I am to hear you say that. That's precisely what I wanted to discuss with you this evening, but didn't know how to approach the subject. Especially since you have done so much for all of us."

Raising his hand, not comfortable having her sing his praise, he said, "Well then, that's settled since we are both in agreement. If you are in need of anything, feel free to tell Miranda and I will see to it that you are well taken care of."

Grateful for his thoughtfulness, she stepped forward and gently kissed him on the cheek.

"You really are such a dear man. How will I ever repay you for all your kindness?"

Smiling at her, he said, "You just did, my dear. Well if there's nothing more, I will be on my way. I know the way out." Turning, he headed toward the door, and said, "Don't worry about a thing, Felicity. Everything is going precisely as I had planned."

Nodding her response, she watched as he made his way through the front door of the rectory, surprised he had left in such a hurry. Then hearing the children and realizing they must have finished their evening meal, she scurried off to assist them to bed.

Outside the orphanage, James stood and watched Felicity's silhouette and rubbed his cheek where she had just kissed him. Just as it had moments earlier, James manhood stirred, recalling her scent as she drew near him. A sinister smile crossed his lips, and he whispered, "Yes indeed! Everything is exactly as I've planned. Only a fortnight to go and I will have you, as mine!"

Meanwhile in front of the rectory, Miranda approached Montgomery and a smile crossed her lips. No longer was she intimidated by his immense size or menacing look. Instead, she regarded him now as a trusted friend. She knew if it had not been for his help, it would have been impossible to harbor Gilbert safely away at the Honeycutt's.

It had become an unspoken rule between them never to mention Gilbert's name when they spoke of him, so instead, she asked, while accepting Montgomery's assistance into the coach, "How is *he* today?"

"Cantankerous as ever," Montgomery somberly replied.

By his tone and the disgusted look Montgomery exhibited, Miranda knew precisely what the driver meant. Of all the men she had ever met, Gilbert O'Flaherty was by far the most difficult. Despite this fact, she had fallen hopelessly in love with him, seeing other attributes in him that she admired and respected far greater than his anger and hostility toward others.

Over the past several weeks while nursing him back to health, she grew to understand that such hostilities were not out of jealousy or envy, but rather from being treated with such a lack of respect.

Upon arriving in America as an indentured servant, he and his sister Margaret-Anne had been forced to endure hardships much like those of a slave. For seven long years, until their contract had been fulfilled, Gilbert, a proud man, had been stripped of his dignity by the hands of his master. He and Margaret-Anne had been reduced to accept the demeaning treatment of his master, or suffer the consequences of extending their contractual time. Margaret-Anne was able to accept those conditions more freely than Gilbert, whose resentment toward those of power grew as each day passed.

Over time, Gilbert's anger grew to hate, especially after fulfilling his obligation, when he discovered he was still viewed as a lower-class citizen, simply because of his heritage.

Was it any wonder that he was so bitter and angry? she thought. Glancing at Montgomery, the thought suddenly occurred to her that perhaps such anger was the reason why this servant showed great kindness to her while treating others with such coldness. Answering her own question, she thought, *Of course it is! We have a special bond between us. He knows that I am looked down upon by some for being a Southerner, just as Gilbert is for being an Irishman, and sadly just as he was, for being a colored man.* Never seeing it in that light before, she smiled warmly at the driver. Noticing he was still awaiting instructions, Miranda immediately apologized.

"Forgive me, Montgomery. I was so wrapped up in my own thoughts I hadn't realized there was something else you wanted to discuss. Has something happened that I should be aware of?"

"No, miss. I just wanted to say that I will miss you when you leave for San Francisco."

Touched by his words she leaned forward and patted his hand. "That was very kind of you to say, Montgomery. I hope you know that I will miss you, too. I take it then that Mr. Sterling has filled you in on my intentions."

"Yes, miss." Then clearing his throat, still uncomfortable to show any emotion to her, he added. "Mr. Sterling has directed me to begin packing a few of your personal belongings. Shall I store them in the passage behind the dumbwaiter in your room, or would your prefer I take them to the basement?"

Confused by his question, she asked, "Passage off the dumbwaiter? I know of no passage."

Judging by the puzzled look on his face, Miranda realized he was surprised at her not knowing and quickly answered, "Beggin' your pardon, Miss Miranda. I thought you knew; you living there so long and all. There is a private passage between each of the rooms for the servants to have easy access. That's how I intended to get to your room without being seen."

The blood drained from her face hearing of such a place, recalling the night Tad had brought her flowers. Realizing that such a passage must have been how Tad had gained access to her room, her heart began to race. Immediately she wondered, *How many other nights had he come into her room uninvited?*

"This private access you speak of Montgomery. Can you show it to me?"

Puzzled by her request, he nodded. "Sure thing, miss. The only problem is, I'm not permitted in the living quarters after nightfall. So, without drawing attention to myself, I will have to come to your bedchamber later this evening through the kitchen or basement."

Nodding, understanding the nature of his concern, not wanting to arouse suspicions, she asked, "Are you saying that this dumbwaiter goes to the kitchen, as well as the basement?"

"Sure enough."

Barely able to breathe let alone talk, her mind buzzing, Miranda somehow managed to find her voice. "I see. After dinner I usually visit with *him* . . . Will midnight be too late for you to show me how this passage works?"

Seeing Montgomery nod and turn to leave, she called to him. "Montgomery, in case I've been negligent in expressing my gratitude to you for all your help . . ."

Turning, he interrupted her. "Miss, that's not necessary. I already know."

"Well, thank you nevertheless. I truly do not know what would have become of *him,* if it weren't for your help. For both of us, thank you."

Nodding, Montgomery smiled then took his position on the buckboard of the hansom cab. As the carriage pulled away from the orphanage, she gazed along the familiar route to the Honeycutt's, grateful to have this time to herself to sort out in her mind more distressing information about the man she had once opened her heart to.

Upon hearing the jaded truth from Gilbert as to why Daniel and Tad had been after him, Miranda was angered as well as sympathetic, too. How dreadful for Tad to think he had been responsible for killing an innocent man. Having lived with the guilt of Joseph's death on her conscience, Miranda knew how agonizing living with such guilt was and had been tempted to ease his troubled mind.

Yet, she also knew, even if he knew the truth--that it wasn't he who had committed such a dastardly deed--Tad would still want to destroy Gilbert out of jealousy, or worse, figure out how she knew. Out of her own need to protect Gilbert, she remained silent. Over time, she began to resent Tad more every day for causing her to make such a choice, and she came to realize that Tad running down Gilbert was deliberate. He had openly sought Gilbert out of hiding to kill him. And that was something she would never forgive him for.

Even after discovering the unthinkable truth, Miranda couldn't figure out why he would do such a thing. For weeks, she had chastised herself for being partially responsible for Tad reacting in such a vile and inhumane way. It occurred to her that obviously he was insecure of her love, or why else would he do such a despicable thing to Gilbert? However, tonight, discovering how Tad had accessed her room, she no longer pitied him or blamed herself for his actions.

Instead, Miranda saw him for what he was, a man with no character. Realizing his lack of integrity caused him to do the things he had done, and the thought of him hovering over her fiendishly while she slept crept inside her mind. *Is there no end to his treachery and deceit?* Then panic filled her heart as she wondered, *Dear God, how can I continue this charade, when he makes my skin crawl?*

Shaking her head in disgust, she recalled Gilbert confessing his part in swindling Tad rather than lie to her. *The differences between these two men far outstretch any class boundaries,* she surmised. *Gilbert may not be as polished or educated as Tad, that much was true. However, what he was lacking in social skills far surpassed Tad in character and integrity. Thank heavens, I found out the truth before it was too late.*

Recalling their passionate embrace several weeks earlier in the garden, she quivered in disgust. *How could I have ever felt close to a man with so few scruples?*

Deep in her thoughts, Miranda had not realized the carriage had turned into the Honeycutt's drive until she spotted Tad waiting outside his grandparents' home As she returned his nod, she planted a smile to her lips for his benefit, while thinking, *Only a fortnight to go . . . You can do this. Smile Miranda.*

"Ah, Miranda dear. I was worried about you," Tad called as the cab paused beside him.

"Worried? Why ever for?" Miranda said calmly, accepting his hand as she stepped out of the cab. "You knew I was at the orphanage."

"You are later than usual."

"Am I?" she asked, avoiding eye contact with him, knowing that he came to meet her only to have a few private moments alone together. Nodding to Montgomery, the servant obediently pulled away and Miranda calmly began walking toward the Honeycutt mansion, determined not to be alone with Tad more than necessary.

"Oh dear, I suppose you're right," she said casually, glancing down at her lapel watch. "Felicity was telling me the news of her cousin Rupert and his newlywed bride, Annabelle coming for a visit. I suppose I forgot the time." Glancing at him, she appeared to be excited, by adding. "It appears they will be returning with Joshua and Elise. Isn't that grand news? You do know that Annabelle is Lavinia's sister don't you?"

"Yes. Of course. Must we speak of them now? It occurred to me that we've not taken a walk in the gardens for quite some time."

"Oh Tad, that does sound lovely. However, considering the lateness of the hour and all, I really need to freshen up before dinner. You don't mind do you? Perhaps another time would be better." Again, she forced a smile to her lips and hoped that her eyes did not betray her.

Gently grasping hold of her elbows, Tad drew her closer to him and huskily whispered, "Are you certain that's the only reason why you are declining my invitation? Lately, I have the distinct impression that you are deliberately trying to avoid me."

Feeling his breath on her neck, the blood drained from her face and she trembled slightly, fearful he had somehow become wise to her deceptions or worse that he was going to kiss her.

"Don't be silly," she whispered, giddily. "Why, I see you nearly every night."

Not releasing her from his grasp, Tad looked deep into her eyes. "Miranda, for weeks after I moved in with father and Sarah, you asked me repeatedly if there was something wrong. Now I am asking you the same. Have you grown tired of my advances and no longer wish for me to court you?"

Tempted to end this farce here and now, but deciding the risk would be too great, she shyly said with the most sincere look she could manage, "Perhaps I have been a little distant of late. I won't deny it troubled me greatly that you had withdrawn from me there for a while, despite you saying otherwise. Nevertheless, I can assure you Tad, my feelings for you are just as strong as before."

Satisfied she had not lied entirely--after all she did dislike him just as she had before he had been courting her--she pasted a smile to her lips as she had seen Elise use countless times before. Then subtlety, she gazed into his eyes to gauge if he detected her insincerity. Judging by the relief she saw looking back at her, Miranda knew she was successful in not arousing his suspicion.

"You know how your grandmother detests lateness, and from the sounds I hear from inside, everyone has already gathered."

Kissing her forehead, he said, "The Sterling's aren't here yet, so she won't even notice if you're running slightly behind. But go ahead, we can talk later."

Entering the mansion, she continued smiling all the while desperately wanting to wash off the grime of a hard day at the orphanage and Tad's kiss from her forehead. Much to Miranda's delight, the evening activities were halted to discuss the arrival of Lavinia's sister, Annabelle, and Rupert Robbins. It was agreed upon right up front that Rupert would feel more at ease with the Honeycutt's, rather than having to choose between staying with his cousin Felicity or his wife's sister.

Clearly excited at the thought of someone so prominent visiting their home, Vivian suggested the welcoming home party already underway should now be a welcome party for both couples. This way, the finest of New York society would have the opportunity to meet 'the war hero' who married her granddaughter as well as the elite of society from Europe. Immediately she began planning to extend her guest list.

While suggestions on who should be included were offered, Miranda impatiently glanced at the clock periodically certain that it must be running slow. Trying to figure a way of checking if the time was correct, her thoughts were interrupted when she heard, "Oh Miranda dear . . ."

Immediately Miranda's back stiffened, knowing by now whenever she was addressed in such a manner, Vivian expected something in return.

"Yes. Mrs. Honeycutt?" she replied politely.

"It suddenly occurred to me that our dear Felicity probably hasn't been out from under those ghastly urchin's feet since Benjamin has been in Washington. Tomorrow, you must see to it that she joins us for dinner. Can I count on you to see to that, my dear?"

Hearing Vivian's comment, Lavinia taking a sip of her wine, started to cough and looked at her friend in shock. An exchange of glances passed between the two women and Lavinia immediately chimed in.

"Yes. How long has it been since *dear* Felicity has been without her Benjamin? When does he intend to return, for goodness sake? Surely Rupert would find it most unsettling to find out his dear cousin has been left alone for so long." Snidely she looked at James and smiled coyly. "Do you know James, darling?"

Raising her hand frantically before her, as if uninterested in James' reply, Vivian looked at her husband frantically. "Alfred, I insist you send for Benjamin and Lucas at once. Why I simply can not allow our dear Felicity to be alone tending to all those children while the two of those men try to change the minds of stubborn bureaucrats. Surely, with all your influence, you could see to it that Benjamin gets the support he needs to run that orphanage properly. Why, when I think of the sacrifices both Benjamin and Felicity have unselfishly made for those children, I'm ashamed that we haven't done more to help ourselves."

Nodding his head, Alfred puffed on his pipe slowly while grinning snidely at his wife. "Mother, why I had no idea you had such an interest in the orphans, or for that matter Reverend Myles and Felicity. However, since you have brought it to my attention, consider the matter closed. I will take care of the situation straight away."

"Thank you, Alfred." Turning her attention back to Miranda, she said, "Well Miranda dear, will you see to it that our dear Felicity dines with us tomorrow evening then?"

Never in all the years that she had lived with the Honeycutt's had she ever heard Vivian refer to Felicity with such endearment, or the orphans for that matter, and Miranda knew precisely why the sudden change of heart. With Rupert Robbins, being first cousin of Felicity, it would not set well with him to know how his cousin had been treated in the past by his hostess. Trying not to show her disgust at Vivian being such a hypocrite, Miranda nodded politely.

"I can't promise Mrs. Honeycutt, but I will certainly try."

Pouting, Vivian nervously tapped her index finger against her lip as if trying to think. Then as if having an idea, she smiled at Miranda. "Come to think of it dear, there is no need for you to say a thing. I'll make a point to drop by in the morning and invite her myself. Why, I will even offer to help with those poor children for a spell. Surely, there must be something I could do that would be beneficial for their upbringing." As if answering her own question, she quickly added. "Ah, of course. I will read to them. What do you think of that, dear?"

No longer masking his amusement by his wife's sudden interest in Felicity Robbins-Phelps Myles, Alfred coughed and looked at Michael then at Sarah, who both tried to refrain from smiling. Shaking his head he said, "As generous as this offer of yours is my dear, perhaps you might want to reconsider. Have you forgotten how children bring on your migraines? I would hate to see you over do it and be laid up for a week."

Red-faced, Vivian glared at her husband. "What an unkind thing for you to say Alfred. Why I love children and you know it." Looking up at her son for support and seeing he had nothing to say, she huffed, "Well I do!"

"Yes, yes of course you do, my dear. However, perhaps it would be best for Miranda to extend your invitation to Felicity after all. Considering all the arrangements that still need your attention, I'm certain that would be best. A fortnight isn't that long and I'm sure your time could be spent making certain our guest's stay will be acceptable."

"Mother Honeycutt, if you would like, perhaps the two of us could go shopping for new bed-linens tomorrow. That is, if you're free." Sarah offered.

Amused at what lengths Vivian would take to make a good impression, and seeing how Sarah was trying to get her attention, Miranda quickly joined in on the conversation of the welcoming-home party. "What was it again Mrs. Honeycutt, you were planning to serve?"

As Vivian prated on about the festivities, Miranda continued to ask her questions to avoid the tradition of Tad reading to her in Vivian's boudoir. Just as she had hoped, as the clock chimed nine, Michael looked at Sarah and Tad.

"Well, it's getting that time. Shall we?" Turning his attention to his father who had stood to send his son off, Michael said, "Dinner was exceptionally interesting tonight. Thank you."

~

An hour later, waiting until she was certain Vivian and Alfred had retired for the evening, Miranda crept through the darkened halls and down to the basement of the Honeycutt mansion. Within minutes of joining Gilbert, she found herself engaged in a heated discussion with him for he managed to upset her again.

"Ah . . . so his lordship didn't get to read to you this evening did he? Tsk tsk, such a pity!" He smirked. "Fret not though, my dear. There's always tomorrow." Acknowledging her scowl, he added sarcastically. "Oh that's right, *my dear* is reserved for his lordship, isn't it, Mandy?" His eyes twinkled at seeing her reaction.

Exasperated, she threw up her hands in despair. "I don't know why I bother to put myself through this. Why does every conversation end up speaking of Tad or you doubting my loyalties? Just you being here should be proof enough. Yet you still question my every encounter with him. Why? Haven't I told you every word that was spoken between us to gain your trust? What must I do to stop your nasty comments to me, which you know will only upset me?"

Sheepishly Gilbert looked at her. "Its not you I don't trust. It's his lordship. And for good reason." Dramatically he raised his arms and spanned the room before turning his attention back to her. "Might I remind you I'm locked up like some peasant in his lordship's dungeon while he runs fancy free to do as he pleases and read poetry to the fair maiden."

"Please Gilbert, enough. You know I only have a few minutes to spend with you. Why must it be spent arguing?"

"Arguing, you say? Why this isn't arguing, lass. I was merely trying to find out how your day was. Can I help it that I find it irritating that you spent so much time with him, after you claim he means nothing to you?"

Inhaling a deep breath to steady her frayed nerves, she continued in a strained whisper. "Well, to my way of thinking, this is indeed arguing. And don't you dare insinuate I have romantic feelings for Tad. You know I can't tolerate him even speaking to me because of you. What perplexes me is why I continue to allow myself to be put through this day after day when it's obvious that my kindness has not been appreciated, nor that you will ever believe me."

Yearning for a sign of encouragement, or words of endearment to justify her decision to run away with him, it suddenly occurred to her that perhaps she had misjudged his awkwardness around her. *What if he didn't show her affection simply because he wasn't interested, rather than not believing he was worthy as she had convinced herself?* Such a depressing thought caused her eyes to well up with tears.

"Jesus, Mary and Joseph, if there ever was a woman who could weep at a drop of a hat it would be you, Miranda. Why would you be crying now, lass?"

Shaking her head, she turned and cupped her head in her trembling hands, managing to mumble, "You wouldn't understand."

"Aye . . . So I'm not as bright as his lordship, am I? Would he be able to understand?"

Angered by such a comment, she turned on her heels and glared at him. "Why you pig-headed fool! Has it ever occurred to you that I was crying because in two weeks you'll be leaving and it troubles me?"

A smile crossed his lips, as he came closer to her. "My, but aren't we the feisty one tonight. Much like that first day we met at the orphanage and I angered you. Remember when you were singing that little ditty with the wee ones?"

Hearing him recall that day, her frown faded and she silently prayed he would at last express the love she hoped he felt for her. "I'm surprised you even recall that day."

"Why is that? I may have been run down, but me head works just fine."

"You're impossible!" She spat in an exaggerated whisper. "I was merely pointing out I was surprised you recall the day we met, considering the fact that you remind me practically every day that knowing me has been a curse."

"Now Mandy, that's not exactly what I said . . ." His eyes dancing merrily as he looked at her, chuckling.

"And that's another thing. Why must you insist on calling me Mandy?" Her tone raised more than she intended.

Smirking and stepping closer to her he asked, "Would you prefer me to call you, my dear, like his lordship does?"

Glaring at him, recalling how Tad had called her that in front of him, she stomped her foot and planted her clenched fists on her hips. Ready to retaliate, Gilbert stepped forward and gently placed his hand over her mouth. "Shh, I hear something," he whispered urgently.

Listening intently, she heard a strange sound and her heart raced in her chest. Fear showed in her eyes as she and stared up at him while clenching his arms. Lowering his hand from her lips, his hand rested on her cheek as they clung to one another straining to hear where the sound originated. As the minutes passed, which seemed like hours, Miranda held her breath frightened for Gilbert's safety but she enjoyed his nearness, the feel his breath on her face. Still gazing deep into one another's eyes Gilbert tenderly began to caress her cheek and slowly trace the edge of her jaw to her chin and finally back to her lips. Feeling his touch, her breathing became unsteady, more like short gasps as her heart raced.

Whispering softly he said, "I call you Mandy, because it suits you when you get all riled up."

Smiling affectionately at him, she whispered, "In that case, I approve. Despite your enjoyment of upsetting me so."

"That I do indeed. You have a real fire in you . . . I pity the poor fool who ever crosses you," he said.

"Then keep that in mind the next time you deliberately try to antagonize me."

"Lass, I'm just havin' a wee bit of fun is all. Just teasing mostly..." Pausing to look at her hand still clinging to his shoulders, he gazed back at her with a hunger she had never seen in his eyes before.

Feeling his breathing intensify she boldly asked, "And now, Gilbert . . . Are you just having fun by teasing me?"

Wrapping his arm around her waist, he brought her closer to him as his lips came crushing down on hers. Eagerly she wrapped her arms around his neck and passionately returned his kiss when suddenly he pushed her from him and coarsely whispered, "This is wrong! You had better be going up to your room, where you belong."

Feeling ashamed and fearful he found her actions vulgar she said, "Why is it wrong Gilbert? I don't understand."

"Are you daft? Isn't it enough that I've sunk so low I've hidden behind a woman skirts to save my own skin like some coward? Do you think I want your pity too?"

Unable to believe he thought himself to be a coward, or that she had kissed him out of pity she whispered, "Look into my eyes, Gilbert. Surely you can see what I feel for you is anything but pity."

"Just leave me be, Miranda. I'm not one of those orphans you tend to. I don't need or want your charity."

"How insulting! Any man who can't distinguish an act of endearment to that of pity or charity is either daft or just pig-headed. In your case, I would hazard to guess that possibly both applies."

Judging by the smirk on his face, Miranda knew Gilbert was not insulted by her comment, but amused by her flared temper. "Aye, so now I'm daft along with pig-headed. Well you might be right lass, but the fact remains that you and I are not suited for one another. So again I ask you, please Miranda, leave me be."

"No! Not until you explain why you push me away either by nasty insults or as you just have done."

"Trust me, you don't want to get mixed up with a bloke like me. What kind of future can I offer someone like you? In case you've forgotten, I'm a wanted man accused of murder. And if that weren't bad enough, I'm hated for being an Irishmen . . . Hell, I can barely write me own name, let alone read poetry or fancy literature to you. All I know how to do is work, and like I said before, your kind has never earned a fair living with his hands in all your life."

There was no mistaking the pain in his eyes as he spoke to her, yet she refused to allow him to say such unkind words.

"I told you before Gilbert, these hands have worked the fields to survive. So don't you dare say such hateful things to me." Angered that he would deny each of them what their hearts desired out of pride, she added sarcastically. "How generous of you to make this decision for the both of us without even consulting me. Do you have such a low opinion of me that you would even think I give two hoots if you are Irish or if you can read or write?" Then softening her tone, she hastily whispered, "What matters to me is your character. I look at you and see a man who never wavered from his convictions or integrity, despite the injustices you've endured."

"Aye, integrity you say. That's why I hide in some dank basement holding my breath every time I hear a strange sound."

"What choice do you have? Go to the authorities? Tell the truth and be hung because your accuser is more powerful than you are? There is no shame or dishonor in what you are doing Gilbert. What matters is that within a fortnight you will have a new start. A real chance to build a life for yourself. Don't you see that?"

Nodding, he said, "What you say may be true, but that still changes nothing between us. Not until I can offer you a life that's deserving, will I ever let what just happened take place again."

Realizing that nothing she could say would change his mind--being as stubborn as he was--she shook her head discouragingly. "Considering the lateness of the hour, I'll say good night. However, before I go, please keep one thing in mind. If what I desired was a man of means, then why am I down here this evening in your arms rather then in Tad's?"

Turning on her heels not waiting for a response, she quietly crept up the stairs. As she approached Alfred's study she paused when she saw a light glowing from inside. Craning her neck around the door, she was surprised to see Alfred sitting in a chair looking directly at her.

"Ah Miranda dear, having trouble sleeping?" he asked, rising from his chair while gesturing her to come inside.

Hesitating for only a moment she nervously said, "Why Mr. Honeycutt, you startled me. I thought I was the only one who couldn't sleep this evening."

"Yes, well I had a few things on my mind. Please shut the door and come sit with me for a spell."

Obediently, she did as he asked and once seated, Miranda looked at him and saw that he was flushed. Concerned, she said, "Mr. Honeycutt, are you sure you are all right?"

"Perfectly, my dear. Just a wee tired is all."

Never hearing him use that term, as the Irish did, she glanced at him suspiciously. Her eyes widened as she detected a glimmer of amusement in his eyes, yet somehow Miranda managed to keep her voice calm while speaking again. "As you should be, working as hard as you do. Shall I get you some warm milk form the kitchen? I find it most soothing."

"No, my dear. That will not be necessary. However, do not let me stop you from getting some for yourself. Assuming that is where you were headed."

Not hesitating in replying, she hastily said, "Actually, I've been in the basement, working on my special project."

"Ah, yes. Your special project. Perhaps it would be better if you moved your project to a vacant guestroom where you would be more comfortable. Surely, the lighting down there is poor. Why, as I recall the last time I ventured down there it reminded me of a dank dungeon."

Realizing Gilbert had said something similar only minutes earlier, her heart raced. *Two comments in less than a minute was no coincident, was it possible he knew?* she wondered while avoiding his eyes.

"Oh I don't mind. It serves it purpose quite well. Thank you for your kind offer though." Then pretending to yawn and covering her mouth, Miranda offered an apology as she stood up. "Excuse me, I must be more tired than I had thought." Smiling in his direction, she headed to the door careful to avoid eye contact with Alfred again.

"Yes of course, Mandy."

Hearing his response, Miranda stopped abruptly. With cheeks blazing and her heart racing, Miranda slowly turned back to face the man who had obviously overheard Gilbert and her. With fear gripping at her heart she asked, "How long have you known?"

"From the day he arrived of course," Alfred replied boldly.

"I see," she whispered, unable to look him in the eyes. Miranda closed her eyes to think of what she could possibly say to excuse her actions, feeling immense shame and fear at the same time.

"Mr. Honeycutt, I'm at a loss for words . . . I never meant to deceive you. Please don't notify the authorities."

"Miranda if that was my intention, I assure you, my dear that would have already been done. Why don't you take a seat and we can discuss why you feel the need to leave with this man you barely know, but obviously care deeply for."

"How do you know . . ." In shock, unable to think clearly, her voice trailed off. Suddenly sick to her stomach and feeling as if the room was spinning around her, through a haze, she saw Alfred stand to take her arm.

"Come over here and sit down Miranda, you're overwrought and exhausted."

Glancing at him as he assisted her and seeing the look of concern on his face, tears welled up in her eyes. "Oh Mr. Honeycutt, I'm so sorry. I never would have dishonored your trust and hospitality if it hadn't been a matter of life or death. You must believe me," she sobbed hysterically.

"Dear, you have not dishonored me. If anything, I owe you a debt of gratitude for saving my grandson from having the blood of another on his hands. If you and Mrs. Myles hadn't reacted so swiftly the night my grandson and his so called confidant ran that man over, I shutter to think what would have resulted from such a heinous act. Not only have you two women saved the life of an innocent man, but in doing so, I have come to know who the true perpetrator of David Sullivan's murder was. And although Tad is not blameless in his actions, at least he has done nothing that cannot be rectified, with the exception of losing you that is. Which was why I felt the need to discuss Mr. O'Flaherty with you tonight."

"I don't know what to say," Miranda said sheepishly through her tears. "Who told you . . . I mean, how did you know?"

"Does that really matter, dear? What matters is that I have taken extra precaution to assure that Mr. O'Flaherty remains safe. Mind you dear, I did not say Tad. What he has done is inexcusable, but he is my grandson. After Mr. O'Flaherty has left safely for San Francisco, and has an opportunity to begin a new life with no fear of retaliation from Tad, I will see to it that his name is cleared of any wrong doing."

"Not that I doubt you, Mr. Honeycutt. But why are you doing this? And how can that be done, without exposing Tad's part in this?"

Smiling at her, he said, "In answer to your first question, do you think you are the only one who possesses scruples and morals Miranda? Throughout my life, I have tried to live by a code of ethics, which I believed were fair and just. In doing so, never once have I set out to physically destroy another man. It shames me that a member of my own family had such a lack of regard for human life that he was compelled to silence a man at any cost. As the patriarch of this family, it is my duty . . . No! It is more than that dear. I truly believe it is the least I can do for Mr. O'Flaherty who has suffered so great at the hands of a Honeycutt. As far as your second question--my dear Miranda--need I remind you that I am a man of means? Money does have a way of remedying even the most delicate situations. It won't be the first time that new information has become available to our noble police force that clears a man of suspicion. So fear not, by the time Mr. O'Flaherty reaches San Francisco, he will be exonerated. Then both he and Tad can put the past behind them and rebuild a new life for themselves."

From an early age, Miranda had witnessed her father manipulating people and situations to get what he desired, and now hearing Alfred justify bribing officials merely to protect his good name and standing in society sickened her. His motivation to help Gilbert wasn't merely to undo the injustices brought down on him, no matter how he tried to sugar coat it to her now. She knew his gestures were ultimately to protect Tad and his loathsome friend from disgrace and shame, and that outraged her.

With Gilbert out of the way across the nation, both men would be free to enjoy life as they pleased while the death of David O'Sullivan would go unpunished. For the first time since she had known Alfred, she viewed him no better than she viewed her father who also proclaimed himself an ethical man.

Hastily she wiped her tears and said, "Excuse me for asking, sir. By your own admission, aren't you also abusing your wealth and position? Please don't misunderstand. I am extremely grateful for your offer to help Gilbert. More than you can know. But by doing what you are proposing, aren't you using whatever is at your disposal to get what you want?"

"Before you pass judgment on me Miranda, might I point out that Gilbert O'Flaherty was not a guest in my home at my request. Rather you brought him here without my consent. So in doing that, you too have used whatever was at your disposal to get what you wanted."

The truth in his words shook her very foundation and she knelt by his feet. "Oh Mr. Honeycutt, I'm so sorry...I don't know what's come over me . . . I'm so confused . . ." Her words broke between sobs.

Leaning forward, he patted her head. As she continued to cry, he whispered softly to the distraught young woman before him. "Get it all out Miranda. Let it go." Taking comfort from his words, she rested her head on his knee while he tenderly stroked her head.

"From the day you entered my life, I have thought of you as a member of our family. I've watched in admiration how you handled the most adverse situations, while maintaining dignity and self-respect. However, my dear, what has always puzzled me over the years is why someone with such breeding as yours has grown to distrust those of prestige and shy away from your inheritable social standings."

Sheepishly, she glanced up at him and whispered, "What you call as my inheritable social standing has come with a price that I'm not willing to pay. My mother, God rest her soul, paid the ultimate price for such prestige and that was her life."

Frowning by such a comment, Alfred said, "I was under the impression your mother's death was from ingesting poisonous mushrooms."

"Oh, that may be what stopped her heart from pumping, but what killed her soul was what society accepted from men of power and means.

Polite society closing their eyes to despicable acts too shameful to discuss aloud."

"Now it is I who am speechless. Clearly, you have been hurt deeply. Perhaps talking about it could help ease the burden you carry in your heart. That is, if you trust me enough to open up to me now."

Tears welled in her eyes as she looked at him in earnest. "Oh Mr. Honeycutt, I do trust you, honestly I do . . . its just I'm so ashamed . . ."

Speaking softly, he interrupted her. "Miranda dear, you of all people know the great shame I bare in my heart having my grandson commit such heinous acts. Surely I am in no position to judge another."

Nodding, understanding for the first time how painful this had been for him, knowing what Tad had done, she relived the painful childhood memories that haunted her. As she spoke of Lucas' infidelities and of her mother's drinking to mask her pain, Miranda was grateful that Alfred showed no reaction of shock or disgust while listening intently to her every word. When she had recalled the accidental shooting of her half-brother Joseph, he stopped her and asked, "Our Elise shot him?"

Realizing by his comment that Alfred had truly adopted all of them in his heart as members of his family--just as he had said earlier--she smiled fondly at him and nodded.

"So now perhaps you can understand why position and power hold little meaning to me. Was it able to save my mother from living a nightmarish existence at the hands of my father's betrayal?"

Softly he replied, "It did not indeed. In truth, I have often wondered what it was that kept you aloof, and now hearing your reasons, I must say you surprise me."

"Surprise? Why is that?"

"From the first day we met I came to realize you were the quintessence of a true belle of the south--shy, well versed in proper social refinement. Yet never had I surmised that beneath your beauty and charm lay the inner strength and determination of a lioness. What you have been able to accomplish with the Underground Railroad, along with aiding Mr. O'Flaherty is astonishing."

"Now it is you who has surprised me. Considering on both accounts I have managed to betray the trust of two men who meant the most to me by being dishonest and conniving. Two very unflattering characteristics for a woman to possess, and for both I am ashamed."

"Nonsense! I won't stand for hearing such rubbish," Alfred said indignantly. "You have nothing to be ashamed of. You reacted from sheer instinct on both accounts for the betterment of others, which shows great integrity and conviction. As I recall, didn't you try only moments ago to convince a rather stubborn man the importance of such fine attributes?"

Blushing again, realizing he had heard nearly their entire conversation she asked, "How do you know that? Was it you we heard?"

Pointing to a screened vent next to the fireplace Alfred said, "What you heard was an old man trying to eavesdrop, and stumbling against the poker. That vent leads directly to the basement."

"I'm so embarrassed," she mumbled, looking down at the floor to avoid eye contact with him.

"No more than I. Please forgive me for invading on your privacy. However, I had to know if you were indeed serious in going to San Francisco with Mr. O'Flaherty."

"Yes, I am. Even though I'm certain he will try to prevent it."

Nodding, he said, "Yes I should imagine he will. Are you certain that this is what you want?"

Sheepishly, she nodded. "I love him and I know he feels the same. It's just his foolish pride that stands in our way."

"Ah yes. Pig-headed I think you called him."

"Oh dear, you really did hear everything didn't you?"

"Not everything, that's why I had to get closer to the vent and clumsily knocked into the poker."

"Judging from the look on your face, I take it you don't approve?" Miranda asked, meekly.

"Before I respond, will you indulge an old man to pry into your affairs and ask a few questions?"

"You're not an old man and you certainly have every right to pry. However, I must warn you, nothing you can say will change my mind," she replied stubbornly.

Raising his hand, he smiled wearily. "I wouldn't dream of trying. I was just wondering what you intend to do once you arrive in San Francisco? Presuming Mr. O'Flaherty permits you to come with him, that is. And then, there is the matter of Lucas. Have you given any thought to how this will affect him?"

Somberly she looked up at him, and took a deep breath. "Mr. Honeycutt, I've thought of little else. Father will be devastated. What I'm relying on is that he risked everything he held dear for such desires, having them once himself, and in time he will come to understand I had to do the same. I intend to write him a letter and have it posted the day I leave, explaining my love and longing to be with Gilbert. As for Gilbert . . . Well in truth, this may prove to be more difficult than Father accepting my decision. He can be so prideful and stubborn, as you've heard." Not waiting for a response, she added hastily. "What I intend to do is point out that the officials are looking for a man, not a husband and wife."

"Ah I see. So you intend to pose as his spouse."

"Yes. I've booked passage for two under the name of Mr. and Mrs. Joseph Hourigan."

Rubbing his brow, looking at her with genuine concern he said, "Traveling across country will be difficult enough. How do you intend to mange keeping others from suspecting that you are not truly man and wife if Mr. O'Flaherty does not agree to this arrangement?"

"Not every detail has been worked out, but I can assure you Gilbert is no fool. Surely, he will see that he has no other choice, or risk being caught and brought up on charges."

Shaking his head, Alfred said, "My dear, do you really believe deceiving him in such a manner is wise? No man, especially one as your Mr. O'Flaherty, will welcome being manipulated in such a manner. You hardly know this man. What if he gets to San Francisco and leaves you? Then what? Your reputation will be ruined, not to mention the fact you will be in a strange place with no one there to protect you."

Looking at him with pleading eyes, she said, "You heard him. He does not believe he is good enough for me. What other choice do I have but to force him to take me along? By the time we reach San Francisco, I should be able to persuade him this was the best for both of us. Once he knows how much I love him, surely he will forgive my deceit."

"There must be a better way." Seeing Miranda ready to argue with him, he raised his hand as if to silence any of her arguments. "Dearest, before you begin arguing with me, please indulge an old man an opportunity to help. Surely, between the two of us, we should be able to work out a more suitable plan. I owe this much to you and your father, not to mention Mr. O'Flaherty."

"Then should I assume you approve?"

"No. I did not say that, my dear. However, I do understand the love you feel for this man. All I hope and pray is that he is worthy of such love."

For the better part of an hour, Miranda, sitting in the chair next to Alfred, listened as he discussed other possibilities for the trip west. While she still feared Gilbert's safety was in jeopardy, she took solace in trusting his and her fate in this man she loved as a father.

~ Fifteen ~

No Turning Back

Exhausted from the evening's events, Miranda, with a heavy heart, slowly tiptoed up the stairs to the second floor of the Honeycutt mansion. Although she was grateful Alfred had offered to assist her traveling to San Francisco, she knew he did not approve. *How could he? When I don't either! No woman should ever throw herself at a man as I'm intending to do. It's degrading. Have you no shame?* She chastised herself, pausing to stare at the vacant room once occupied by Tad.

Without warning, memories flooded her mind of the tenderness she and Tad had once shared. Unable to move from where she stood, stinging tears welled up in her eyes as she recalled the deep pain Tad had caused her by his deceit. Such betrayal Miranda knew she would never be able to forgive.

As a tear streamed down her cheek, Miranda began to question her motives to leave the life she had made for herself in New York to run off with a man she barely knew. Was it possible she had deluded herself into believing she was in love with Gilbert simply to avenge the deep-seeded pain Tad had caused her? Stunned by such a revelation, she immediately rushed up the remaining steps to the privacy of her own room. *Dear God, am I capable of such treachery?* Cupping her head in her hands, leaning on the wooden door of her bedchamber, she softly wept.

Hearing a cough from the other side of the room, she trembled.

"Miss Miranda, it's me. Please don't fret none."

Squinting across the dimly-lit room, Miranda was able to make out the silhouette of a man rising from a chair and she hastily wiped her tears. "Oh Montgomery, you startled me!" she whispered. "With all that has gone on this evening, I completely forgot we were too meet. How long have you been waiting . . ." Her voice trailed off as she increased the flame of her kerosene lamp. "Why it must have been hours. I'm so sorry . . ." She added apologetically.

"I was startin' to worry some. Mr. Gilbert didn't hurt you now, did he?"

"No. Of course not," she answered quickly, wondering why he would think such a thing and then realizing he had seen her cry.

Miranda smiled warmly at him. "How kind of you to be concerned about my well being Montgomery. But no need. It's been a long day and

I'm a bit out of sorts, is all. Especially, since I've just found out Mr. Honeycutt . . ." Miranda's voice trailed off realizing it must have been Montgomery who had informed Alfred that she had befriended Gilbert and was harboring him. She quickly added. "How foolish of me to forget the bond between a servant and his master, or in this case employee and employer."

The servant, clearly taken off guard, sheepishly glanced down to avoid eye contact with her, not saying a word. Realizing his actions confirmed her suspicions, she hastily added, reassuringly. "It's alright Montgomery. I'm not angry with you. It just would have been easier if I had known . . ." Then finding her words amusing, she nervously chuckled. "Who am I fooling? I never intended for Mr. Honeycutt to know, and if I had, I would have told him myself."

"Miss Miranda, I didn't mean to deceive you . . . but, both Mr. James and Mr. Alfred made me promise not to tell you."

Shocked hearing James also was in on this, she whispered, *"Mr. James . . ."*

Seeing the concerned look in the servant's eyes, Miranda cleverly changed her tone so as not to let on that he had mistakenly broken a confidence.

"Mr. James and Mr. Honeycutt have had my best interest at heart all along and I'm truly grateful for all of your help. Especially yours, Montgomery. This must have been extremely difficult for you."

"No trouble at all, miss. I sure am glad the cat's out of the bag though."

Not having heard that expression in some time, she smiled fondly at Montgomery, reminiscing how Chester, her former slave, used to say the same thing.

"Yes . . . Well it is getting late. Where is that passageway you were speaking of earlier Montgomery?"

"Right here, miss," he said eagerly, walking only a few steps to the corner of the room next to her dry sink and wardrobe. Judging by the tone of his voice and mannerisms, Miranda knew she had been successful in concealing he had spoken out of turn.

Before she had time to figure out why James Sterling would benefit from keeping the truth from her, Miranda's attention was drawn to Montgomery. There before her, she observed the servant lean over slightly and with great ease slid what she had thought to be a wall behind the wardrobe.

"Oh my! Why, I had no idea," she gasped. Walking closer to the opening in shock, she asked, "Now am I to understand you correctly.

Didn't you say that every bedchamber is equipped with . . . with . . ." Not knowing what exactly to call such a devise, she motioned to the opening. "One of these things?"

Nodding his head, he smiled. "Yes, miss. Every bedchamber has a dumbwaiter. Come step inside and see for yourself."

Hesitantly, Miranda walked closer to the passageway and saw in the center of a small area what looked to be a three-sided box made of metal suspended in mid-air. The platform, sides, and back were connected to two ropes on either side with a large pulley. Eager to demonstrate, Montgomery gently tugged on one of the ropes.

"See, this is how you go down. And if you want to go up, all you do is pull on this cord.'

Fascinated, and not believing she had no knowledge of it until now, she looked about the small room and noticed to the right of the metal platform what looked to be a narrow tunnel.

"Ah I see . . . and where does that go?" Miranda asked.

"Why that goes to Mr. Tad's old room, and if you head the other way, all the way down to the last chute, that takes you to Mrs. Honeycutt's room."

Confused and intrigued at the same time, she glanced from where she imagined the tunnel ran in her room and then back into the dark opening.

"But why can't I see that tunnel from my room? There are windows right there . . ." Her voice trailed off, looking back inside her room again. Then as if answering her own question, she smiled, whispering to herself, "The window seat! In all the rooms, a seat stretches across the wall to mask the tunnel. How ingenious."

"Mighty easy on the help too. Years past, before there were dinner parties every night, the Missus and Mr. Alfred would have their meals brought up to them. Rather than having to cart their trays up and down the stairs, the maids used this here dumbwaiter instead. It goes directly into the kitchen or can go to the cellar too."

"Really? I wouldn't imagine anyone could walk, let alone carry a tray in such a small area."

"Oh there's plenty of room. Come closer and see for yourself." Pointing at the darkened alleyway, Miranda noticed that from where she stood, no floor could be seen. Confused, she looked at Montgomery hoping for an explanation.

"The floor of the passageway is down a few feet, right over Master Alfred's library and the dinning room."

Closing her eyes, Miranda visualized the rooms below her and realized that the ceilings of those two rooms had lowered panels along the outer perimeters, which she had always thought was for decorative effects. Never had she realized they were multi-functional. Directing her attention back to the dumbwaiter, she asked, "Is this devise strong enough to hold the two of us?"

"Nah." Montgomery shook his head. "But if you like, I can pull on this here rope and you can take a ride for yourself and I'll come down right quick."

Nodding, Miranda stepped inside the iron chute, holding tightly to the metal rails just below the large pulley and ropes.

"Now don't be moving about none, and keep your head still, for there ain't no light down the hall so it's going to get mighty dark," Montgomery warned. "The kitchen doorway stays open some so as you pass by you'll see a little light, but when you reach the basement you will have to step out and open the door to the cellar yourself. Can you do that, Miss Miranda?"

She nodded, then asked, "Where will the door to the basement be exactly?"

Listening carefully, Montgomery gave her directions, like that of a parent to a child and she smiled, never seeing this side of him before.

"You can't miss it. Just as soon as you step off the platform, feel to the left and pull on the handle. The door will open right quick--it's good and oiled so as not to stick. Be sure to send the dumbwaiter back up and I'll meet you down there in a few minutes." Looking about the room, he lifted his finger as a gesture to wait for a second. Judging by the look on his face Miranda assumed he found what he was searching for and left for a few moments, returning with an unlit brass hurricane lamp.

"Here miss, you take this here candle and be real careful now." Miranda took the candleholder in hand while Montgomery searched inside his pocket for matches. Once the light was lit and the glass dome securely replaced in the holder, he looked anxiously at her. "You ready?"

Taking a deep breath, Miranda nodded and smiled nervously at Montgomery as she watched him pull gently on rope to her right. With every pull, the platform glided downward with ease. The further she descended, the darker it became and she was grateful Montgomery had thought to send her along with a light. Within a few moments she passed the small opening which she assumed was the kitchen. Nervously she looked at the candle's reflection that flickered as an eerie glow against the wooden tunnel leading to the basement. Being careful not to move as Montgomery had warned, Miranda became anxious wondering how much longer this would take. Luckily within moments the platform came to a halt and holding the candle firmly in one hand, Miranda nervously stepped out of the dumbwaiter onto the basement floor. Then spotting the handle precisely where Montgomery had said it would be, she opened the door with ease.

Breathing a sigh of relief, Miranda turned back and began pulling the rope to send the platform back where it had originated. Just as before, the dumbwaiter moved stealth-like with ease. Realizing that Montgomery was now pulling on the rope from his end, Miranda stepped away from where she stood and looked about the cellar. Rows of canned fruit and vegetables lined wooden shelves, with bushel baskets of potatoes and carrots stacked neatly against the other walls. Turning to face the other opening, she realized the door was locked from the inside.

Cautiously walking forward, she unlatched the hook from its eyehole and gently opened the door. Much to surprise, she heard voices, tiptoed out of the cellar, and gasped at hearing Alfred's voice.

"Be reasonable, Mr. O'Flaherty. Surely, a man of your keen perception can see I mean you no harm. All I am proposing is a business deal. Nothing more."

"Suggesting I marry Miranda ain't no business deal! Beggin' yer pardon, sir. But why are you so hell bent on getting' rid of her, too? She ain't done you no harm. She was just trying to mend me broken bones is all, which yer grandson and that no count friend of his caused, I might be addin'."

"You misunderstand me, Mr. O'Flaherty. I have no desire to see Miranda leave this home. On the contrary, nothing would please me more to see her and Tad one day wed, yet that seems highly unlikely under the circumstances."

Unable to believe what she was hearing, Miranda's hands began to tremble while she inched her way closer, anxious to hear Gilbert's reply.

"And what circumstances would that be, sir?"

"Isn't it obvious, Mr. O'Flaherty? Miranda took great risks, not only to her own person by bringing you here, but to her position and reputation if you were ever discovered. She could have easily hid you at her friend's home, where your sister lives. With the Carmidy's abroad, and your sister more than capable of tending to your wounds, I think you would agree this would have been the most logical of solutions. That is, if all Miranda cared about was your safety. No, I think Miranda's unselfish actions speak volumes. She clearly cares deeply for you, and if you want to admit it or not, the facts speak for themselves. And judging by your present condition and living conditions, I would also assume these feelings are reciprocated. Otherwise, why else would you risk living under the very roof of the man who accosted you?"

Hearing Alfred's declaration, Miranda's heartbeat quickened. *Dear God this can't be happening!* Clenching the handle of the lamp, she inched closer, determined to hear Gilbert's response.

"Look sir, beggin' your pardon, but you know nothing of me. What you're suggesting is ridiculous. Hell, I don't know the first thing about packaging fruit, besides, a man just don't go up to another and offer him a job and then say, 'oh and by the way, why don't you marry this lass too'? Even if I were so inclined--not saying I am, mind you--but for argument sake let's say I was. Who says Miranda would agree to such a marriage?"

Before Alfred had a chance to reply, his attention was directed to the entrance where Miranda stood dumfounded. "Ah, Miranda dear," Alfred said, stretching his hand out for her to join them. "As you can see, I've taken the liberty of introducing myself to our guest."

Feeling the blood drain from her face, she slowly stepped closer, her eyes never leaving Gilbert's. "I didn't mean to eavesdrop . . . I just found out this very evening about the dumbwaiter . . . er . . . When I heard voices, I came to see where they were coming from." Her words broken, she was clearly shaken and unnerved at what she had overheard.

Taking Miranda's hand as she approached, Alfred lovingly patted it and tenderly said, "Yes well, our business was just about over."

Turning his attention back to Gilbert, Alfred said sternly, "Mr. O'Flaherty, I'm a man of business and don't make it lightly when offering a man employment. As I said before, with the proper training, I'm certain you would be an asset to my food brokerage company outside of San Francisco. It will be hard work, but a man like yourself doesn't strike me as the kind who runs from a challenge. Think on it some and I'll get back with you tomorrow for an answer. As for my other suggestion, well . . . Why don't you and Miranda sit for a spell? I'm sure you two have plenty to discuss."

Gilbert's eyes trailed from Alfred to Miranda, and he blushed as their eyes locked. Just then Montgomery walked out of the cellar and upon seeing him, Alfred turned and smiled fondly at Miranda. "Well, if I had known it was going to be so crowded down here this evening, I would have had cook prepare us a snack."

Turning his attention back to Gilbert, he raised his eyebrow. "Tomorrow afternoon while Mrs. Honeycutt is away, perhaps you and I could visit again."

Nodding, Gilbert said, "Yes, sir."

Then patting Miranda's hand again, Alfred smiled warmly at her and winked. "Well my dear, it's late. Before long, cook will be up making us breakfast, so do be cautious."

"I will," Miranda whispered.

Turning to leave, Alfred said, "Ah, one more thing. Do see to it that you don't use that dumbwaiter during the day. Cook will be wondering why, and be inclined to investigate." With that, he turned to Montgomery. "Come, old friend, we've got a few things to discuss."

Both Miranda and Gilbert speechlessly watched as Montgomery assisted Albert up the wooden stairs leading to the main floor. Slowly turning back to Gilbert, she looked sheepishly at him, praying he would say something to break the tension between them.

"He's quite a corker that one. Did you know he was coming here tonight?"

"No. Of course not!" she replied indignantly. "Why, I just found out only a while ago that he even knew you were here. Why do you ask?"

"Nothing, except when he saw you, he wasn't surprised."

"What are you implying Gilbert? That I sent him down here to ask . . ." Unable to say the words, and angered by his innuendoes, Miranda glared at him before continuing. "It just so happens that when I returned from seeing you this evening, Alfred confronted me. In a most embarrassing manner, I might add. Not that you would care." She spat indignantly.

Glaring back at her, he chuckled. "Don't be raising your voice to me and getting your nose out of joint. All I'm trying to find out is why that man had to come down here in the middle of the night offering me a position and proposing . . . Well you heard what he was saying, you stalking about like some grave digger and all."

Outraged by his implications, she shouted, "How dare you! I was not stalking about. Don't you dare speak to me in that manner Gilbert O'Flaherty. I won't stand for it, I tell you. Not now or ever again." Clenching her fists at her side, she glared at him. "It just so happens I don't know why Alfred came to see you this evening. I was too busy finding out how Tad had been able to stalk me while I slept."

Seeing the rage in his eyes at hearing Tad's name, she knew she had said too much. In a horse whisper he said, "What did you just say?"

"Nothing. It doesn't matter. It's been a long day and I'm tired. Far too tired to be arguing with you over Tad. So, goodnight." Turning to leave, he grasped her arm and looked pleadingly into her eyes.

"Miranda, please. Tell me what you meant by his lordship stalking you in your sleep." Every instinct in her told her to run, but she knew if she did, Gilbert would only badger her later, so she took in a deep breath.

"I'll tell you everything as long as you promise me not to lose your temper."

"Just tell me, Miranda."

Quivering from the fierceness of his glare as his eyes penetrated her very being, Miranda felt her cheeks grow red and slowly began to explain her comment.

"The night you and Tad got into that scuffle, he came home quite late and had words with his father. After he had gone to his room, I went to him. Only to tend to his wounds." Miranda paused. Seeing his jaw pulsate, she quickly added. "Nothing more. I swear Gilbert."

"Go on." His voice was barely audible.

Never had she seen Gilbert react like this. She found herself growing more anxious, avoiding his green eyes that were boring a hole through to her soul. "The following morning I found a vase of flowers and a thank you note on the bed-stand, next to my bed. It struck me as odd, since I was certain I had locked my door."

Again, Miranda paused seeing how his eyes reacted to hearing her words. Nervously she placed the candle she was still carrying on a nearby table and hastily added. "Until this evening, when Montgomery was driving me home from the orphanage, did I come to realized that Tad had probably entered my bedchamber through the tunnel that leads from each of the rooms on the second floor."

His icy-cold glare continued, and she looked up at him pleadingly. "You must believe me Gilbert, I knew nothing of the dumbwaiter, or for that matter, I had no idea Alfred intended to speak with you this evening let alone what he was going to propose. I swear."

Saying not a word, Gilbert turned and sat on the edge of his bed then bent over and started to remove his boots. Stunned by such a reaction, Miranda watched in astonishment.

"What are you doing?" she asked.

From her vantage point, she could make out that his jaw was still clenched as he leaned over to put his boots next to the wooden chair beside his bed. Standing, he glared at her while unfastening his trouser buttons.

"Unless you fancy stalking me like his lordship, I suggest you leave. I'm tired and I need my rest if I'm to be fit to travel in a few weeks."

"Are you serious? Aren't we going to discuss this further?" she asked, resenting him for dismissing her like some child.

Shaking his head defiantly as a response, he brazenly continued to unfasten his trousers.

Shocked, Miranda somehow found her voice. "If you are angry with me then say so. But don't you dare try to intimidate me, Gilbert O'Flaherty. Because it won't work. Have you forgotten I've seen you undressed already?"

"Ah, have you now? And when would that be, lass? It was Montgomery who undressed me after my accident. You said so yourself. Or was that just another lie?"

"Are you accusing me of being a liar, again?" She spat while stomping her foot and clenching her fists by her side. "As I told you before, I have no reason to lie to you. What I said, was that Montgomery assisted me, so I could tend to your wounds. Can I help it you assumed he unclothed and bathed you too?"

Hearing her words, Miranda saw the anger in his eyes as he glared at her.

"Aye, now that wouldn't be trying to twist the truth to suit ya, now would it lass? Is that what ya learned in all those fancy books that his lordship reads to ya most every night? How to twist the truth rather than being earnest and straight forward?" Shaking his head in disgust, he pulled off his shirt and tossed it across the arm of the chair. "Leave me be, Miranda. I've had a belly full of yer kind."

Outraged by such a comment, she asked indignantly, "My kind? And just what is that supposed to mean?"

Glaring at her, he stepped closer. Undaunted by his obvious anger, Miranda remained planted firmly where she stood and defiantly glared back at him.

In a coarse whisper, he spat indignantly, "Ya let that sons 'a bitch read sweet nothin's to ya nightly. Ya let him kiss ya occasionally, always insisting it's to protect me, and now I learn that he's seen ya undressed, in yer nightdress too." Standing only inches from her, he asked, "Just tell me Miranda, what will be next? Are ya going to let him bed ya too?"

His words cut through her heart. Never had anyone defiled her with such hateful words, and she raised her hand to strike him. Before she made contact, Gilbert grasped it tightly in his own, and she winced, feeling his strength as he squeezed her hand in his.

Their eyes locked and she gasped seeing such hatred and anger. As if he had nothing more to say, Gilbert silently released her hand and turned back to his bed where he sat resting his head in his hands.

Stunned and outraged, she looked at him, bewildered. "What have I done to deserve such treatment? Except, risk everything to nurse you back to health so you could insult me and cast me aside, as if I was some cheap strumpet."

Hearing no response, it suddenly occurred to Miranda that what bothered Gilbert the most was that Tad had seen her in her dressing gown rather than the fact that he had violated her privacy. Outraged that she was viewed by these two men as nothing more than some prize to be won, she began to shake uncontrollably.

In that instant, Miranda vowed she would no longer be willing to stand by meekly while those she loved continued to hurt her--like her mother had allowed her father to do. In her current state, the voice of her mother taunted her, recalling how Catherine had repeatedly said to her as a child. *"Be a good girl, Miranda. Mind your manners, Miranda."* Defying her rearing, and as if answering her mother's commands, she shook her head defiantly. *Not this time! Not ever again. Being a good girl has only broken my heart.*

Glancing at Gilbert and seeing him still sulking, Miranda somehow managed to find her voice and calmly said, "You know what Gilbert? I've just figured out this very second why we continue to argue. It's not really me you're angry with, or for that matter, what has happened to you. What angers you is that Tad has gotten away with it and you can't do anything about it. Nothing I say to you or a well-respected man as Alfred Honeycutt means little to you where Tad is concerned. All that matters is your wounded pride and competing against a man who you despise."

Fine Gilbert! It bothers you that Tad has seen more of me than you have. Well I'll even the score then. Bending over, she swiftly untied her shoes and stepped out of them. Impulsively, she began to unfasten the buttons to her skirt, and releasing them from their restraints, she let the skirt fall around her feet. "You've been in competition with him from the day you met and I've been foolish enough to think that over time things would change . . ."

While still speaking angrily at Gilbert, Miranda hastily began unfastening each button. "Let's see if I've gotten it straight. Tad calls me a special name, and so you have to come up with one too. Then Tad kissed me and of course, you had to as well. Now you learn that he violated my privacy, but rather than be concerned for my welfare, or try to console me when I needed you, all you could think of was that he has seen me in my nightgown. How pathetic is that?" she spat indignantly.

Angered more than she had ever been before in her life, she flung her blouse to the floor, and added. "Since Tad has never seen me in my pantaloons and corset, will you think you're ahead in this twisted and warped game you two insist on playing?" Glancing at him, and seeing no response, Miranda tugged at the cords of her hooped skirt until it too become free while she angrily called to him. "What? No clever response or hateful unjustified accusation?"

Pausing, she glared at him, waiting for him to respond. Hearing none, she angrily planted her fists squarely on her hips and boldly said, "Answer me damn-it! I deserve that much."

Slowly he raised his head, and judging by the shocked look on his face, Miranda knew he was as surprised to see her partially clothed, as she was, in herself for disrobing in front of him.

Rather than backing down, Miranda looked him squarely in the eyes and defiantly asked, "So tell me Gilbert, is the score even? Or are you ahead since I willingly disrobed for you without having you sneak into my room in the dead of the night to leer at me? I'm confused, how would you rate this?"

Taking in a deep breath and shaking his head, an impish grin of admiration crossed his lips. "I said it before and I'll say it again. You are a feisty one, I'll give ya that much. But let me warn ya Mandy, I won't be just fiendishly leering over ya while ya sleep, if ya keep standing like that much longer."

Hearing him say such a thing, her breathing intensified as her chest rose up and down in short thrusts. "So now are you suggesting I bed you, rather than Tad. Yes. I guess that would put you ahead, wouldn't it Gilbert?"

Then glaring at him, not waiting for a response, she knelt to retrieve her blouse. "Well you can go to the devil! Right alongside Tad, because I'm tired of being your prized token while you break my heart."

Picking up the garment, she hurriedly pulled the sleeves right side out so she could put it back on, while she added. "Why come to think on it, Tad has never seen me dress either. My, but you really are ahead aren't you? Pity that only you'll know how far ahead you were, since Tad will be here and you will be thousands miles away in San Francisco. How about me relaying the message for you? Will that help to heal your pride, because God knows how hard I've tried to heal your wounds?" On the verge of hysteria, Miranda, shaken to her very core started trembling uncontrollably.

Standing up, Gilbert started to step closer to her and instinctively Miranda grasped her blouse to her exposed chest and neck. Her heart bounded so hard in her chest, she was certain he could hear it.

"I'm sorry Miranda. I wasn't thinking clearly," he whispered, slowly inching his way closer to her. "It's just when I think of him touching ya or looking at ya, I go a little mad."

Painfully aware of his bare chest and opened trousers, and how appealing he looked, Miranda began to inch farther from him, while pleading desperately, "Please Gilbert, don't come any closer. Turn around and let me escape from this humiliating and embarrassing moment. I beg of you. This was a mistake . . . I don't know what came over me. I just wanted to prove that I'm not some prize that you two can fight over."

Coming closer, Gilbert said solemnly, "I am truly sorry Miranda. Will ya please just answer me one question?"

Shaking her head from side to side, clutching at her blouse she whispered, "If it's about Tad, so help me Gilbert . . . I'll scream."

"I swear to ya, I'll never bring up his name again. That is, if ya answer me this one question."

Timidly she asked, "What is it?"

"Did Mr. Honeycutt come down here tonight to offer me a job and suggest I take ya with me because of somethin' ya said to him?"

Hearing his question, Miranda knew instinctively that if she admitted to what had actually been said, she stood the chance of angering Gilbert further, so reluctantly she said, "I swear to you Gilbert, I did not ask him to do that."

Inching even closer, Gilbert shook his head and softly said, "That's not what I asked ya, Miranda."

"Please Gilbert, don't pressure me . . . What I spoke in private with Alfred was never meant to go any father than between him and me."

"Do ya trust me Mandy?" he whispered, only inches from her partially exposed body.

Tenderly, their eyes locked and she nodded her head. "Yes, you know I do. With my life. But must you humiliate me further?"

Seeing she was on the verge of tears, he tenderly pulled her to him, his bare arms wrapped around her, and timidly, she released the blouse that she still clung to and allowed herself to take comfort in his arms. Clutching him, leaning her head on his shoulder, Miranda could feel his heartbeat quicken as he grasped her tighter in his arms, his hands tracing the curvature of her spine.

"Christ ah mighty, ya have no idea what ya doing to me. Yer skin feels as soft as the mornin' dew on a rose petal."

Glancing at him, no longer angry, but relishing in his touch and his words, their eyes locked and Gilbert tenderly said, "I know I can be difficult at times, prone to think the worst of people, but ya must never again think I was interested in ya because his lord . . . er . . . What I mean to say is, yer was never a prize to win. From the moment I saw ya, I loved ya, and if the Saints will bless me, you'll say ya love me too."

Pulling slightly from him with tears running down her cheeks Miranda said, "Oh Gilbert, I do love you--with all my heart."

"Then ya must learn to confide in me, as ya have with Mr. Honeycutt."

"I can't. You will be angry with me," she muttered.

"Don't ya know that yer just made me the happiest man in the world? How can I possibly be angry with ya when yer gave me your heart?"

Timidly she looked up at him wanting desperately to be able to confess what she had planned without his consent, but fearful if she did, she risked ending this moment of blissful tenderness.

As if sensing her awkwardness, Gilbert drew her in his arms and whispered, "I meant what I said Miranda. I love ya. You *do* believe me, don't ya?"

Feeling his breath on her cheek and hearing him declare his love for her again Miranda timidly nodded her head while nestling closer to him. "Oh Gilbert, if you only knew how often I've prayed you would say those words to me. Even when you were so cruel, picking fights with me, I kept praying that the day would come when you realized that you loved me as I loved you."

"My love for ya was never in question. Don't ya see Miranda, I had nothing to offer and my love is so deep for ya, I could not allow me own selfish needs come before what was best for ya. Even now, as much as I want this to happen, I know . . ."

Anticipating his words, she pulled from him and placed her fingers over his lips. "Please don't even think of such things Gilbert. What you didn't take into consideration all the while you pushed me away, was that when a woman truly loves a man, as I love you, such love isn't measured by worldly possessions or standing in society. I say this not out of the throngs of passion, nor from a lack of not knowing a privileged life. We both know I was more fortunate than you were in this regard. For months, I've been prepared to gladly to give up everything to be with a man that I admire and respect but most of all, love. You may be stubborn Gilbert O'Flaherty, but what you must come to understand is I too, can be equally stubborn when I believe in something. And I believe in you, and in us. Especially the life we could share if you would only let it happen."

Tenderly caressing her cheek, he said, "What kind of life could I possibly offer someone as perfect as ya? Even if I were wealthy, Miranda, the fact remains in this country I'm judged by not who I am, but where I came from. I cannot bring such pain and misery down on ya, simply because ya love an Irishmen. So please be a good lass and go back to yer fine room, back to the life where ya belong and let me have this memory untarnished forever."

"No. Please don't push me away again. I'm here where I want to be, where I belong."

"Oh Mandy, I'm only a man, and as God is my witness, I can't just hold ya without wanting to make ya mine. So before I can't stop myself, ya better leave."

Stubbornly she shook her head. "If you force me too, I'll beg because where you're concerned, I have no shame. I want you to make me yours."

Hungrily his mouth came crushing down on her, and she matched his passion by clinging to him, moaning softly, feeling his hands pull her body firmly against his. Hearing him groan, swept away with his desire for her, Miranda gasped breathlessly. "Oh please Gilbert, love me."

Pulling slightly from her, their eyes locked and he breathlessly said, "Heaven help me, after tonight in the eyes of God ya will be my wife. From here out, I promise to do all in my power to deserve the love and trust ya have in me."

Seeing a tear run down Miranda's cheek, Gilbert tenderly wiped it with his thumb before continuing. "Perhaps, yer friend Mr. Honeycutt could bring by a parson tomorrow to make it legal. That is, if ya will honor me by sharing a life together and becoming my wife. But before ya answer, ya must know Miranda, that marriage is sacred to me. In the eyes of God, we will be one, so there will be no more secrets between us, no hidden meanings in yer words, or no more being alone with another man who wants ya as much as I do."

Hearing his words, she lifted her head and gazed into his eyes. "Gilbert O'Flaherty, nothing would make me happier than to be your wife and for us to build a life together."

Saying not a word, Gilbert tenderly swept her into his arms and carried her toward his bed, while Miranda silently leaned her head on his shoulder. No longer was she fearful that she was incapable of loving another. Casting aside what she had been taught of morality and decency, she clung to him wanting only to give herself completely to the man she loved.

Upon reaching the bed, Gilbert knelt on the edge and gingerly released her. A tender smile crossed her lips as their eyes locked on to one another, and she traced his broad chin with the tips of her fingers, as he inched his way next to her.

Dreamily she said, "That first day we met at the orphanage--even though you angered me so--hours later, all I could think of was your eyes. And although I saw in them such anger and hate, somehow I knew you had a great capacity of tenderness too. I was then as I am now, bewitched."

Smiling, he placed her hand in his, then looking down at it as if it were a delicate and rare art object, he leaned forward and softly began kissing it tenderly. Feeling his lips move slowly across her arms sent immediate rushes of desires through her. Pausing, he huskily growled, "Bewitched ya say? Was that before or after ya walked away from me in a huff?"

A smile crossed her lips, recalling the look of merriment she had seen in his eyes that morning when he knew he had gotten her goat. Gazing into his green eyes now she saw a glimmer of amusement along with a longing that took her breath away.

"Huff, you say . . ." she cooed, enjoying the sensation of his hands slowly tracing her shoulders and inching up her neck that heightened as Gilbert slowly began to kiss her skin where his hands had just been.

Leaning slightly further into the featherbed, she stretched her head back and closed her eyes, drinking in the splendor of such sensual caressing. Being aroused by his touch, Miranda inhaled deeply and slowly finished her sentence. "As I recall . . . you were deliberately trying to provoke me."

"Aye. And now, am I still able to arouse ya, Mandy girl?" he asked suggestively as he leaned in to kiss her. Feeling his mouth on hers, Miranda responded eagerly to his tongue as it parted her lips while his hands began to explore her petite frame. Never had she felt such longing, and urgently and she grasped her hand tightly around his neck. Feeling the hardness of his body next to her, aware that his hand had found its way into her corset and was fondling her breast, Miranda moaned softly, causing Gilbert to pull away from her and sheepishly apologize.

"Forgive me for hurting ya. I didn't mean to be so rough."

Brazenly, with trembling hands, she began to untie the cord that fastened her corset and said, "You weren't hurting me . . ."

Needing no prompting, Gilbert placed his hand over hers. "Please let me," he huskily whispered. Nodding her head, Miranda leaned back on the bed, allowing herself to feel the full sensation of his touch as his hands loosened the garment.

"My, but ya wear a lot of clothing, don't ya?" Miranda smiled as he caressed her breasts through her lacy camisole. Obligingly, Miranda raised her arms as Gilbert removed that as well. Tilting her head back, her spine arched, she gasped feeling his hands trailing down her breasts, softly caressing her abdomen. Without prompting, she raised her hips as he slid the lace-trimmed pantaloons over her thighs and gently removed her stockings.

Completely exposed to him, Miranda rested her head on his pillow, watching Gilbert remove the remainder of his clothing, finding it erotic. Her heart raced seeing his aroused manhood. Never had she felt such desire as she stretched her arms out to him.

Gingerly he returned beside her, the length of his body firmly pressed next to her as their mouths hungrily sought the other. As their desires increased, their hands voraciously began exploring the newness of the other's nakedness, all the while urgently kissing each other through their gasps of pleasure. As Gilbert inched his body closer to her--Miranda eager to become his-- completely grasped his neck as he slid his body over hers. Parting her legs so Gilbert could enter her, she moaned feeling his enlarged manhood inside the warm crevice of her body, and immediately their bodies moved in perfect unison, intertwined until they reached ecstasy.

Between gasping for air, Gilbert, huskily whispered, "I love ya, Mrs. O'Flaherty."

Hearing his words, Miranda clung to him, and said hoarsely, "Oh Gilbert, I love you."

While still inside her, Gilbert leaned to one side and Miranda did the same, contently lying nestled in Gilbert's arms. Feeling their oneness, she smiled radiantly at him.

"Now that I am yours completely, if you truly need for me too tell you what Alfred and I spoke of, I will tell you, so there will be no secrets between us."

"What ya spoke of earlier with Mr. Honeycutt was as Miranda Brown, and as much as I want ya to confide in me, that's one secret ya can take to yer grave if ya wish."

Tenderly caressing his chest, she smiled, thinking what a wonderful man she had just given herself too. "No. I want to share everything with you from here out. I'm just embarrassed and a little frightened that you'll think badly of me."

"Oh Miranda, never worry about that, especially when ya just made me feel like the luckiest man in the world."

Hesitating, she whispered, "After Alfred confronted me, explaining he had known you were here and that you were leaving for San Francisco, I told him I was going with you."

"Oh, were ya now? And how were ya intending to do that lass, prey tell?"

"It had occurred to me that if the trains were being searched for an Irishmen traveling alone that you could be in danger, so I booked two tickets, first class as Mr. and Mrs. Joseph Hourigan."

"Joseph Hourigan, ya say?" Clearly Gilbert was shocked hearing that name in particular. "That was me mother's da name."

Timidly she said, "Yes, I know. Margaret-Anne told me."

"Ah, so the plot thickens. Ya've gone to me own sister to conspire against me too."

She gazed into his eyes to gauge if he was angry with her or teasing her. Seeing a twinkle in his eyes while tenderly caressing her breast, Miranda said, "Not to conspire against you, but rather explain my intentions and to tell her that I loved you. It was her suggestion I use your mother's maiden name so you would know that I had spoken to her."

"You told her ya love me?"

"Yes. Just as I told Alfred the same tonight. Where you and your safety is at stake, I've already told you, I'm shameless. Nothing was going to keep me from you and nothing ever will again. Not Alfred, my father or anyone else, not even your stubbornness."

A smile passed over his lips. "And you call me stubborn?" he whispered. "Oh Mandy, ya too good to be true. As soft and beautiful as rose, and a heart as pure as an angel. Sweet Jesus, I may not have anything to offer ya, but having ya, I have all the riches a man could ever want or need. And one thing ya can be sure of, ya have my heart and all my love."

"That's all I ever wanted or will ever need. The rest we will leave in God's hands."

Tenderly their lips found the other, and as their passion increased, they culminated their love for one another again, bringing each other to fulfilling rapture in the splendor of their love and desire.

Hours later, still nestled firmly in Gilbert's arms, Miranda dreamily said, "Oh Gilbert, this is paradise. Please tell me again about your homeland. Do you ever want to return there?"

"Of course I do! When I've made a name for myself. You, me, and the children can go there and spend as long as ya like," he whispered, tenderly kissing her forehead while fondling her breasts.

"The children? As in more than one?" Miranda smiled sheepishly, not at all embarrassed of her nudity or what they had done.

"Of course! The more the merrier," he whispered. "Oh Mandy, yer goin' to love Ireland!"

While Gilbert described the beauty of his homeland, Miranda turned and snuggled closer to him as his hand moved over her shoulder hugging her softly. Leaning down to kiss his bare chest, she marveled at how much at ease they were with one another. Never had she felt so much at peace.

Feeling suddenly tired, Miranda closed her eyes but jerked awake, hearing a muffled coughing from above their heads. Pulling away from him, she whispered, "Darling, I must leave you. I'm certain that is Alfred I hear. His library is directly above us."

Tenderly kissing her forehead, he nodded. "When will ya be returnin'?"

"That really depends on Alfred, I suppose. I'll make my excuses with Felicity and be home early. I promise."

"Home? To our palace in paradise?"

Preferring his playful sarcasm to antagonizing her, Miranda ignored his comment and hastily withdrew from his bed and started to dress. Gilbert watched in silence, smiling at her as she stepped across the room to retrieve her other garments. After securing her blouse inside her hooped skirt, while slipping back into her shoes, she hastily reminded him that Alfred could hear everything they said. Then tiptoeing back to his bed she leaned over and kissed him tenderly. "I'll return as soon as I can."

Nodding, he whispered, "I love ya, Mandy."

"I love you more," she whispered while caressing his cheek.

"Impossible," he growled. "Now be off and do what ever ya have to do, before I change me mind."

Hating to leave him, but knowing she must, Miranda bent down and kissed him again. "Don't tempt me, Mr. O'Flaherty."

Lovingly he raised his eyebrow, and chuckled. "Now who's bewitching who, Mrs. O'Flaherty?"

Groaning playfully, she turned and tiptoed up the stairs, praying she could make it to her room without being detected. As she passed Alfred's study, seeing the door closed, Miranda hesitated, not wanting to spoil her bliss by having words with him, but knew she must speak with him. Adjusting her hair, she timidly knocked gently at his door.

Hearing his gruff reply of "Enter", Miranda suddenly wished she had waited. Then realizing she was still in the gown she wore to dinner the previous evening, her cheeks grew red. *Oh dear I should have changed first. He's sure to notice.* Before Miranda had a chance to react, the study doors opened wide and Alfred looked at her in surprise. "Miranda, why what a pleasant surprise. Come in."

"Only for a moment," she said meekly.

Much to her surprise, Alfred did most of the talking while pacing, as she sat quietly and listened. When he announced that after being down in the basement last night for the first time in years, he had to agree with Gilbert--it was dank and dismal. Her heart raced, fearing the worst. Instead, she was relieved to hear that other arrangements were being made for Gilbert to be moved to the servant's quarters in Montgomery's room, where the two of them could have more privacy. Although he said nothing directly to her, just by his remark of them requiring privacy, she knew Alfred had guessed why she hadn't changed from her gown.

Only being in the servant's wing once, Miranda recalled that Montgomery had his own entrance to the gardens as well as the main house, and she smiled, thanking him. Blushing, Alfred then addressed other concerns on his mind, the first being if she still intended to go with Gilbert to San Francisco.

When she replied yes, explaining she and he would like to be wed as soon as possible, Alfred immediately nodded his head and said he would make the necessary arrangements. However, he insisted that the wedding be detained for a few days until Benjamin had returned, since Alfred was concerned in letting any others find out they were harboring a wanted man for murder. Agreeing with him, and grateful for his keen perception of the situation, she asked, "Is there anything else you care to discuss with me before I make my leave?"

Looking at her, she knew what he was about to say troubled him by the look on his face. Bracing herself for a lecture Miranda took in a deep breath.

"Considering the lateness in the hour and when you did not answer your door to your bedchamber earlier, I took it upon myself to send word to Mrs. Myles that you have taken ill today."

Hearing him say he had visited her room and knew she was not there, Miranda blushed but said nothing, listening to his every word.

"This so-called illness should suffice for a few days, my dear, by being excused from dinner and other situations where you would be required to be in contact with Tad. With Joshua and Elise arriving with the Robbins' early next week and the preparations for the party keeping everyone preoccupied, I should venture you'll have ample excuse not to be alone with Tad. Nevertheless, we still have the end of this week to get through. Are you certain you will have the courage to continue this charade?"

Puzzled by such a comment she said, "Of course. Haven't I done so until now?"

Tuning to face her, he looked tenderly at her. "It has suddenly occurred to me that in my zest to help, I may have caused you and Mr. O'Flaherty more harm than good by not waiting to speak with him next week."

"I'm sorry Mr. Honeycutt, but I'm not following you . . ."

Raising his hand to silence her, he added. "I wasn't finished. You see, there is a certain glow a woman possesses when she loves and she knows she is loved in return. And my dear, you radiate. If I can see it, I am positive that a certain young man who already thinks you're beautiful, will see it too. Therefore, from here on out, until you leave us Miranda, you must be doubly careful. It goes without saying that myself and Montgomery will help wherever we can, and I'm sure after I explain the complexities of the situation to Felicity, she too will assist you as well. However, we cannot be with you every moment of the day. Now more than ever before, we must do nothing to arouse the suspicions of Tad or the temper of Mr. O'Flaherty. Not that I think your fellow would do anything unwisely, mind you. But a man in love is apt to do anything, especially if he must protect the woman he loves from his enemy."

Seeing her ready to object, Alfred hastily added, "Miranda, I know what I'm talking about here." As if the matter had been settled, he added. "As I was saying, as wonderful as it is to have you confide in me, there are certain matters you need to discuss with a woman. Mrs. Myles, being worldly and as levelheaded as she is, would be my first choice. Not to mention, with Vivian hell-bent in rekindling an alliance with Felicity, for the sake of impressing Rupert Robbins, we can use this to our advantage. Don't you agree, my dear? So I've urgently requested she come early tonight, before dinner."

Realizing he was right and trying to be as delicate as he could, she nodded. "As you wish, sir. Is there any thing else?"

"Just one. Please be happy, my dear. You and Mr. O'Flaherty deserve that much."

After thanking him again, Miranda crept silently to her room. While freshening up and changing into another gown, a smile crossed her lips as the last of Alfred's words sprang to mind. Although he had never said it formally, she instinctively knew Alfred approved of her choice in men.

~ Sixteen ~

New Beginnings

Anxious passengers made their way toward the gangplank to meet their loved ones, while Joshua and Elise stood on the deck looking out onto the harbor nostalgically.

"Well Mrs. Carmidy, did you enjoy your wedding trip?" Joshua whispered huskily, holding Elise close to him, his arms wrapped around her waist as they looked out over the harbor.

Smiling at him, Elise cooed, "It was perfect. I almost wish it didn't have to end."

"Even traveling the rough seas?" Joshua teased.

"Oh you . . ." she whispered lovingly, tapping his hand. "I could do without that I suppose."

"Indeed. Are you feeling better now?" he asked concerned.

"Oh much better now that we've docked. I'm so sorry I spoiled our last few days . . ."

"You did nothing of the sort." Joshua interrupted. "I rather enjoyed tending to you for a change. Although, as I recall, I was a far better patient after we were ambushed than you were these past few days."

"That's because you were unconscious," she replied sarcastically.

Chuckling, Joshua kissed her head and asked, "Have you decided if we should share our news right away, or wait a few more months?"

Knowing what news he was referring too, and loving him for allowing her to make this decision, Elise leaned back into his shoulder enjoying his nearness. "Oh darling, as much as I'd love to share our good fortune with our family, let's wait for just a while. After all, with Rupert and Annabelle here, I wouldn't want to distract from their visit."

Nestling closer to his wife, Joshua smiled. "Who are you kidding Elise? You enjoy being the center of attention. Do I need to remind you how you used to sashay around your mother's parlor to be certain you had captured all the men's hearts?"

Playfully slapping his hand, she said, "Oh you do exaggerate so. Besides, I've already captured the only man I'll ever need or want."

"Yes you have, my pearl."

Turning to face him with concern in her eyes, she said, "Darling, before long I'm going to be fat. Will you still love me then?"

Chuckling, he kissed her forehead. "I'll love you more."

Satisfied with his response, she cooed, "You always did know how to turn my head."

Seeing that the Robbins' were on their way to join them, Joshua hastily whispered in her ear, "Behave yourself, you shameless hussy."

Smiling at him with a twinkle in her eye, she innocently asked, "Is that anyway to speak to the mother of your child?"

Turning his attention to Rupert, who had now joined them with Annabelle on his arm, Joshua ignored her last comment, directing his attention to their new friends. "All packed and ready to meet everyone?"

"Well, we're packed. But in truth, suddenly I feel a bit apprehensive." Annabelle said shyly. "We've had such a lovely trip. Do you suppose we could remain on the ship instead?"

"Oh fiddlesticks, Annabelle. It won't be so bad." Elise said reassuringly, while taking her arm. "If Lavinia so much as looks at you crossed-eye, why I'm apt to forget I'm a lady!" Then hugging Annabelle, Elise mischievously giggled. "You know, with me not having my sea legs and all, she might have an unfortunate accident," Elise exclaimed, while exaggerating a shifting motion of her hips followed by Elise clasping her hands around her cheeks as if shocked. "Mercy sakes, now wouldn't that be a sight! Her splashing about in all that murky water below might be quite memorable, not to mention most amusing. Why, I should imagine even the pristine and beautiful Lavinia would find it difficult to keep up appearances in those conditions."

Chuckling nervously, Annabelle embraced her new friend. "Yes, but you wouldn't really do such a thing. Would you, Elise?"

Tucking her arm through Annabelle's, Elise snickered while cocking an eyebrow. "Well, I have been prone to be a might cantankerous from time to time, when provoked." Leaning closer as if sharing a secret, Elise said, "Did I ever tell you of the time when Joshua made me so upset that I threw my shoe at him?"

"Oh you didn't!" Annabelle replied with a broad smile.

"I most certainly did. It was back at my Mama's boardinghouse in Fairfax."

Lagging behind their wives, Rupert looked at Joshua. "Your wife really is quite special."

"That she is," Joshua said, proudly grinning in her direction, admiring Elise's ability to put people at ease, even under the most difficult situations. Turning his attention back to Rupert, he added. "I'd say we both were damn lucky men."

"Indeed," Rupert proclaimed.

With that, the four of them stood in line with the rest of the passengers ready to disembark. Once on the gangplank, Elise began scanning the crowd of people waiting for the passengers. Spotting her mother in the group below, she began waving frantically.

"Look Joshua. Mama and Michael are here. Oh, and there are your folks, too. See them?" she asked excitedly.

"Yes dear, perhaps it might be wise not to jump about in your condition though. After all, you could fall."

Squishing up her nose and acting as if she were annoyed, Elise pouted while clearly enjoying his pampering. "Oh pish-posh. You're no fun! Honestly Joshua, ever since you found out, you've been hovering about like some old nursemaid."

Turning her attention to Annabelle, she said in an exaggerated whisper, certain that Rupert could hear her as well. "By the way, we've decided not to bring up the baby just yet. You will keep our secret won't you?"

Nodding her response, Annabelle's eyes drifted to the crowd below and she discreetly scanned where Elise had been pointing. Spotting Lavinia among the crowd, her heart began to race as the blood rushed to her cheeks.

Glancing at Annabelle and seeing her friend's concerned look, Elise reassuringly patted her arm. "Don't fret, Annabelle. She can't cause you harm as long as Rupert's by your side."

"A very wise and accurate assessment," stated Rupert, proudly.

Raising her eyebrow, Elise timidly looked at Rupert with a smile pasted to her lips. *Oh my, this should be interesting,* she thought while politely nodding as they made eye contact.

As soon as the four of them stepped outside onto the dock, they were immediately surrounded by family. After exchanging hardy hellos to her family, Elise watched shamelessly as Annabelle and Lavinia grazed each other's cheeks without any hugs or excited greetings as she and Joshua had with their folks. Instinctively she knew this strained welcoming had nothing to do with the English being reserved, acting as passing acquaintances rather than family.

From Elise's vantage point she marveled at how cordial Rupert had been with James rather than with his wife's sister. He boldly said, "James, you old scoundrel. Good to see you again." He shook his hand vigorously while Annabelle nodded saying a polite hello. Again, Elise's interest piqued noticing how Annabelle had addressed her brother-in-law as Mr. Sterling rather than by his Christian name.

How peculiar, Elise thought, looking away so as not to appear rude by staring at them. However, she did notice that as polished as Rupert was-- seldom exhibiting emotion in public--he made no attempt in concealing his disappointment at discovering that Felicity was not able to welcome them.

"And why is it again that our cousin was not able to be here, Mrs. Honeycutt?"

Obviously flustered that he was asking her the question rather than Lavinia, Vivian said, red faced, "Why Rupert, just as I explained. With she and our dear Miranda welcoming Reverend Myles and Miranda's father back home, there simply was no time. Why, if we had not received your telegram late this afternoon, telling of your early arrival, I dare say we would have all missed this joyous occasion. Isn't that right Alfred?" Vivian said, looking for support from her husband.

Not lending the encouragement Vivian had wanted, he replied by asking, "Why is it that you decided to take an earlier ship, Mr. Robbins?"

Speaking up, Joshua said, "Actually, it was our idea, sir. Elise was a little under the weather and I wanted to get her home safely."

"Oh dear," Sarah exclaimed, hugging her daughter nearer to her. "Are you alright dear?"

"Mama, don't worry. I'm fit as a fiddle. Joshua was just being overly cautious, is all." Judging by Sarah's concerned look, she didn't believe her daughter, but smiled at her anyway.

As they started to make their way to the coaches, Elise's ears perked up upon hearing Rupert address Felicity's absence again.

"Shall we be seeing our cousin tonight then, Mrs. Honeycutt?"

"Why yes, of course. She promised me as soon as Benjamin and Lucas arrive they will come straight to our home. As a matter of fact, they should be there now."

"Right. I was under the impression that when Reverend Myles traveled, Felicity accompanied him. Am I too assume she has been residing with you Mrs. Honeycutt, in Benjamin's absence?"

Clearly flustered by his questions, Vivian replied, "As it was, Felicity preferred to stay at her own home. She really is quite devoted to the children you know."

Having spent the last six weeks with the Robbins', Elise knew that the glance they had just shared between one another was more than idle curiosity.

Reaching the coaches, it was decided Elise and Joshua would travel with both of their parents, while Rupert and Annabelle would accompany the Sterling's along with Alfred and Vivian. Smiling reassuringly at Annabelle, Elise stepped into her coach and took a seat by her mother.

As soon as Elise was situated, Sarah leaned closer to her and whispered, "Don't you think for one minute you're fooling anyone, missy. A mother always knows."

Smiling sweetly at her mother, acting naïve, Elise coyly said, "Mama, for the life of me, I don't know what you're referring too." Grateful for the diversion as Mary Carmidy entered the coach, Elise cooed, while patting the seat and sliding over.

"Come sit beside me, Mother Carmidy."

"Why certainly, dear. As long as I won't be crowding you. As I recall when I was in your delicate condition, I just hated to feel closed in."

The blood drained from Elise's face as her eyes opened as wide as saucers, quickly glancing between her two mothers in complete shock. Seeing Joshua enter the coach, Elise looked over at him pleadingly and said, "I swear, darling. I didn't say a word!"

With a triumphant grin, Mary patted Elise's hand and looked at her son. "It's true! As soon as I saw that glow to her and then looked at you all puffed up like some rooster, I just knew."

"*We* just knew!" Sarah chimed in.

"Knew what?" William and Michael asked as they took their seats across from the three women.

"That we're soon to be grandparents!" Both mothers exclaimed enthusiastically. This immediately sent great cheers of laughter erupting from inside the coach that echoed throughout the crowed street. While in the Sterling's coach that followed closely behind, no such excitement existed. Instead, the silence between the six of them was deafening.

As soon as the coaches pulled in front of the Honeycutt's mansion, instinctively everyone remained in the background while Rupert and Annabelle was greeted with great enthusiasm by Felicity. With tears welling in her eyes, Elise smiled as she watched Felicity embrace Rupert and Annabelle.

"How good it is too see you both," she exclaimed hugging them again, tears running down her cheeks. "If I had known you were arriving today, I would have welcomed you at the dock." Seconds later, Benjamin joined his wife and shook Rupert's hand vigorously, then patted him on the back.

"Congratulations and welcome to America, old friend." Turning to Annabelle, Benjamin hugged her fondly as she did him in return. Turning his attention to Rupert he jokingly said, "You're a lucky man, my friend.

How did you ever manage to persuade such a lovely creature as this to become your bride?"

Glancing to his once sister-in-law, Benjamin said sincerely, "I've never seen you look more radiant Annabelle."

Bashfully, she smiled and warmly said, "How kind of you to say so Benjamin. It's so good to see you again."

From the look on Annabelle's face, it was clear to everyone that her words were sincere, and Elise glanced at Lavinia. Judging the sour look on Lavinia's face, Elise knew instinctively that she was not enjoying the reunion of these four people who obviously cared deeply for one another. As Lavinia and Elise's eyes locked onto each other, Elise extended a cordial smile to her, which was not returned. Nearly ready to burst out giggling, Elise politely glanced back at the Myles' to hear what Benjamin was saying.

"Speaking from our hearts . . ." Pausing and extending his arm for Felicity to join him, Benjamin continued. "Having you both here means more to us than words could ever express."

As they all hugged one another again, Elise noted what a contrast this reunion was to the one at the docks.

Alfred, seeing Miranda and Lucas watching from the steps, cleared his throat and motioned them to join him. "Mr. and Mrs. Robbins, I would like to introduce you to Lucas Brown and his dear daughter, Miranda. The Brown's are old friends of the family. Perhaps my granddaughter told you that she and Miranda grew up as neighbors in Fairfax, Virginia?"

Hearing Virginia, Rupert looked at his cousin. "Virginia? That was where you were raised Felicity."

Tucking her hand in his arm, she said nostalgically, "Oh Rupert. What a dear man you are--you remembered. Yes. Mama and Papa were old friends of Mr. Brown's, too."

Nodding, making the connection, Rupert smiled while extending his hand to Lucas, who accepted it and shook it vigorously. "How good it is to make your acquaintance, sir."

Pleased by the warm gesture, Lucas smiled and nodded respectfully at Annabelle, then said to Rupert. "I had the pleasure of knowing your aunt as well, Mr. Robbins. A mighty fine woman--a mighty fine woman indeed."

As Felicity introduced Miranda to Rupert and Annabelle, Elise felt a twinge of jealousy proclaiming her a dear friend. Feeling Lavinia's eyes on her, Elise deliberately avoided eye contact with her, and joined them by tucking her arm around Miranda's waist.

"I'll only share her with you Felicity, since you were so kind to introduce me to your dear friend, Annabelle."

The four woman giggled softly and Annabelle, said, "Well, it would appear we shall all be friends then."

Clearly able to see that her friend and confidant was an outcast to these four women, Vivian glanced at Lavinia, discreetly gesturing her to join them. Seeing Lavinia make no attempt to join the circle of friends, Vivian pasted a smile to her lips and said, "Dearest Felicity, why don't you show our guests into Alfred's study and we will continue this lovely reunion in comfort."

Following their hosts into the study, everyone began to mingle freely, chatting amongst themselves as the servants brought refreshments. Sitting on a padded ledge overseeing the gardens and facing the other guests, Elise smiled cordially, listening to Joshua recount their trip abroad to their parents. She was intrigued by how the Myles' and Robbins' immediately huddled together, catching up on each of their lives, while the Sterling's sat quietly on the opposite side of the room keeping Vivian company. Elise, nodding at Miranda, who smiled at her while chatting with Alfred and her father, noticed how lovely her friend looked. *Miranda's in love*, she thought to herself and then looked about the room and realized Tad was not present.

"Excuse me, Michael." Elise interrupted. "I've just realized Tad's not with us this evening. Will he be joining us for dinner?"

"Yes dear, of course. He had errands to run. In truth, I haven't seen him all day. So he will be pleasantly surprised to see that you all have arrived earlier than expected."

"Ah . . ." Elise answered absent mindedly, watching Alfred make his way across the room to speak with Benjamin in private, far removed from the other guests. From the look on her grandfather's face, Elise got the distinct impression he was troubled by something. Watching discreetly, she saw the two men excuse themselves and head toward the gardens. As they passed, she nodded at her grandfather, who smiled fondly back at her while escorting Benjamin outdoors, without stopping to say a few words.

Hmm, how odd, Elise thought. Wondering what could be so urgent that he wouldn't take the time to chat for a spell, she glanced at Miranda, hoping to get her attention so she could gesture for her and Lucas to join them. Instead, Elise observed Miranda who was too preoccupied watching the Reverend Myles and Alfred to even notice her.

Curiosity getting the best of her, Elise immediately tapped Joshua on the shoulder and whispered, "Darling, I think I'll stretch my legs and get a breath of fresh air for a spell."

Nodding, Joshua leaned closer to her and asked, "Shall I join you?"

"Heavens no. You find out all the news I know that you're dying to hear, while I have a nice chat with my dear friend, Miranda."

Politely excusing herself from Sarah and Mary, Elise went directly to Miranda and hugged her, while saying to Lucas. "Mr. Brown, why don't you visit with Michael and Joshua, while I steal Miranda away for one of our chats."

Chuckling, he boisterously said, "I was wondering how long it was going to take for you two to get your heads together."

"Come Miranda, let's take a stroll in the gardens."

"The gardens you say . . ." her voice trailing off while smiling sweetly at her friend. It was obvious to Elise that Miranda was stalling, which only heightened her interests further.

"As lovely as that sounds, it seems so selfish of me to occupy all your time when you've just returned. Perhaps after dinner we could sneak away."

Leaning closer to Miranda, Elise whispered softly, "I may have been away for a spell, but I know when you're trying to keep something from me. The way I see it, we can go to the gardens now and discuss our secrets. Just as we have since we were babes, or I can find out on my own. The choice is yours." Smiling sweetly she leaned into the flustered Miranda and continued. "Oh please don't be a ninny, Miranda. You know, I mean you no harm. I'm just curious as to what has you so keen on Grandfather Honeycutt and Reverend Myles going to the gardens, and why you don't want me out there."

Still smiling, Miranda looked at her friend and shook her head whispering coyly, "Dearest Elise, your imagination is running away with you. What possible secrets would I have, for goodness sakes? It just so happens, when I saw Alfred going to the gardens I was just wondering if he had an opportunity to complete a special surprise we have for you and Joshua's homecoming, is all. So don't you dare try to wiggle it from me. My lips are sealed."

Not fooled by the ploy Miranda was trying to use on her, having used it countless times herself in the past, Elise smiled and applauded softly not to draw attention to them.

"Bravo, Miranda. Well done. Why, I don't believe I was ever as convincing as you were just then. However, my dear, it isn't wise to use one of my own tricks on me. I see right through them."

Seeing Miranda's smile fade, Elise added. "Why must you insist on taunting me by trying to conceal something from your oldest friend? As soon as I saw you, it was obvious you were trying to hide that you have found love. You radiate with the glow as only a woman can who has found true love. Who is he Miranda?" she whispered.

Giggling nervously, Miranda said, "He? Whatever are you babbling about?"

"You're in love and loved in return. Don't try to deny it Miranda." Leaning closer, she whispered enthusiastically, "Is it Tad?"

Shaking her head, Miranda for the first time since they had been chatting, looked sincerely at her friend. "I'm sorry to disappoint you Elise. Although Tad and I have been courting, we are not in love like you, and your Joshua . . . Which reminds me, I really must speak with Alfred. Promise you will act surprised. I'll be right back for that chat."

With that, Miranda turned and scurried away before Elise could stop her. Watching her friend, Elise shook her head gently. *Fine Miranda, run from me now, but I know something is not right, here. And by gosh, I intend to find out before the night is over.* Turning her attention to Felicity, Elise decided that perhaps she might find out something from Miranda's newest friend. Smiling cordially, she joined Felicity and Annabelle as they chatted softly sitting on the settee arm in arm.

Seeing Elise approach, Felicity asked, "My, but you look so distracted Elise. Are you well?"

Keeping the pasted smile to her lips, she cooed, "Yes. Quite well, thank you Felicity, dear. It's just so close indoors, after all that delightful sea air. Perhaps you two would care to join me for a stroll in the gardens?" Elise asked, while glancing at Annabelle, who nodded in agreement.

As the three of them strolled past Lucas, the Honeycutt's and the Carmidy's, Elise was aware of the watchful eye of her husband as he continued conversing with Michael about current events.

"So am I to understand you correctly? The latest theory is that Booth shot the President from a personal vendetta, rather than a hopeful restoration of the Confederacy?"

Returning Joshua's smile, Elise glanced at Annabelle and whispered, "That's one thing I sure didn't miss while we were abroad."

Confused by such a comment, Felicity said, "What's that?"

"All that talk of poor Mr. Lincoln's death. Why it's depressing."

The three women rushed past the crowd gathered around William Carmidy and heard him reply, "According to eyewitnesses, Booth was seen with Lucy Hale the morning of the assassination at the National Hotel. Rumor has it, their meeting was to inform Booth that their engagement was to end, since she would be traveling with her father, John Hale to his newly appointed assignment as Ambassador of Spain. That, by the way, Lincoln had appointed him too that very day!"

Caught up in the conversation, Joshua said, "Really father! Why I wasn't aware Booth was even engaged. The last I had heard, he was quite a womanizer."

Anxious to bring Joshua in all the latest news, Michael said, "According to my sources, not only was Booth and Lucy engaged, but he was insanely jealous of an involvement between Lincoln's son Robert Todd, and his betrothed."

Hearing the latest comment as she left Alfred's study, Felicity smiled at her friends. "Thank heavens we don't have to worry of such betrayal from our husbands."

Nodding her head, Annabelle added. "Yes, indeed. I shudder to think though how close I was to choosing unwisely."

Knowing whom she was referring too, Elise said, "I know precisely what you mean."

Slightly distracted by not seeing Benjamin, Alfred, or Miranda anywhere in sight, Elise turned her attention back to her friends and smiled to mask her curiosity. "Although in truth, there was never anyone else for me but my Joshua. Nevertheless, I feel lucky knowing I would never end up so happy, if I had chosen another path."

"Oh don't be so sure it was luck, Elise. I have come to believe firmly that what happens in our lives is not luck, but rather is all in God's plan. You and Rupert, Joshua and Elise and my Ben . . ." Pausing, suddenly feeling very awkward, Felicity glanced sheepishly at her friend.

Sensing her friend's awkwardness, Annabelle tucked her arm through hers knowingly, and warmly said, "No two people belong together dear friend, more than you and Benjamin Myles. Thank heavens, your dear Auntie had the wisdom to break tradition."

Seeing Felicity well up with tears in her eyes, Elise suddenly felt as if she were intruding on them and tried gracefully to excuse herself. Recognizing why she was excusing herself, the two women insisted she remain, explaining they had no secrets Elise hadn't already heard, being a trusted friend. Reluctantly, Elise listened soberly, nodding occasionally as Felicity explained in detail how she and Benjamin were reunited. In return, Annabelle recounted the years they had been apart beginning with the death of her father, her ill-fated infatuation with Francois and how Rupert had been there to mend her broken heart once again when she discovered what a scoundrel Francois actually was.

Hearing them speak of such intimate details, exposing their hearts and the love they had for their husbands, it was clear to Elise these two women shared the same friendship that she and Miranda had. Time apart from one another had little effect on the way they felt for each other, or the ability to sense the other's thoughts. Precisely why as Elise sat listening to Annabelle and Felicity rekindle their friendship, her thoughts were on Miranda.

No matter what her friend said, she knew Miranda had found love. *If not with Tad, than who?* she wondered. So caught up in her own thoughts Elise hadn't realized that Annabelle had asked her a question. Hearing no chatter amongst her companions, Elise looked at them and seeing the strange look on both of their faces as they stared at her, blushed.

"Oh, do forgive me. Seeing how you two speak so freely with one another has made me start to worry about Miranda."

"Worry you say? Whatever for Elise?" Felicity asked, fanning herself to cover the warmth in her cheeks she suddenly felt by having Elise bring up Miranda now of all times. Especially, since she knew that Benjamin had probably already joined her and Gilbert in holy matrimony. Hastily, Felicity added to help ease Elise's troubled mind.

"Although we're not as close as you and she are, I can assure you, Miranda is very happy."

"Yes. She does have that certain glow to her, doesn't she?" Elise asked suspiciously, aware of Felicity's sudden uneasiness. Guessing that Miranda had confided in her made Elise jealous, but she refrained from showing her disappointment and waited for Felicity to respond.

"Glow you say? I guess I didn't see any change in her appearance, since I see her nearly everyday at the orphanage." Seeing an opportunity to change the direction of the conversation, Felicity hastily added. "Oh dear, I do hope Miranda's not having a relapse. You know, she was quite ill last week and missed several days at the orphanage."

"No I wasn't aware of that," Elise replied politely, all the while thinking, *Who are you fooling? Miranda's no more sick than you or I am.*

Hearing of the orphanage, Annabelle quickly asked, "With Miranda ill and Benjamin away, how did you manage, Felicity?"

Glancing at Elise before she answered, Felicity wondered if her feeble attempt of redirecting the conversation had been successful. Unable to gauge by the look in Elise's eyes or in her mannerisms, Felicity surmised, *You must have been an excellent spy.*

~

Not more than one-hundred feet away, inside the small servant's quarters that was now being used to harbor Gilbert, Benjamin smiled warmly at Miranda.

"As you can guess, I'm equally surprised and honored to perform this ceremony for you and Mr. O'Flaherty, Miranda. And although it is quite pleasant that Mr. Honeycutt and Gilbert's sister, Margaret-Anne are here to witness this joyous occasion, I would be amiss in my duties by not stating the obvious and that is your father's absence. Are you certain you want him to miss such an important occasion, Miranda? Especially when he's so near?"

Looking at Benjamin, Miranda nodded. "Yes, Benjamin. I'm certain. As hurtful as it will be for both father and I, for years to come, I truly feel this is for the best."

Inhaling a deep breath and looking at Alfred then back at the intended bride, Benjamin hesitantly nodded his head. "Very well, as you wish."

Taking a moment as if gathering his thoughts, Benjamin closed his eyes before glancing back at Miranda and Gilbert. "Often times, before joining two individuals as one into one of God's holiest ordinances, I remind couples that the vast differences of their past must never be forgotten. Today, looking at the two of you, never have these words seem so poignant. As you embark on this new journey, not as two individuals but rather one, be certain to bring with you the essentials of a strong union. Patience, respect, and above all, love. The love you feel for one another, your patience to see the other's points of view and respecting each other, as individuals, with their own unique personalities along with different heritages will make for a strong and lasting bond. My solemn prayer for you both is that if you honor these commitments to one another, your life as man and wife will flourish as each day passes."

Pausing, Benjamin smiled fondly at Miranda.

"Dearest Miranda, moving thousand of miles away from the protection of your loved ones may be painful and exceptionally hard on you. Are you prepared to forsake the life you once lived and cleave only to Gilbert, all the days of your life?"

Solemnly, Miranda glanced at Gilbert and said without hesitation, "I am. We shall build a life from our love with the help of God."

Nodding as if satisfied with her response, Benjamin directed his attention to Gilbert.

"And you, Mr. O'Flaherty. As you stand beside your intended this afternoon, with your future uncertain, are you prepared to place Miranda's needs and desires in front of your own?"

Hearing his question, Gilbert glared at Benjamin. "I'll not be giving any explanation to some Englishmen, despite that collar, Parson."

Shocked by such a comment, Miranda gasped while Albert, shouted, "That will be quite enough, Mr. O'Flaherty. How dare you speak to Reverend Myles in such a vile manner?"

Turning his attention to his host, Gilbert said apologetically, "Forgive me, sir. I meant no disrespect to ya. But I'll be damned if I'm going to answer such an intimate question to the likes of him." He scoffed, coldly nodding at Benjamin.

Confused by his sudden outburst, Miranda looked pleadingly at Gilbert while reaching for his arm. "Why are you saying such things, Gilbert?"

Sheepishly looking over at her, the anger faded from his eyes and he smiled lovingly at her before responding in a soft whisper. "I already told ya Mandy, the day God brought us together was the most blessed day of my life and I will cherish ya until the day I die."

"Then why are you so angry? Benjamin has done nothing against you. He is here at my request, because he's a trusted friend."

Rubbing his hands through his hair, Gilbert glanced at Benjamin then back at Miranda and he tenderly smiled at his bride to be. "I know how much it means to ya that we are legally wed, and so out of respect for ya, Mr. Honeycutt, and even that collar the parson wears, I will answer any question he asks. But mind ya lass, this will be the last time I will ever be judged by some Englishmen, who knows nothing of me, or answer questions regarding my devotion to ya."

Before Miranda had a chance to respond, Benjamin coughed politely and smiled warmly at the man before him. "Mr. O'Flaherty, forgive me for being so intrusive on your privacy. And although, I do not know you personally, it is clear that the love you feel for Miranda is one of great depth. Will you kindly allow me the honor and privilege to join you as man and wife in the eyes of God and all his holy saints?"

Nodding at Benjamin then looking at Miranda, Gilbert smiled. "Nothing would make us happier, Parson."

Taking a deep breath to steady her nerves, Miranda accepted Gilbert's hand. Although, she had no idea why he had taken such an instant dislike to Benjamin, she knew that despite Gilbert's obvious objections, what mattered most to him was her happiness. A loving smile replaced her frown and as they were legally joined as one. She took great solace in knowing that in spite of the anger he harbored in his heart towards others, Gilbert loved her more.

~ Seventeen ~

Watching Eyes

Paralyzed were she stood, Miranda found it difficult to contain the rush of emotions that swept over her as she glanced at family and friends gathered in the Honeycutt's study after her wedding. Secretly she hoped someone would realize her whole life had changed, all the while praying no one would discover her secret and jeopardize Gilbert's safety.

In a daze, she wondered how was it possible that those in attendance could chat idly after what she just did. She was now a married woman aching to share her joy and jubilation with those she loved, yet she was forced to act as the single most important event of her life had never happened.

As her eyes rested upon her father, whose laughter rang out above the rest, immense guilt and sorrow gripped at her heart. Pleadingly she thought, *Oh Papa, please don't hate me for hurting you. It wasn't intentional.* In her distraught state of mind, Miranda continued to plead her case, although her father would never hear her words. *Surely, you must remember what is felt to love another? Such love cannot be denied.*

Hearing her own thoughts of denied love, Miranda found her mind connecting the love she felt for her husband to the love she imagined her father must have felt for his slave. Shocked by such a revelation, Miranda stared at her father more intently and wondered, *Was it that way for you too, Papa? Is that why you continued to have an affair with Elmira all those years? You couldn't stop your heart from feeling as it did.*

Knowing instinctively the answer to her questions, the resentment and anger that Miranda had harbored against her father seemed to dissolve. Surprisingly, Miranda found herself able to understand in part how difficult it must have been for Lucas to love and lose both women in his life. Such a revelation made her feel closer to her father than she had ever felt before. A tender smile crossed her lips as she watched him conversing with his friend, Michael Honeycutt.

Papa, you don't know it yet, but I truly am your little girl. Not only am I strong-willed and a might stubborn at times, I also have a great capacity for loving, too. Unfortunately, like you, I too have hurt others I love, just as you hurt Mama. I hope that someday you will come to understand my actions were not those of an angry child, defying her father, but rather of a woman trying to protect the man she loves. Looking up to heaven she hastily added, *And God willing, a far sight better than Papa was able to protect Mama and Elmira.*

Realizing she had included Elmira in her prayer, and the tragic fate of both women, Miranda closed her eyes and hastily added, *Dear God, please let the similarities of my father and I end there. Please don't let my loved one perish as Papa's did.*

Unable to think such despairing thoughts, knowing she would burst into tears, Miranda looked about the crowded room for a distraction. Glancing at Elise and Joshua, her fears subsided as she watched Joshua stand tentatively near her friend's side, his hand resting around her waist as if it were the most natural thing to do in the world. *My, but you two have come so far together,* she mused to herself.

Recalling, their turbulent relationship back in Fairfax, and how Joshua and Elise were able to overcome their vast differences, a sense of hope filled her. *If they can do it, I just know Gilbert and I can too,* she thought as Benjamin's words, echoed in her mind. *As you embark on this new journey, not as two individuals but rather one, be certain to bring with you the essentials of a strong union . . . patience, respect and love.*

Taking comfort from his words--which took on a deeper meaning--Miranda vowed again that from here on out, not only would she love Gilbert, but she would learn to be patient and respect his inheritance. Still puzzled as to why he had reacted so adversely to Benjamin, she became aware that Elise had motioned her to join them.

Knowing she couldn't bring herself to join in casual conversation, Miranda declined with a subtle shaking of her head. Feeling incredible guilt for not sharing her secret, even now with her dear friend, she silently prayed. *Oh Elise, please don't be angry with me for too long when you find out.*

Seeing the concerned look in Elise's eyes, Miranda smiled reassuringly back at her, amused that even now after starting a new life of her own, her dear friend still hovered over her like an old mother hen. *Dear Elise, even after you have children of your own, I suppose you will keep trying to look after me.* The thought of Elise mothering her own children sparked the memory of them growing up together and the pledge they had vowed to one another. Remembering that pledge, Miranda looked away with stinging eyes. *I didn't break my promise Elise. Honest I didn't! No one else was my maid of honor.*

Chastising herself for becoming so emotional, Miranda tried desperately to regain composure. *Get mad, Miranda,* she told herself. *Get good and mad just like Elise taught you to do countless times before.* Almost able to hear her friend's words, Miranda nodded her head feeling her tears rescind as she took in a deep breath and put the blame where it belonged. *This is Tad's fault. All of it! He cheated you out of your day!*

As anger and rage replaced her guilt, she observed the man who had caused her so much pain, enter the room. Hatred mounted in her heart as she watched Tad being introduced to the Robbins' by Vivian, as if he were royalty or someone equally fine. Unlike those who gathered around him, Miranda was no longer impressed with Tad's striking good looks and polished mannerisms. What she saw as she glared at him from across the crowded room was a depraved bastard, whom she now loathed.

So engrossed in watching his every move with contempt in her eyes and in her heart, Miranda hadn't realized that Alfred, seeing her react so adversely to Tad's presence, had come to her side. Lovingly placing his hand on her shoulder, Miranda jumped and turned toward him.

"Oh Mr. Honeycutt . . ." She gasped, pausing to catch her breath, her heart pounding in her chest. "You gave me such a start!"

"I'm sorry, dearest. By the look on your face I thought you needed rescuing."

Blushing, suddenly ashamed of her behavior, Miranda smiled at the man she had truly began to think of as a second father. "Was I that transparent?" she asked sheepishly.

Nodding his response, he said, "Hell has no fury like a woman's scorn, they say. And if a woman ever looked at me, as you just did my grandson, I would run from the room for protection."

"I can't help it. I hate him . . . I hate him for what he's done to Gilbert. For ruining what was supposed to be the happiest day of my life. I mean it, sir. No matter how much I try not to, I can't stop myself. I hate him!" Her voice became louder with every declaration of her immense loathing of his grandson.

"Shh," Alfred whispered discretely. "You must get a hold of yourself, my dear. Otherwise, everyone will become suspicious."

On the verge of hysteria, Miranda looked pleadingly at Alfred. "I'm trying too . . . honest I am. But the pain is so strong."

"Do it for that fine husband of yours, Mrs. O'Flaherty," Alfred whispered softly, smiling tenderly at her.

Hearing him refer to Gilbert as a fine man and calling her by her new name, Miranda nodded her head obediently. "He is a fine man, isn't he?" she asked timidly, desperately needing his approval.

"Indeed he is, dear one. I never say anything I don't mean and I'm telling you, despite his temper, I like your husband very much. He has a fine character and obviously loves you. And that my dear, is what I admire most in him. When a man loves as he loves you, everything is bound to work out."

Tenderly he patted her cheek, than looking solemnly to avoid being seen showing too much emotion, Alfred continued in a soft whisper, "All you need to do now, is try to keep this charade up for a few more moments. Afterwards, I will see to it that for the next several days, you and Mr. O'Flaherty will not be disturbed."

Confused by his last comment, Miranda frowned. Seeing him nod in the direction of the door, Miranda's eyes followed his. There she saw Montgomery standing proudly at the entrance and discreetly grinning at her.

"My dear, it would appear you are about to have a dreadful relapse of your mysterious illness of last week, and for precautionary measures mind you, I must insist that you be quarantined to the third floor."

Puzzled, she asked, "Relapse . . . Quarantined? Whatever do you mean?"

"What I mean is, you and your husband need time alone together. No two people so much in love should be separated from one another, especially on their wedding day."

Seeing her eyes start to well up with tears, he leaned closer and whispered sternly, "Now don't you dare cry on me, Miranda! Or you'll spoil everything I've taken great care to plan out."

Seeing the merriment in his eyes, she nodded and tried desperately to oblige by fanning herself, hanging onto his every word, feeling suddenly giddy as a schoolgirl.

"Montgomery has just successfully moved all your personal effects, along with the few things you've manage to purchase for Mr. . . . for Gilbert, to the third level. It's my private suite as you know, and I have the only key, or should I say Gilbert has the only key now. He's there waiting for you, my dear. Before you go to him though, I must discuss a few things with you. So please hear me out."

Seeing the seriousness of his look, Miranda leaned closer to him. "I'm listening."

"As much as I approve of your choice in men. I do not approve of your plan. So . . . I've taken the liberty of altering it some." Raising his hand to silent any objection she might try to give him, Alfred hastily added. "There is no point in arguing, my dear. The matter is finished. Beside, we have only a few more moments."

"Go on," she whispered, trying not to appear to anxious, knowing that others may see her and come to find out why before Alfred had finished.

"First off, Montgomery will be accompanying you and your husband to California. This was his choice, not mine. Although I will miss him terribly, I know he will serve you well. Secondly, after this week, your husband's sister, Margaret-Anne, will no longer be a servant. If I know your husband, he would prefer she too begin a new life and so I've given her a small, but adequate dowry so she can begin a new life for herself. Finally, when you arrive in San Francisco, you are to go to your new home. Montgomery knows the address. It's a modest home, but should do you both nicely as you begin a new life together."

Stunned, her head reeling, Miranda desperately wanted to burst into tears and hug this wonderful man who truly had thought of everything. Rather than try to think of the right words to describe her gratitude Miranda softly said, "I love you. Thank you for caring for me as if I were your own."

Smiling at her, and obviously touched by her words of endearment, Alfred's voice cracked as he said, "As far as I'm concerned, you are, my dear." Then glancing up and noticing Tad approach he hastily added, "Now wipe that smile off your face and look as if you are going to faint, because Tad is on his way over here."

Turning to see her nemesis, Miranda's smile faded with no further prompting from Alfred. Feeling suddenly nauseous and lightheaded, Miranda managed to turn and face Alfred while feeling the room spin around her. Mumbling incoherently, Miranda said before slumping into Alfred's arms, "No need to pretend . . . I truly am not feeling *well*."

Stunned, Alfred reacted by motioning for Montgomery, while protectively wrapping his arms tightly around Miranda, preventing Tad from lifting her into his own arms. Sternly, Alfred said, "Tad, let Montgomery tend to Miranda." Giving no explanation for his sudden outburst to his grandson, Alfred turned his attention to the others that had gathered around them, seeing Miranda faint.

Motioning to his guests, he hastily said, "Stand back, please. Give her some air."

By then Montgomery had arrived to assist Miranda. Alfred, seeing Felicity, politely asked, "Mrs. Myles, would you be kind enough to assist Montgomery in making Miranda comfortable?"

Nodding and without hesitation, Felicity obligingly said, "Yes, of course."

"Good God, is she alright?" Lucas bellowed as he rushed to his daughter's side, holding her hand. Turning to Alfred, he demanded an explanation.

"What in tarnation, happened Alfred?"

Just then Vivian pushed through the crowd of people, looked at her husband, raised her eyebrow and said, "Yes indeed. What has happened to our dear, Miranda?"

"We were talking and she swooned. Fear not though, I'm sure she will be fine in no time at all. Thanks to the keen observation of Mrs. Myles--who informed me earlier that she feared Miranda was still under the weather--I took the liberty of having her things moved to my private suite on the upper floor. After she is settled in, I'll send for the doctor straight away."

"Thank you, Alfred," Lucas called out as Montgomery carried her toward the entrance, all the while scolding the servant with every step he took. "Be careful with her. Damn it man, must you walk so fast?"

"Sir, Margaret-Anne is already upstairs fixing up her new room. I'm sure she and Mrs. Myles will take good care of Miss Miranda, right nicely."

Lucas nodded in agreement, paused allowing the servant to proceed, while Elise rushed past Lucas to be at her friend's side. Following closely behind Elise and Montgomery, concerned for his wife's well being was Joshua, who managed to catch up with her.

"Darling, do you think that's wise?" he asked, tenderly placing his hand on Elise's shoulder. "After all, you don't know the extent of Miranda's illness and you have to think of your own heath, especially now."

Pausing, Elise turned and looked at him pleadingly. "She needs me! Miranda's like a sister to me."

"I know, sweetheart," he whispered soothingly. "But our baby needs a healthy mother too."

Nodding, Elise begrudgingly allowed Joshua to escort her back inside to the parlor. Upon reaching both of their mothers, Joshua shook his head disapprovingly and jokingly said, "Keep a close eye on her while I find anchors to weigh her down. She's as fast as lightning."

As both mothers consoled Elise, Joshua stepped over to Michael and his father. "Damn, I thought keeping track of a platoon was tough! That was easy compared to my little spit-fire." Chuckling amongst themselves,

Joshua glanced at Elise and winked as she pouted while her mother continued to fuss over her.

Alfred, amused hearing his granddaughter's husband's comment, smiled while extending his arm to Lucas. "Let's you and I crack open a bottle of some aged brandy, old friend, and let Mrs. Myles tend to our Miranda."

"Good idea," Lucas exclaimed, pulling out his handkerchief and wiping the perspiration from his brow. "When I saw her swoon . . . Hell, I'm not too proud to admit it. I felt as helpless as the day I found out her mother had left us."

Knowing what Lucas meant, Alfred patted him on the shoulder and said reassuringly, "There's nothing wrong with Miranda that a few days of rest won't cure."

Glancing at the staircase, Lucas nodded. "God, I hope you're right. She's all I have left."

Across the room, seeing the concerned look exchanged between Rupert and Annabelle, Vivian rushed to their side. "Let me assure you, your rooms are far removed from Miranda's. You have nothing to be fearful of."

Obviously offended by her comment, Rupert said curtly, "Mrs. Honeycutt, I assure *you*, our concern was not for our welfare, but rather that of Felicity's friend. Now if you'll excuse us."

Taking his wife's arm, Rupert promptly escorted Annabelle where the Carmidy's and Honeycutt's were gathered. Humiliated, Vivian's cheeks turned crimson and she latched onto her grandson's sleeve as he started for the stairwell.

In a strained whisper, Vivian said, "Don't you dare leave my side Tad! Or so help me, I'll never give you another red cent."

Raising his eyebrow and then cordially smiling at her, Tad snarled in a hushed whisper, "Now grandmother dear, that wouldn't be a threat, would it?"

Returning the same fraudulent smile, she said coldly, "Why Tad. I wouldn't dream of ever doing such a treacherous act as blackmailing my own grandson."

Hearing the word blackmail, Tad's smile faded. "Grandmother, I'm warning you. If you do anything, and I do mean anything for Grandfather to discover . . ."

Raising her hand slightly and pointing her index finger in front of him, she said, "Careful, dear boy. When someone, such as yourself needs funds to pay off a hefty ransom, it clearly isn't wise to offend the one who has been footing the bill with blood money, now is it, dear Tad?"

As the two of them actively engaged in conversation they, along with everyone else in the room, were being monitored closely by Lavinia. Perched like a Persian cat on the window-seat that looked out to the gardens, she smiled sheepishly. *Well, well, well,* she mused to herself. *Seems little Miranda has been far more craftier than I gave her credit for. There's much to be said for being an observer. You do find out the most intriguing things . . .*

Glancing to where the Carmidy's and Honeycutt's were gathered, it was obvious to Lavinia by the way everyone congregated around Joshua and Elise and paying special attention to Elise, that she must be expecting. Not the least bit interested in such news, other than amused that before long she was going to become fat, Lavinia thought, *How droll!* Then Lavinia paused, as she witnessed her sister and Rupert join them. Judging by how Annabelle was reacting, it was clear to Lavinia that the Robbins' were in on their little secret, too.

A quick glance at Vivian, Lavinia surmised her hostess knew nothing of the joyous event or otherwise she would have already made a big announcement. Snickering to herself, she thought, *Poor Viv, too busy with that no-count grandson of hers to notice this would have been her first opportunity to connect with that boring husband of my sister.*

Looking back at Annabelle, she smiled grimacing, *Little will-robber, enjoying being brought in on that back wood, no-account secret, are we? Well, when I'm through with you, I'll wipe that smug smile right off that amusing face of yours!*

Feeling eyes on her, her focus drifted to Rupert. *You traitorous bastard,* she thought cordially extending a smile back to him. *You might have out-foxed me back in England, and even won my sister's heart but I'll be damned if you'll ever spend a cent of Father's money that is rightfully mine!* Seeing him glance away made her feel victorious. *Rupert Robbins, if it takes me a lifetime, I will make you pay for betraying Father and me for the likes of Benjamin Myles!*

Thinking of her ex-husband, her eyes trailed to where he and James were huddled close together. Surprised, she wondered, *What possibly could James have to say that would interest that dull, do-gooder?* Observing the knowing nod James and Alfred exchanged between them, she surmised Alfred was in on it too and Lavinia frowned.

Hmm, what possibly could the three of them have in common? she wondered. Then recalling Miranda's dramatic scene moments earlier and how she had witnessed her fainting spell brought on by seeing Tad--rather than an illness as Alfred had tried to convey to everyone, Lavinia's mind began to race. Looking about the room for any noticeable clues, her eyes rested on Vivian. Judging by Tad's expression, it was obvious Vivian was holding something over his head. *But what?* she asked herself.

Unable to piece the puzzle together, she glanced back at her husband. *No wonder you've been leaving me alone, you've been too busy plotting with Alfred.*

Knowing James as she did, and realizing he only did things that would benefit him in the end, she concluded that somehow all of this had something to do with Felicity, too. Scanning the room quickly to see if Felicity had returned, and seeing so sign of her, Lavinia's attention returned to James. While hastily thinking what information she was certain of, and how it could benefit her, a plan started to form in her mind. Gingerly sliding off the cushioned bench, Lavinia slowly approached the unsuspecting James, all the while her mind raced.

"Benjamin, you wouldn't mind if I stole my husband away for just a while, would you?" she cooed sweetly. "The naughty man has neglected me all afternoon."

"Right," Benjamin, said cordially, glancing apprehensively at James, recognizing that particular look in Lavinia's eyes, but unable to say or do anything. Instead he headed toward Rupert. "Ah old friend, so tell me how are Edward and Anne?"

"In truth, not as well as I would like to report. Anne and the children are well, but Edward on the other hand has had a recurring bout of influenza . . ."

As curious as Lavinia was in hearing the news of the Spencers', she had more pressing interests. Tucking her hand around James' arm, she suggested a nice stroll in the gardens. Seeing her husband start to object, she smiled at him while coyly raising her eyebrow.

"Fine, James. We can stay here if you like, but I thought you would prefer some privacy considering I know that you, Alfred and that little tart you lust for, have been helping Miranda plot against Vivian's grandson. Perhaps I'll just go speak with my dear friend, instead."

Starting to walk away and feeling him pull her back, Lavinia knew she had hit a nerve and smiled triumphantly. Turning and seeing the surprise in his eyes, she brazenly said, "Why James, you honestly didn't think you could keep a secret from me. Did you?"

Needing no more prompting, James hurried his wife off to deep within the garden and turned her to face him. With no one able to hear him--feeling no need to keep up a pretense of polite conversation--he demanded, "And just what is it precisely, you think you know Lavinia?"

"Evidently I know more than you want me too, James darling. Or why else would you rush me out here and act so indignantly?"

Glaring at his wife, ready to walk away calling her bluff, Lavinia said, "Is that really wise James? Considering, I know that this so-called courtship between Tad and Miranda has been nothing but a farce."

"You're delusional! First we're conspiring and now you're accusing someone as innocent as Miranda of perpetrating such a heinous act."

"Ah yes, dear innocent Miranda. Who just happened to faint when Tad approached--if that was real, that is--or perhaps another elaborate scheme to prevent other's from seeing the hate she feels from a man who has been trying to win her heart."

"Hate? That's preposterous! Why for weeks we've seen her and Tad cozy up to one another, stealing glances at each other . . ."

Shaking her head, enjoying rattling James, watching him struggling to throw her off the scent, she interrupted him and said, "Oh I know when a woman hates a man alright James. She looked at Tad, much as I do when I look at you. She loathes him. Moreover, Alfred's feeble attempt of coving up her so-called illness, is nothing more than an elaborate hoax. What puzzles me though, is why does dear, sweet Miranda, need a few days locked up on the third floor? What is she hiding?"

Seeing the stunned look on his face, she began to walk past him, snidely saying, "Never mind, I'll ask Vivian."

Grasping her arm, James said, "What do you want, Lavinia?"

Inhaling deeply, yanking free of his grasp, then raising her eyebrow, she glared at him. "Want? In exchange for my silence, or in general, James?"

"Both!" He snapped, his voice traveling over the hushed surroundings of the garden.

Enjoying turning the tides back on him, Lavinia smiled victoriously. "Oh, James darling, do keep your voice down. You wouldn't want the Robbins' to think you've lost your senses, now would you? Even though Rupert detests me, he would be forced to rescue his sister-in-law if for nothing more than good form."

A disgusted grin crossed James' lips, and he bowed to her. "Bravo!" He snarled while sarcastically applauding her. "You managed to win a minor battle, my dear. However, not the war! So, name your price. That is what you want, isn't it Lavinia? Money? The question is how much?"

"James, you have no idea what I want and what I intend to have. However, in exchange for my silence, a nice tidy sum of let's say . . . ten-thousands pounds, placed in a private account will do nicely for the time being."

"Ten thousand pounds . . ." he said, shaking his head. "You are mad!"

"That's my price. Either you pay it, or I shall not only speak to Vivian, but I'll be forced to go to Benjamin and tell him how you've been secretly lusting over that tart wife of his. And then all your scheming, having Benjamin off in Washington while you and that alley cat grew closer, was for not. Which by the way was my idea as I recall, so that in itself is money due me, don't you agree, James darling?" Pausing for the effect, enjoying watching James' face redden she added in a low purr, "Wouldn't that be such a shame, if all your manipulating and scheming, worming your way into that little tart's heart was foiled?"

"Fine, Lavinia. I'll pay your price. Not for the reasons you think, but rather in payment for what you've taught me."

"And just what would that be, James?" She spouted indignantly.

"No matter how elegant the attire a woman wears or how beautiful she is, a whore is still a whore. And you my dear, are nothing but a high priced whore! Willing to sell your soul if the price is right."

Outraged by such a comment, she immediately retaliated by striking him across the face. Seeing him lunge at her as if he were going to strike her, Lavinia quickly stepped back and saw in the corner of her eye Rupert standing off the path, clearly within hearing distance. Taking full advantage of such a perfect opportunity, she cried out, "Go ahead James hit me. It can't be any worse than you threatening to have me put away in an insane asylum, after I caught you lusting over Felicity. Are you that jealous over Benjamin that you have to seduce his new wife too, as you did me? Well I won't stand for it, I tell you. If you force me too, I'll go to Rupert and Annabelle and tell them everything."

"Go right ahead, you whore! Sell your soul to them too. However, if you think that spineless traitor will believe a word you have to say, after the disgrace you and that drunken father of yours brought down on the good name of Bailey-Smythe, you're crazier than I thought. Rupert Robbins would rather see you rot in hell than listen to a word you have to say. Need I remind you of the cool reception you got at the dock?"

Satisfied that James had said enough to warrant Rupert's sympathy she leaned forward. Lowering her voice, certain that only James could hear her, she said, "That comment of yours will now cost you twenty-thousand pounds, darling. I'll expect it transferred first thing in the morning."

Stepping out from behind James, Lavinia looked surprised as she hailed Rupert. "Why Rupert, for goodness sakes! Whatever are you doing out here?"

"Oh I needed a little fresh air. It's rather close indoors."

Sympathetically, Lavinia said while making her way to Rupert's side, "It took me quite sometime to get used to the difference in climates."

"Right. Judging by the color of your cheeks, perhaps not fully though?" Rupert said calmly, while leaning closer to her, to assure he was not overheard. "Are you alright, Lavinia?"

"Please don't make this any more unpleasant then it already is by pitying me. If there is one thing I've learned from being banished to the colonies for my past foolishness is that I can adapt well to even the most adverse situations."

Then dramatically Lavinia turned her attention back at her husband, and called to him, "Coming, James?"

Unable to hide his shock in seeing Rupert, and realizing that Lavinia had probably known he was near and had goaded him into saying more than he ever intended Rupert to hear, he waved her off. "No, I think I'll enjoy the breeze, for a while. Rupert ol' man why not join me?" he asked cordially.

Hesitating before responding, to glance at Lavinia and seeing her nod, Rupert whispered to her, "We must talk."

Smiling up at him, and detecting the concerned look in his eyes, Lavinia knew she had been successful in gaining his allegiance. If not for her sake, Lavinia knew that Rupert would do anything for the cousin of his that he loved so much.

"Yes. More than you know. Perhaps tomorrow when James is away?"

Nodding, he headed toward James while Lavinia turned and motioned to her husband and stretched out her hands, exhibiting all ten fingers. Closing them tightly, she raised them again, signifying twenty. Knowing he understood what she meant, Lavinia turned smiling, victoriously thinking, *Now for Vivian . . .*

As Lavinia glided toward her next victim, upstairs on the upper-level of the Honeycutt's mansion, Gilbert leaned by the side of the bed holding his wife's hand, having been visibly shaken by seeing Montgomery carry her into their temporary shelter.

"Are you certain ya don't require a doctor, Mandy?"

Smiling reassuringly at him, conscious that Felicity was still close by, Miranda softly whispered, "Positive. All I need is a little rest and I'll be fit as a fiddle in no time at all."

Hearing her comment, Felicity approached the bed. "You gave us all quite a scare, Miranda."

"I don't know what came over me. One minute I was speaking with Alfred and the next the room was spinning around me . . ."

Nodding, Felicity smiled at her and said sympathetically, "It's understandable, especially with all that is on your mind. Try to get some rest and I'll check on you before I leave."

"Thank you," Miranda said, smiling at her friend.

Turning to leave, Felicity paused hearing Gilbert call to her. "Mrs. Myles, please wait." Reaching her side, he whispered, "I'm grateful for yer help. Are you sure she's goin' to be alright?"

Touched by his concern, Felicity patted Gilbert on the shoulder. "All she needs is to be here, with you. And please, call me Felicity. We're practically family, now that you're my dear friend's husband."

Nodding, he watched as Felicity closed the door behind her. Rubbing his hands through his hair and shaking his head in disbelief, he returned to Miranda's side and lovingly looked down at her. "Should I get ya something?" he asked timidly. "Some water . . . or . . ."

"Darling, please." Miranda chuckled raising her hand for him to join her. "I'm fine, really."

A smirk crossed his lips and he raised his eyebrow while gingerly leaning next to her. "Now I know yer sick. Ya called me darlin', rather than a pig-headed fool."

Wrapping her arms around his neck, Miranda pulled him closer to her and cooed, "If you can call me your Mandy, surely I can use a term of endearment for my wonderful husband." The word husband still sounding so new to her that she smiled again. "That is if you approve?"

"It's perfect. Just as ya are, lying there in yer pretty, little frock. Is it new?"

Glancing down at her gown, she smiled. "This isn't a frock silly. It's a dressing gown . . ." Anticipating an adverse reaction from him, recalling how he had reacted discovering Tad had seen her in such a gown, she hastily added. "A *new* dressing gown that I purchased just for you."

Glancing at her in her lacy garment with admiring eyes, Gilbert huskily said, "As lovely as ya look in it Mandy, perhaps, we should take it off to save it for later."

"Later? But why? I thought you would like it . . ." Then seeing the look in his eyes, she stopped questioning his comment and smiled knowingly back at him. "Hmm, yes, I see what you mean" she whispered seductively raising herself from her pillow to draw him closer, eagerly parting her lips as their mouths hungrily sought each other.

Pulling slightly away from her, he growled, "There'll be none of that ya little temptress! Or yer won't be gettin' none of that rest Felicity said ya needed."

Shaking her head, she said, "Felicity said no such thing. What she said was, all I need was to be with you." Gliding a lace strap off her shoulder, Miranda smiled seductively up at him. "And she was right." Removing her other strap and allowing the dressing gown to slip down around her waist, she looked up at him wantonly. "Darling, would you deny your wife what she wants, only hours after promising before God never to do such a thing?"

Shamelessly Miranda reached for Gilbert's trousers, and with shaking fingers, she began to unfasten each button, aware of his enlarged manhood protruding from beneath the wool material of his pants. Needing no further coaxing, Gilbert hastily finished undressing as Miranda removed her gown. Smiling at her while gliding the length of his naked body next to her creamy white skin, he held her tightly to him and kissed her forehead.

"Mandy, let's just lay still, holding one another for a while. Me heart is still pounding, seeing ya bein' carried in here like that. What happened?"

Nodding, Miranda snuggled closer to him, enjoying his nearness as his hands gently began caressing her skin. Slowly she began to explain how she had reacted upon seeing Tad approach her after telling Alfred how much she loathed him.

"Ya really told him that?" he whispered lovingly.

Detecting no anger in his voice, Miranda felt relieved to be able to discuss Tad with him without risking an outburst of jealousy. "I did. Several times in fact, as I recall. It was so hard for me to watch my father and friends interchange with one another and not share with them my greatest joy. Then after Alfred had explained what he had planned for us, I must have been overcome with emotion. Joy, sorrow, hatred all at once, and it made me dizzy I suppose. Thinking back at the last thing, I remember . . . Maybe seeing Tad and fearing he would try to steal this happiness from me too, I became overwrought. The next thing I knew, you were calling my name and realizing I was safe, here with you, I wasn't frightened any more," she whispered.

Wrapping his arms tighter around his wife, Gilbert huskily whispered, "Oh Mandy, I love ya."

Miranda nestled close to him with tears in her eyes, hearing the depth of his love.

Saying not a word, the two of them blocked out the rest of the world and clung to one another, allowing themselves to bathe in the splendor of their love.

~ Eighteen ~

Calm Before the Storm

August 1865

As Felicity stood listening pensively to James going over the last details to free Gilbert, she felt no joy or relief that the elaborate cover-up that had involved so many was nearly over. It made little difference to her now, that if it had not been for her and Miranda, an innocent man would have probably died at the hands of those who had actually framed him for murder. Or, that those of power and wealth risked public ridicule and possibly jail time themselves if discovered they had been harboring a fugitive.

What concerned Felicity now was that after tonight, it was quite possible a friend she had grown to love like a sister might be the next victim in a series of good intentions gone bad.

In her heart, Felicity knew that what she and Miranda had begun that fateful afternoon months earlier, protecting Gilbert from his hunters, was the right thing to do. Yet now, knowing all that had transpired from that one act of kindness, Felicity couldn't help but wonder if given the chance to do it again--knowing the end result--would she still be willing to help. And that's what troubled Felicity the most.

From the moment she woke that morning, a sense of doom plagued her. Flashes of the fire that had taken her parent's life while aiding run-away slaves had flashed before her eyes. The image of her beloved Aunt Gwen on her deathbed haunted her. Felicity knew her aunt's life had been shortened by traveling to America so that she and Benjamin would be brought together. And as grateful as she was to her aunt for making such a sacrifice, even now several years later, Felicity felt guilty.

All three of her loved ones had risked their own lives to help others and what Felicity feared most, *Was history repeating itself again*? Could it be possible that she was destined to lose yet another loved one out of her need to help others?

Unable to bear another hardship, and fearful she was the cause for the loss of their lives, she asked James timidly, "Surely, there must be someone else that could be used as a ruse for Miranda? Someone far more experienced or shrewder in such matters than I am. Not that I am backing out mind you, because I'm not. It's just I can't help but wonder if there might be a simpler way to free Gilbert."

Seeing the look of disappointment in James eyes, she hastily added. "It just seems to me, simplicity would be wiser with so much at stake. Mind you, I'm hardly in a position to know such matters, but why is it necessary for Miranda's excuse to leave the party be my sole responsibility? What if I'm not convincing enough? You, yourself know that Elise already suspects Miranda is hiding something and has been badgering me for answers ever since she returned."

Sensing her tension and realizing Felicity was on the verge of hysteria, James interrupted her. "What better excuse for Miranda to be excused from this social event than for her to escort you home and tend to you? Just as you have been presumably been caring for her these past few weeks. Trust me, it is the most natural thing in the world for her to help you. Especially, since Benjamin will need to stay behind to represent family unity. Otherwise, if Benjamin left to escort you home, chances are Rupert, being as devoted to you as he is, might feel the need to leave as well. Which hardly seems appropriate, since this little function is partially in his honor."

"Precisely my point. Rupert is my cousin. A very important part of my life and I would no sooner disappoint him or dear Annabelle at such an important occasion."

Interrupting her once more, he said calmly, "Of course you wouldn't, unless you were truly ill. Don't you see Felicity, no one would fault you in leaving early or be suspicious either. Even if Tad, Elise and Lavinia, for that matter, have suspected something peculiar in Miranda's need for seclusion these past few weeks, you becoming mysteriously ill too, should ease even the most cynical mind. You really need to trust both Alfred and me on this. It really is the most logical and safest way."

Need to trust . . . James words haunted Felicity. For an instant she heard her father's voice saying those exact words to her mother who had been apprehensive in harboring runners in the abandoned barn on their property. Even his wealth or influential position in the community hadn't protected them from being killed. Again, she relived in her mind the sights and sounds of that afternoon as she watched her parents murdered at the hands of their longtime trusted friends. She began to shake. *If only you knew . . . Nothing is ever fail-proof. Good decent people can still be killed.*

Hearing Benjamin's familiar cough from the next room, and realizing he needed silence if he were to complete his resignation to hand it to the bishop this evening, Felicity stepped closer to James. Pushing her tormenting memories from her mind, she whispered, "I do trust you and Alfred, James. Honestly, I do . . . I'm just being a ninny, I suppose."

Taking a deep breath to help settle her nerves, she continued. "Forgive me for being so contrary. The plan is well thought out. Perfect in fact. You and Alfred truly have thought of everything. By the time anyone even suspects that Miranda is missing, she and her beloved Gilbert will be miles away from here. Far from the clutches of Tad and his fiendish friend, I know that . . . It's just I feel so strange--foreboding almost about tonight."

"Nonsense! What possibly could go wrong? I think what you are feeling is premature anxiety at the thought of never seeing a dear friend again. Besides, Benjamin has agreed as well."

"I know, he told me earlier this made perfect sense." Seeing the concerned look on James' face, Felicity tried to smile as reassuringly as she possibly could. "It's funny you should say that, because Benjamin said nearly the same thing to me just this very morning. As a matter of fact, he's suggested that perhaps before the weather turned too bad for traveling, we might make a trip to San Francisco to see Miranda and Gilbert."

"Really? Why I would have thought by now, good old Rupert and Annabelle would have convinced you both that England was where you two should be and go back with them on their return passage."

Shocked by his astuteness, Felicity blushed and wondered, *How could he possibly know that Benjamin and I are intending to return to England with them?*

To mask her apprehension, she asked softly, "Return passage, you say? Why I hadn't heard that Annabelle and Rupert had already planned a date."

Mistaking her uneasiness with concern at the thought of Rupert and Annabelle leaving, James quickly went to her side. "Forgive me, Felicity. My intention was not to upset you further. On the contrary, I'm here today simply to help ease your mind. In answer to your question, I've heard no mention as to when the Robbins' intend to return to England. However, I should think they would want to stay here in America for several months. After all, this is such a vast country with much to see. Certainly since they are on their honeymoon, there should be no hurry in returning to England."

Realizing she had managed to conceal her and Benjamin's secret from him for the time being, Felicity smiled fondly at James. "Yes. I'm sure you're right."

Glancing at her and seeing her trembling fingers, James leaned closer and placed her petite hands in his. "As you know Felicity, I'm not in favor of women partaking frequently in the consumption of spirits--having a lush for a wife--however, I do feel there are particular circumstances that a few nips at some brandy might be welcoming to steady one's nerves. This being one of them, since this whole affair with Miranda has obviously upset you more than you are saying."

"Surely, you can't be suggesting I use alcohol to get through this evening, James? Why, that is completely irrational and I would think you and Alfred would want me in top form rather then dimmed by the effects of brandy."

At times like this, when James had the opportunity of being alone with her and capable of seeing just what an extraordinarily fine woman she really was, he found it exceedingly difficult not to exhibit his true feelings for her. Especially when she reacted in such a manner as she just had, using logic while not being overbearing. Admiring this quality in her, he smiled adoringly at her.

"Dearest Felicity, I'm not suggesting anything more than we take a few nips at Benjamin's finest brandy for medicinal purposes, and who knows-- if we are lucky--we might find it a fine elixir."

Shocked by him making such an innuendo that they should share in a magic potion together, Felicity pulled her hands from his grasp feeling suddenly uncomfortable by his nearness. Seeing the hurt look in his eyes and surmising the strain of tonight's events must be putting them both under a great strain, she asked sweetly, "Do you really think it wise? What I mean to say is, if you honestly think a few sips of brandy might steady my nerves then of course I will consider it."

"Absolutely, it would help. And if it lessens your guilt, perhaps you would pour me one too."

Smiling at how skillful he was at convincing her to share a drink with him, which she normally reserved only to indulge in the privacy of her home with her husband, Felicity turned to retrieve Benjamin's only vice. As she walked the few steps across the small room, so deep in thought about the risk they all faced if caught trying to free Gilbert, Felicity was unaware that James watched her every move.

With every minute that passed, James knew the time was drawing nearer to when he would finally take this woman from Benjamin and claim her as his. If only for the moment that he would bed her.

As Felicity bent down to retrieve the crystal decanter from the locked cupboard, James' breathing became irregular. Standing in the small lounge of the orphanage, with Benjamin only a few feet from them, James fantasized what it would feel like to come up from behind Felicity and pull her naked flesh next to his.

Even watching her delicate fingers pry open the lid of the bottle to pour some of the contents into a glass was an aphrodisiac to him. As Felicity innocently glanced at him for his approval, his craving for her grew. He became acutely aware he had a full erection, and immediately took a seat. Still drinking in her every move while pouring a second brandy, he warned himself, *Pace yourself, old boy. Don't spoil it now, like some over-zealous schoolboy out of control, or all that you have done to win her confidence, was for not.*

As Felicity, took a seat beside him, James, aware of how nervous she was acting in his presence, calmly suggested she take a sip of the brandy to help settle her nerves. Obliging, after several minutes of polite conversations and another round of drinks to help prime his unsuspecting victim, James watched with keen interest as the seemingly shy and always pristine Felicity began to feel the effect of the drink and slowly let down her defenses.

"I'm so grateful for all the help you've given to Miranda and Gilbert. Why I still cannot imagine why you would risk harboring a fugitive from the authorities as you have. All I can say is, you have no idea what your kindness has meant to both Benjamin and me. We shall never forget it."

"Dear Felicity, as I told you before. I was only too happy to help."

Hearing Benjamin stir from his office and realizing the lateness of the hour, James stood as his host entered the room. "Old Man, not only have I overstayed my welcome this afternoon, I've taken the liberties of introducing the nectar of the Gods to my fair hostess."

James paused to raise his glass to Benjamin and nod his head to Felicity before continuing. "Who was overwrought with anticipation and anxiety, but thanks to this fine vintage, has since found herself to be quite relaxed."

Disgusted at watching Benjamin lean over the back of the chair where Felicity sat and tenderly kiss the crown of her head, James lifted his glass and belted back the remaining contents of the glass. The brandy quickly soured in his mouth hearing Benjamin speak softly to his wife.

"My poor darling. I've neglected you, haven't I?"

Felicity leaned further into her chair and stretched her neck back while looking up at her husband lovingly. "Never," she exclaimed.

From where James stood, never had he heard her voice sound so seductive, and he became hypnotized by the contours of Felicity's long slender neck. Shamelessly he stared at the woman he hungered, as she gingerly raised her arm and caressed the side of Benjamin's face and beard.

"I trust you were inspired to complete the task at hand, my dearest?" Felicity asked warmly, knowing how difficult it was for Benjamin to write a letter asking the Bishop to find someone else to replace him at the orphanage as soon as possible.

Nodding, he smiled knowingly at her. "Indeed. I had guidance from above."

"Good." Aware that they were being watched, Benjamin coughed and pulled on the gold chain dangling from his front waist pocket to retrieve his watch. Glancing down at it, he raised his head in disbelief. "My, but the party is in less than two hours."

Shocked, Felicity bolted from her seat. "You can't be serious, Ben. Why, I haven't even freshened up, let alone fix my hair . . ." She mumbled, feeling to see if her hair was still tightly curled from this morning. Obviously flustered, Felicity then turned to James. "Please do forgive me. I really must excuse myself this very moment. Thank you for keeping me company this afternoon and calming my nerves. You really are such a dear man..."

Not finishing her sentence, she dashed from the room leaving Benjamin and James chuckling amongst themselves. Noticing Felicity had reached their bedchamber, Benjamin lovingly called to her. "I'll be in shortly to help you, my dear."

Turning to James, he added. "With only hours to go until Gilbert is finally a free man, I would be amiss if I didn't convey to you, my heartfelt gratitude in all your efforts regarding Miranda and Gilbert. You're unselfish kindness means more to Felicity than mere words can say."

Before James had a chance to respond, Felicity called out to her husband. "Oh Ben, please do excuse the interruption. Dearest, were you intending to wear your blue or brown suit this evening?"

Smiling at James, Benjamin turned and called to her. "Neither darling. I thought we agreed on the black silk that you commissioned for me."

Hearing Benjamin's words of how Felicity had spent money from her inheritance to have a suit specially tailored for him, James' back stiffened, fighting the impulse of glaring at the man before him that he had come to loath. Thinking Benjamin no better than some educated, peasant Gigolo, who preyed on rich women pretending to be God-like, James pasted a smile to his lips to cover up the contempt he felt.

"Of course! How silly of me." Felicity called from behind the closed door. There was no mistaking the tension in Felicity's voice, and James looked at Benjamin wondering why such a fine woman allowed this man to use her as he did.

"Well, I'm sure you too need to freshen up too, so I won't keep you by rambling on about our gratitude for all you've done, James. Just one quick thing before you go. Speaking for both Felicity and myself, I can honestly say that both of us value your friendship, more than you know. And, if there is anything we can do for you in the future, don't hesitate to ask."

Accepting Benjamin's hand, he shook it cordially all the while thinking, *You phony bastard! Let's see how superior you act when a second wife of yours discovers what it's like to be with a real man.*

Such thoughts caused him to smile and James said, "Right. Since there's little time to spare, I should be making my leave."

"Indeed." Benjamin nodded, while gesturing his guest to the door.

Hearing the door close, Felicity, still anxious over tonight and unable to shake this feeling of pending doom, pulled back the lace curtains to see James enter his coach. Closing her eyes, still feeling the effects of the brandy, she leaned against the window and said a silent prayer. *Dear Lord, please protect Gilbert and Miranda and help them find the peace and happiness they deserve.*

Caught up in her own thoughts and fears, Felicity had no idea that James, leaning back into the seat of his hansom cab, eyes glistening with anticipation, watched her like that of a hunter, as he spotted his prey. Whispering to himself, he said, "Yes, indeed! Tonight you will be mine!" Then with a sinister chuckle, he taped the roof of the cab signaling his driver to commence.

~

Across town, Elise, unable to draw the cords of her corset tighter around her protruding waist, cried out in despair. "Oh fiddlesticks! Megan please help me, otherwise I'll never fit into my gown."

Obligingly, the young maidservant placed the mantel she had just brushed across the foot of the bed. Turning, the young servant, sheepishly said, "Mrs. Carmidy, beggin' your pardon, didn't Mr. Carmidy instruct me not to make your corset so tight? You wouldn't want me to be sacked, now would ya?"

Entering their bedchamber, hearing the maid's plea, Joshua proclaimed, "Why certainly not Megan. That will be all. I'll tend to my wife this evening."

Disgusted that once again Joshua was underfoot, Elise rolled her eyes. "Mercy sakes, Joshua. Can't a girl have a moment's peace without you lurking about? Might I remind you that you are no longer a Union officer tracking some Southern spy's whereabouts?"

Chuckling silently at seeing his wife stand before him, fists planted firmly on her hips, he walked behind her and tenderly whispered in her ear. "That may be so, but some things never change. I see you're still as feisty as ever." Nuzzling his cheek next to hers, he tenderly kissed the nape of her neck.

Feeling her respond to his nearness by leaning closer to him, Elise's tone softened. "And you my wonderful husband, still believe I can be tamed like some wild stallion."

Kissing her neck again and sliding his arms around her expanding waist, Joshua huskily whispered, "Not a stallion my dear, a mare."

Immediately hearing his comment, Elise's back stiffened and she slapped Joshua's arm. "Well how flattering to compare your wife to a horse!"

Ignoring Joshua's smirk, looking at her reflection in the mirror, Elise turned to face Joshua on the verge of tears. "It's no wonder you think of me as some horse. Just look at my backside. Why, it's getting as big as Maggie's!" she wailed in despair.

Unable to conceal his amusement in her comparing herself to that of her horse, Joshua laughed out loud. "Oh Elise, I've seen plenty of horse's backsides and I can assure you, never once have I ever been aroused by them as when I look at yours. Now come back over here and let me help you get into your gown or we'll be late for our own party."

Still pouting, Elise shook her head defiantly. "That's the whole problem. You can't help me into my gown, because it doesn't fit me anymore!"

Because Elise was truly upset, Joshua looked down at the lovely gown she had worn only a month earlier. Immediately he became concerned, wondering if it was normal for a woman to already be getting so large so soon into her pregnancy, but rather than worry her needlessly, Joshua glanced at Elise reassuringly.

"I never did fancy that gown, if truth be known. Why not pick out another. Didn't you just show me a gown you and your mother picked out the other day?"

Nodding, her lips trembling she said, "I can't wear that to a party, Joshua. That's a gown for expectant mother's to be."

"And aren't you?"

"Yes. However, no one knows it and besides, I won't wear it. It makes me look big and fat."

Walking over to her, Joshua lovingly placed his hand on her rounded torso and tenderly rubbed it before looking up at her. "When I see our baby growing inside you, I don't see someone gaining weight, but rather the woman I love who is carrying my son or daughter, and it takes my breath away. Never have I desired you more, so please no more talk about being fat. You look radiant to me."

Cupping her arms around his neck, she cooed, "Oh Joshua, you always could turn my head with your words."

Several minutes later, after convincing Elise that she looked beautiful in her new dress without the corset that bound her, Joshua also managed to convince his wife that tonight would be the perfect time to announce their joyous news. As they made their way to the Honeycutt's, earlier than usual so that Elise could have the chance to share her news with Miranda first, Joshua made a mental note to speak with his mother regarding Elise's condition.

~ Nineteen ~

Lives are Changed, Forever

As soon as the front door opened to the Honeycutt home, Elise headed directly to Miranda's bedchamber rather than having her mantel placed in the cloakroom. Joshua went in search of Alfred, having been told they were the first to arrive. Standing outside Miranda's room, Elise paused a moment when she felt a fluttering in her stomach. Startled, she gasped and her hand went immediately inside her mantel to rub her protruding abdomen over her silk skirt.

"Mercy sakes, what was that?" she whispered. In that fleeting moment her maternal instincts came alive and she spoke softly to the child growing inside her.

"Hello little one. Was that you?" Wanting to run to Joshua in hopes what she had felt was the baby, but certain she wasn't far enough along to feel movement, she stood silently and rubbed her stomach in wonderment. Hearing noises coming from behind the closed door, Elise quietly knocked and smiled when Miranda opened it.

Ignoring the surprised look on her friend's face, Elise rushed past her and squealed, "Oh Miranda, I'm so glad you're alone. Can we please chat for a spell before the party begins? I must tell you something before anyone else finds out."

Shutting the door behind her and glancing about the room to make sure there was nothing left about that would draw suspicions from her curious friend, Miranda smiled at Elise. "My, this must be some news if you didn't have your mantel checked. Shall I take it for you?" Miranda asked, stretching out her arms ready to take her friend's wrap.

Instead, Elise herself ran to Miranda and hugged her tightly. "Oh Miranda, it's so good to see you. Ever since you took ill I wanted to check on you, really I did. But Joshua and Mama thought it unwise."

"Oh don't fret none about that, Elise. I'm sure getting accustomed to your new surroundings and home was far more pressing than to nursemaid an old friend. Besides, there wasn't anything you could have done for me. I just needed rest. And as you can see, I'm as fit as a fiddle now."

Pulling slightly away from her friend still holding onto her waist, she smiled warmly. "That you are, my dear friend, that you are. I mean this, Miranda, I've never seen you look so beautiful."

Lowering her head embarrassed, Miranda still noticing Elise was wearing her mantel, asked again, "Are you chilled, Elise? It's hotter than blazes this evening and you've still got your mantel on. Maybe you're coming down with something?"

Snickering, realizing her friend was right, she stepped back and begun pulling on her drawstring. "It is a might close in here, tonight. But I didn't want anyone else to see my gown until you did."

Puzzled by such a comment, Miranda asked, "Is your dress the important news you wanted to share with me?"

"Well, not exactly . . ." Elise said coyly, dramatically turning around and taking off her mantel, letting it drop to her feet. Turning slowly back to face her friend, in anticipation, she stood there beaming as Miranda's eyes scanned Elise's new dress. Immediately her hands went to her mouth in shock and began to squeal in delight.

"Oh Elise, how wonderful. You're going to have a baby!" Immediately the two women hugged one another as Elise nodded her head enthusiastically.

"Can you believe it? I'm going to be a mama."

"Does your Mama know?"

Planting her hand squarely on her hip, she scuffed, "Why, I didn't even get off the boat before both she and Mother Carmidy had guessed. I swear it was the most peculiar thing. There I was, trying to be so secretive, but they both knew. I guess, just like I knew the moment I saw you in Alfred's study the other day, that you had found true love."

Desperately wanting to share her news with Elise, but knowing it was too risky, Miranda shook her head. "I swear Elise, when you get something in your head you're as stubborn as an old mule. Can't we just please take a few minutes to share in your joy?"

Raising her eyebrow, Elise cocked her head and looked at her friend. "No sense in trying to get me all riled up by calling me names, Miranda. This old stubborn mule ain't budging, until you tell me who the lucky man is." Then tapping her foot, she looked at Miranda just as she had countless times before when she expected an answer.

Breaking out in a giggle, Miranda said, "Just look at you. Standing there tapping your foot like you're going to give me a whoppin' or something. You old bossy thing, you really are going to be a great mother."

Hearing Miranda referring to her in such a way, Elise's attention was diverted and she asked, "Do you really think so?"

The thought crossed Miranda's mind that this may be the last time she would share one of these heartfelt chats with her oldest and dearest friend, and tears welled up in her eyes. "Take it from someone who knows, you always looked after me as a mother would. That little baby is going to be the luckiest child alive."

Needing no prompting, both women rushed to each other and again hugged tightly. Just then a knock at the door alerted them that their few minutes alone together had come to an end. Wiping a tear from her eye, Miranda softly said, "Come in." Seeing it was Montgomery, she smiled fondly at him.

"Miss Miranda, Mr. Honeycutt wishes to see you in his private suite."

"Thank you, Montgomery. I'll be there in just a few moments." Bowing politely, the chauffeur turned and left. Miranda looked at Elise solemnly.

"Tomorrow, after the party is behind us, I promise all your questions regarding the love of my life will be answered. However, I can't discuss anything right now since I'm expected to see Alfred, and you--my dear--shall be announcing that you are to be a mama. Just please know I love you."

Smiling triumphantly, Elise raised her brow. "Ah so you are in love. Just tell me one thing before you dash off, does he deserve such a wonderful woman as you?"

"Oh Elise, it is I who find myself wondering how lucky I am to have found such a man as my Gilbert. He's handsome and strong willed, but mostly he is a man of honor and integrity who loves me. I'm certain my Gilbert, genuinely loves me. Now don't you dare breathe a word of this to anyone, hear me?"

Crossing her index finger with her middle finger and placing it over her heart, just as she and Miranda had done as children, Elise whispered earnestly to her friend, "I cross my heart. Just promise you'll tell me everything by morning or I'll surely burst!"

As Miranda left her room, she wondered if she should have confided in Elise as much as she had. Knowing her friend as she did, and knowing by her in confiding as little information as she had, Elise's appetite of finding out more about Miranda would be quenched for the time being.

Climbing the steps to the third floor, and knowing Alfred was with Gilbert, she wondered why he had called for her. Especially since they all had agreed she wasn't to go to the room again. Suddenly fear gripped at her heart that something was gravely wrong.

As she entered the room she and Gilbert had called theirs for the past several days, Miranda was stunned to see Alfred standing by the window obviously upset, while Gilbert sat with his head in his hands.

Glancing at Alfred and then to Gilbert, she closed the door and went to her husband. "Darling, what is it?"

"Mandy, all the weeks ya cared for me, tending to me wounds, I saw in yer eyes a love I had no right to. Every day then as I have these past few weeks, I've etched every detail of ya firmly in me mind, so years from now I would still have the memory of yer smile, yer scent, and yer laughter to remember."

Miranda gasped and glanced at Alfred. Returning her attention to Gilbert she said, "Remember? For heaven sakes why . . . I'll be with you."

"That seems to be the problem. Mr. O'Flaherty seems to believe that you should remain here while I send him back to Ireland rather than to San Francisco as arranged."

"What?" Miranda felt dizzy and glanced back at Gilbert, leaning in front of him. "Why would you ask such a thing? How could you hurt us like this . . . Has everything that has happened been a lie?"

Apparently not the least embarrassed at discussing something so private in front of Alfred, he said, "Christ a' mighty, am I the only one who understands the life I have to offer ya is not deserving of someone as fine as ya? Don't ya understand, until that evening ya overheard Mr. Honeycutt and I discus his job offer and ya . . ."

Pausing, not willing to discuss that portion of the evening in front of Alfred, Gilbert hastily continued. "Durin' all those weeks of ya carin' for me, never had I allowed meself to even dream that someone like yer could ever be mine. However, from that first night . . . to this, I have come to know what God intended when he created man and woman, through yer love. Such a love, I never dreamed existed, let alone that I would find. Every time ya have looked at me, yer eyes have shown the love I had no right too, but selfishly I took it, prayin' to God that ya would never regret lovin' me. And until tonight, I believed ya had no regrets. That was until earlier when ya were writin' yer letters to yer father and yer friend Elise. And when I saw the regret in yer eyes, I knew ya would be better here with yer kind."

Miranda, saying not a word, stood up and asked Alfred for a moment alone with Gilbert. Alfred immediately stepped inside the bedroom area of the suite and as the door closed, Miranda glared at her husband, her hands planted firmly on her hips.

"My kind? How dare you Gilbert O'Flaherty speak to me of love in one breath and insult me in the next. Well I'll have you know, not only are you pig-headed, but by insisting you know what's better for me and my kind, you are sentencing not only me but your child to a life of unbelievable shame and ridicule."

Stunned by her words, he stood up and clenched her arms. "Me child? What are ya sayin'?"

"What I am saying is I think I'm going to have a baby, and now I discover my baby's father doesn't want us!"

Dazed, Gilbert's eyes locked onto hers. "How . . . We've been only together a short while . . . Surely ya are mistaken?"

"Over a fortnight is more than ample time to make a baby Gilbert, and I can assure you, a woman knows these things. As sure as I'm standing here, I can tell you I'm with child. So, go ahead, run off to your precious Ireland. All the while wallowing in your self-pity and degradation believing that you are being chivalrous for my sake, and I'll see to it that your child is raised with more confidence in women then apparently you have in me."

Judging by the look on Gilbert's face, he didn't know what to say or do as he gazed at her. Unrelenting, Miranda raised her brow. "You do realize, I can't stop you from going to wherever it is you want to go. However, just keep one thing in mind Gilbert O'Flaherty. As God is my witness, I will not ever deny your child his inheritance. And although I will forbid you from ever setting eyes on our child or me if should leave tonight without us, know this--our baby will be raised to know just how lucky he or she is to be Irish-American."

Not waiting for a response, she walked to the door of where she was certain Alfred was eavesdropping and swung it open. As she suspected, Alfred nearly fell into the room. Not commenting or giving him a chance to explain, Miranda hastily said, "Mr. Honeycutt, thank you for alerting me to what my husband has intended to do. Please be so kind and inform me what his final decision is, while I attend to *your* guests who are surely arriving as we speak."

Turning her attention back to glance at Gilbert, she said, softly, "I love you Gilbert O'Flaherty and I always will."

Then hastily before she lost her nerve, she stormed out of the room leaving both Gilbert and Alfred in stunned disbelief. Closing the door behind her, she held her breath and trembled. *Dear God, let him choose me!*

Within moments, Miranda was cordially kissing Elise as she and Joshua were walking up the stairs leading to the third floor.

"Sorry Miranda, but we've come to look for someone to greet the guests who are arriving. Where is everyone hiding? Poor Benjamin went in search of someone in the gardens leaving Felicity, who looks dreadful I may add, in Alfred's study, and I haven't seen Mama or Michael."

It was obvious Elise was confused, so Miranda calmly said, "Well, I suppose everyone is getting their last instructions from Vivian before being announced formally. Let's you and I sneak inside Alfred's study and check on Felicity and then wait to see how the night unfolds. I'm sure it will be anything but dull."

"What a strange thing for you to say, Miranda. Are you alright? Why you're trembling."

Before Miranda could explain, Joshua urged Elise to take a stroll with him in the gardens as well. Glancing at him perturbed, she flatly refused.

"Oh fiddlesticks, Joshua. Felicity isn't ill, she's drunk for goodness sakes. Now you go find your parents and I'm going with Miranda." She spat indignantly. "I promise I'll be careful."

Seeing the fire in her eyes, Miranda pressed a smile to her lips all the while glancing up the stairs to the third floor wondering what Alfred and Gilbert were discussing. Joshua kissed his wife tenderly on the cheek then Elise and Miranda made it down the stairs and quickly dashed into Alfred's study unnoticed by arriving guests.

Seeing Miranda and Elise come into the study, Felicity, feeling a sudden flash of heat rush through her veins from all the liquor she had consumed, started waving a fan in front of her face. "Don't worry about me Miranda. I'm just fine. My, but it is warm in here, isn't it?" All the while praying, *Dear Lord, please don't let me faint. It's not time yet.*

The smell of brandy filled the air, and Elise and Miranda, recognizing the scent having smelled it on Catherine Brown's breath countless times in their youth, glanced at the other. And Elise smirked at her friend as if saying I told you so.

Never being shy, Elise knelt down beside Felicity and whispered, "Why Mrs. Myles, I do believe you are tipsy."

"Oh dear, you can tell? I needed a bit to steady my nerves." Felicity, bringing her hand to her lips apologetically, glanced at Miranda. "I was so nervous about introducing Rupert to New York society with Lavinia here and recalling my own introduction party . . ." Felicity cleverly added as to mask her real reason for being so nervous.

Elise and Miranda immediately comforted her by patting her on the shoulder as Felicity looked pleadingly at them. "Please don't let Rupert or Annabelle see me in such a state. Why I'll die of embarrassment."

"Don't fret Felicity, we will tend to getting you something to nibble on," Miranda said as Elise called for a servant.

"Bring us some coffee at once."

Hearing Elise's comment as James entered Alfred's study, Miranda rushed to his side, as if to spare Felicity any embarrassment. "Oh James, I was just this very minute on my way to find you. Could you please be a dear, and go fetch Alfred from his private suite and explain to him, his guests are arriving and that Mrs. Myles is not herself this evening?"

James, looking at Felicity, and seeing the glazed look in her eyes, smiled and whispered, "Oh dear, poor Felicity looks intoxicated."

"She is, but please go upstairs and see if Gilbert is alright. I don't have time to explain. but I've just left him and I can assure you he is far from being ready to follow through with our arrangements."

A look of concern filled James' eyes. At once he left the study and went directly up the stairs while Miranda returned to Felicity and Elise who was pouring Felicity a cup of coffee.

Without showing any interest in where her husband had gone in such a hurry, Lavinia skillfully managed to her make her way into Alfred's study without anyone noticing.

Silently she watched as Felicity whispered to Miranda, "Don't worry dearest, the bird will escape from the nest unscathed, even though the cat is prowling about."

"Bird?" Elise said, glancing at Miranda. "What on earth is she babbling about?" Then bringing the cup of coffee to Felicity, Elise said, "Please Felicity, drink this."

Felicity smiled at Elise then pointed to the doorway where Lavinia stood. At once Miranda stood and greeted Lavinia, knowing full well what Felicity had meant.

"Well hello, Mrs. Sterling. It appears poor Felicity, after taking such good care of me, has become ill herself, so perhaps it wouldn't be wise of you to come any closer."

"Nonsense! I never get sick. I have a constitution as strong as a horse."

Seeing Elise stand up and noticing her attire, a smile crossed her lips. "Ah well, Elise dear, I see you are with child. How lovely for you and Joshua, which reminds me--where is that devilishly handsome man of yours? Perhaps I should go and find him and tell him you're attending to a sick woman in your delicate condition."

Not wanting Lavinia Sterling anywhere near Joshua or he being alarmed, Elise said, "How kind of you Mrs. Sterling, but I was just on my way to find my husband myself. Why don't we both go in search of our wayward spouses?"

Turning to look at Felicity, Lavinia's trained eye raised as she turned her attention back to Elise who hastily whisked her from the room. *Why the prim and proper Mrs. Myles is intoxicated. Oh this may prove amusing.*

Smiling sweetly at Elise, Lavinia whispered, "You know, some women in your condition fear their husbands may find them unattractive; dreading they might seek comfort in the arms of a more pleasing woman to look at. But in your case my dear, I'm certain you have nothing to be worried about."

Elise not giving Lavinia the satisfaction of seeing how her comment hurt her, smiled. "Oh I know, I just can't imagine any woman being so vain, but then again it's probably because her husband never really loved her as my husband loves me. Speaking of husbands, where is Mr. Sterling this evening? Funny how I never see you and he together."

Seeing Joshua coming toward them, Elise beamed and immediately went to his side, tucking her hand into the crook of his arm. Leaning over to her, he whispered, "Back so soon? I was just going to see if you were behaving yourself, my delicate pearl."

Sickened by his comment, Lavinia excused herself as Elise drew Joshua away from the others explaining Felicity's predicament. "Darling, after Rupert and Annabelle are announced, you must keep him preoccupied until we can get Felicity away from here. Now don't worry, I'll do nothing to over exert myself. Come let's say hello to your dear parents."

Back in the study, Felicity, turning to Miranda upon seeing James and Alfred enter the room, said, "I'm fine really. I just need to rest for a spell."

Before Miranda could say a thing, Alfred said, "Miranda, don't be alarmed. Gilbert is safely tucked away as originally planned. By God, young woman, you do have a way of getting what you want, don't you? Not that I approve of what you just did mind you, but remind me never to cross you."

Felicity drank more of the hot coffee as ordered and looked at her friends with tears in her eyes. "I'm so ashamed, please forgive my foolishness. I hope I haven't spoiled everything."

Before Miranda had a chance to answer, James said, "Listen to me, we don't have much time. I saw Lavinia lurking about."

"She's already been here."

Shaking his head, James said in a strong and urgent voice, "Benjamin is with Rupert explaining that you have taken ill, and since they are planning to make their introduction within the half hour, there is no time to spare. Especially since Tad and Vivian are expected to be announced before them. As for you Felicity, you're doing splendidly. It may not be the illness we had planned, but you certainly don't look yourself, so follow my cue."

His voice became gentler as he looked into Felicity's eyes. "Just don't begin weeping and spoil everything."

Alfred opened the study doors and called for a servant to retrieve Montgomery while he motioned for Miranda to join him on the terrace, so he could have a few moments alone with her before she left.

As he and Miranda were saying their farewells, Miranda discreetly passed him the letters she had written earlier. James, meanwhile spoke privately to Montgomery, going over the last minute details to assure everything was going precisely as planned. Lavinia, seeing that Felicity was alone, discreetly entered the study while everyone else was preoccupied, and caring a glass of punch, offered it to Felicity.

"I've instructed the cook to bring along some broth for our ill patient. I see you have some coffee. I should think that might be rather harsh for you. Here Felicity, why not try the punch instead. I've poured it especially for you, *dear*." Lavinia, nearly choking on her own syrupy words smiled at Felicity.

Not wanting to appear ungrateful, Felicity took the goblet of punch from her and said sweetly, "How kind of you to make such a fuss over me Lavinia. I'm fine though, really!"

Thirsty, from the effects of the brandy and detested coffee, Felicity took a rather large swallow of the punch, nearly choking. By this time Miranda, Alfred, and James saw Lavinia near Felicity and went to her side nonchalantly. Still coughing from the punch, Miranda took the goblet from her passing it to James as she patted Felicity on the back. James' eyes locked onto Lavinia's who smile immediately changed her look to that of concern.

Suspicious of his wife, James sipped the punch himself, and when he discovered it was vodka with a splash of punch for color, he scolded her, "Are you mad? This is straight liquor!"

"Why James, I don't know what you referring too?" Lavinia appeared to be shocked. "I was only trying to help. How was I to know that the punch was spiked?"

"I'm sure there is no harm done. I think though, under the circumstances I should get Felicity home," Miranda hastily said.

In agreement, Felicity nodded her head as she tried to regain her composure through the coughing spell. "Yes," she gurgled.

Glaring coldly at his wife, James, in a stern voice demanded, "Lavinia and I will accompany you." His voice softened as he looked at the other two women. "It's not safe for two women to wander the streets alone at night. Besides, we haven't helped the situation much anyway, have we, dear?"

His glance returned to Lavinia and she gasped. "And miss the entire ball?" she whined. "No. I simply cannot miss my own sister being announced into New York society. What would people think? You go with them and I'll stay here and represent the family."

Glaring at her, his tone now that of disgust, James said, "As you insist, Lavinia. Miranda, you ride with Felicity and I'll follow you safely home and then I'll meet you back at our home following the party, my dear. I have work to attend to and I'll not be returning to this gala event."

Lavinia, in a huff, turned sharply on her heels. "In your present frame of mind, that will suit me just fine."

Both woman sighed relief after Lavinia left and Alfred said, "By God, James, you gave me such a fright. Why on earth would you suggest she come with you?"

"Simply because if I hadn't, Lavinia would have thought something amiss and would have insisted on coming along."

Shaking his head, Alfred said, "Well, by God, you could have warned me. My heart can't take anymore surprises tonight." Then looking at Miranda, he said, "Are you ready, my dear? I believe there is a very anxious man waiting to speak with you."

Smiling at Alfred, she said, "Yes. I'm anxious to speak with him as well."

As the four of them made their way to two the carriages, James directed his driver as Alfred helped Felicity into the other carriage after saying his good-byes to Montgomery. Alfred, pale and visibly shaken, turned and said to Miranda, "Don't worry, my dear, I'll see to it that Lucas receives your letter in Washington. I'll send a courier straight away."

Kissing him lightly on the cheek, she whispered, "Thank you, for everything. I love you."

"And I love you. Now be off with you and be kind to your family, dear one. Especially, that stubborn one inside who loves you with all his heart."

Smiling knowingly at what Alfred was referring to, Miranda stepped inside the coach and lovingly gazed at Gilbert who was lying across the floor of the carriage. After taking a seat next to Felicity, Gilbert withdrew the blanket from his head and glared at Miranda.

"Mrs. O'Flaherty, don't ya be thinkin' that yer goin' to be getting' away with walkin' out of the room as ya did earlier, without me havin' a chance to say anythin'."

"We'll have plenty of time to be discussing whatever you like, Mr. O'Flaherty, all the while we're traveling to our new life in San Francisco. But in the meantime darling, please do be patient until we're safe."

With that, Montgomery pulled away from the curb of the Honeycutt's mansion following James Sterling's cab. With Gilbert safely tucked away inside, only minutes from freeing the man they had rescued months earlier, Miranda and Felicity clutched each other's hand, scared to death.

Lavinia, who had been watching her husband from the window of Vivian's private suite, observed as their driver, once safely off the Honeycutt's property and down the street a few doors, pulled over to the side of the road.

Wondering why they had stopped, Miranda and Felicity gasped and waited in the coach bursting with anxiety. Gilbert, lying hunched over at their feet, moved about slightly. Miranda whispered, "Stay still darling, Mr. Sterling is approaching."

James then called to his driver, "Good man please assist me with Mrs. Myles, she's poorly this evening, and I'll care for her in my coach after all."

The coachman looked curiously at him but did as he'd been instructed. As James took Felicity's elbow, he winked at Miranda, who looked as if she'd seen a ghost.

"Mrs. O'Flaherty, it just occurred to me, there will be no way for your carriage to be returned with Montgomery accompanying you. Rather than go through the inconvenience of fetching it tomorrow and since Felicity is truly not herself, why not say your good-byes now? I'll take Felicity back to the orphanage myself and have my driver return Alfred's coach after you're safely aboard the train."

Miranda looked at Felicity hesitantly, fully aware that other carriages were arriving in front of the Honeycutt's and she felt very apprehensive they could be discovered harboring Gilbert. "Are you alright with this?"

"Of course, dear. It makes perfect sense."

Holding Miranda in her arms, Felicity said, "Please be happy. You both deserve to be." Then smiling at Gilbert, she added. "Take good care of her. She's very special."

Accepting James' hand, feeling as she were ready to break down and cry, besides feeling the effects of the alcohol even more than before, Felicity stepped out of the carriage. She leaned slightly on James while he gave directions to his driver who had joined Montgomery on the buckboard.

Waving to Miranda as Montgomery pulled away, Felicity, distraught, wept silently in James' arms as he led her inside his carriage, before taking his place on the buckboard.

Lavinia, still watching from the window, glared at her husband. *You will rue the day you chose her over me, James.* She sashayed away from the window in search of Rupert.

As Montgomery proceeded down the cobblestone road leading to Union Station, Miranda's heart, beating as quickly as the wings of a dove as it just learned to leave the nest for the first time, sighed. Once the carriage was well out of sight, she watched Gilbert slide from the floor of the carriage and retrieve a topcoat, hat, and riding gloves from the boxes that were placed on the seat across from Miranda.

"Well Mr. O'Flaherty, don't you look exceptionally handsome today. Every bit a fine dapper gentlemen."

"Mr. Hourigan, lass. And don't yer dare be tryin' to sweet talk me just now. Not after what ya just pulled off."

Detecting a hint of amusement in his eyes, she practiced her Irish accent. "Aye, so I'm to receive the silent treatment again, am I? Well I'll be havin' none of that laddie!"

Shaking his head and smirking while taking a seat beside her, Gilbert chuckled. "That is the sorriest excuse of an Irish accent me ears have ever heard. Is it any wonder I've decided to make sure me son knows how to speak with a true Irish brogue?"

Grateful this nightmare was finally coming to an end, and feeling Gilbert place his arm around her lovingly, Miranda leaned back in the seat and smiled. "Your son? And how are you so sure you'll have a son, Gilbert? Perhaps our baby might be a girl, have you ever thought of that?"

"A father knows. Why didn't ya tell me, Miranda? Have ya already forgotten our promise never to have secrets?"

"Darling, I swear as I held onto Elise today, and was congratulating her for being in the family way, I just knew I was having a baby, too. So I didn't keep any secrets from you. I told you as soon as I felt it. Besides, I may be wrong . . . ."

"Aye, but even if yer not now, we've got a whole lot of time to make sure ya are before we get to San Francisco," Gilbert said, huskily winking at her suggestively.

"So then, you're not angry with me for saying such cruel things to you earlier?"

"Now don't be pushin' yer luck there Mandy, girl. Ya were a might harsh, but I'll be forgivin' you this once, on account what ya said made a wee bit of sense. So, let's not be worrin' that pretty head of yers anymore about what was said in the past. Have ya not forgotten we have our whole lives ahead of us?"

Minutes later as the coach approached Grand Central Station, she, Gilbert, and Montgomery stepped on board the train, and after finding their assigned box-cars on the Erie, Gilbert looked at Miranda.

"It's over. We're finally out from beneath the clutches of the past and no harm can come to us now."

"I know, I was just thinking the same," she said softly. "No more, hiding or being frightened that someone will find you. By tomorrow your name will be cleared of the killing of David Sullivan, so if you choose, we can start using our name as soon as we reach San Francisco."

"It can wait, I'm as much a Hourigan as I am an O'Flaherty, I suppose. Just how long will this train take us to get all the way to San Francisco?"

"Oh darling, I'm afraid we're going to be on several different trains, didn't I tell you? From what Alfred said, we'll stay of this one until we reach the Mississippi and then we'll have to make some changes. If memory serves me right, we'll go on The Central Pacific then on The Union Pacific. I can pull all the tickets if you like."

"No, tomorrow we can look at them. Let's just enjoy our freedom tonight. To do as we please, not hidden from view."

"Yes darling, anything you like. Besides, San Francisco isn't going anywhere, I don't believe."

Gilbert smiled. "Aye, looks like we will definitely have a great deal of time on our hands. And there's not much room in this sleepin' car . . ." Smiling knowingly at her husband as he took her in his arms, feeling the train leave the station, Gilbert asked, "Any regrets?"

"None. What possibly do I need other then what I have right here?"

~

As the carriage pulled up in front of the orphanage, James stepped down off the buckboard to find Felicity resting in the back of the coach. After securing her inside her home and seeing she was still quite distraught over Miranda's departure, he convinced Felicity what she needed most was rest. After convincing her another shot of brandy would help her sleep, Felicity, already intoxicated and feeling the effects of all the liquor she had consumed that afternoon, reluctantly agreed. Starting to feel uneasy that James was still there, he politely saw himself out while leaving the door open for easy access later. The unsuspecting Felicity, feeling dizzy, went directly into her and Benjamin's bedchamber and began to disrobe while

James stood outside the small home, watching her silhouette as she struggled with her clothing.

After changing into her dressing gown, Felicity lay across her bed, feeling the effects of the liquor. She closed her eyes feeling the room begin to spin.

Within minutes, James reentered the small dwelling, and locking the door behind him, made his way into the room where Felicity was lying on the bed, nearly passed out. Quickly he disrobed, all the while watching his prey. Naked and standing in the darkened chamber, with only the moonlight shining over the bed, James inched closer and traced her cheek and neck with his index finger.

She stirred and moaned softly. "Oh, darling, you're home so soon? I must have dozed off."

Unable to lift her head, she moaned again feeling his hands on her breasts through her gown and feeling his urgency grasping them with such force, unlike what she was accustomed too. Felicity slowly opened her eyes. Trying to focus on the reflection of the man standing over her and seeing the face of James Sterling rather than her Benjamin, she began to scream. However, James' reflexes were quicker than Felicity's in her current condition, and she felt his hand immediately cover her mouth and nose.

Trying desperately to get away from him, struggling beneath the weight of his hand, with her fists, she struck him repeatedly while James forcibly pushed her head back onto the bed. Seemingly, he was not hurt by her attempt to fight him off. His left hand held her down, while his right hand grabbed at her gauze dressing gown. He knelt beside her, hovering over her petite frame. His nakedness gleamed in the moonlight and Felicity, seeing his erection screamed again.

"No one can hear you, Felicity. Don't fight me, I'm only repaying a dept to your beloved husband, the swine."

Not understanding, Felicity cried out, "No. James, please stop . . . No." While still trying desperately to fight off her attacker, her blows became stronger as she scratched and tried to bite at his hand while he ripped her gown exposing her breasts.

"God you are, perfect . . ." he growled, groping at her naked skin, trying to pull her garment up past her hips. Feeling his hands press up against her inner thighs, Felicity violently began thrashing her legs trying to escape from him. Fully aroused at seeing her delicate skin and the mound of hair below her taunt stomach, James forcibly pried her legs apart and mounted her with all his force.

Feeling his enlarged manhood penetrate inside the moist crevice of her body, Felicity jerked, scratching relentlessly, pushing him from her screaming, while the rest of his naked body crushed down on her.

Trapped and helpless against his weight, Felicity continued screaming and crying, to no avail. His grip over her mouth was drowning out her pleas and suffocating her at the same time, and her arms no longer were able to fight back.

With every thrust of his enlarged erection, causing him to enter her deeper, Felicity heard him groan as his pleasure increased. Silently she prayed this vile act was a nightmare and that James wasn't actually ravishing her like some wild beast.

Numbly, knowing she could do nothing to prevent him from defiling her, Felicity struggled to breathe. James, rocking harder and quicker to satisfy his longing, caused the pressure of his hand over her face to intensify. Feeling no oxygen to her lungs, only his sharp thrusts as his body crushed against hers, Felicity glanced up at the ceiling as the room became darker.

As fear crept inside her heart that she would suffocate by the hands of her attacker, James continued taking pleasure from her weakened and still body, until Felicity heard him cry out, being gratified. His grip around her face lessened as he lay motionless over her.

"James stop . . . I can't breathe . . ." she gasped.

Spent and hearing her call out his name, James looked down at her, seeing her lying there, not screaming any longer, and whispered, "If I release my hand Felicity, will you promise not to scream?"

Nodding through her tears, James hesitantly released his hand from her face and she gasped for air, choking and coughing.

Lifting his shoulders far enough to gaze down at her, Felicity immediately turned her head, cringing, feeling him touch her breasts, his touch repulsive and vile to her. Hovering over her, Felicity trapped beneath his weight, James kissed her cheek and she jerked her head and spat into his face.

"Get out! You've taken everything from me you wanted, now get off of me you barbarian!"

Calmly wiping the spit from his face and seeing blood from where she had scratched his face, slowly James pulled himself from her and stood watching her from the edge of the bed. As Felicity tried to cover herself with her torn dressing gown, ashamed and helpless, she hovered in a ball on the center of her bed, sobbing softly. As he placed his shirt over his back he winced, feeling the pain of the gouges she had afflicted. Looking at her now, it struck him that she wasn't the alley cat, who had dug her nails into his flesh causing him to hunger her more. Lying there now, he saw only a frightened kitten who needed comfort and tenderness after what he had done to her.

Wanting desperately to give her the consolation she needed, but knowing she would never allow him to be near her, James dressed hastily. As he was ready to leave, he hesitated and knelt beside Felicity.

"Whether you want to believe me or not, I do love you, Felicity. I am truly sorry that you had to suffer for the sins of your husband. But, a man must avenge his wife's honor, even if he doesn't love her. So it had to be like this, me taking you from him, just as Benjamin had taken Lavinia by force with no consent from me, back in England. You do see that, don't you Felicity? Why should that swine be allowed to live in bliss, when he destroyed Lavinia's and my relationship forever?"

Pulling her throbbing head from the bed, Felicity screamed, "Get out!"

Seeing him leave her room, his words haunted her, and Felicity fell back onto her bed, sobbing hysterically for her beloved Ben.

~ Twenty ~

Restitution

Following the first set, while the orchestra took a short break, Rupert excused himself politely from Elise, his partner from the last dance, and went in search of Annabelle and Lavinia.

Angered that his wife's sister had tried to sabotage their announcement into New York society by insisting she speak with him immediately, and insinuating that if he didn't, the consequences were something he would have to live with, Rupert was outraged though he concealed it well from others. *How dare she try to spoil Annabelle's chance to shine, just as she ruined Felicity's years earlier,* he thought.

Seeing Lavinia and Annabelle across the crowded dance floor chatting amongst other guests, Rupert walked over to them and calmly kissed Annabelle's cheek softly, while glaring at Lavinia. "Ah, my darling wife, having a good time?"

"Wonderful. I do wish though Felicity hadn't become ill. Having her here tonight would have made it perfect."

"Right. Well it seems your dear sister, tried to nurse her back to health earlier. Didn't you Lavinia, dear? How terribly thoughtful of you." Rupert's words sounded pleasant, but his eyes reflected anything but.

Realizing that Elise must have said something to him, she smiled politely at Rupert. "Yes. However, dear brother-in-law of mine, I did ask to speak with you earlier . . ."

"Ah, so you did. Well, as we seem to have a few minutes now, perhaps you might care to take a stroll in the lovely gardens of our hosts." Smiling reassuringly at Annabelle, who suddenly looked alarmed, Rupert said softly, "Dearest, I shan't be long. Why not go and find our dear friend Elise, to keep you company?"

Annabelle nodded seeing Joshua and Elise coming toward her and said, "Ah, Elise I was just on my way to find you . . ."

As the Carmidy's kept Annabelle occupied, Rupert lead Lavinia out to the gardens, nodding politely at guests as he took her further along the path for privacy. Finding the perfect place--far removed from anyone--he immediately demanded an explanation for her actions.

"First you give alcohol to a woman already under the influence and then you try to disrupt Annabelle's one chance to outshine you. By God, Lavinia, when will your insatiable jealousies ever end?"

"It doesn't surprise me that you would think so poorly of me, but this time you couldn't be farther from the truth, Rupert. Whether you want to believe me or not, I came to you earlier, fearful what James would do to poor Felicity."

Hearing this had something to do with his cousin, Lavinia had gotten his full attention, and quickly she explained what she had witnessed, including why she had not gone to Benjamin, who had for the past several months been fooled into believing James was his friend. All the while she had heard from James herself how much he detested him while lusting after Felicity.

"Why didn't you say anything to me earlier, or for that matter tell Benjamin of James' hatred?"

"You heard for yourself, James is insane I tell you. First he threatened to lock me up in a sanitarium. He has accosted me, threatened to beat me. Why even now, I'm fearful if he finds out that I've confided in you, I'll have to endure his wrath. But I'll gladly risk such unpleasantness to protect your cousin, despite my past differences with her."

Never had Lavinia given such a convincing performance, and at once, Rupert understanding the gravity of the situation, grasped Lavinia's elbow. "Come let's find Benjamin at once."

Within minutes of speaking to Benjamin, discovering the nature of James' secret involvement, and the need for Felicity to appear sick and leave with James while helping her friend Miranda, Rupert--not taking the time to understand what precisely had transpired leading to such an elaborate hoax and fearing the worst--demanded they leave at once to check in on Felicity.

Excusing himself, explaining he had to be certain that his cousin was not gravely ill to his hostess, the Robbins', Benjamin and Lavinia left the Honeycutt's party and headed directly to the orphanage.

As they entered the church grounds and seeing no lamps glowing from inside the small home, Benjamin immediately jumped from inside the coach as if sensing something was wrong, knowing Felicity always left a light on for him.

"Benjamin, wait. Let Annabelle go to her," Rupert said. "Lavinia, you wait here. Benjamin, let's have a chat inside your office so I fully understand what has transpired causing my cousin to be put in such a compromising situation."

As Annabelle entered the small dwelling, the sounds of muffled crying came from behind the closed door she knew to be the bedchamber, fear gripped at her heart. Seeing Benjamin and Rupert go to the office, Annabelle lit a kerosene lamp and crept inside the room. Her heart stopped beating seeing Felicity crouched in the fetal position on her bed.

Hearing the door creak, Felicity jumped thinking James had returned to accost her again. Seeing Annabelle, she cowered from her, too ashamed to be seen.

Immediately placing the lamp on the table, Annabelle took the frightened and hysterical Felicity in her arms. At once it was clear to Annabelle by Felicity's torn gown and her bruised face that she had been raped. She tenderly consoled the trembling woman while taking the quilt off her bed and wrapping it around lovingly.

"Dear Felicity, we need to get you out of these clothes and clean you up before Benjamin becomes alarmed and comes in."

"He's here?" she asked dazed and confused.

"Yes, dearest. Rupert has him in his office trying to find out why James was allowed to be alone with you."

"Oh Annabelle please . . . Don't let Benjamin know what has happened. Please! I beg of you. I'm soiled. He'll never love me again . . ."

"I promise Felicity, but you are not soiled. You've been attacked by a monster who should be killed for what he has done to you."

Again, Felicity wept uncontrollably—shaking--relieving the pain and humiliation she had suffered. "It's my fault. I was helping Miranda . . . ."

"This is not your fault! That depraved bastard forced himself on you. So I will not hear another word that you had any blame in this. Now come and let me help you change."

Numbly, Felicity tried to rise from the bed, but her legs were weak and her head throbbed. Recalling his words, saying he had only done what Benjamin had done to Lavinia, Felicity felt suddenly nauseated and ran to her dry sink and vomited. The smell of soured brandy filled the room and Annabelle went to her side to tenderly comfort her. Her heart ached for her friend, unable to fathom that her brother-in-law could have done such a vile thing.

Sobbing again, Felicity unable to stand, was led to the side of her bed. Annabelle tenderly washed her and helped her into a fresh gown. After securing her safely in her bed, she told Felicity she would be right back to make sure Benjamin would not disturb her.

Leaving the bedroom, she immediately called for Rupert. Hastily explaining what had happened, and the condition Felicity was in, Rupert eyes widened. "I'll kill the bastard!"

"No, dearest. Felicity never wants Benjamin to know the shame she has been put through, and if you truly love Felicity then you will respect her wishes and keep her secret."

"And let James get away with what he's done? No!"

"Shh, Rupert. Please darling, Benjamin will hear you. Now I did not mean that James should not suffer for the pain and humiliation he has brought down on Felicity. But there are other ways a man can suffer for such vile things he has done. It is up to you my dearest to see that he pays, and pays dearly for what he has done to our Felicity."

Seeing the tears in Annabelle's eyes, Rupert took her in his arms. "Can I see her? Is she badly hurt?"

"Felicity doesn't want to see anyone, not even Benjamin. How can we keep him from her for a few days? Benjamin needs to tend to the children . . ."

"The hell he does. We shall set sail on the next ship and if need be, I'll hire a staff to take care of this orphanage until the Bishop finds his replacement."

Nodding in agreement, it was decided amongst them that it would be best if Annabelle stayed with Felicity for the evening, promising to stall Benjamin from seeing her for the time being. After kissing his wife goodbye, Rupert immediately went back to the office.

"Benjamin old friend, it would appear our Felicity is quite ill. Since Annabelle has already been exposed to her, and since you have to think of the children, I'm afraid seeing Felicity this evening is out of the question."

Seeing Benjamin try to object, Rupert calmly placed his hand on his shoulder. "Old boy, let her have tonight with Annabelle. She's having a bad time of it, not accustomed to so much to drink, and she has made quite a mess of herself. Let her hold onto her dignity. Surely one night apart won't matter to you, but it will mean everything to her."

Benjamin consented, certain that Rupert was holding something back from him regarding Felicity's condition, and was only following her wishes not to see her right now. Hearing that Annabelle would remain with Felicity, and knowing she would be well cared for, Benjamin finally agreed to Rupert's request.

"Need I remind you that my sister-in-law is waiting for us in the carriage?"

"Right." Benjamin said frowning, consumed with worry for Felicity's welfare, knowing it had to be gravely serious if his beloved Felicity wouldn't want him with her. Numbly, Benjamin glanced to the closed door where Felicity was hiding from him.

"Come along with me, old boy," Rupert softly said. Obligingly, Benjamin did as Rupert and Felicity wanted and left his home while he and Felicity suffered deeply.

On the ride from the orphanage to the Sterling's, Benjamin said not a word. The events of the past few months processed through his troubled mind. Recalling the first time James had approached him speaking of how he had preformed sexual acts with Lavinia while thinking of another, he wondered if that woman he had lusted after was his Felicity. And remembering on countless times since that day, how he had seen James look at Felicity with such admiration, he felt sickened. *What kind of man couldn't even protect his own wife?*

Closing his eyes, he earnestly prayed that what he feared had never happened. *Dear Lord, please, I beg of you let my thoughts be wrong. Have I been so naive and so preoccupied with my own selfish needs that I've allowed another man to harm my wife?*

Before he had a chance to question Rupert further, their carriage arrived in front of the Sterling's residence. Rupert, glancing at Benjamin said sternly, "Stay here Benjamin. I will only be a few moments."

Assisting his sister-in-law from the coach, Rupert refrained Lavinia from going inside by using her key, and knocked at the door instead.

"Rupert, the servant's are asleep."

"I know. I wish for James to answer." Puzzled, Lavinia said nothing, waiting suddenly fearful of Rupert's reaction.

As soon as James answered the door, Rupert viewing the scratches on his face and neck, calmly gripped his left hand on James' shoulder as if extending a warm greeting while raising his knee forcibly into the unsuspecting James' groin. Taken completely off guard, both Lavinia and James gasped. Bending over in excruciating pain, James began coughing as Rupert clenched his right hand into a fist planting a firm blow against his jaw. At once James was knocked to the ground, and Rupert calmly said, "Close the door, Lavinia!"

Frozen to the spot where she stood, her mouth opened, she stared down at her husband who lay beneath Rupert's boot pressed firmly against his larynx. Lavinia started to argue with him, seeing James struggling for air, twisting on the floor at their feet.

"I said, shut the door!" Rupert demanded.

From the carriage outside, Benjamin witnessing what had just transpired, suddenly knew that his fears had been right. James had taken Felicity as his, and judging by the scratches on his face, he knew Felicity had fought off his advances. Unable to bear the thought of her body being gratified by the man he had thought was his friend, and imagining what pain she must have endured, Benjamin became violently ill.

Rushing out of the carriage, vomiting onto the street as he wept, he knew he had not protected the only thing that mattered to him, and that was his wife. Loathing himself for allowing such a thing to have happened, and grieving his wife's pain, Benjamin sunk to his knees. "Why God, why? She did nothing wrong but love me."

At the exact moment inside in the Sterling's home, Rupert glared at Lavinia and calmly asked, "I shall only ask you this once, Lavinia. Do you want to return to England with us, or do you wish to remain here and married to this heathen?"

"England of course, but how will I survive. I have nothing..."

Pressing his boot harder on James' larynx, seeing the veins protrude from his neck and throat, and hearing him gasp for air, Rupert said, "James will be more than happy to provide for his wife. Isn't that right, James?" Shaking his head, unable to speak, James clutched at Rupert's boot.

"Go to the carriage Lavinia, and we'll return tomorrow for your things."

Meekly, she said, "You're not going to kill him, are you Rupert?"

"Go to the carriage Lavinia."

Fumbling for the door knob, she hastily ran outside, and seeing Benjamin kneeling in prayer, she ran up to him. "You pathetic bastard, all you can do is pray as Rupert is killing James? Well, God have mercy on your soul, Benjamin Myles!"

Hearing her comment, Benjamin snapped out of his grief and ran to the front door to hear Rupert say, "As God is my witness, if you ever step one foot near any of my family again, I'll kill you, you uncivilized savage!"

Releasing his foot from James neck, he turned and walked from the landing just as Benjamin approached. Seeing James crouched over, gasping for air, Benjamin struggled to get inside to finish off what Rupert had begun, but was pulled back by Rupert. "Remember your vocation!"

"No damn it, get away from me Rupert." Ripping his collar from his neck, Benjamin shouted, "God has forsaken me and is punishing me for my past sins through Felicity. He deserves to die, and by God, I'm going to kill him, for what he's done!"

"Think of Felicity. She'll need you to be near her, to love and comfort her, and how can that happen if you're locked away in prison, or hanging by a noose. No Benjamin. It takes a stronger man to help your wife than to satisfy the need in you to avenge her. If you truly love Felicity, then walk away for her sake."

Shaking--never feeling such hate in his heart--desperately wanting to end James' life, Benjamin glanced up at Rupert and said, "Fine. Not for God, or you, only for Felicity."

~ Twenty-one ~

After the Pain

Following the party, discovering from Rupert what had happened following Miranda's daring escape to free Gilbert--although Rupert had not explained precisely why it was necessary for Lavinia and Benjamin to seek lodging at his home--Alfred could only imagine. Calling a family meeting in his study, seeing the concerned look on everyone's face, he said nothing to relieve their minds. Waiting in silence as the last servant shut the door, trying desperately to know where to begin, Alfred cleared his throat. "Tonight, many things have transpired that will undoubtedly change our lives and those we love forever. Until I have completely said all there is to say, please I must not merely insist but demand, that everyone hold their comments until I have finished."

Without waiting for a response from his family, Alfred began. "This evening, with the assistance of myself along with others I care not to mention, Miranda has successfully left New York, with her husband--a fine man by the name of Gilbert O'Flaherty."

At once everyone gasped and Tad stood up protesting that Gilbert was nothing but a murderer. Alfred shouted, "Sit down, Thaddeus. And I do mean now!"

At Michael's insistence, Tad did take his seat, jaw clenched and face red, while glaring at his grandfather who returned his look.

"Mr. O'Flaherty, as I was saying before I was so rudely interrupted, is a fine and decent man who was framed for a murder he did not commit and was deliberately run down by the actual murderer. This, thank heavens, was witnessed by Miranda, and through her persistence and foresight, not only managed to save his life, but prove his innocence as well--discovering the truth of who actually ended the life of Mr. O'Flaherty's friend."

Alfred paused and looked at Tad before turning his attention to Elise who was crying softly in Joshua's arms. "My dearest Elise, Miranda has a letter for you that I shall give to you following this meeting. But let me say this on her behalf--not sharing with you, in particular--her greatest joy and happiness has caused her great pain. Precisely why she was ill, the stress was far to great on her. However, if she hadn't done what she did, an innocent man more than likely would have been murdered since the individuals who committed such heinous acts were still actively trying to kill Mr. O'Flaherty. So as you can see, she had little choice but to protect the man she loved and to begin a new life elsewhere. And I must say, the courage and determination that Miranda has shown has made me very proud of her. And Mr. O'Flaherty who could have, at any given moment, turned in those who tried to silence him, chose not to for reasons I will not discuss at this time. So you see why I am very fond of the man Miranda has chosen to share a life with."

"Is that it, Grandfather?" Tad asked still glaring at him.

"No, actually that is not it. The latter part of this week, the Robbins' will be returning to England along with Mr. and Mrs. Myles, and Mrs. Sterling. Again, I look at you Elise, because I'm certain Felicity and Annabelle will want to say their good-byes to you, in particular. It would appear my dearest granddaughter, that your charms have spread across the Atlantic, and you will be missed terribly."

Smiling warmly at her, he asked, "Dearest, I'm sure you will want to read your letter in private. So why don't you and Joshua go to your home, but before visiting the Robbins' or the Myles', please come and see me tomorrow so I can tell you of Miranda's wedding. By the way, she asked me to tell you, she never broke her promise to you--there was no maid of honor. Only myself and Gilbert's sister were in attendance, and strictly as witnesses." With that, Elise stood and ran to Alfred who kissed her tenderly then handed her the letter.

Following Elise and Joshua's departure, Alfred insisted everyone else remain. He immediately informed Tad it was not he who had killed David O'Sullivan as he had thought, but was in fact, Daniel Hobbs. Michael stunned, held Sarah's hand listening intently as his father continued. While Alfred shook his head glancing at both Tad and his wife, he had discovered that Vivian had been paying Daniel money to silence a blackmailer, who at the time they had believed was Gilbert.

Reassuring them that was impossible since Gilbert had been living under their roof since Tad and Daniel had run him down, Alfred pointed out that the money was probably paid directly to the murderer. The murderer, who by now, he was certain was on his way to a poor-farm where he would work for his room and board since his father had disowned him for what he had done.

Directing his attention to his grandson, Alfred eyes warmed. "Tad, you have chosen unwisely and it cost you more than the blood money your grandmother paid for you. You lost the love of a fine woman. Until Miranda saw you help Daniel run Gilbert down, you had her heart. All she needed or wanted in return was a man with integrity who would not lie to her or break the trust she had placed in you. And Tad, as much as it pains me, rather than trust in her and her love that she genuinely had for you, you sought to kill another man whom you feared was a threat, never realizing the only thing that threatened your relationship with Miranda was you. Tad, I pleaded with you that night you came home after you had thought you took a man's life that you could either choose to be swallowed up by self-hatred and become bitter, or you could learn from your mistake. I pray Tad at last, that you will learn to be the man both your father and I know you can be."

Excusing himself, not saying a word, Tad went to his old room and immediately went through the secret passage that connected to Miranda's room. Sitting on the edge of the bed, her scent still lingering in the room, Tad wept for the love he had let slip through his fingers.

~

Felicity, still quite upset, lay next to Annabelle as she spoke of the events that had led to her attack and why she had felt so safe with James. No longer crying or shaking, Felicity at last felt safe near her dear friend.

"So do you think all those months he had planned this?" Annabelle asked, assured by Felicity that it helped by talking freely.

"I honestly don't know. It makes no sense. For weeks at a time, Benjamin has been gone and at anytime during the past few years if he had wanted to attack me, he would have had the opportunity now that I think about it."

Frowning, Annabelle said, "Oh Felicity, you know how much I care for Benjamin, but surely he had to have known it wasn't safe for you alone here?"

"Alone?" Felicity smiled. "Dear Annabelle, I'm hardly alone. Why we have over a hundred children that we tend to."

"Yes, and none of them were able to prevent what happened tonight. I'm sorry if that hurt you, but promise me, you will never be alone again, no matter what. When you return to England, I do hope you will stay with Rupert and me for a spell. I know Anne will want you with them of course, but before we go to France for the season, I do hope you'll spend a little while with us."

"Oh Annabelle, how can I possibly think of England, after what has happened? Don't you see, nothing will ever be the same between Benjamin and me? If he were to find out, how could he ever hold me in his arms, knowing that another man had soiled me? Or worse, every time he did, I'd be worried he was thinking about what James did to me. On the other hand, if I don't tell him, I am willingly and openly lying to my husband. So as it turns out, James was right. He has spoiled it for us forever."

Felicity had no more tears to shed, her heart was broken as was her spirit, and Annabelle tried desperately to show her that one night could not erase the love that Benjamin and she shared.

Nodding as if in agreement, Annabelle knew her friend was merely appeasing her, and the two of them lay side by side both pretending to sleep.

As Felicity lay there, suddenly it all made sense to her. *James had chosen that night in particular, since it was Annabelle and Rupert's introduction to New York society.* Especially knowing that by Rupert proclaiming Benjamin's innocence--the true perpetrator--Lavinia's father was made public, which ultimately banished Lavinia from England's society. Recalling James' words as he left her, Felicity winced. *Had Benjamin taken Lavinia by force? Was it possible her tender, loving husband was capable of such a vile act against Lavinia when they were married?*

Felicity couldn't bring herself to believe Benjamin capable of such an act of violence. Surely, it was Lavinia who had lied to James, telling him that Benjamin had forced himself on her to excuse her from being intimate with Benjamin.

Realizing that Lavinia would do such a thing, and understanding how deeply it must have hurt James to think the woman he loved had been abused in such a manner, Felicity still couldn't excuse him from committing such an act himself.

How could a man, after violating her in such a despicable manner, say he loved her as James had, and then in the next breath excuse his actions?

Felicity had to understand why he would do such a thing if she ever were to find a moment's peace, so she forced herself to process what she knew to be true, rather than focus on the act itself. As if her mind was trying to heal her body by logically figuring out why she had been violated, she thought, *Obviously James had harbored such hate in his heart all these years. Seeing her and Benjamin happy, while his and Lavinia's marriage was anything but blissful only had added to his hate and jealousy toward Benjamin.*

Recalling James say as much following his attack on her, the pieces began to fall into place. This made sense in some sick and twisted way, since James, after committing such a heinous act, had made it a point to tell her he had a right to do it.

What better way to avenge his wife's honor then to make certain Rupert suffered as his wife had, and pay back a dept he felt Benjamin owed him. One dastardly deed took care of both men whom he despised for causing Lavinia's torment, and what he believed was the cause of his ill-gotten and tumultuous marriage.

God have mercy on your soul, James Sterling, because I never shall! You can go straight to the devil where you belong!

~

The following morning as Rupert had promised, he took Lavinia to her home to gather what personal belongings she wanted to take with her back to England. Arriving there, longing to have an opportunity to be alone with James, she glanced at Rupert wondering how she might accomplish such a feat without jeopardizing her current standing with her brother-in-law. Much to her amazement, Rupert made it easy for her.

"Lavinia dear, after last night's incident, perhaps it would be wise if I wait for you here. That is if you feel safe with your husband, this one last time."

Nodding, she said, "Perhaps you're right, Rupert. Just knowing you're near if I should need you is reassuring. After last night, I should think neither you nor James should ever be alone with one another again."

Climbing the stairs, she glanced back at Rupert who stood tall and erect by the carriage, to show James he was near, she imagined.

As a servant answered, Lavinia, said, "Where is Mr. Sterling?"

James replied as he walked from the parlor, his head and neck wrapped in bandages. Glancing out the door as the servant shut it, he said, "Ah, so I see you've brought the guard dog with you. No need Lavinia, your belongings are packed and ready for you, and all I can say is good riddance."

Turning back to the parlor, Lavinia directed her attention to Andrew, their butler, before following her husband. "See to it all my trunks are taken to my brother-in-law's carriage at once."

Andrew paused and looked for direction from James, who nodded to him before following Lavinia's directions.

Chuckling, Lavinia said, "James darling, don't tell me you had directed the servants to protect you from Rupert. Were you afraid he'd finish off what he started last evening, after you viscously attacked his beloved cousin?"

Turning at her, he glared. "Allegedly attacked, my dear. I would hate to have to bring a lawsuit of slander against my own wife, who stood by and did nothing as her brother-in-law viciously attacked me without provocation."

"You must think of a far better excuse than that darling, if you think anyone in this god- forsaken country is ever going to believe you."

"What do you want, Lavinia?"

"Want? Why James, how considerate of you to think of my needs when obviously you're in so much pain. My only question is who hurt you more, your precious little tart, or her cousin, after finding out you attacked her? This by the way, truly was an act of sheer genius on your part, and especially on Annabelle's welcoming into America's society. I couldn't have planned a better or more befitting way to destroy such a joyous occasion for the little will-robber. Thank you so much for assuring my welcome back into England society after my exile. Too bad you won't be able to attend my victorious return as the poor helpless wife of an unscrupulous brut who made my life as miserable as he did his first wife."

Not responding to Lavinia, James walked over to his liquor cabinet and poured himself a stiff brandy and winced as he gulped it back then promptly poured himself another.

"Oh dear James, does your throat hurt this morning? Why how silly of me, of course it must, having Rupert's boot pressing on it as he did or was it that punch in the jaw? Tsk, tsk, tsk, pray tell, James, was bedding that precious tart worth the pain and humiliation it has caused?" Lavinia's amusement was undeniable by the twinkle in her eyes and James raised his glass to her.

"I can assure you my dear, it was indeed! Especially after bedding such a droll and cold woman as yourself."

Hearing his remark, Lavinia's smile faded, she glared at her husband and said in retaliation, "To bad though you felt the need to avenge my honor, James, considering there really was no need. You see darling, Benjamin never forced himself on me. On the contrary, that puritan had to be seduced before he would take advantage of even his own wife. But I can assure you, once I sufficiently aroused him, Benjamin found bedding me more than enjoyable. As I recall, I too scratched him rather deeply as I clung to him while he excited me beyond anything I ever felt with you. That is, I'm assuming your lusty little tart scratched you out of enjoyment."

"Get out!" James yelled in a strained voice.

"Oh I shall. Just keep this in mind, James, while I'm basking in my homeland, and you are banished in this god-forsaken country with your lusty little tart nearby, you can be assured that everyday I will make sure her life is a living hell for what she has done and there will be nothing you can do about it."

With that, Lavinia turned and James threw his glass across the room then slumped in a nearby chair, saying, "Christ, what have I done?"

~ Twenty-two ~

Bitter Sweet

Late October, 1865

Lucas Brown, standing outside a hotel room in Buffalo, New York took a deep breath before knocking softly, hearing a man's voice call from behind the door.

"Mandy girl, times a wastin', lass. Better be getting yerself up and ready, Montgomery's already here."

Lucas knew he was at the right door hearing the male's voice having an Irish brogue, and his daughter being referred to as Mandy. Bracing himself to meet the man who had stolen his daughter from him, Lucas held his breath as the door swung open.

Immediately Gilbert's smile faded as he saw the stranger standing where he thought Montgomery would be. "Can I help you?" Gilbert asked politely.

Eyeing the rugged man before him, Lucas said, "Yes, Mr. O'Flaherty you can. May I come in please? I'm Lucas Brown, your father-in-law."

Stepping aside, allowing Lucas access into the room, he immediately extended his hand. "Pleasure to meet ya, sir. I've heard a lot about ya from yer daughter."

Taking his hand in his, Lucas, said, "Is that right? I unfortunately can't say the same since my daughter never spoke a word of you to me."

"Aye." Gilbert nervously gestured toward a chair for Lucas to take then added. "Beggin' yer pardon sir, but how did ya know where we were?"

From behind the closed door, both men turned when Miranda called out, "Darling, please tell Montgomery I'll be out directly."

Gilbert, hearing his wife speak, and ready to tell her that her father was there, stopped when Lucas said in a hushed voice, "Please Mr. O'Flaherty, let us have a few minutes to get acquainted."

Nodding, Gilbert awkwardly took a seat beside Lucas and said, "Sir, under the circumstances, perhaps ya should call me Gilbert."

Not responding to Gilbert's request, Lucas said, "In answer to your first question, Mr. O'Flaherty, Alfred Honeycutt was kind enough to inform me that the two of you were here. From what I understand, my daughter was too ill to travel on the train. Is that right?"

Noting that Lucas had still called him by his last name, Gilbert said, "Aye. The motion of the train made her a wee sick, so I thought it best to stay here in Buffalo for a spell."

Rather enjoying seeing the man before him, feeling uncomfortable trying to explain that not only had he stolen his daughter from him, but had impregnated her as well, Lucas applied more pressure to his son-in-law. To see if what he had heard about this man from Alfred was true, he cleverly goaded him by saying, "Is that right? How peculiar, as I recall Miranda has a strong constitution and never has a train made her ill before."

Clearing his throat and rubbing his hand through his hair before answering, Gilbert said, "Well, I wouldn't be knowin' about that, sir, but I do agree Miranda is a strong-willed lass."

"Indeed. How clever of you Mr. O'Flaherty, to remind me of my own daughter's character."

"Look sir, we seem to be getting off on the wrong foot here . . . I meant no disrespect, obviously ya know yer daughter far better than me. Considerin' everythin' that has happened, and if I were in yer shoes, I'd be ticked off. But I can tell ya sir, no man could love yer daughter as much as I love Miranda. As soon as I'm able, I'll do right by her. But I'll be damned, if I'm going to sit here and let ya or any other man try to make me feel as if I'm not good enough for my wife. Cause I am. I make Miranda happy and I'll keep on makin' her happy with my last dyin' breath."

Immediately, Lucas erupted in laughter, and hearing the familiar sound of her father's voice Miranda--brushing her hair in the other room--dropped her hairbrush. "Papa?" she whispered. The blood drained from her cheeks, she tiptoed to the closed door and listened intently all the while trembling.

"Well your reputation supersedes you, lad. You're every bit as independent and stubborn as Alfred said you were and it's clear to me that you love my daughter as much as I've heard."

Dumfounded by Lucas, remark Gilbert sat speechless across from him, trying to size him up, as Lucas had just done to him.

Glancing at his son-in-law, Lucas said, seriously, "I apologize, Gilbert, for putting you through that, but I had to be certain you truly loved my daughter as I had heard from Alfred. Which by the way, he's your greatest ally and coming from a man like him, that's quite a feat."

"I have no qualms with Mr. Honeycutt, he's a rightly kind man. Decent and honorable and I owe him a lot."

"Yes. Well since we both seem to agree on another point, and since if I know my daughter, she is probably listening at the door by now. Let me get directly to the point as to why I wanted to speak with you before being reunited with Miranda."

Pausing to clear his throat, he said, "Gilbert, I don't know if Miranda told you or not, but when I married her mother, Catherine Mason, I was not a wealthy man. I married into wealth."

Standing up, obviously angered by what Lucas was implying, Gilbert said, "Well if that's what ya think I've done . . ."

Chuckling, and raising his arms at seeing the fiery temper Alfred had spoken of, Lucas said, "Sit down Gilbert, and let me finish, please. I think you owe me that much."

Respectfully, Gilbert sat down while Lucas continued. "Alfred was right again, you do have a temper, which I'm not opposed to, mind you. As a matter of fact, I've been know from time to time to be a might stubborn myself, if provoked. As Miranda's father, I'd like to imagine that's what attracted her to you in the first place . . ."

Clearing his throat, again feeling suddenly very sentimental, Lucas said, "That's neither here nor there--my point was--whatever your intentions were, the fact remains, Miranda comes from a wealthy family. And, as the sole heir, and being a woman, her holdings when I pass will automatically resort to you. Now Gilbert, what you do with them after I'm dead I'll have little say in the matter. You can let them all resort back to the government, which would pain me deeply, but obviously there won't be a damn thing I can do about it. So, I was hoping that today I might persuade you to please consider for Miranda's sake, and take her back to Virginia where she belongs, rather than begin a new life for both of you in San Francisco. This isn't a gift, Gilbert, there's not much left of my holdings but the land. And by God, I'm just too old and I no longer have the drive or the heart to work it properly. So what I'm proposing is that you build a life for you and my daughter on the land of her birth. There is over five-hundred acres that need to be worked, and by God I'm asking--no, I'm begging you--to raise my grandchildren on the land of their ancestors."

Gilbert's eyes locked onto Lucas while Miranda stood breathless, waiting for his reply.

"Mandy told me her family home was now an orphanage. I won't be havin' me wife tend to other children or live under another man's roof."

"I can abide by that, besides, Glenbrook needs to remain a school. What I had in mind is . . . That is if you agree, of course, is you and I pick out a fine location to build a new home for you and your family. One that is solely yours and hers. Maybe alongside the brook that travels along the backside of the property. As a child, Miranda and Elise used to sneak down there and catch pollywogs . . ." Recalling his daughter as a little girl, his eyes welled up and he looked pleadingly at Gilbert.

"Fine, Mr. Brown I'll work yer land and build a home for Mandy and the wee ones, but not because I want it for meself, but for her."

"Thank you, Gilbert, and please call me Lucas, son." Gripping his hand, Lucas shook it heartily and then called out, "Missy, come on out of there and give your father a hug."

Without any further prompting, Miranda ran to her father, tears running down her cheeks. "Oh Papa. I love you. I'm so sorry I've hurt you." Kissing and hugging him excitedly, she glanced at Gilbert and whispered, "Thank you."

As Lucas pulled away from her, he said, "Let me get a look at you." Seeing she was indeed carrying a child as he had been informed by Alfred, he softly said to her, "My, but being married and in the family way suits you my dear. I've never seen you look more beautiful. And don't be frettin' none about hurting me, seems to me we've all been hurtin' long enough. After I found out what you had done, and after getting over the anger and shock, it occurred to me, Miranda, what an incredibly brave and strong-willed woman I had raised. Fearing I had lost you too, when I heard you were here with your husband, I came at once. And the whole way here, I didn't know how I was going to be able to tell you just how much I love you and how proud I am of you. But seeing you now, obviously happier than you've ever been, it suddenly occurred to me, words aren't what matters. What truly is important is showing you. Not only do I have my daughter back thanks to your fine husband, I have a son, and soon a grandson who deserves some happiness as well. And by God, his papa and I are going to make damn sure he gets it. Isn't that right, son?" Lucas glanced at Gilbert for confirmation that he would allow him into their lives.

"Aye, sir."

Overcome with joy, Miranda smiled through her tears. "Grandson? Just how are you and Gilbert so certain this baby is going to be a boy?"

"A father just knows these things, daughter."

Immediately, Miranda and Gilbert laughed hearing Lucas say that and once finding out Gilbert had said the same thing after realizing out she was expecting, Lucas said, "Ah, so another thing we see eye to eye on, Gilbert."

For the remainder of the afternoon, traveling plans were made for their trip back to Virginia including Montgomery, who had agreed to work with Gilbert--not just as an employee but as a trusted friend. With Lucas having already scheduled to meet Michael in Fairfax on business, he would travel ahead by rail while the other three would go by coach for Miranda's sake.

Gilbert, agreeing to the location Lucas had described by the brook--rather fond of the thought that his own child would be playing where his mother had as a child--it was agreed Lucas would begin the construction on their new home before their arrival. Settling on late November, giving them able time to make the trip by not pushing Miranda in her delicate condition, Lucas set off for Fairfax with a smile on his face and at last peace in his heart.

~

April, 1866
Pixie Halt, Devon England

Anne, watching her cousin as she and Rupert took a walk through the gardens, sighed. "Oh Annabelle, are you certain Felicity isn't homesick? She's so sullen, not the least bit happy, although she does make a brave attempt for appearance sake."

"She's just having a rough pregnancy and with her and Benjamin's home still not completed, I'm sure that adds to her worries."

Shaking her head, Anne said, "After years of not having been blessed with a child, and now that she and Benjamin actually are going to have a family, you would think Felicity would be bubbling over with enthusiasm. However, it's just the opposite. Why, she was more excited picking out gifts for Elise and Joshua's twins then picking out something for her own child. It was Benjamin who purchased what meager things they have for that poor little thing, and heaven knows the baby could come anytime now."

Annabelle, wanting desperately to change the subject, said, "Speaking of Elise and Joshua, did you receive a photograph of them in the post?"

Smiling proudly, Anne said, "Indeed I did. Wasn't that so kind of them to send one along to Edward and me? It tickles me to think Elise has two little ones to contend with. I was just telling Edward this very morning, seeing how proudly Joshua was holding his little daughter, Sarah Tess, and Elise smiling as only she can while holding her little son, Andrew Michael, just how fortunate they truly are. When I think how she could have miscarried after her dreadful fall down those stairs, I shudder."

"Yes, they were very fortunate indeed..." Annabelle's voice trailed off recalling the letter she had received from Elise, following her accident and how Joshua, who had blamed himself never left her side.

For months, Elise had been cooped up in the house, only occasionally going to the Honeycutt's or her and Joshua's parents' home for dinner.

Bored and miserable from her condition, having grown exceptionally large with child, Elise had insisted Joshua stay home with her more. This was impossible since he had been called upon to help his college buddy, William Maxwell Evarts to defend the president, Andrew Johnson, from impeachment.

Outraged by Joshua's lack of tentativeness when he was leaving for the office, Elise reaching to grab his arm, lost her footing, and rolled down the stairs, knocking herself unconscious. Grief stricken and blaming himself for her accident, Joshua stayed by her side for the duration of her pregnancy, turning over all his findings to his father and Tad, who was an apprentice at his father's law firm.

Anne, clearing her throat, noticing Annabelle lost in her own thoughts, said, "Were you thinking of Elise and Joshua, or your babe?"

"Both I suppose," Annabelle said, smiling rubbing her protruding stomach. "How ironic that all four of us--Elise, Miranda, Felicity and I--will be new mothers at the same time. I just hope that we all will be able to accept motherhood and our new life as well as Elise and Joshua seem to have adjusted. Earlier, when I read Elise's letter and she wrote, 'Well at last my Joshua and I've not only weathered the storm through a war by our love, but we've finally learned how to bind that love through daily life as man and wife'. I couldn't help but wonder if all of us will be as lucky as Elise and Joshua are."

"Why Annabelle, I'm shocked! Never have I heard you speak so negatively. Surely you aren't suggesting you and Rupert are having problems . . ."

"Oh no. Rupert and I couldn't be happier, despite Lavinia constantly being under foot."

"Which reminds me... Just how long are we to be graced with her company? I know she just returned from the winter in London, but must she remain here the entire summer?"

As Annabelle and Anne continued their conversation, Rupert and Felicity had taken a seat amongst the rose bushes her late aunt had planted. Feeling the child growing inside her, feeling a kick to her ribs, she winced. Just as she had when the child's father had impregnated her.

Realizing Rupert was watching her, she smiled and softly said, "I've longed for the spring to finally come so I could come here. Auntie Gwen loved her roses." Felicity said, nostalgically. Suddenly feeling as if her aunt were near her, recalling how often the two of them had come to this very spot, Felicity thought, *Oh Auntie Gwen I need you so. What am I to do?*

Her heartache was deep, and Felicity needing advice, desperately looked at the budding roses, preparing to bloom.

"You made Gwendolyn very happy in her last years Felicity. In fact, you've made so many happy."

"Oh Rupert, how kind of you to say, but somehow I don't feel as if I've been able to make anyone happy these days. Least of all Benjamin or myself."

As he glanced at his cousin, Rupert desperately wanted to ease her burden. Having already discussed with her on numerous occasions after Felicity had discovered she was pregnant and that there was no chance the child she was carrying could be Benjamin's, it had been extremely hard for Felicity to admit that the two of them had not been intimate for weeks before the attack, with Benjamin in Washington. And then following the attack, although Benjamin had been affectionate and attentive, he had respectfully never come to her, sensing she wasn't ready.

Once discovering she was pregnant with another man's child, Felicity couldn't allow herself to be intimate with Benjamin. Feeling unclean and that her body had betrayed their marriage in the most perverse way conceivable, she found it even difficult to allow Benjamin to hold her, for she was too ashamed. This all resulted in Felicity punishing herself from being loved by the man she desperately needed.

"Dear Felicity, from early on in our relationship, the one thing I valued most was our ability to discuss whatever was on our minds. And now, more than ever, I would like to speak from my heart."

Sighing, fearing that Rupert wanted to speak of the child she carried and her lack of enthusiasm, she said, "Oh Rupert, if this is another discussion about the baby and how I'm dealing with carrying James Sterling spawn . . . ."

"That is precisely what I'm worried about. That child growing in you is not just James' child, but he or she is yours, too. Now I've respected your wishes by not discussing with Benjamin yours and his relationship, but surely, you know he realizes the child isn't his, especially after he saw what happened the night Annabelle found you. I'm not proud of the way I behaved that evening, but Felicity, by you refusing to discuss that night with Benjamin, or the child you are having, the distance between you is growing. Why I can't recall the last time I saw you and he have any physical contact with one another."

"Please Rupert, don't you think I know that? But I cannot bring myself to allow him to touch me. I feel so dirty and cheap. And I certainly cannot discuss the attack, not after all this time--especially now that my nightmare of that night lives on as everyday this child grows inside me. Every time I feel it kicking me . . . I think of how it was conceived and I cringe."

"I can't imagine the pain you carry in your heart. Yet, I would be amiss if I didn't point out to you Felicity, the prison you have forced yourself and Benjamin to live in, is of your own doing. Your husband loves you and loathes himself for not protecting you. And don't tell me you haven't noticed. He's a lost man without his faith. A preacher without God in his heart is a shell of a man, and only you Felicity, can release him and the bondage you have placed each other in.

"It is obvious to me that Benjamin thinks of this child as only yours, loving you has he does. Has it not been he who has prepared for the birth of your child? Which is admirable, but knowing Benjamin as I do, I wouldn't expect anything less of such a fine and good man.

"I implore you Felicity, please think of your love for Benjamin. He may not be the man who created your child--that much is true--but if you allow him to be, he will be your child's father. And no better father could that babe ever have. You and only you are keeping Benjamin out of your life. And far more will be lost then what has already taken place on that dreadful night. The love you and Benjamin shared will be lost too."

Felicity, in tears, sat starring out into the garden and Rupert kissed her forehead. "Sit among your dear aunt's garden, my dear, and please think of what your aunt sacrificed to bring you two wonderful people together. Surely, if your love was able to endure all that you and Benjamin went through to be joined together, your love can get beyond this as well."

~

Returning to the home of her grandmother's family which had been boarded up for decades until Felicity and Benjamin had returned to England, she looked about for any sign of Benjamin. Seeing a light in the carriage house, Felicity made her way over the meadows and watched her husband from the doorway. Her heart filled with love for this kind-hearted man who knelt on the ground as he painstakingly sanded what appeared to be a cradle and tears welled up in her eyes.

After several minutes of watching him, and thinking about what Rupert had told her earlier, she softly said, "Hello darling, what are you making?"

"Felicity, my love. I didn't hear you arrive." Standing up in front of the wooden cradle, shielding it from her, Benjamin said, "Just a little something for the babe. I had hoped to surprise you."

Noting that Benjamin referred to the child, as he always did, she said, "You did. I've a confession to make. I've been standing here watching you for sometime. Why didn't you tell me you were making the baby's cradle?"

"And spoil the surprise?" Benjamin smiled lovingly at her.

Missing his smile, Felicity, not remembering the last time either of them smiled, asked, "Benjamin, will you do me a favor, darling?"

"Anything, my love."

"Will you please come and hold me."

Immediately, Benjamin brushed off the wood dust from his hands and his coat, and came to Felicity. Tenderly he placed his arms around her and feeling her tremble, held her closer to him. It had been weeks since she had seemed remotely interested in him and feeling her next to him now, Benjamin closed his eyes, taking in her scent.

Pleadingly Felicity looked up at him with tears in her eyes. "My dear Ben, do you know how much I love you? And how lucky I feel knowing what a wonderful father you will be to my baby?"

"Oh Felicity . . ." His words garbled, as he held her close. "I love you. Can you ever forgive me?"

Glancing at him and brushing his face, seeing specks of wood shavings in his beard, she placed her finger to his lips and softly said, "There is nothing to forgive. You are my husband and I have selfishly locked you out of my heart when I needed you the most, and you have needed me. Can we please darling, put the past behind us, never speaking of the pain we've caused each other and please just let our love for one another build a future together?"

Kissing her fingers and paying extra attention to her thumb, he kissed it tenderly just as he had done the night he had proposed to her. Overcome with emotion, Felicity grasped onto Benjamin's neck. "Oh darling, I love you so."

Feeling the baby kick inside her, she pulled slightly from Benjamin and taking his hand in hers, brought it to her stomach.

"Little one, this is your father. The most wonderful man I have ever known."

Benjamin, being allowed to feel the life growing in his wife's womb had long ago stopped thinking of the child as James Sterling's, but only as Felicity's and a tear ran down his cheek. "Oh Felicity, I swear to you, I will be the best father I can for the child God has finally blessed you with. Our child."

~ Twenty-three ~

Restless Spirits Laid to Rest

Hearing his wife scream out in pain again, Gilbert jumped up from his seat and looked at Chester, Lucas Brown's elderly former slave. "Christ almighty, what's takin' them so long?"

"Sit on down there, Mas'sa Gilbert. They be back with the doc when they be back, and all the pacing around you doin' ain't gonna bring them here none the faster. Tess and Bessie is in there with yer missus, and she'll be just fine. Reminds me of the night, Miz Catherine had our little Miranda. Mas'sa Lucas, he nearly wore out the rug just like you are now."

From upstairs came the sounds of Miranda's screams once again, followed this time by Bessie calling out to her, "Push honey child, you can do it! Come on Miranda girl, let your Bessie see her babe."

Gilbert jumped from his seat and began climbing the stairs leading to their bedroom, pausing upon hearing Chester calling to him. "Now Mas'sa Gilbert, you 'no they ain't gonna let you in there till they good and ready. So come on back down here."

Wringing his hands through his hair, Gilbert looked anxiously at Chester. "Jesus, Mary, and Joseph, I can't just do nothin' when my Mandy needs me."

"Miz Miranda's got her Bessie and Tess with her. Ain't no need for you to see her likes that. Now come sit back down before ya makes me get on up out of this here chair and come and make ya. I ain't about to get Bessie riled at me."

Smiling wearily at the older man who could barely walk, Gilbert did as he asked. Hearing his wife cry out again, he swore, "Damn it, Lucas, where in the hell are ya?"

Not more than three miles from their home, Lucas, along with Michael, Montgomery, and Doc Watson were fighting for their lives surrounded by men on horse back with white hooded sheets carrying torches and guns.

"Get on down from there, you uppity nigger!"

Michael recognizing the voice of the man hollering up at Montgomery, shouted, "Thomas, is that you? Christ, what in the hell is wrong with you?"

The man Michael was directing his attention too, still mounted on his horse, with a whip in his hand, dressed in a white hooded sheet, looked down at him and Lucas who stood alongside the carriage. "Get on back inside that fancy coach of yours Honeycutt, or you'll die alongside this here bastard."

Without warning, the hooded man cracked his whip, striking Montgomery across the neck and face, causing the injured man to yelp out in pain. Just then the other men circled the buckboard yelling and grouping at him until one managed to get Montgomery off balance and he fell to the ground.

At once, Michael ran to protect Montgomery, shielding him with his body. "Get out of here Thomas. This man has caused you no harm."

Hearing a gun hammer cock, and looking up at the man Michael believed was the man he had hired to oversee his wife's home following the war, Michael calmly said, "Is this the way you repay my kindness, Thomas?"

"I have no beef with you Honeycutt, it's him we want."

Another man yelled, "Shoot 'm both, Thomas. He ain't nothing but some Yank anyway!"

"Shut up!" And with that, Thomas' horse reared up and the other man, already aiming his gun, shot his pistol, hitting Michael in the shoulder. Seeing his friend being shot, Lucas, taking his cane, began striking at the hooded men that were approaching him, and in the scuffle Lucas took a bullet in the stomach.

Doc Watson, who had been inside the coach until that time, and hearing other horses approaching, stepped out of the coach with gun in hand and yelled, "Get out of here, Thomas Hastings! War hero or not, so help me God I'll shoot you down as sure as I'm standing here."

Taking aim at the doctor who had treated him for his wounds after he had been ambushed during the war, and those of his injured men, Thomas yelled, "Get on back inside the coach, George. Let me and my men do what we gotta do."

"No. Damn it!" George Watson yelled. "There's been enough bloodshed." Seeing Thomas point his revolver back toward Michael and Montgomery, taking aim, the doctor who had saved so many lives in his career shot Thomas in the head and he immediately fell from his saddle.

With Thomas' slain body covered in a white sheet, now dripping in his own blood, lying on the dirt road, and with another buggy approaching, the other hooded men rode off into the dark of night, yelling they'd be back. George Watson, still holding the revolver that had taken a life, stood staring at the hooded man he had once saved from multiple gunshot wounds in stunned disbelief.

Jumping from Montgomery's body, Michael went to Lucas who was leaning against his carriage, grasping at his stomach. "Get me to Miranda, old friend. I've got to see my grandson before I die," Lucas gasped, obviously in great pain.

With the other buggy approaching, Michael with the aid of George, who had since dropped his revolver, helped Lucas back inside the carriage. Glancing at Montgomery, Michael said, "Are you okay to drive?"

"Yes, sir." Boarding the buckboard and hearing George Watson say he'd stay there with Thomas' body until authorities could be alerted, Montgomery cracked the whip and the carriage raced back to the O'Flaherty's newly constructed plantation.

Back at the O'Flaherty's, Gilbert knelt beside the bed of his wife, lovingly kissing her forehead and gazing down at their son.

"Oh Mandy, he's beautiful . . . like his mother."

Smiling, she said, "Handsome, darling. And I think he looks like his papa."

"I told you he was a boy."

Hearing the sounds of horses and Michael's voice calling for Bessie and Tess, Gilbert stood and asked Miranda, "Darling, can I take our son to introduce him to his grandfather?"

"Yes. That would be nice. I need some rest anyway. Please darling, tell Papa the name we've chosen."

Nodding, Gilbert tenderly took his son in his arms and kissing his wife affectionately, spoke lovingly to the baby, who looked up at him sucking on his fist.

"Hello there little man, what a strapping fine lad ya are."

Walking slowly from the bedroom and down the hallway, Gilbert's happiness soon faded upon seeing Lucas, bleeding, slumped over and being led into the parlor by Michael and Tess. Tucking his son closer to his chest, Gilbert descended the steps and walked into the parlor, asking, "What the hell has happened?" Fear gripped at his heart seeing the man he had grown to love who was bleeding profusely from his midriff.

Lucas glanced up at Gilbert and seeing him with a child in his arms, whispered, "Son, come closer and let me see my grandchild."

The blood draining from his face, Gilbert stunned, obediently walked over to Lucas and knelt beside the pale man who was gasping for air, and said, "Da, meet your grandson, Lucas Joseph O'Flaherty."

Hearing Gilbert call the baby in his arms by his name, his eyes welled up and he gazed lovingly at the small child. Lucas said in a raspy voice, "Thank you, Gilbert for naming him after me. You're a good man, better than I deserve. You make damn sure he grows up to be like the fine man his father is and not after his namesake, hear?"

Gilbert nodding, asked Lucas if he wanted to hold him and Lucas whispered, "No son, just seeing him was all I needed. Now you take good care of him and my daughter. And tell them both I love them."

Glancing at his grandson, Lucas breathed his last breath. Seeing his head slump over, Bessie fell to her knees wailing, "Oh Mas'sa Lucas."

Chester, consoling his wife, patting her shoulders listened to Gilbert as he said, "Please everyone, me Mandy girl has just given birth to our son and is restin' upstairs. She doesn't know she's just lost her father. Please, don't let her find out this way."

Bringing his child closer to his heart, he looked at Michael standing solemnly at the doorway. "Mr. Honeycutt, will you kindly take care of things down here while I go to my wife and tell her?"

"Certainly, Gilbert."

As Gilbert climbed the stairs leading to his bedroom, holding his son near to him, tears rolled down his cheeks. Feeling little Lucas stir in his arms, he whispered, "That was Grandda, son. He loved ya very much. God rest his soul."

Moments later, after Gilbert entered the room where his wife lay resting from just giving birth, the chilling scream of grief rang out from behind the closed doors, followed by the soft cries of Lucas Joseph O'Flaherty.

~ Twenty-four ~

Closure

A week later, Michael had picked up his wife and family at the train station. After telling them the events that had lead up to Lucas' and Thomas Hastings', deaths, Sarah lovingly glanced at her husband, his arm bandaged and in a sling.

"And you darling? Are you healing from your gunshot?"

"Me? Yeah, sore, but I'll be fine. Poor Montgomery will be left with a nasty scar, though. He's damned lucky it missed his eye. Half an inch higher and he would have lost it."

Sarah, shaking her head, said, "My God, I can't believe it. Why didn't you tell me the White Camellias that I had read about in Versus' letter were so dangerous? I surely never would have allowed you and Tad to be down here for so long if I had known."

"Precisely why I didn't say anything. You were needed with Elise, and do you think I would allow you down here under these circumstances? Fairfax is no longer the lovely sleepy town we left a year ago. The hatred in the hearts of these men are possibly worse then during the war. This secret organization, the Ku Klux Klan members don't proudly wear a uniform, they shroud themselves in sheets and strike at night most of the time. So you don't know who they are. It could be any of your friends or trusted neighbors, which makes them doubly sinister. The fear they have brought down on honest law-abiding citizens is unbelievable."

Elise, sitting next to Joshua holding her son, as Joshua held his daughter, looked at Michael. "And, you say that Thomas was a member of this organization?"

"Not just a member, but evidently the leader in these parts. That's why Mammy Tess left Doves Landing. It just wasn't safe for her there any longer."

"And now? Where is Mammy Tess?" Sarah asked.

"Oh since Tad came down last month, she has moved back in to the old boardinghouse of course, tending to Clarisa, her daughter-in-law, who apparently had been beaten so badly they don't think she'll ever walk again. Jessie won't come by the house at all, not even to see his wife. Blames himself for not protecting her, I suppose."

Inhaling a deep breath, Sarah glanced out the window as they passed Glenbrook. A smile crossed her lips seeing the children running about the grounds.

"Well at least the Brown's old plantation looks good. Why, I don't recall it looking so nice in years."

Seeing a newly-constructed fence where none had been before, she looked at Michael, and asked, "Is that the dividing of the grounds? I see the cemetery is on the other side of the fence."

"Gilbert insisted that the family plot remain a part of Miranda's and his portion of the property."

"That was very thoughtful of him. How did Gilbert and Lucas get along?"

"Surprising well. Lucas took to him straight off. As a matter of fact, when Lucas died, Gilbert was by his side, bringing little Lucas closer to him, so he could see him."

Sharing with them, Lucas' last words, Elise glanced at her son sleeping in her arms. "I'm glad Mr. Brown got to see his grandson before he died. That must be a great comfort to Miranda."

Pulling up in front of Gilbert and Felicity's plantation and seeing the immense size of the Georgian mansion, she gasped. "Oh my, I had no idea Lucas had built such a large home for Miranda. What on earth is she ever going to do with such a big place?"

"It was Lucas' wishes, trust me. Before she and Gilbert had arrived, he had already begun the construction of it. You should have seen poor Gilbert's face as he tried to keep his temper. There he was--red as a beet-- with Miranda jubilant, and I thought the man was going to burst. I genuinely felt sorry for him."

As the carriage stopped, Bessie and Tess ran out the doors and instantly welcomed Sarah, Elise and Joshua while each of them took a baby in their arms, cooing and fussing over the twins.

After kissing Mammy Tess and Bessie, Elise went directly to the door where stood a man she presumed was Gilbert. Stretching out her hand to him, she said, "Hello, I'm Elise Carmidy."

"Aye. I suspected as much. Welcome. I'm sure glad yer here. My Mandy girl has been needing her best friend." Hearing him refer to Miranda by his pet name and saying such a kind thing, Elise impulsively leaned forward and hugged him.

"Thank you kindly. Where might I find Miranda?"

"She's upstairs in the nursery with little Lucas--second door to your left. Go on up while I welcome the others."

Nodding, Elise went straight up the stairs. Without knocking, she opened the door and finding Miranda nursing her son, lovingly smiled at her friend.

"Hello Miranda," Elise said, while rushing over to her and kissing her forehead as she looked down at the baby contently drinking his mother's milk. Elise, cooing at him, caressed his forehead and pulled up a chair. Neither woman seemed the least bit embarrassed that Miranda was nursing her child.

Elise said, "I met your Gilbert. I like him. Why didn't you tell me how good looking he is?"

"Oh, I don't know . . . I suppose, I failed to tell you lots of things, didn't I?"

It was clear to Elise that her friend was extremely melancholy and was suffering deeply from the loss of her father. "Well, give me my little godson, Miranda. Looks like he has had plenty to eat. Besides, before long, Mama will be up here and then I won't ever get to hold him, with Sarah Tess and little Michael wanting to be fed."

Smiling, Miranda removed her son from her nipple and as she placed him in Elise's arms, she smiled, watching Elise place him over her shoulder and tenderly pat his back.

"My, just look at you, Elise. Why you're an old pro at this."

As Elise sat rocking the wee baby in her arms, Miranda hastily buttoned her black blouse.

"I see Bessie's been by sealing all the windows and mirrors in black taffeta," Elise said.

"Yes. I suppose some things never change."

"Oh, I don't know about that. From what I heard from Michael, your Papa sure did. Sounds like he and Gilbert had a wonderful relationship."

Nodding, Miranda smiled and said, "They did. Papa truly loved him I think. It was so wonderful these past few months . . ."

"Time well spent, I'd say. I'm happy you were able to make peace with Lucas." Hearing the baby burp, Elise wiped his mouth with a cloth handing it back to Miranda, she added. "Well little man, you sure were a lucky little boy weren't ya? You got to meet your grandpapa before he went to heaven."

Smiling fondly over at her friend, Miranda said, "I'm so glad you came, Elise. I don't know if I could have made it through the funeral without you. Beside, it's only right that you're here to say goodbye to Papa, he loved you so."

Calmly rocking little Lucas in her arms, smiling down at him, seeing him drift off to sleep Elise said, "And I loved him. Lucas was like a father to me, and these past years seeing him . . . Well, let's just say it does my heart good to know that he finally found true happiness in his heart through you and your family."

"He did, didn't he?"

"You sure made him proud of you, Miranda. We all are. Which by the way, I'm not liking it one little bit, my sister out-shinning me like that. So from here on out there will be no more heroics out of you."

Chuckling, Miranda smiled through her tears. "God, I love you, Elise. Only you could make me smile the day I lay my father to rest."

"Miranda, honey, your Papa lived a full life and thanks to you his last days here on earth were happy ones. So don't be sad for him. Lucas Brown was to proud a man--far too proud to let his little girl grieve over his passing. I can hear him just as if he were standing right here beside me, 'Missy, you just take this sweet child on down to that there cemetery and let me rest, because I live through you and little Lucas'."

Nodding, Miranda said, "He would have said that. Thank you, Elise. I truly needed you here today, especially since I'm certain Tad will be in attendance and it's hard enough seeing that man when I'm having a good day . . ."

"I heard he's been in Fairfax. Mama even mentioned he was seeing Constance Hildebrandt."

"Is he? I wouldn't know and I don't rightly care, either. I just hope Constance knows what she's up against. If I were a better friend, I'd probably warn her against the likes of him."

"She wouldn't listen to you anyway. You know Constance, she always had a mind of her own."

Again, Miranda chuckled. "Why Elise Carmidy, I can't believe my ears. Coming from one of the most stubborn women I have ever know . . . Why, I'm flabbergasted."

"Me?" Elise said smiling. "Why you should talk Miranda dear, or need I remind you how you ran off with Gilbert, without so much as a how do you do?"

Then Miranda raising her eyebrow, smiled and said, "Well, I suppose you're right. It must run in the family, little sis."

Hearing her own children crying Elise said, "Well come on Auntie, let's you and me go introduce little Lucas here to his cousins. And then later this afternoon, just when the sun sets--Lucas' favorite time of the day--we'll lay him down to rest next to those he loved."

"Papa would like that."

The two of them left the nursery, arm and arm, and hearing the door open, Joshua stood at the foot of the steps with Sarah Tess in his arms crying to be fed.

"Hello, Miranda. I'm so sorry at your loss."

"Thank you, Joshua, especially for bringing Elise and my niece and nephew here. It means the world to me."

"It was my pleasure." Looking over at his wife, he hastily added. "Thank heavens darling, you came down when you did because my little princess here is just like her mother, impatient as they come."

"Hmm," Elise said teasingly, leaning into Miranda, she said, "Oh, and by the way, I'm one up on you little sis, so you and that good looking husband have some catching up to do."

Gilbert, standing under the stairwell, able to hear every word Elise had said, stepped out so he could be seen looking up at her and his wife. He smiled hearing his wife snicker. Already he knew he was going to like Miranda's friend, and said, "Aye. Da, God rest his soul, sure gave us a large enough house now didn't he?"

As they all went inside the parlor, the Honeycutt's, Carmidy's, and O'Flaherty's rejoiced in Lucas' legacy, knowing he would have loved having those he cherished most celebrating his life and accomplishments.

THE END

Linda Daly

As a child, I recall sneaking a flashlight into bed so I could finish reading under the covers a book from the school library before it had to be returned the following day. As a teen, my English teacher read *Johnny Tremain* by Ester Forbes having everyone in my class, including myself, mesmerized upon discovering how a fictional boy from the Revolutionary War is maimed for life following a tragic accident. I remember gasps by my classmates as the bandages were taken off Johnny's wounded hand and his discovery that his fingers had grown together.

As I studied my own hand, imagining what it must be like to have webbed fingers, I understood fully the significance of weaving a good tale--a tale that could take the reader on a holiday for the mind.

It is my sincere hope that as you read the third installment to the *Doves Collect* series, you will be swept away to another place and time and fully enjoy discovering more about the lives and times of these fictional characters during America's most tumultuous era in history.

The "Doves Collect" series will continue with. . .

Soiled Doves

    In the forth book of the series life isn't always as we expect. . . The past and the evil that lurks in the hearts of some will dramatically change the future forever, especially the innocent.